CRAVING
SUPERNATURAL
CREATURES

Series in Fairy-Tale Studies

General Editor
Donald Haase, Wayne State University

Advisory Editors
Cristina Bacchilega, University of Hawaiʻi, Mānoa

Stephen Benson, University of East Anglia

Nancy L. Canepa, Dartmouth College

Anne E. Duggan, Wayne State University

Pauline Greenhill, University of Winnipeg

Christine A. Jones, University of Utah

Janet Langlois, Wayne State University

Ulrich Marzolph, University of Göttingen

Carolina Fernández Rodríguez, University of Oviedo

Maria Tatar, Harvard University

Jack Zipes, University of Minnesota

A complete listing of the books in this series can be found online at wsupress.wayne.edu

CRAVING
SUPERNATURAL
CREATURES

German Fairy-Tale Figures in
American Pop Culture

CLAUDIA SCHWABE

WAYNE STATE UNIVERSITY PRESS
DETROIT

ISBN 978-0-8143-4196-4 (paperback)
ISBN 978-0-8143-4601-3 (hardcover)
ISBN 978-0-8143-4197-1 (e-book)

Library of Congress Control Number: 2018966275

Published with the assistance of a fund established by Thelma Gray James of Wayne State University for the publication of folklore and English studies.

Wayne State University Press
Leonard N. Simons Building
4809 Woodward Avenue
Detroit, Michigan 48201-1309

Visit us online at wsupress.wayne.edu

Dedicated to my parents,
Dr. Roman and Cornelia Schwabe

CONTENTS

ACKNOWLEDGMENTS

F irst and foremost, I would like to thank my amazing mother, Cornelia Schwabe, for the many hours and afternoons she spent with me discussing the contents of this book over a latte macchiato. Our conversations were extremely stimulating and her input and encouragement to write *Craving Supernatural Creatures* was invaluable. I want to thank my father, Dr. Roman Schwabe, for always believing in me and loving me as much as any father could. I am also extremely grateful to my wonderful husband, Christopher Gibson, for lending me a patient ear whenever I needed it, for his consistent and unwavering support in everything I do, and for his infinite love.

During my work on this book I was greatly assisted by Anne Duggan, Lisa Gabbert, and Barbara Mennel. All of them have been superb mentors and made significant contributions at different stages of this volume. Furthermore, I owe a special thanks to Jeannie Thomas who inspired me to write about supernatural creatures in the first place. The anonymous Wayne State University Press reviewers were both kind and helpful in their recommendations. I thank them for their generous readings of my manuscript and for their candid comments and individual suggestions. I also thank Jack Zipes, Don Haase, Christine Jones, Cristina Bacchilega, Jill Terry Rudy, and my dear friend and USU colleague Christa Jones for their ongoing warm encouragement along the way. Exchanges with these scholars and with my fellow "sisters" from the Coven des Fées, including Christy Williams, Jeana Jorgensen, Sara Cleto, Brittany Warman, and Veronica Schanoes, have greatly enriched the perspectives behind this book.

Finally, I want to express my sincere gratitude for the entire editorial, production, and marketing team at Wayne State University Press, which was crucial for the successful editing, design, and advertising of the book. It has been a tremendous joy to work with them, especially Annie Martin, Marie Sweetman, Emily Nowak, Kristina Stonehill, Jamie Jones, Rachel Ross, Sandy Judd, Carrie Teefey, Ceylan Akturk, and Rachel Lyon. All of these publishing professionals, along with other talented members of the team at Wayne State University Press, were unflaggingly dedicated to shepherding this volume through its various stages, copyediting the manuscript, designing the text, preparing the index, and designing the striking cover. Producing a volume such as this is a team effort, and I thank all members involved for their meticulous work.

INTRODUCTION

T he inspiration for this study came to me in 2013 as I was browsing the toy section in one of America's most popular retailers. When I entered the aisle for girls' toys, my eyes fell onto Frankie Stein, Clawdeen Wolf, Cleo de Nile, Draculaura, Ghoulia Yelps, and Lagoona Blue, fashion dolls from the American franchise Monster High launched by Mattel in 2010. These ghoulish dolls are bone-thin "goth barbies" equipped with monstrous attributes, such as fangs, stitches, wolf ears, fins, bandages, and snakes. Appearing more diverse than their "normal" Barbie sisters, the Monster High dolls display various skin tones ranging from blue, green, and brown to orange and pink. These freaky doll creations by Garrett Sander were unlike any dolls I had ever seen before. Although the dolls are promoted as the daughters of such popular monsters as Frankenstein, the Werewolf, the Mummy, Count Dracula, Medusa, and so forth, they have little in common with them other than their outlandish looks. Draculaura, for instance, cannot stand the thought of blood because she is a vegetarian and turned off by meat. The teenage dolls, which look like the underfed love children of Tim Burton and Lady Gaga, attend a school for creepy creatures called Monster High. The idea behind the brand is that we all are somehow "monstrous" because of our idiosyncrasies, perhaps quirky characteristics, and individual flaws. As Lori Pantel, Mattel's vice president for marketing global girls brands, emphasized, "The Monster High brand uses the monster metaphor to show girls that it is ok to be different and that our unique differences should be celebrated" (Business Wire). The school Monster High represents a highly heterogeneous space where everyday learning coalesces with lessons in mutual tolerance, overcoming stereotypes, and diversity. Although the dolls' doe-eyed, Twiggy-style appearances may raise concerns about body image, just as their classic Barbie predecessors did, the brand highlights the positive character traits of its creations, including compassion, determination, and intelligence.

The logo of the franchise, a skull with eyelashes and a pink bow tie, feminizes death on the one hand and beautifies or trivializes the monstrous on the other. The logo, together with the slogans of the franchise, "(Where) Freaky Just Got Fabulous!" (2010–11) and "Be yourself, be unique, be a monster!" (2011–16), suggests that monstrosity and the freak or the Other represent marketable concepts in contemporary North American society. The marketability of such monstrous, supernatural creatures goes hand in hand with their promotion as desirable and "cool" dolls. Today, the franchise includes different consumer products, from various toys, stationery, bags, key chains, and play sets to video games, TV specials, a web series, and direct-to-DVD movies. A spin-off line of dolls that Mattel introduced in 2013 is Ever After High. In this line, the characters are based on fairy tales and fantasy stories instead of monsters, featuring the offspring of Snow White, Sleeping Beauty, Cinderella, Rapunzel, Red Riding Hood, the Evil Queen, Pinocchio, the Little Mermaid, the Pied Piper of Hamelin, and many more. Among the faculty are popular fairy-tale-inspired characters, including Rumpelstiltskin, Mr. Badwolf, Baba Yaga, and the brothers Milton and Giles Grimm (a direct allusion to the infamous Brothers Grimm). Remarkably, Ever After High unsettles the simplistic dichotomy of good and evil fairy-tale characters and subverts the idea that malignity is hereditary and a predestined path for the offspring of traditionally villainous fairy-tale characters. The show features the character Raven queen, for instance, as the daughter of the evil queen from "Snow White," who is not vicious or so much as mean but kind and considerate. In the adventures of Ever After High, she actively rebels against prejudice and her unjust reputation by taking actions toward self-determination and autonomy. The line has spawned a web series (2013–present), several feature-length presentations (2013–present), and two book series (2013–present).

Mattel's franchises Monster High and Ever After High are prominent examples of how the US consumer goods industry caters to the demand of primarily teen and tween girls for fantastic creatures. The target audiences of other companies—for instance, Hasbro and Walt Disney–owned Marvel Entertainment—consist of children and adults alike who are "hungry" for superheroes and mutants of the Marvels Universe. Of course, humans everywhere have always brought mythical creatures, legendary beasts, fairy-tale characters, and supernatural beings to life in stories, songs, and works of art, so it may not come as a surprise that these creatures continue to thrill, terrify, entertain, and inspire us today.[1] Since the early twenty-first century, however, the craving for fantastic creatures in popular culture appears to have reached new dimensions. This craving for the fantastic is reflected, for instance, in the numerous media productions in film and television featuring heroic supernatural beings to satisfy the consumer demand, such as Marvel's X-Men, Wolverine, the Avengers, the Fantastic Four, or the Guardians of the Galaxy. In addition, within the past two decades, a wave of fairy-tale-infused characters has swept over both the small and silver screens, from the rehabilitated dark fairy Maleficent, the wizard boy Harry Potter, and the comical ogre Shrek to fantastic beasts hidden in plain sight, romanticized werewolves, adventurous Hobbits, pugnacious dwarfs, and semi-emancipated, live-action Disney princesses.

People's craving for fantastic creatures goes hand in hand with what Jack Zipes describes in *Grimm Legacies* (2015) as "contemporary hyping of fairy tales" (67). The relationship between the fairy-tale hype produced by the mainstream culture industry in America and the public's craving for supernatural beings appears to be of reciprocal dynamics: the more hype is created, the higher the demand, and the higher the demand, the more hype follows. Indeed, more than ever before, or so it seems, fantasy creatures are in vogue and omnipresent in today's popular culture in the form of television shows and commercials, films, theater performances, online websites and social media, novels and fan fiction, poetry, comic books, video games, toys, clothing and fashion accessories, school supplies, jewelry, cereal boxes, and other merchandise. In *Grimm Legacies*, Zipes has sharply criticized the negative effects of the current hyping of fairy tales and their paratexts, which lead to "shallow products" (68), such as the fairy-tale "blockbuster" films *Mirror Mirror* (2012), *Snow White and the Huntsman* (2012), *Frozen* (2013), and *Maleficent* (2014), that "'thrive' parasitically by draining meaning and from warping memetic stories" (73). Whereas Zipes deplores the ways in which these media productions "tend to distort source stories" (2015, 73), it is precisely this dissonance between the supernatural creatures featured in contemporary fairy-tale adaptations and their source tales that I find intriguing and worth analyzing. I believe that the ways in which supernatural creatures are portrayed in today's consumer culture are significant because they reveal relevant information about society's views on marginalization, diversity, and Otherness within a hegemonic culture. Specifically, I argue that there is a growing trend in North American popular culture that moves toward the celebration and exaltation of fantastic Otherness, the anthropomorphization of and identification with supernatural beings, and the rehabilitation of classic fairy-tale villains and monsters. This development becomes evident, as I will demonstrate in this study, when examining contemporary fairy-tale adaptations and their representations of fantastic creatures. By saying "contemporary" adaptations, I refer to the time frame of the late twentieth century, when the trend took its nascent form, and the early twenty-first century, when the trend found traction.

Although many different terms have been deployed in fairy-tale scholarship to discuss contemporary fairy-tale adaptations (e.g., postmodern fairy tale, recycled fairy tale, fairy-tale remake, fractured fairy tale), I choose "adaptation" as my preferred denotation in the sense of Cristina Bacchilega's use of the term. In *Fairy Tales Transformed? Twenty-First-Century Adaptations and the Politics of Wonder* (2014), Bacchilega uses "adaptation" as her operative construct "to emphasize that the fairy-tale web is not only an inter/ hypertextual, but also an intermedial and multimedial, symptomatic, and possible transformative reading practice" (35). Whereas some adaptations are postmodern retellings of traditional tales based on single plot structures, others take the form of a fairy-tale pastiche, also referred to as fairy-tale mash-up, mix, or montage, without relying on a single fairy-tale plot. As Jeana Jorgensen noted, pastiche is "a relevant concept for studying popular revisions of fairy tales that contain more than a single fairy-tale plot, or no traditional plot at all, in addition to countless references to fairy-tale motifs" (2007, 218). In a pastiche work, various story worlds, fairy-tale motifs, and characters may intermingle and blend with other figures, tropes, and genres of folklore, such as fables, myths, and legends, while coexisting in one cosmology. A fairy-tale pastiche may contain elements of parody and satire, mocking the fairy-tale genre, characters, or tropes, or it may celebrate the work it imitates in the form of a tribute or homage. DreamWorks's popular *Shrek* films (*Shrek*, 2001; *Shrek 2*, 2004; *Shrek the Third*, 2007; and *Shrek Forever After*, 2010) are a good example of a satirical fairy-tale pastiche, whereas Tarsem Singh's *The Fall* (2006) illustrates the latter in the form of a fairy-tale homage.

In this study, I focus on contemporary North American adaptations that are transtextually linked to German source tales and their fairy-tale creatures of the Romantic tradition of the early nineteenth century mainly for three reasons. First, German source tales influence a great number, if not the majority, of fairy-tale adaptations in American visual culture of the twentieth and twenty-first centuries. Second, I needed to narrow the analytic scope of my study to a selection of specific tales and fairy-tale figures within a large "fairy-tale web" of cultural productions. Third, I have a personal interest in German folk and literary fairy tales in particular because I am German and grew up with the fairy-tale corpus of German writers. Of course, we must bear in mind that, similar to individual fairy-tale motifs, common fairy-tale characters (e.g., the witch, the monster, or the dwarf), are archetypal figures that are universal and cannot be tied to a certain "birthplace" or country of origin. Already Jack Zipes has emphasized that fairy tales, and hence their creatures, "have been in existence as oral folk tales for thousands of years and first became what we call literary fairy tales during the seventeenth century" (2002, 2). In fact, the Brothers Grimm omitted the words "German" and "folk" from the title of their *Kinder- und Hausmärchen* (*Children's and Household Tales*), published first in 1812, presumably aware that many of the tales in their fairy-tale collection are not of particular German origin and are of literary rather than oral roots (Bosch-Roig 2013, 317). Although it is legitimate to assume that the creators of American adaptations are familiar with the popular Grimms' tales, one cannot simply surmise that about the German *Kunstmärchen* or literary fairy tales written by the German Romantics (e.g., E. T. A. Hoffmann, Ludwig Tieck, Achim von Arnim, or Wilhelm Hauff). Therefore, in my examples I will not only carve out the hypertextual relationships between the German hypotexts, the supernatural creatures, and the American adaptations but also cite direct references, such as quotations and allusions, when applicable, to demonstrate any intertextual connections to German literary fairy tales. Occasionally, I will point out transtextual relations to fairy tales in the larger European tradition—for instance, "Beauty and the Beast" and "Pinocchio"—but will discuss those connections more lightly due to the main focus of this book on German *Märchen*.

My understanding of "transtextuality" is based on Gérard Genette's theory of textual transcendence, as everything that brings a text into relation, whether manifest or hidden, with other texts ([1979] 1992, 81). Genette describes intertextuality and hypertextuality/hypotextuality as subtypes of transtextuality. The type of transtextual relation between a contemporary

American fairy-tale adaptation and a German source tale can vary significantly, from fairy-tale "fragments," such as memetic objects (e.g., red hood,
glass slipper, poisoned apple, magic mirror), symbolisms (e.g., sexual, religious, psychological), narrative plot, functions, and characters (e.g., prince,
princess), and supernatural creatures (e.g., talking frog, fairy, dwarf, witch)
to direct quotes. A case in point for the latter is the television series *Grimm*
(2011–17), which opens every episode with an intertextual reference to
a particular fairy tale. The episode "Mr. Sandman" (season 2, ep. 15), for
instance, begins with the citation "'Now we've got eyes—eyes—a beautiful
pair of children's eyes,' he whispered," from E. T. A. Hoffmann's 1816 literary
fairy tale "Der Sandmann" ("The Sand-Man," 2008, 188). Other openings
consist of text excerpts from various tales of the Brothers Grimm, including
the less popular tales "Hans mein Igel" ("Hans My Hedgehog"), "Der Krautesel" ("Donkey Cabbages"), "Die Alte im Wald" ("The Old Woman in the
Wood"), or "Die drei Schlangenblätter" ("The Three Snake Leaves").

    Although I devote some attention in this book to theater performances,
comics, video games, and visual art, in the field of contemporary fairy-tale
cultural production in North America, most of the fairy-tale adaptations
I analyze are cinematic and televisual. The reason for this selective scope
is that these media platforms are among those with the broadest distribu-
tion and visibility within the twenty-first-century "fairy-tale web" as they
appeal to mass audiences.[2] Within fairy-tale scholarship, popular fairy-tale
productions and revisions in the cinematic and televisual landscapes have
been the focus of several landmark studies and pioneering edited collec-
tions. Pauline Greenhill and Sidney Eve Matrix's *Fairy-Tale Films: Visions of
Ambiguity* (2010) gathers essays on hybridity, commodification, and feminism in American films. Jack Zipes's *The Enchanted Screen: The Unknown
History of Fairy-Tale Films* (2011) offers a comprehensive overview of fairy
tales and their historic influence on film beyond Disney and DreamWorks.
Dani Cavallaro's *The Fairy Tale and Anime: Traditional Themes, Images and
Symbols at Play on Screen* (2011) links European fairy tales and Japanese

animated films. Pauline Greenhill and Jill Terry Rudy's international collection *Channeling Wonder: Fairy Tales on Television* (2014) demonstrates
the wide range of fairy tales that make their way into televisual forms. Jack
Zipes, Pauline Greenhill, and Kendra Magnus-Johnston's *Fairy Tale Films
Beyond Disney: International Perspectives* (2015) presents essays on fairy-
tale film from every part of the globe. My edited collection *The Fairy Tale
and Its Uses in Contemporary New Media and Popular Culture* (2016) considers fairy-tale transformations in today's "old" and "new" media, including
fairy-tale-inspired YouTube parodies, films, television series, commercials,
comic book series, and fan fictions.

The four chapters of this book are structured around different supernatural creatures, beginning with my examination of the automaton, the
golem, and the doppelganger, which emerged as popular fairy-tale figures
in the German tradition of Dark Romanticism in the early nineteenth century. E. T. A. Hoffmann, Achim von Arnim, Joseph Eichendorff, Adelbert
von Chamisso, Ludwig Tieck, Wilhelm Hauff, and other Romantic writers
portray these three supernatural creatures in their *Kunstmärchen* as embodiments of the uncanny, as terrifying agents, and as diabolic harbingers of death.
By drawing on Sigmund Freud's fundamental essay *Das Unheimliche* ("The
Uncanny," 1919) and conceptions of "the fantastic" in Tzvetan Todorov's
The Fantastic: A Structural Approach to a Literary Genre (1973) and Rosemary
Jackson's *Fantasy: The Literature of Subversion* (1981), I demonstrate how the
automaton, the golem, and the doppelganger in German literary fairy tales
can be read as personifications of the uncanny and unfamiliar Other. I then
move on to contemporary North American visual culture to illustrate how
fairy-tale-infused films, such as *Edward Scissorhands* (1990), *A.I. Artificial
Intelligence* (2001), *The Stepford Wives* (2004), *Harry Potter* (2001–11), and
Frozen (2013), and television series, such as *The Simpsons* (1989–present),
The X-Files (1993–2002; 2016–18), *Sleepy Hollow* (2013–17), *Once Upon
a Time* (2011–18), and *Grimm* dramatize, humanize, and infantilize these
"uncanny" characters in multifaceted ways.

Chapter two explores supernatural fairy-tale villains, foregrounding the popular figures of the evil queen and fairy-tale witch in contemporary retellings of the Grimms' fairy tale "Snow White." I examine the portrayals of today's fairy-tale female villains in American film, television, and theater, and demonstrate how these productions twist, distort, trivialize, and subvert the depictions of the archetypal evil queen and witch in German fairy tales. In particular, I am interested in the question of why audiences gravitate toward these reimagined villainesses as desirable figures that allow for personal identification. I not only carve out transtextual connections between the Grimms' literary "Snow White" and its postmodern adaptations but also explore the nature of the queen's wickedness in the different variants, including *Snow White and the Seven Dwarfs* (1937), *Snow White: A Tale of Terror* (1997), *Once Upon a Time* (2011–18), *Mirror Mirror* (2012), *Snow White and the Huntsman* (2012), and *The Huntsman: Winter's War* (2016). Beyond the "Snow White" corpus, I also include the popular Disney production *Maleficent* (2014), which is rooted in the tale "Sleeping Beauty." In my analysis, I consider mental illness, psychosis, narcissistic personality disorder, addiction, and traumatic experiences of abuse to be possible sources of the fairy-tale queen's evilness and highlight how contemporary adaptations redeem "evil" women through motherhood.

The third chapter deconstructs the concept of the monstrous Other in fairy tales by scrutinizing the figure of the Big Bad Wolf. Traditionally, the lupine creature that is known for preying on Little Red Riding Hood and her grandmother incarnates the dangerous, scary, wild, and ferocious Other. North American pop culture, however, does not "monstrify" this classic fairy-tale beast and perpetrator, but instead portrays the supernatural creature in a more positive light, either as rehabilitated, appealing, sexy, and likable werewolf figure or as funny, infantilized, anthropomorphized "good" wolf. I begin this chapter with an illustration of how German fairy tales connote physical human-animal transformations negatively and magical mutations of human body parts into animalistic extremities as disadvantageous.

A hermeneutic or close reading of the Grimms' popular tale "Little Red Cap" exposes the wolf as a life-threatening, monstrous Other and highlights parallels to Sigmund Freud's concept of the uncanny. I then concentrate on postmodern representations of the wolf as they emerge in the character Monroe in *Grimm*, the figure of Ruby/Red in *Once Upon a Time*, the protagonist Valerie and her lover Peter in Catherine Hardwicke's *Red Riding Hood* (2011), the tritagonist Wolf W. Wolf in *Hoodwinked!* (2005), and Bigby Wolf in Bill Willingham's *Fables* comic book series (2002–15) and the spin-off video game *The Wolf Among Us* (2013–14).

In chapter four, I explore the supernatural figure of the fairy-tale dwarf, claiming that North American adaptations today emphasize the diversity of dwarfs' personalities and celebrate the potency of dwarfs' physicality. Departing from the idea of fairy-tale imps as deformed, emasculated, infantilized, asexual people, contemporary films and television shows increasingly draw on regular-height actors to portray traditional fairy-tale dwarfs in multifaceted and, at times, sexually charged roles. Beginning with an introduction to the role of dwarfs in Norse and Germanic mythology, I analyze the ambivalent role dwarfs play in German Romantic fairy tales, including "Snow White," "Rumpelstiltskin," and "Snow White and Rose Red," drawing on source tales by the Brothers Grimm, Karoline Stahl, E. T. A. Hoffmann, and Wilhelm Hauff. Ann Schmiesing's pioneering study *Disability, Deformity, and Disease in the Grimms' Fairy Tales* (2014) serves as an important reference work in this chapter. For my examination of the dwarf in contemporary media productions, I survey Peter Jackson's *Hobbit* (2012–14) trilogy, *Snow White: A Tale of Terror*, Caroline Thompson's adventure television film *Snow White: The Fairest of Them All* (2001), Joe Nussbaum's teen romantic comedy *Sydney White* (2007), Tarsem Singh's family comedy *Mirror Mirror*, Rupert Sanders's action-loaded fantasy film *Snow White and The Huntsman*, and ABC's popular drama television series *Once Upon a Time*. Remarkably, the figure of the fairy-tale dwarf in postmodern visual and pop culture appears less and less as a marginalized, oppressed identity that is socially constructed as a "disabled," abnormal Other.

My study is timely and important because it not only demonstrates how postmodern fairy-tale adaptations in North America are redrawing the lines about what is considered Other but also traces an ideological shift in how we view and value diversity in society today. The fairy-tale adaptations examined in this book are more than just twists on old stories and more than newly spun tales with creative embellishments. They serve as the looking glasses of significant cultural trends, changes, customs, and social challenges. Is it a coincidence that positive representations of supernatural creatures in pop culture are arising at a time when racism and xenophobic violence by right-wing extremists, white supremacists, and neo-Nazi groups are on the rise across the United States? One of the more recent fairy-tale films, *The Shape of Water* (2017) by Guillermo del Toro, is an erotic monster tale that addresses Otherness in a favorable light by introducing audiences to a sexualized, heroic amphibian man-beast as an embodiment of the noble savage. Yet, the film implies that monsters, who are portrayed to be more humane than are common people, are still considered threats in North American society, and that there is no place for them, just as there is very little space for immigrants from "undesirable" countries. Whereas the fairy-tale adaptations that I analyze suggest that Otherness can and should be fully embraced, they also highlight the yawning gap that still exists between the representation and the reality of embracing diversity wholeheartedly in twenty-first-century America.

1

Reimagining Uncanny Fairy-Tale Creatures

Automatons, Golems, and Doppelgangers

"Alle Geburten unsrer Phantasie wären also zuletzt nur wir selbst."
(All creatures born by our fantasy, in the last
analysis, are nothing but ourselves.)[1]

—Friedrich Schiller

German fairy tales are tales of wonder and terror, of marvelous transformations and horrific images, of delight and disgust. Whether we speak of folk fairy tales penned by the Brothers Grimm or literary fairy tales penned by the German Romantic writers E. T. A. Hoffmann, Ludwig Tieck, Achim von Arnim, Wilhelm Heinrich Wackenroder, Clemens Brentano, Novalis, and Wilhelm Hauff, these stories have the power to tug at our heartstrings by appealing to some of our most basic emotions, which Philipp R. Shaver and his colleagues identified as love, joy, surprise, anger, sadness, and fear (1984). From rags-to-riches stories and narratives featuring heroic quests with happy endings to scenarios of social injustice, human tragedy, and uncanny encounters with supernatural creatures, German fairy tales are not only known to enthrall but also to shock readers. In

November 2014, Jack Zipes published *The Original Folk & Fairy Tales of the Brothers Grimm*, a new translation of the Grimms' tales that reveals to its Anglo-American readership how "extremely dark and harrowing" some of the stories really are (Zipes "Today's Fairy Tales"). Indeed, the Grimms' fairy tales are heavily saturated with gruesome topics such as cannibalism, mutilation, murder, and incest. And yet, the Grimms' fairy tales remain an expression of German Romanticism. But perhaps even grimmer than the Grimms' fairy tales are those tales that belong to the movement of Dark or Black Romanticism (hence *schwarze Romantik* in German, *le genre noir* in French). Emerging at the end of the eighteenth century, this undercurrent of Romanticism favored themes such as night, nature, magic, the monstrous, and death. Thus, it hardly comes as a surprise that supernatural creatures in German folk and literary fairy tales of that period, in particular the figures of the automaton, the golem, and the doppelganger, loom large as demonic, eerie, and sinister agents of calamity.

The movement of Dark Romanticism arose as a countercurrent to Weimar Classicism and as a rejection of Enlightenment reason. One of the principal goals of the Enlightenment was the elimination of fear (Apel 1993, 145). Everything that caused unreasonable fear and thus hindered rational thought and progress, such as superstitions, the belief in magical powers and creatures, and nature's unpredictability and dangers, should be abolished and replaced by rational forms of knowledge. As Michael David Bailey points out, "the eradication of superstition in all its forms became the battle cry for the Enlightenment thinkers, especially the French philosophes," for example, Denis Diderot and Voltaire (2007, 209). By superstition, these philosophers understood not only common beliefs in magic, spirits, ghosts, and demonic powers but also organized religion, "especially the Catholic Church, with its claims of effective ritual drawing down active divine power into the world" (209). In Germany, Immanuel Kant emerged as a major authority of the Enlightenment. In his essay "What is Enlightenment?"

(1784), Kant "challenged the citizens of his day to break free from the chains of superstition and 'dare to know'" (Jackson 2002, 293).

The Dark Romantics, and above all E. T. A. Hoffmann, rejected the principles of Enlightenment to focus on the darkness of the soul, the unfathomable reaches of the human psyche, and produced works of gloomy, macabre, scary, demonic, or satanic character. In a way, they juxtaposed the "light" of the Enlightenment with the "dark" side of Romanticism. The writers of the movement thematized hidden fears, dreams, and the grotesque and emphasized irrational, melancholic traits. In their aspirations to penetrate the mysteries of life, the Dark Romantics were also fascinated by the formation of human madness and "evil." By fusing reality with the fantastic, the rational with the irrational, empiricism with mysticism, and the natural with the supernatural in their novellas and fairy tales, the Romantics transcended the narrow genre boundaries of their time. Adherents of Friedrich Schlegel's philosophical credo of a "progressive universal poetry" (*progressive Universalpoesie*) (Schlegel, vol. 2, 182), Romantic writers strove to create poetic works that were framed paradoxically as universal yet forever without closure. In contrast to the proponents of Enlightenment, the Romantics valued the heart over the head and were attracted by the inexplicable, the hidden, the dark, the subconscious, the unknown, and everything that was not open to rational comprehension. Thus, the enigmatic quality of wonder tales, the mysterious nature of fantastic creatures, and the marvelous, ancient aura of the fairy-tale genre corresponded to the underlying foundations of Romantic convictions and philosophies.

Whereas in the German Romantic period the figures of the automaton, the golem, and the doppelganger were viewed as uncanny, disturbing figures, their significance transforms in twentieth- and twenty-first-century American media culture. Hence, although German folk and literary fairy tales of Romanticism code the figures of the automaton, the golem, and the doppelganger as uncanny, terrifying agents and diabolic harbingers of death, contemporary visual culture in America portrays these characters in a dramatically different light. In fact, these supernatural beings resurface in postmodern media productions as transformed, dramatized, humanized, and infantilized characters, oftentimes with positive connotations and equipped with profound emotional depth that invites a spectator's empathic response in return. At the same time, the grim themes of the Romantic works that were intended to shock and fascinate the readers of the nineteenth century still capture our imagination and interest today.

Ulrich Scheck ties this ongoing fascination with Romantic novellas and fairy tales to their depiction of strange and terrifying events "that unearth the darker side of the human soul" (2004, 101). Scheck highlights how contemporary film and television series echo the mysterious topoi of the Romantic texts:

> Indeed, for today's readers who receive an almost daily dose of the supernatural via television and motion pictures, the wondrous occurrences in these texts could have come straight from the twilight zone of the X-Files: a knight loses his sanity and life when he finds out that his marriage is based on an incestuous relationship; young men succumb to the seductive powers of marble statues and female automatons, protagonists make deals with evil forces and trade their shadows and hearts for material wealth. (101)

As this chapter makes clear, the automaton, the golem, and the doppelganger are particularly illustrative of the ways in which the uncanny figures emerging out of nineteenth-century German texts resonate in twentieth- and twenty-first-century North American media. In order to highlight the different treatment of these three figures, the chapter first examines their emergence within the framework of the nineteenth-century German literary field before considering the important transformations these creatures undergo in North American media culture. American films, such as *The*

Stepford Wives (1975, 2004), *Edward Scissorhands* (1990), and *A.I. Artificial Intelligence* (2001) provide us with new perspectives on these figures treated by the German Dark Romantics. We might understand these twentieth- and twenty-first-century films in terms of Pauline Greenhill and Sidney Eve Matrix's notion of adaptation:

> *Adaptation,* understood as "repetition without replication," may involve a degree of faithful homage in its alteration or translation of the text, but fidelity may just as easily reside in critique as it does in imitative tribute (Hutcheon 2006, 7). Many modern fairy tale films and examples of cinematic folklore are best understood as transfigurations or transmutations of folktales since they incorporate varieties of transtextuality—embedded interlinked texts—theorized by Gérard Genette (1997). Once the focus of the fairy tale film expands beyond the classic Disney animations, it becomes immediately apparent that there are numerous examples of the kind of resolutely unfaithful cinematic folklore adaptations that Robert Stam would describe as "less a resuscitation of an originary word than a turn in an ongoing [intertextual] dialogical process" through which the filmmaker engages with the source (2004, 25). (13)

In its first section, for instance, the chapter explores live-action films with adult themes that are fairy tales in disguise. To narrow the scope of research, the chapter focuses on contemporary media productions of the last few decades that feature postmodern manifestations of the automaton on the one hand and qualify as fairy-tale films on the other hand. In a similar fashion, the corpus of the following two sections unfolds in this chapter concerning the golem and the doppelganger emergent in fairy-tale-inspired media productions of the twentieth- and twenty-first century. To identify a film as a hypertextual fairy-tale adaptation or as a film with intertextual references to a specific source fairy tale requires some familiarity with tale types and fairy-tale motifs. The films *The Stepford Wives*, for example, can be read as a "Bluebeard" tale type, *Edward Scissorhands* appears to be a modern interpretation of "Beauty and the Beast," and *A.I. Artificial Intelligence* provides us with an updated version of Carlo Collodi's children's novel *Le avventure di Pinocchio* (*The Adventures of Pinocchio*, 1881–83), in addition to making direct intertextual references to the fairy-tale-inspired *Pinocchio* narrative. Already Maria Tatar observed that "no fairy tale text is sacred" (1992, 229), and Greenhill and Matrix have noted that, even if the idea of a fairy-tale film is stretched, the "consideration of fairy tale connections can greatly enhance both the fairy tale and the film as intertext" (2010, 17).

The focus of this chapter will revolve around the three supernatural creatures of the automaton, the golem, and the doppelganger, as the reimaginings of these figures, from dangerous monsters that instill fear to nonthreatening, pitiable creatures that evoke sympathy in readers, listeners, or spectators, are part of a larger trend in North American media culture and a response to the forces of globalization that create multicultural awareness. This trend reflects North American society's changing attitude toward "the Other,"[2] toward what is considered strange and different and therefore frightening. Because we live in a postmodern time of global exchange and increased cultural diversity, Otherness and alterity have become integral parts of our everyday life. American fairy-tale-inspired films and television series promote the idea that just because someone is different, this does not make this person a monster. By humanizing supernatural creatures—that is, by stripping them of their monstrous features and endowing them with feelings, personality, and positive character traits—they become creatures to relate to and can engage audience empathy. As Christina M. Gschwandtner aptly notes, "What is other or different or strange or incomprehensible is scary, unsettling, and fearful. The stranger has always been a threat on some level. So what do we do when something or someone is 'strange' or 'different'? Either we destroy: try to eliminate the scary stranger, to wipe out anything that induces fear. Or we assimilate, comprehend (encompass), make like us—so the stranger really becomes merely another version of the self" (2012, 42).[3] To put my claim in in a nutshell, postmodern pop culture metamorphoses the monstrous Other featured in German fairy tales into fantastic figures with which to identify. In a way, this transformation also represents the overcoming of what psychiatrist Ernst Jentsch and later psychoanalyst Sigmund Freud have termed "Das Unheimliche" (the uncanny). Zipes summarizes the concept as "the uncanny in life, so that which is strange becomes familiar and we feel comfortable with it" (2006, 198).

The Otherized supernatural creatures in German Romantic fairy tales can be read as personifications of the uncanny, a term associated since the 1970s with the foundational works on fantasy, or "the fantastic," of literary theorist Tzvetan Todorov and, since the 1980s, with the works of Rosemary Jackson. In his definition of the fantastic in literature, Todorov draws on the German term *unheimlich*, which translates literally to "unlike home" and, because there is no English equivalent, is referred to as "unfamiliar" or "uncanny." In *The Fantastic: A Structural Approach to a Literary Genre* (1973), Todorov defines "the fantastic" as a moment of hesitation between belief and disbelief of the supernatural. It is a moment of uncertainty between the uncanny and the marvelous. According to Todorov, the uncanny is experienced upon encountering something that is at once both strange and familiar. The marvelous, by contrast, is the more traditional view of fantasy. Todorov claims that the uncanny is characterized by a character's response—often fear—toward something seemingly inexplicable, or impossible. He argues that the marvelous does not require a response from a character, only that the fantastic event occurs. The suspension between the uncanny and the marvelous makes the literature fantastic.[4]

In *Fantasy: The Literature of Subversion* (1981), Jackson suggests that the fantastic is not a literary category and should therefore be referred to as a *mode* rather than as a genre placed between the marvelous and the uncanny (35). According to Jackson, the fantastic uncanny leans toward explanations that can be elucidated by logic and rules of the world as we know it, whereas the fantastic marvelous does not question the supernatural. In contrast to Todorov, Jackson emphasizes in her seminal study that the uncanny has both philosophical and psychoanalytic meanings and draws on the works of Martin Heidegger, Sigmund Freud, and Helene Cixous. Whereas for Heidegger the uncanny is the "empty space produced by a loss of faith in divine images," a space that is neither God's nor man's, for Freud the uncanny "uncovers what is hidden and, by doing so, effects a disturbing transformation of the familiar into the unfamiliar" (1981, 63, 65). Jackson cites Cixous to argue that the uncanny represents our terror at the possibility of nonexistence and nonsignification: "*Das Unheimlich* [*sic*] is at its purest here, where we dis-cover our latent deaths, our hidden lack of being, for 'nothing is both better known and stranger to though than mortality. . . . 'Death' has no shape in life. Our unconscious has no room for a representation of our mortality'" (1981, 68).

Whereas Todorov does not explore the different German meanings of the term *unheimlich*, Jackson draws on Freud to examine the two different levels of the term, which are vital for an understanding of his theory in relation to fantasy. Further, the two different levels are also crucial for how the term is understood and applied in this chapter and throughout the book. The unnegated adjective *heimlich* is ambivalent, as it encapsulates two different meanings: "homely" and "secretly." On the first level of meaning, it signifies that which is homely, familiar, comfortable, positive, protective, safe, friendly, and cheerful. It is also connected to the noun *Heimat* (homeland) and the adjective *heimisch* (native). Hence, its negated form *unheimlich* summons up anything that is alien, strange, uncomfortable, not familiar, and unknown. On the second level of meaning, it signifies that which is concealed from others, including everything that is hidden, obscured, and secreted with potentially disturbing powers. According to Jackson, "The uncanny combines these two semantic levels: its signification lies precisely in this dualism. It uncovers what is hidden, and by doing so, effects a disturbing transformation of the familiar into the unfamiliar" (65).

North American media culture takes the *unheimlich* or uncanny fairy-tale figures of German fairy-tale tradition, the automaton, the golem, and the double, and recasts them as *heimlich* creatures that appear familiar, "more like us," and therefore more human. As a result, the viewers are in the position to better understand the fantastic characters and to empathize and connect with them on a personal level. At the same time, what is familiar and known is inevitably less threatening and frightening than what is unfamiliar and unknown. In his essay *Das Umheimliche* ("The Uncanny," 1919), Freud interestingly describes fairy tales as excluding the uncanny: "Fairy tales quite frankly adopt the animistic standpoint of the omnipotence of thoughts and wishes, and yet I cannot think of any genuine fairy story which has anything uncanny about it" (1917–19, 246). What is problematic about this statement is Freud's notion of what accounts for a "genuine fairy story." Freud associates only those stories in which the world of reality is left behind from the very start with fairy tales, such as the tales by Hans Christian Andersen and, presumably, the Grimms' tales. In these stories, Freud argues, "feelings of fear—including therefore uncanny feelings—are ruled out altogether. We understand this, and that is why we ignore any opportunities we find in them for developing such feelings" (1917–19, 252). Yet, Freud cites E. T. A. Hoffmann's *Kunstmärchen* (literary fairy tale) "Der Sandmann" ("The Sandman," 1816) and Wilhelm Hauff's literary fairy tale "Die Geschichte von der abgehauenen Hand" ("The Severed Hand," 1825) as prime examples of the uncanny. Although this inconsistency of Freud's argument is noteworthy, the idea of the uncanny in the form of the supernatural Other plays a significant role in this chapter's analysis of the different portrayals of the automaton, the golem, and the doppelganger.

The Automaton in German Fairy Tales

This section sheds light on Hoffmann's employment of automatons as uncanny Others in his literary fairy tales and then moves on to demonstrate how contemporary North American media productions reinterpret the theme of the artificially created human in new and innovative ways. Although there are common tropes, such as the eyes as windows to the human soul, the artificial woman as a projection of man's imagination, and the scientist or inventor of the automaton, shared by Hoffmann's tales and the American films, there are also significant differences. Whereas Hoffmann's automatons are predominantly soulless mechanical creatures associated with madness, monstrosity, and fear, North American retellings feature automatons as comedic or sentient beings inviting audience empathy. Beginning with Hoffmann's fairy tales, we will see a development from automatons resembling toys and dolls, to automatons in American media productions in the roles of subjugated housewife-slaves, and finally to automatons emerging as sentient, creative, and artistic beings. Besides this development of the automaton from mindless machine to sentient being, I will also demonstrate how the figure of the diabolical and uncanny scientist or inventor in Hoffmann's tales is recast in American films. Postmodern reimaginings range from evil men who murder their wives to form a patriarchal society to the gentle, father-like creator, reminiscent of elderly Mister Geppetto from *Pinocchio*, who invents a sentient, feeling being rather than a monstrous machine, even if others may view the character as monstrous.

The desire of humans to become godlike by taking creation into their own hands is as old as humankind itself. Indeed, the imaginative notion of the simulacrum of women and men that come to life is a recurring theme in literature, art, and other media, from the legends and mythologies of ancient Greeks to modern science fiction. Artificially created humans, so-called automatons or automata, usually come into existence in three different ways: as creations at the hands of gods (for example, in Greek mythology, the story of Pygmalion and his statue Galatea as described in Ovid's narrative poem *Metamorphoses* or the golden robotic handmaidens designed by the blacksmith god Hephaestus), by the use of magic (for example, the medieval golem of Jewish folklore or the mandrake in Achim von Arnim's "Isabella von Ägypten" ["Isabella of Egypt"], 1812), or by the use of science, either with mechanical (for example, the doll Olimpia in E. T. A. Hoff-mann's "The Sandman") or nonmechanical artifice (for example, the monster in Mary Shelley's *Frankenstein; or, The Modern Prometheus*, 1818, or the Homunculus in Goethe's *Faust, Part Two*, 1832). Artificially created humans continue to captivate people's imagination, and postmodern media productions confirm this ongoing fascination with the mechanical Other.

Automatons, which I identify with humanoid robots or "androids" as they are commonly referred to in today's science-fiction genre, have a long tradition in the world of North American film and television.[5] They are featured in Ridley Scott's *Blade Runner* (1982), the *Terminator* films (1984–2015) and television series (2008–9), Tim Burton's *Edward Scissorhands*, Steven Spielberg's *A.I. Artificial Intelligence*, and Alex Proyas's *I, Robot* (2004), to name but a few examples. So-called gynoids or fembots, the female counterpart to androids, have appeared in Fritz Lang's German expressionist epic *Metropolis* (1927), Bryan Forbes's thriller *The Stepford Wives* (1975) and Frank Oz's comedic remake in 2004, and more recently in Alex Garland's *Ex Machina* (2015). Although sophisticated robots, such as Data in Gene Roddenberry's television series *Star Trek: The Next Generation* (1987–94), have existed largely in the domains of science fiction, fantasy, fairy tales, and mythology, the concept of the mechanical human and the fascination in developing robots that can mimic human morphology is rooted in historical fact, as hinted at by Martin Scorsese's *Hugo* (2011). In effect, humanoid automata can be demonstrably traced back as far as the Middle Ages and the complex constructions by Muslim polymath Ismail Al-Jazari, which he described in *The Book of Knowledge* in 1206. Several centuries later, in 1737, French engineer Jacques de Vaucanson invented *The Flute Player*, the world's first successfully built biomechanical automaton. Other eighteenth-century automaton makers include the prolific Frenchman Pierre Jaquet-Droz and the Swiss mechanic Henri Maillardet. Their automaton creations were capable of producing programmed artwork, such as playing music, drawing pictures, and writing poems.

The German Romantic tradition incorporated numerous stories based on the literary theme of the automaton. On many levels in Romantic discourse, the automaton or pure mechanism is regarded with fascination, but it is equally an uncanny object of suspicion that instills fear.[6] As Samuel L. Macey notes, the Romantics were both intrigued and alarmed by "the possibility that man might not merely imitate God, but, in doing so, might even eliminate his functions" (1987, 97). At the same time, the German Romantics believed that the rise of rational philosophy represented an attack on the imaginative faculties of the artist and writer. Lieselotte Sauer has argued that automatons represented "the incarnation of materialistic and rational forces threatening man's innocent imagination" (1990, 293). One way of rebelling against the dominant movement of the reason-based Enlightenment and of reclaiming imagination, nature, and innocence was for the German Romantics to write *Kunstmärchen* that portray automatons negatively. In E. T. A. Hoffmann's fairy tales "Nußknacker und Mausekönig" ("The Nutcracker and the Mouse King," 1816), "Das fremde Kind" ("The Strange Child," 1817), and "The Sandman," the automaton becomes not only the symbol of a repetitious, purely mechanical, and dull world but also a symbol of the uncanny, threatening Other that forebodes the hollow existence of living death or inanimate life without imagination.

Imagination, of course, is the magic wand of childhood that transforms ordinary sand into fairy dust or an old tree trunk into a sparkling palace. In the fairy tale "The Strange Child," which was published in the second volume of his collection of children's fairy tales *Kinder-Mährchen* (1817), Hoffmann pays homage to Jean-Jacques Rousseau's "notions of a natural education that would allow children to flower" (Zipes [1999] 2013, 102). It is a didactical tale that prioritizes nature, imagination, and the fantastic over artificiality, memorized knowledge, and reason. At the beginning of the tale, the siblings Felix and Christlieb, two poor children who live in an idyllic country setting, succumb all too easily to their artificial toys, a mechanical harp player, a hunter, and a doll, which they receive as gifts from their rich, automaton-like relatives.[7] After carrying the toys off into the forest, the children quickly realize how monotone, boring, and useless these playthings are, and throw them into the bushes and a pond. Here they meet the strange child, a fairy princess and androgynous messenger of the land of fantasy, who reminds them of the magical secrets hidden in nature. Inspired by the beauty and variety of their natural surroundings, the children now use their imagination and play with the things nature offers to them. However, when their private tutor, Master Inkblot (Magister Tinte), attempts to civilize and functionalize Felix and Christlieb with his pedantry, the little toy automatons reappear once more as symbolic representations of rational thought, mechanization, and control. In the end, the children are forced to leave their home after the death of their father, but since the strange child remains alive in their dreams, they are still able to enjoy the marvels from the otherworldly realm.

Hoffmann animates inanimate objects in "The Strange Child" by transforming simple toy automatons into eerie, self-controlled machines, which are not only able to speak and move but also physically attack the children Christlieb and Felix. Although the little mechanical harpist, the hunter, and the doll should be fun and harmless for the children to play with, the toys turn out to be no innocent playthings at all. As threatening supernatural creatures and faithful servants of the antagonist Master Inkblot, the toys come alive when the children are trying to escape from a storm in the woods:

Christlieb was weeping with fear, but she did as Felix said. However, as soon as they were sitting in the middle of the dense bushes they heard harsh, rasping voices right behind them. . . . Felix looked around, and he felt his flesh creep when he saw the toy huntsman and harpist he had thrown away rise form the undergrowth . . . the huntsman even levelled his little shotgun at Felix. . . . The rain was now pouring down, thunder was rolling overhead. . . . Christlieb's big doll rose from the reeds into which Felix had thrown her and said in a grating voice "Silly things, simple minded creatures—despised me—didn't know how to treat me! . . . You just wait, boy, you just wait, girl, we are Master Ink-blot's obedient pupils, he'll soon be here, and then we'll make you sorry you defied him!" (Hoffmann 2010, 188–89)

A closer look at the vocabulary reveals just how scary Hoffmann portrays the automatons in his fairy tale. Hoffmann describes them as "ugly," "uncanny," and "horrible," staring at the children with "dead eyes," and causing a "horrific spook" that leaves Christlieb "half dead." It is up to the reader's imagination to picture what the automatons would do to the children if Master Inkblot would catch them. By juxtaposing the extreme weather conditions of the natural forces, the pouring rain, the rolling claps of thunder, and the roaring of the storm with the unexpected attack of the non-natural forces, the uprising automatons, Hoffmann creates a climactic moment in the fairy tale. The tension between the organic and the lifeless, between nature and the machine, is further intensified by the fact that the controllable automatons, which represent the rational, have become uncontrollable and thus add to the irrational forces of nature in this dramatic scenario.

With startling and deceptively simple ease, Hoffmann manages in his fairy tales to blur the boundaries between the fantastic and reality by merging and contrasting the grotesque, uncanny, bizarre, and mysterious with the prosaic, familiar, known, and normal. He does so by enlivening inanimate objects, such as toys and dolls (e.g., the toys in "The Strange Child," the nutcracker and toy soldiers in "The Nutcracker and the Mouse King"), and by giving the reader the impression that living beings are in reality mechanical creatures (e.g., godfather Drosselmeier in "The Nutcracker and the Mouse King") or vice versa (e.g., Olimpia in "The Sandman"). It is this amalgamation and juxtaposition of the animate and the inanimate that account for much of the horror beneath the surface. The reader is alarmed, suspicious, and ultimately shocked upon the realization that the world of the supernatural and the fantastic is not comfortably removed from everyday existence. Hoffmann's literary fairy tale "The Nutcracker and the Mouse King," which has become a holiday staple for theaters across the United States, unfolds in the overlapping realms of reality and fantasy as domains with ambiguous boundaries. Just like Marie Stahlbaum, the chief protagonist of the tale, the reader may find it difficult to distinguish the two realms.

In this tale, the siblings Marie and Fritz celebrate Christmas Eve with their godfather Drosselmeier, who is an inventor of mechanical toys. Marie becomes fond of her gift, a wooden nutcracker. When the nutcracker's jaw breaks and Drosselmeier promises to fix it, the face of the wooden puppet seems momentarily to come alive. Marie is frightened and at night believes she sees the nutcracker and her brother's toy soldiers fight a battle against the mouse king and his army. Marie rescues the nutcracker by throwing her slipper at the mice. On the following day, Drosselmeier fixes the nutcracker and tells Marie the story of Princess Pirlipat and Madam Mouserinks. Marie learns that the nutcracker is really Drosselmeier's nephew, who had been cursed by the witch Madam Mouserinks to transmute into an ugly nutcracker, and Princess Pirlipat banished him from the castle. To break the spell of his enchantment, the nutcracker has to kill the mouse king and must find someone who falls in love with his ugly visage. Marie helps the nutcracker defeat his enemy and follows him into the doll kingdom. When she returns home, she tells Drosselmeier's nephew that she would love him and thus breaks the curse. He proposes to her and Marie becomes the queen of the doll kingdom.

Similar to what happens in "The Strange Child," toys, dolls, automatons, all soulless, artificial creatures, and children, as representations of life and imagination, play a central role in this fairy tale. Just like Christlieb and Felix's relatives, who give them mechanical playthings, it is godfather Drosselmeier who surprises Marie and Fritz with fascinating toy automatons. Hoffmann presents the inventor and judge Drosselmeier as a mysterious and sinister man. Drosselmeier's entire appearance as an ugly, short, old, dark pirate look-alike with a wig reflects his uncanny and artificial nature, which in turn is also expressed in his occupation: "Supreme Court Justice Drosselmeier was anything but handsome. He was short and scrawny, his face was covered with wrinkles, and he wore a big, black patch instead of a right eye. He also had no hair on his head, which is why he sported a very lovely periwig made of spun glass and very artistic. Indeed, the godfather was altogether a very artistic man, who even knew a thing or two about clocks and could actually build them" (Hoffmann and Dumas 2007, 3). Drosselmeier's uncanniness is tied to his appearance, reflecting artificiality and a type of masquerade that not only identifies him as a maker of machines but also renders him "machine-like." One of Drosselmeier's gifts for Maria and Fritz is a clockwork castle with mechanical people moving about inside it. The children, however, get easily bored by the repetitive dancing automatons and openly show their contempt for the dullness of the new playthings. The stark oppositions between imagination and creativity versus reason and monotony come to the fore in this particular scene. Fritz deprecatingly remarks, "If those small polished things in the castle can only keep repeating themselves, then they're not worth much, and I don't especially have to call for them" (8). Instead of the castle construction with the teensy automated dolls, Fritz prefers his hussar soldiers, which are much better suited for imaginative play. In an aggravated tone, Drosselmeier realizes that his artistic work "is not meant for senseless children" (8). Put another way, the rational world of adults, with its technology, is incompatible with the child's world of imagination.

Hoffmann constantly challenges the boundaries between human and automaton in "The Nutcracker and the Mouse King." The tale compares Drosselmeier, for instance, time and again to a spooky mechanical doll and ugly string puppet. He not only moves "as if he were a marionette" but also makes humming, whirring, and purring mechanical noises (see quotes further below) (24). If we follow Jentsch's argument that the feeling of the uncanny arises where we are in doubt as to "whether an apparently animate being is really alive; or conversely, whether a lifeless object might not be in fact animate," it helps us understand why this destabilization of Drosselmeier as a human being might awaken certain fears and anxieties in the reader revolving around the question of human agency (qtd. in Freud [1919] 2003, 135). Of course, ever since the age of automation and industrialization, one major fear has been that human beings may not be very far ahead of their mechanical doubles. Machines that simulate human performance to perfection can easily replace their human counterparts. This begs the question of how exactly human beings differ from machines. Furthermore, Eric Wilson has pointed out that the automaton of Romanticism manifests two related psychological dimensions: "the uncanny psychic tension between the fear that everything is a machine and the hope that nothing is inorganic" (2012, 112). Hoffmann, the "unrivalled master of the uncanny in literature," as Freud put it, alludes to this tension in his fairy tale by defying easy polarities and by shifting back and forth between Marie's perceptions of reality, dream, and fantasy (Freud [1919] 2003, 141). In the middle of the night, Marie experiences fear when she encounters an automaton version of her godfather sitting on top of the grandfather clock, preventing it from striking. Not only has Drosselmeier replaced a mechanical bird as part of the clock, or rather, the two have transformed into one entity, he also speaks like a wind-up doll or externally controlled marionette and is thus stripped of any human agency:

Marie looked up. The big, gilded owl perching on the clock had lowered its wings, covering the whole timepiece and poking forth the ugly cobblestone with the hooked nose. And the noises grew louder, and words could be made out: "Clock, tick, tock, clock, tick tock! And everyone has to hum softly, hum softly. After all, Mouse King has a fine ear. Hummmmm, hummmmmm, hummmmmm. Strike, chime, do / Soon there will be few!" And the humming resounded dull and hoarse twelve times! Marie shuddered dreadfully and she would almost have dashed off in horror if she had not spotted Godfather Drosselmeier, who sat on the wall clock in lieu of the owl, his yellow coattails dangling like wings on both sides. However, Marie pulled herself together and she exclaimed, loudly and tearfully: "Godfather Drosselmeier, Godfather Drosselmeier, what are you doing up there? Come down to me and stop frightening me, you nasty Godfather Drosselmeier." (Hoffmann 2007, 15)

Is Drosselmeier a real person or is he a machine? Is he an ally or adversary of imagination? Hoffmann leaves these questions open for speculation. In "The Myth of Persephone in Girls' Fantasy Literature" (2012) Holly Blackford calls Drosselmeier "an unnatural, perverse, and deformed being" (48). It is no coincidence that Marie thinks she sees a resemblance between the ugly godfather and the nutcracker doll with its oversized head and spindly legs. In another scene, Drosselmeier evokes the image of a scary string puppet:

But Drosselmeier was making very bizarre faces and he spoke in a snarling and monotonous voice: "Pendulum, had to hum, softly hum, bells boom, bells blast, limp and lame and honk and hunk, doll girl, don't worry, scurry, ring the bell, bell is rung, bell is sung, to drive away Mouse King today, now the owl comes flying fast, pack and pick and pick and pack, chimes are jingly, clocks, hum, hum, pendulums have to hum, pick wouldn't stick, hum and hum and purr and purr!" Marie gaped at Godfather Drosselmeier because he looked very different and far uglier than usual, and because he kept swinging his right arm as if he were a marionette. She would have been truly horrified at the godfather if the mother hadn't been present. (Hoffmann 2007, 24)

Yet, despite his ugly appearance, frightening demeanor, and negatively coded, automaton-like character, Drosselmeier fulfills an ambivalent function in the tale. After all, he is described as a "kind" and "dear" godfather, and the children are, for the most part of the story, very fond of him. According to

Lieselotte Sauer, the mysterious mechanic must not be seen in a completely negative light as the adversary of an exalted imagination (1990, 294). Sauer hints at the fact that Drosselmeier is also the producer of the nutcracker, which is animated by Maria's imagination and accompanies her voyage to the realm of fantasy. However, as Blackford has correctly observed, the text never directly reveals whether the nutcracker toy is Drosselmeier's gift (2012, 52). The stark contrast between Drosselmeier's sophisticated inventions and the simple nutcracker also sheds doubt on this assumption. But it is Drosselmeier who tells Marie about the enchanted nutcracker and who introduces his goddaughter to his handsome nephew from Nuremberg. At the end of the tale, Marie breaks the curse by loving the nutcracker despite his ill-favored looks, a variation of the "Beauty and the Beast" or "Cupid and Psyche" theme. Thanks to Marie, the wooden toy nutcracker turns back into a man and thus love conquers ugliness, beauty redeems the monster, and human life triumphs over the machine.

Automatons in German fairy tales are most terrifying when they are most lifelike (Sauer 1990, 292). This is the case with the androids in Hoffmann's literary fairy tales "Automata" (1814) and "The Sandman" (1816). The androids in these tales are abhorrent, yet "fascinating symbols of life's deception," which are "often used by hostile powers to lead man into temptation" and ultimately death (Sauer 1990, 292). Like Drosselmeier, Professor X in "Automata" is a skilled inventor of automatons. His android, "the Talking Turk," reminiscent of Wolfgang von Kempelen's chess-playing Turk, is a mysterious prophet automaton dressed in a Turkish costume that excites the townspeople in the story. When people ask the automaton questions, the quasi-human figure mysteriously comes up with an answer that demonstrates its knowledge of the questioner's inner life and therefore appears to look into the soul of his interlocutor. The two main characters of the tale, Ferdinand, a poet, and his friend Ludwig, a musician, echo the ambivalent attitude of the Romantics toward pure mechanistic science: fascination on the one hand and suspicion and critique on the other (Riou

2004, 222). At least at the beginning of the tale Ferdinand views the automated oracle primarily as a piece of art, whereas Ludwig expresses his distaste about this caricature of life and man:[8]

> "All such figures," said Ludwig, "that emulate a person less then they mimic the human, these true still images of a living death or a dead life are abhorrent to me to the highest degree . . . it is the oppressive sense of being in the presence of something unnatural and gruesome; and what I detest most of all is the mechanical imitation of human motions. I feel sure this wonderful, ingenious Turk will haunt me with his rolling eyes, his turning head, and his waving arm, like some necromantic monster when I lie awake nights." (my translation)

This tale depicts androids such as "the Talking Turk" as imperfect, soulless imitations of human beings—they are nothing more than an incoherent mixture of life and death. By emphasizing the discrepancy between mechanism and supposed spirituality, Hoffmann intensifies the tension between inorganic artificiality and organic nature. For Ludwig the automaton represents a monstrous creature that haunts him at night, which thrusts the automaton into the realm of the supernatural. Ludwig's association evokes Marie's nightly encounter with her scary, ghostlike godfather Drosselmeier. The figure of the Sandman in Hoffmann's eponymous literary fairy tale is also a nightmarish phantom.

The enigmatic tale of "The Sandman" is one of the most popular German fairy tales that employs the motif of the automaton. At the heart of the story is an early-childhood terror of the protagonist Nathanael, who is caught observing the alchemical experiments of his father and the nightly visitor Coppelius, a frightening, large, and malformed lawyer. Nathanael sees in Coppelius the Sandman, a fantastic character who is said to steal the eyes of children who would not go to bed. The Sandman then takes the eyes to his owl nest on the crescent moon and uses them to feed his children.

Working together, Coppelius and Nathanael's father are engaged in the Faustian endeavor of creating an artificial being, a homunculus. Coppelius takes "shining masses" out of the fire and hammers them into face-like shapes without eyes. Nathanael's sudden scream betrays his presence. As punishment for the unwelcome observer, Coppelius threatens to throw embers into Nathanael's eyes. When his father pleads for mercy, Coppelius instead twists Nathanael's hands and feet and tortures him before he passes out. A year later, Nathanael's father dies during one night of experiments. When Giuseppe Coppola, an Italian trader in barometers and lenses, arrives at his rooms, Nathanael believes he recognizes Coppelius in him and he is determined to take vengeance.

Frustrated and feeling misunderstood by his lover Clara for acting like a "lifeless automaton," Nathanael, now a student, is taken with Olimpia, the "daughter" of his university professor Spalazani. After moving into a new accommodation across from Spalazani's house, Nathanael buys a spyglass from Coppola to observe Olimpia's "heavenly beauty" more closely, believing her to be a human being. He is unaware that Olimpia is an artificial construct, and her strangely staring eyes, the dull mechanical music she performs, and the few sounds she is capable of make her for Nathanael an ideal woman who is superior to all other women. Whereas Olimpia becomes more and more vivid and lively in Nathanael's eyes, Clara appears increasingly like an automaton. When Nathanael decides to propose to Olimpia, he barges in on a fight between Coppola and Spalazani during which Olimpia is thrown down the stairs. Nathanael witnesses his ideal woman shatter into the automated puppet she really is. The realization that Olimpia is, in fact, an automaton, an empty shell, and a wooden doll drives Nathanael into madness, which culminates in suicide.[9]

There have been so many different attempts to interpret Hoffmann's "The Sandman" that, according to Rudolf Drux, the sheer number of interpretive approaches "appears to constitute its own special literary discipline in which representatives of all methodological directions partake" (2009, 59, my translation). Of central importance to this literary fairy tale is the trope of the "eyes," proverbially known to reflect man's soul. Hoffmann ties this leitmotif to the automated woman Olimpia and to the Sandman as described by Nathanael's nurse. In her tale, the Sandman is "a wicked man, who comes to children when they won't go to bed, and throws a handful of sand into their eyes, so that they start out bleeding from their heads. He puts their eyes in a bag and carries them to the crescent moon to feed his own children, who sit in the nest up there. They have crooked beaks like owls so that they can pick up the eyes of naughty human children." The nurse's story can be seen as a form of anti–fairy tale because it inverses the depiction of the mythical Sandman figure in central and northern European folklore, who is a friendly and loveable character bringing good dreams to people by sprinkling magical sand onto their eyes. If we understand the "eyes" theme as a metaphor for mirroring man's soul, then the wicked Sandman robs children in this anti-tale not only of their eyesight but also of their souls. The soul, in turn, is the one thing the automatons in Hoffmann's fairy tale lack. Hence, the Coppelius-Coppola's automaton creatures, and Olimpia in particular, have a need of eyes, as their empty sockets indicate that they are really nothing but soulless chimeras.

Freud has extensively interpreted the anxiety of losing one's eyes in his essay "The Uncanny" as fear of castration. But besides this psychoanalytic perspective, one can tie the fear of going blind also to the process of alienation, of losing sight of what is fact and what is fantasy. As Patrick Bridgwater has so eloquently stated: "It is the eye that is the organ of control, not the one-eyed monster of Freudian dogma" (2013, 321). In other words, Nathanael's childhood trauma, his fear of losing his eyes, alludes to the fear of losing his grip on reality. Throughout the tale, Nathanael's gradual estrangement from reality is closely tied to his perception of the automaton's eyes. At the beginning, Olimpia has "staring eyes," almost as if she has "no power of sight," which scares Nathanael. Hoffmann uses the term "uncanny" to describe Nathanael's feelings about his first sight of Olimpia.

However, throughout the tale, Olimpia's "dead eyes" appear to become more and more lifelike, and when Nathanael gazes through Coppola's spyglass, "it seemed to him as if moist moonbeams were rising in Olympia's eyes. It was as if the power of seeing were being kindled for the first time; her glances flashed with constantly increasing life." Nathanael is not only increasingly deceived into believing that the automaton is a living being but is also alienating himself further and further from reality. The machine becomes more human and real to him than his actual human fiancé, Clara. By believing that Olimpia's eyes beam back at him "full of love and desire," Nathanael ascribes emotions to the automaton and thereby falls victim to his own wishful thinking. Nathanael's blinding to reality culminates when his apotheosized automated woman with her "heavenly eyes" is suddenly unmasked for the fraud and deception of life she truly is. The unexpected disillusionment and realization of the truth affect the protagonist's physical and mental state adversely: "Nathanael stood paralysed; he had seen but too plainly that Olimpia's waxen, deadly pale countenance had no eyes, but black holes instead—she was, indeed, a lifeless doll . . . madness seized him [Nathanael] with its burning claws, and clutched into his soul, tearing to pieces all his thoughts and senses" (Hoffman 2008, 37–38).

The figure of Olimpia as the perfectly pleasing artificial woman introduces the trope of gender in relation to the uncanny automaton. Olimpia is the product of male manufacturing, namely, the invention of Coppelius-Coppola and her "father" Spalazani, and thus can be read as a mere projection of man's imagination of ideal femininity. For Nathanael, Olimpia's beautiful looks, her stiff posture and statue-like appearance, her tasteful and rich clothing, her perfect musical abilities, and her "heavenly eyes" are all factors contributing to Olimpia's charm and attractiveness. Nathanael misinterprets Olimpia's utter passivity and her painful lack of words—or rather her obedience and silence—as indications of a deep, noble mind and poetic soul. Of course, the notion of men artificially creating an ideal woman has a long literary tradition, and robotic women in contemporary works of fiction have been seen as an extension of this theme. Such gynoids or fembots are designed according to cultural stereotypes of a "perfect" woman and are often unique technological inventions made to fit a particular man's desire for a submissive and obedient sex object. The concept of creating dull, obedient, mindless, and sexually attractive women reemerges in Ira Levin's 1972 satirical thriller novel *The Stepford Wives* and the two films that followed in 1975 (directed by Bryan Forbes) and in 2004 (directed by Frank Oz). Whereas Hoffman's nineteenth-century literary fairy tale describes Nathanael as a mad man who mistakes an artificial doll for a real woman, the female robots in Levin's twentieth-century novel can pass as real women in our world, and their artificial bodies are preferred by men to their human wives.

The Automaton in American Media

In Levin's *The Stepford Wives*, husbands are portrayed as preferring obedient, mindless, and docile housewives to independent, vital, diverse, and intelligent spouses. By resorting to technological means, husbands replace their human wives with zombie-like gynoid substitutes that are obsessed with motherhood and household chores. Dressed in big hats and party dresses, these full-size Barbie dolls are perfectly happy to wash, wax, polish, clean, cook, iron, and shop all day long. Without having a mind of their own, the Stepford wives exist solely to satisfy their husbands' every need. But the result, a "picture-postcard" flawless suburban society, comes at a costly price and gruesome truth: the human wives are transformed to robotic lookalikes through murder. Even the protagonist of the story and new resident of the town Stepford, the talented photographer Joanna Eberhart, cannot stop the conspiracy. After becoming suspicious of the "Stepford Men's Association," Joanna realizes that the Stepford women are nothing but robotic duplicates of women killed by their husbands and ultimately becomes another Stepford wife victim. Daniel Dinello, who sees the story as an allegory of male chauvinism of the period, has noted that *The Stepford Wives* "extends the master/slave relationship to husbands and wives and effectively symbolizes a vision of homogenized suburbia where women become manufactured products, providing domestic and sexual service to their husbands" (2013, 78).[10]

The film adaptations of *The Stepford Wives* are hypertextually linked to Hoffmann's "The Sandman" with regard to the male-created, artificial woman and the trope of the eyes as mirrors of the human soul. In both the 1975 and the 2004 film versions, the protagonist Joanna is shocked when she witnesses her duplicate gynoid with soulless, black, empty eye sockets. The scene of the 1975 horror film is reminiscent of "The Sandman" and the moment when Nathanael discovers that Olimpia is nothing but a mechanical doll. In contrast to the passive, inanimate, and ultimately fragmented puppet Olimpia, the female duplicates in Bryan Forbes's film version actively triumph over human life. They are uncanny, soulless creatures and programmed killing machines, designed by men, which are shown to take the lives and eyes—that is, the souls—of their victims. Indeed, it is the Joanna-automaton who brandishes a phone cord and strangles the real Joanna to death.

In Frank Oz's 2004 adaptation, starring Nicole Kidman in the lead role as Joanna Eberhart, the gynoids are portrayed in a very different light, as stultified, ridiculous characters. The artificial woman no longer appears

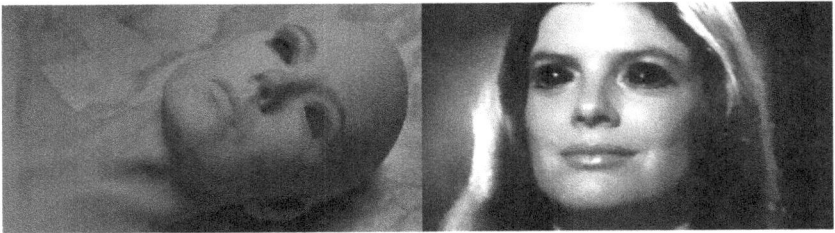

The Joanna automatons in the 1975 (right) and 2004 (left) film versions of *The Stepford Wives* are depicted as soulless creatures with black, empty eye sockets evoking the theme of the eyes in Hoffmann's "The Sandman."

as threatening or uncanny Other but supplies comic relief as a walking appliance instead. Although the automatons are still sexually attractive, dull, obedient, and compliant, corresponding to a 1950s male fantasy of the perfect woman, the robotic creatures are presented as silly and bizarre mechanical "Barbies" with an "off" switch and a remote control operated by their husbands. In contrast to Olimpia in Hoffmann's "The Sandman," the mechanical features of the gynoids in the film are intensely overdrawn to trigger a humorous response in the viewer. At a square dance scene, for instance, Stepford woman Sarah Sunderson (Faith Hill) blows a fuse and starts spinning at an abnormally high velocity. She repeats the same words, "Yippee-ki-yay" and "Do-si-do," over and over until she suddenly falls to the ground with a loud bang, twitching like a broken robot and giving off sparks. To intensify the comedic effect, the scene is followed by a quick joke made by Joanna's friends, Roger Bannister (Roger Bart), a flamboyant gay man, and Bobbie Markowitz (Bette Midler), a writer and recovering alcoholic. "She is drunk," Roger speculates about Sarah's strange behavior, and Bobbie replies sneeringly, "She is blonde." In another scene, Joanna's husband, Walter (Matthew Broderick), attends a meeting of the "Stepford Men's Association." One of the husbands demonstrates to Walter that his wife is capable of dispensing money like an ATM machine and gives her his credit card. The Stepford woman first puts the card in her mouth, appears to process it, beeps, and then ejects twenty dollars. This is the crucial moment when Walter realizes for the first time that the Stepford women are, in fact, machines. But instead of showing any signs of shock or madness, as does Nathanael in "The Sandman" when he recognizes that Olimpia is a wooden doll, Walter cracks a joke to demonstrate to the other husbands that he is "on board" with the ideology of Stepford. "She gives singles!" Walter remarks, followed by approving laughter, applause, and shoulder patting from the other men.

Examining the film through the lens of gender, the figure of the ideal female robot as a projection of male fantasy takes center stage. The Stepford women, who never age, are ever-willing sexual servants to their husbands.

At Sarah's house, Joanna and her friends overhear an unrealistically long, shrill scream of orgasmic ecstasy coming from the upstairs bedroom and Sarah's joyous exclamations to her husband, "I am so lucky" and "You are the king!" With the push of a button, men even have the power to inflate the breasts of their wives. Although the husbands enjoy mastering their automated women through remote controls engraved with their wives' names, the gender power balance is reversed at the end of the film when the viewer learns that a woman, namely the town's leading lady, Claire Wellington (Glenn Close), initiated the Stepford master plan. She explains her intentions behind establishing the community of Stepford with the following conviction: "All I wanted was a better world. A world where men were men and women were cherished and lovely." As Marion Gymnich and Klaus Scheunemann have pointed out, Claire is the only female character who voluntarily adopted the conservative gender role and the lifestyle of Stepford. "The fact that the Stepford community is the idea of a woman alludes to the potential complicity of women with conservative gender stereotypes, which may be fueled by a feeling of nostalgia for a supposedly idyllic past" (2010, 194). The viewer also learns that Claire, a former brain surgeon, created a mechanical duplicate of her dead husband, Mike Wellington (Christopher Walken), whom she killed in a jealous rage over a love affair. The final scene of the film does not foreground an uncanny, fearful, or menacing automaton but the love of a human woman for an artificial man. It is an emotional and dramatic moment about the loss of a beloved spouse that invites viewer identification. And yet, the automaton is wedded to the notion of death, as in Hoffmann's "The Sandman." After Joanna decapitates Mike with a candlestick, revealing him to be an android, Claire holds up Mike's severed robotic head and electrocutes herself by kissing it passionately.

Whereas Oz's *The Stepford Wives* puts a comedic twist on the representation of gynoids by overstating the robotic features of mindless artificial women, the films *A.I.* and *Edward Scissorhands* portray automatons endowed with apparent feelings and a sense of self-awareness. In contrast to Hoffmann's simple toy-automatons and mechanical puppets and in contrast to the mechanical but more lifelike Stepford wives, the androids in *A.I.* and *Edward Scissorhands* are much more sophisticated, technologically advanced, and able to display a rich panoply of emotions. Because they can laugh, cry, and get angry, sad, jealous, or scared, and also know how to communicate such sensations to their surroundings, these humanoid robots appear to be ensouled, sentient beings. Their sentimental responses on the screen allow the audience to connect with the automatons as emotive, humanized subjects rather than inanimate objects. The films encourage spectators to identify with the artificial creatures by empathizing with the automatons' tragic fate as misunderstood outcasts and victims isolated from the rest of society. Spielberg's *A.I.* presents a special case study in my analysis of the automaton in contemporary fairy-tale films because the protagonist, David (Haley Joel Osment), is a child automaton. Whereas the German Romantics viewed machines and the mechanical critically as the embodiment of cold reason and materialist science that compromise man's innocent imagination, the film *A.I.* portrays the android boy David as personification of innocence, love, and imaginative spirit.

The narrative of the film unfolds against the backdrop of a not-so-far future in which the human race has advanced to the point of being able to create realistic automatons, called mechas, to serve them. David, the first highly advanced robotic boy programmed to love, is adopted as a test case by a Cybertronics employee (Sam Robards) and his wife, Monica (Frances O'Connor), as a substitute for their biological son, Martin (Jake Thomas), who remains in cryostasis, stricken by an incurable disease.[11] To provide David with a companion, she gifts him Teddy, a robotic teddy bear and "super toy." When Martin unexpectedly returns home after a cure is discovered, friction develops between him and David as they both seek favor with Monica. Jealousy grows among the siblings, and Martin asks Monica to read them *Pinocchio* to force the issue of human boy versus artificial boy. David becomes enamored with the fairy tale, in which the wooden puppet becomes a real boy thanks to the story's Blue Fairy. At Martin's birthday pool party, an act of self-preservation by David is misinterpreted as an attempt to drown Martin. Monica tries to return David to Cybertronics for disassembly but has a change of heart and abandons him in the woods instead, along with Teddy. After David embarks on an adventurous journey to discover where he truly belongs, the film jumps two thousand years forward in time.[12] Advanced mecha rescue David and Teddy from an icy tomb. Since humanity has died out, the mecha are intrigued by David's experiences of living with humans. After downloading his memories and reviving David, they fabricate a reality with a character resembling the Blue Fairy. She explains to David that although the future mechas cannot turn him into a real boy or bring Monica back to life, they can use the DNA from a lock of Monica's hair, which Teddy had saved, to create a clone of Monica that will live for one single day. The next day, David spends a day of perfect bliss with his "mother," who tells him at the end that she loves him and has always loved him. With this knowledge, David falls asleep content and peacefully beside her.

The film *A.I.* features a world in which automatons exist as material commodities, merchandise, private property, and service providers, functioning as surrogates for affection, both psychologically and physically. Joe (Jude Law), a mecha male prostitute who befriends David, evokes the gynoid sex servants of Stepford. His looks are dashing, he has charm, and he flatters a female client by telling her "you are a goddess." Joe tries to convince David that humans, including his mother, cannot love mechas because they are merely considered consumer goods: "She loves what you do for her as my customers love what it is that I do for them. But she does not love you David." By highlighting the fine line between sophisticated androids programmed with emotions and humans, the film calls into question the nature of consciousness and personhood. Based on his external appearance, David is an eleven-year-old boy with brown hair who weighs sixty pounds and is four feet, six inches tall. But it is David's ability to love and feel, whether artificial or natural, that distinguishes him from other mechas and positions him in the category of *he* instead of *it*. David's artificial intelligence as a marvel of cybernetic progress along with his performance or simulacrum of humanness elevates his status from an emotionless automaton to a sentient being. Indeed, David's profound love for his mother, his capability to hope and dream of finding the Blue Fairy, and his determined wish to become a real boy set him apart from the mindless, monotone, negatively coded automatons of German Romanticism. He is also further "developed" than the subdued, mechanical Stepford wives, who are under the complete control of their husbands. In contrast to the externally controlled, nonautonomous fembots, David's actions demonstrate a free will comparable to that of humans.

Although Spielberg's *A.I.* incorporates significant portions of Collodi's fairy-tale-inspired novel *Pinocchio* and of Disney's animated *Pinocchio* (1940) adaptation, Greenhill and Matrix point out that *A.I.* is not universally or instantly recognized as a fairy-tale film because: "Disney's animators have stamped a cartoon vision of the boy puppet on the popular imagination in indelible ink. Theoretically speaking, moving from animation to live action is already a step outside the Disney paratextual boundary" (2010, 10).[13] The same can be said about Burton's gothic fairy-tale film *Edward Scissorhands*, which might not be immediately recognized for its allusions to "Beauty and the Beast" thanks to Disney's popular 1991 animated version.[14] *Edward Scissorhands* is a film about being on the outside as an isolated, albeit sentient "monster." The unfinished automaton, Edward (Johnny Depp), who has scissors for hands, evokes dismemberment and mutilation reminiscent of Olimpia's fragmented body in Hoffmann's horrific tale "The Sandman." Just like Drosselmeier in Hoffmann's "The Nutcracker and the Mouse King," Edward's gothic, scar-faced appearance is uncanny and frightening. Yet, Edward appears as an innocent, naïve, misunderstood, and neglected creature and thus resembles in many ways the child-automaton David. Edward, or the "Pinocchio-like monster," as Linda Badley refers to him in *Film, Horror, and the Body Fantastic* (1995), does not think with his head, he thinks with his heart: his responses to situations are immediate and unmediated (96). In spite of his inherent ability to slay anyone he comes across, the android is a gentle soul whose only wish is to be loved. When he is "adopted" into a 1950s middle-class American family, he falls in love with the gorgeous neighborhood sweetheart, Kim Boggs (Winona Ryder), who must come to see the inner beauty of the lonely, outcast "Beast."

Throughout the film, Edward transforms from what appears to be a cold creature to an android with human character traits and facial expressions that reflect his emotional state, such as happiness, surprise, fear, embarrassment, anger, and confusion. Everything is new to him, a fact that is expressed in the character's wide-eyed wonder and little subtleties like the way Edward quivers his scissor hands whenever he is nervous or curious. As he associates with the people in his environment, he begins to socially mature and his ability to feel emotions intensifies. Edward's social awakening coupled with his childlike clumsiness due to his physical handicap and inexperience of life allows viewers to feel sympathy for the character and to empathize with him as a misunderstood, sensitive creature. Because of his razor-sharp fingers, Edward is incapable of directly touching anyone and thus becomes the physical manifestation of isolation.[15] Unlike Hoffmann's automatons, Edward possesses creative potential and ultimately becomes a true artist after exploring different ways of applying his artistic skills. At first, Edward begins by trimming the hedges in the backyard of his host family in the shapes of people and animals. Then, he starts grooming the neighborhood dogs, and soon after he is cutting the hair of the suburban housewives with great sophistication and extravagance. By the end of the film, he carves beautiful ice sculptures and in the process creates an effect of falling snow. His sculptures are evidence of his imaginary mind and innovative creativity in sharp contrast to Hoffmann's "stiff and soulless" automaton Olympia, whose harpsichord playing and singing have "the unpleasantly correct and spiritless measure of a signing machine, and the same may be said of her dancing" (Hoffmann 2008, 34). Edward's artistic capabilities also supersede the programmed performances of the Stepford wives, whose "creations" in cooking or baking, for example, are the results of neither their own creativity nor ingenuity but rather the output of an engineered coding.

The film's portrayal of Edward's creator, an old scientist played by Vincent Price, not only evokes Mary Shelley's gothic novel *Frankenstein; or, The Modern Prometheus* (1818) but also recalls Hoffmann's emphasis on the inventors of automatons in his literary fairy tales, including Drosselmeier ("The Nutcracker and the Mouse King"), Professor X ("Automata"), and Spalazani-Coppelius-Coppola ("The Sandman"). Burton's scientist, however, is not a spooky character in the Hoffmannesque sense. The inventor, who suffered a fatal heart attack and died before he could give real hands to Edward, is portrayed as a benevolent father figure reading Edward poetry and teaching him etiquette rules. It is through the positive impact and care of the inventor that Edward "discovers" his first emotions and learns how to smile. His character has more in common with Collodi's Mister Geppetto, who teaches Pinocchio how to walk, than with Hoffmann's eerie scientists. Unlike many fairy tales, *Edward Scissorhands* does not feature a happy ending between the two unequal lovers. Believing Edward to be guilty of a terrible crime, an angry mob of local townspeople eventually thwarts his romantic attachment to Kim. As a misfit hero, there can be no acceptance into society for Edward, who returns to the old, decrepit castle where he was first created and lives as a recluse, carving magnificent ice sculptures with his artistic gift. Given the fact that the pale automaton does not age, similar to a vampire, and the fact that he is the only mechanical specimen of his kind, he is doomed to loneliness in the long run. The ending of the film invites spectators to feel sympathy for this isolated, misunderstood creature who is denied a fairy-tale happily ever after. A noteworthy fairy-tale allusion that is made in Burton's romantic dark fantasy production is the framing of the film, which emphasizes the fairy-tale genre: the main story is bookended by a prologue and an epilogue featuring an elderly woman telling her grand-daughter a bedtime story of where snow comes from.

The automaton is not the only fairy-tale figure that has "developed" from an uncanny, mindless toy and one-sided, creepy, mechanical "monster" of nineteenth-century Romantic imagination. Another artificially created supernatural creature, the golem, appears in German Romantic fairy-tale tradition in a similarly negative light as a rather sinister, dark, and nega-tively coded figure. We find other examples of texts centering on the fig-ure of the golem in Hoffmann's "Meister Floh" ("Master Flea," 1822), and Arnim's "Isabella von Ägypten, Kaiser Karl des Fünften erste Jugendliebe" ("Isabella of Egypt, Emperor Charles the Fifth's First Young Love"), which Arnim published in 1812 as part of his best-known novella collection (com-monly referred to as *Novellensammlung von 1812*). Like the reimaginings of the automaton featured in postmodern North American visual culture, the golem is recast as a humanized Other equipped with positive character traits such as sentience, self-determination, compassion, and the ability to love. In my discussion of contemporary media representations of the golem, I will again focus only on the last few decades to narrow my scope of research, but instead of focusing on fairy-tale films I will zoom in on particular episodes of popular television series, such as *The X-Files* (1993–2002, 2016–18), *The Simpsons* (1989–present), and *Sleepy Hollow* (2013–17), that feature differ-ent golem reincarnations.

The Golem in German Fairy Tales

The golem is a popular Jewish folkloric character. It is a supernatural but man-made humanoid creature, a quasi-magical automaton, usually created of soil and approximately life size. The term "golem" is first used in the Bible, where it appears once in Psalm 139:16: "Thine eyes did see my 'golem.'" According to ancient Talmud literature (a collection of rabbinic texts that constitute the religious authority for traditional Judaism, compiled in the fifth and sixth centuries C.E.), these words were spoken to Adam by God and referred to a man before he acquired a soul (Bilski 1988, 10). Thus, at a certain stage in his creation, Adam was a soulless golem creature or, differently put, a human being in an incomplete, primordial state. The golem "assumed its present connotation in the Middle Ages, when many legends arose of wise men who could bring effigies to life by means of a charm" or of "a combination of letters forming a sacred word or one of the names of God".[16] According to legends, there are different ways of bringing the golem to life—for example, by "inserting God's name into the golem's mouth or affixing it to his forehead" (Leviant 2007, xv). The letters' removal deanimates the clay creature again. In early golem tales, the artificially created being is usually a perfect servant who performs all sorts of physical labor for his master, but it is also a source of danger because, once created, the golem continuously grows in size and strength. In 1674, Johann Christian Wagenseil, German polymath, Orientalist, and professor of history, published an account of how to create a golem, the danger it poses, and its eventual destruction, which he found in a letter by German folklorist and Christian author Christoph Arnold (Bilski 1988, 13). In this reprinted Latin letter, translated into German by one of Wagenseil's students, Arnold accused Polish Jews, in particular rabbi Elijah Ba'al Shem or Elias Baal Shem (Elias, Master of the name, 1550–83), of sorcery. The anti-Semitic claim went hand in hand with the Gothic imagination of the golem as the "monstrous mirror image of the Christian self, a haunting manifestation of the inassimilable other" (Gilbert 2015, 377). This account of the golem, recorded by German Orientalist Johann Jakob Schudt and published in 1714 in Frankfurt, provided the basis for the modern conception of the golem in popular culture (Gelbin 2011, 8).

Not only did Schudt's publication of the tale of a dangerous golem have "tremendous ramifications," his book also became the source for Jacob Grimm (Bilski 1988, 14). On April 23, 1808, Grimm published a version of the golem story in his *Zeitung für Einsiedler* (*Journal of Hermits*), which, in turn, significantly impacted the German Romantics, who incorporated the legendary figure into their writings. Grimm narrates the tale as follows:

> After saying certain prayers and observing certain fast days, the Polish Jews make the figure of a man from clay or mud, and when they pronounce the miraculous Shemhamphoras [the name of God] over him, he must come to life. He cannot speak, but he understands fairly well what is said or commanded. They call him golem and use him as a servant to do all sorts of housework. But he must never leave the house. On his forehead is written *'emeth* [truth]. Everyday he gains weight and becomes somewhat larger and stronger than all the others in the house, regardless of how little he was to begin with. For fear of him, they therefore erase the letter, so that nothing remains but *meth* [he is dead], whereupon he collapses and turns to clay again.
>
> But one man's golem once grew so tall, and he heedlessly let him keep on growing so long that he could no longer reach his forehead. In terror he ordered the servant to take off his boots, thinking that when he bent down he could reach his forehead. So it happened, and the first letter was successfully erased, but the whole heap of clay fell on the Jew and crushed him. (Scholem 1969, 159)

Jeffrey Miller describes Grimm's golem story as "a sort of bridge, showing the transition from mysticism to legend," which firmly entrenched a unique method of destroying the creature (2013, 187). He labels the mute golem a "domestic Frankenstein," who, in a religious mystical sense, is an artificial, nonhuman creation due to the lack of speech capabilities: "if creation is Word and language separates man from animal (in older, non-scientific belief, at least), only God created man may speak" (188).

This argument evokes an earlier discussion about the legal status of the golem between two scholars specializing in Jewish law. Two descendants of Elijah Ba'al Shem, a rabbi of the Polish city Chelm who is credited with creating the first golem with a *shem* (hence his last name), Rabbi Tzvi Hirsch ben Yaakov Ashkenazi (known as Chacham Tzvi) (1656–1718) and his son, German talmudist Rabbi R. Jacob Emden (known as Ya'avetz) (1697–1776), concluded that human form and a sense of intelligent understanding alone are insufficient attributes to make something human. Furthermore, according to the Polish version of the golem story told by Ashkenazi and recorded by Emden in a book published in 1748, the destructive potential of the golem might destroy the world or universe (Scholem 1969, 201).

Shortly before Grimm came across the golem tale, as Scholem suspects, the Polish legend about the rabbi of Chelm moved to Prague and attached itself to the popular figure of Rabbi Judah Loew of Prague (1525–1609) (202). In this version, perhaps the most famous narrative in popular culture today, Loew creates a golem to defend the Prague ghetto from false accusations about the ritual murdering of children, anti-Semitic attacks, and pogroms. Fashioned out of clay from the banks of the Vlatva River, the golem becomes a protector figure of the Jewish community suffering under the reign of Rudolf II, the Holy Roman Emperor. Because all creatures rest on the Sabbath, Loew turns the golem back into clay every Friday evening by removing the piece of paper with the *shem*, the name of God, from its mouth. When he forgets to remove the *shem* one Friday, the golem runs amok, destroying everything that comes its way. Loew throws himself in front of the golem and removes the *shem*, whereupon the creature crumbles into clay pieces. The rabbi then goes on to bury the remains in the attic of Prague's Old New Synagogue, where they are said to lie to this day. According to the legend, the golem will come back to life if needed.

Thanks to the influence of Grimm's golem tale, the legendary golem creature became a literary motif. In addition, Heinrich Heine's discussion of Arnim's literary fairy tale "Isabella of Egypt" in his books *Zur Geschichte der neueren schöneren Literatur in Deutschland* (*On the History of the Recent Belles Letters in Germany*, 1833) and *Die Romantische Schule* (*The Romantic School*, 1836) gave the golem wider currency (Bilski 14). Because of the prevailing anti-Semitic sentiments of the German Romantic period, during which Christian writers played a decisive role, the golem appeared in a predominantly negative light as a sinister figure, including in Arnim's "Isabella of Egypt," in highly distorted form in Hoffmann's "The Sandman," "Die Geheimnisse" ("The Secrets," 1821), "Der Elementargeist" ("The Elementary Spirit" 1821), and "Master Flea," in Tieck's fairy-tale novella *Die Vogelscheuche* (*The Scarecrow*, 1835), and in Anette von Droste-Hülshoff's poems "Die Golems" ("The Golems," 1844) and "Halt fest!" ("Hold On Tight!" 1844). The portrayal of the golem in these works has little to do with the world of mysticism but rather with the realm of the fantastic. The works portray the golem as a supernatural creature, much like an evil witch, a screaming mandrake, a monstrous giant, or a devious dwarf, and place it in a universe of doppelgangers and simulacra.

In the writings of Hoffmann and Arnim, the golem imitates a living person or serves as a shallow substitute for a real character involved in a romantic affair. In "The Secrets," Theodorus, a vain, elegant freedom fighter for Greek independence from the Ottoman Empire and lover of a beautiful Greek noblewoman, is replaced with a golem created by the mysterious kabbalist Gregoros Seleskeh from Smyrna. The artificial creature is a young, handsome man called Theodor von S. Confusingly, Hoffmann refers to the golem as "Teraphim," a Hebrew word from the Old Testament to denote small images or cult objects used as domestic deities or oracles by ancient Semitic peoples. The *Kunstmärchen* describes "Teraphim" as an artificial image that imitates life by drawing on secret powers from the world of spirits. But a talisman and the touch of the Greek princess are enough to make the false and shallow creature collapse into dust. Cathy S. Gelbin sees in the golem's disintegration "an image suggesting the lacking essence in Jewish modes of creativity" and a "sign of failed cultural authenticity" (2011, 35). Catherine Mathière emphasizes that the cork-constructed simulacrum Theodor von S. is a "disembodied figure with no tangible reality" who lacks the solidity of clay and instead "walks hesitantly, with jerky movements"

(1992, 474). Thus, the golem appears as a flawed construct of inferior design, a false replica that is incomplete and unstable, without any real substance.

Interestingly, in Hoffmann's "Master Flea" and Arnim's "Isabella of Egypt" the figure of the golem is a woman. Hoffmann's golem, or rather Tera-phim, is the mysterious Dutch beauty Dörtje Elverdink, a supernatural, dev-ilish being disguised in human form. Reminiscent of the automaton Olimpia in "The Sandman" who becomes a motionless doll if not wound up regularly, Dörtje is a "lovely, charming little doll" whose life depends on the flea stings by Master Flea to regularly revitalize her lifeless body and reanimate her blood circulation. These artificial, life-sustaining treatments are necessary because Prince *Egel* (Leech), a vampiric bloodsucker, killed Dörtje once by draining her body completely of blood. Dörtje's character frequently crosses the borders between life and death and between the two realms depicted in the fairy tale, the realist world of Frankfurt, Germany, and the fantastic land of Famagusta. Her strangely lifeless and empty eyes evoke Olimpia's automaton features, and her erratic, uncoordinated movements in one situa-tion conjure up the image of a malfunctioning, mechanized puppet. Her "convulsive laughter" is not comedic but grotesque and, together with her uncontrollable leaping around the room, makes her resemble an "uncanny spectacle."

Dörtje is also associated with the motif of the doppelganger. Her double identities consist of the princess Gamaheh in the magical realm, who is also a tulip, and the witch-like, ugly, old nanny Aline in the nonmagical world. Dörtje is thus a hybrid figure, conflating human, supernatural, and botanic elements. In contrast to the traditionally formless and sexless mythi-cal golem, Dörtje is a seductive woman who knows how to play her charms and manipulate men. Peregrinus Tyß, whose alter ego is the Indian king Sekakis in Famagusta, is madly in love with Dörtje until he realizes that she is merely a distraction from a higher truth and that she only pretended to love him. Based on Peregrinus's sensation of guilt after this realization, Mathière interprets the golem as "an unconscious projection of the self torn away from the true individual" (1992, 476). Another negative connotation of Dörtje is her incestuous desire to pursue a love relationship with Peregrinus, since, in the world of Famagusta, the tulip princess Gamaheh, alias Dörtje, is the daughter of king Sekakis, alias Peregrinus. If Dörtje is aware of this family connection, which is not made clear in the tale, then the golem character is guilty of breaking a grave taboo. Described by Hoffmann as the "Serpent of Paradise," the seductive female golem in this tale is imbued with metaphysical symbolism, evoking the Genesis creation narrative as well as the Fall of Man. The serpent, of course, also stands for betrayal, seduction, lust, sex, evil, and the devil. These associations are reiterated in the tale during one of Peregrinus's dreams when he hears the following words: "Wretched King Sekakis, because you have neglected to understand nature, dazzles by evil charm and the cunning devices of the evil, you have contemplated the deceitful appearance of the Teraphim instead of contemplating the true spirit."[17] Diametrically opposed to Dörtje is the "angel of light" virgin Röschen Lämmerhirt (the name "Little Rose Lamb Herd" implies her character traits), a naïve, poor, modest, *Biedermeierian*[18] woman who ultimately becomes Peregrinus's bride.

Preceding the demonized female golem Dörtje in Hoffmann's "Master Flea" is the evil doppelganger-golem woman in Arnim's *Kunstmärchen* "Isabella of Egypt." Inspired by Jacob Grimm's golem legend in the *Journal of Hermits*, Arnim, publisher of the journal, dedicated his literary fairy tale to the Brothers Grimm (Bilski 1988, 48). Set in the early sixteenth century, the complex narrative begins in medias res with the heroine Isabella (Bella), a young and beautiful "Gypsy princess," who has just learned about her father's death.[19] Now, all hopes of Bella's people lie on the heroine and the prophecy of her son, born from Bella's union with a Western emperor and destined to unite the Gypsies by leading them back to Egypt, the legendary land of their origin. Bella lives with her old guardian, Braka, in an abandoned house on the river at the outskirts of town in what would be Belgium today. Following Braka's advice, Bella seeks the magical root that sprouted from the tears of her hanged father and grows it into a mandrake, an ugly miniature automaton who calls himself Cornelius Nepos.[20] They travel to Ghent, where Bella hopes to win the heart of the young archduke Charles V, with whom she has fallen in love. In Ghent, Charles meets with Bella, returns her affection, and arranges for a nocturnal encounter. To distract the jealous mandrake, Charles enlists the help of an old Jewish magician who creates a female golem and exact replica of Bella. Although identical in appearance to the heroine, the copy is merely a soulless and shallow apparition. Cornelius falls in love with the golem Bella, but so does Charles. Since he cannot tell the two Bellas apart, the archduke sleeps with the doppelganger-golem. Eventually, Charles realizes the truth and destroys the golem by erasing the first syllable of the word *emet* on her forehead. After a maze of misunderstanding, scheme, and intrigue, Bella and Charles become alienated from each other. Bella, now pregnant, abandons Charles one night and returns to her people.[21]

The notion of the artificial woman in this tale no longer corresponds to the Romantic conception of sublime womanhood, where the carnal features of the female body are turned into an artistic ideal. Instead, the golem Bella represents danger, corruption, and betrayal, distorting the Romantic image of the divine bride, transforming her into a dark and devious femme fatale. As Michael Andermatt stated: "But in the Venus statues, dolls, and automata of Arnim, Hoffmann, and Eichendorff, the divine tips over into the monstrous, the spiritual becomes sexual, and life once intensified by art becomes an enervated mechanism of death" (2008, 209). Indeed, the Romantic figure of the aesthetic marble statue has been replaced with a figure of clay, a type of soil sullied by the sins of man. The Jewish magician replies to a question on how to create an animate being:

. . . and Man, the image of God, can bring forth something similar when he knows the right words that God used. If there were still a Paradise, we could make as many people as there were clumps of earth there. But since we were driven out of Paradise, our humans are that much worse, in the same way that the clay here is inferior to that in Paradise. (Arnim 1997, 54)

Because the earth used to construct the golem Bella is inferior to that in the Garden of Eden, the creation of the Polish Jew is an imperfect one resulting in a creature that lacks compassion and the ability to feel true love. According to Gad Yair and Michaela Soyer, Arnim considered the female golem to be "the embodiment of opposition to natural life" (2008, 21). This is made clear in the fairy tale when the artificial woman is referred to as "lifeless puppet" (*leblose Puppe*), evoking Hoffmann's female automaton in "The Sandman." Similar to Dörtje, golem Bella is a deficient, flawed being, undermining the idea of Jewish creativity, artistic creation, and cultural production. By equipping his creature solely with the "crude embodiments" (*plumpe Verkörperungen*) of "haughtiness," "voluptuousness," and "meanness" (*Hochmut, Wollust, Geiz*), Arnim's anti-Semitic stance comes to the fore, echoing the anti-Jewish sentiments and stereotypes of his time.[22] In fact, Arnim's golem Bella has a "Jewish heart" (*Judenherz*) and mind, and fears that the real Bella could either replace her or cost her money when Bella seeks refuge at the golem's house.

In contrast to Grimm's golem legend and Jewish folklore, the golem Bella does not rise against her master, the Polish Jew, but rather against her doppelganger, the genuine Bella. The animated dummy threatens to physically harm Bella by scratching "her false, lying face to ribbons with her nails" (Arnim 1997, 64). At their final encounter, the clay creature attacks Bella with a golden, arrow-shaped hairpin, attempting to stab her victim, and yells: "Do I have to see you again, you pre-creation of God? Do I have to doubt my own existence in your presence?" (Arnim 1997, 76). Driven by her jealousy of Bella's living body and God-given soul, the undead, soulless dummy attempts to eradicate the Gypsy queen before Charles manages to undo the magic that created the golem. Defined by her spiritual love, her innocence, and her frugality, Bella is synonymous with Romantic love and the sublime, whereas her opposite, the artificial simulacrum, stands for the destructive potential of the profane, sexual lust, and carnal desire. As a creature that knows merely materialist wants, pride, and lust, golem Bella represents the Other, the Janus face that reverses Bella's positive virtues. The "accursed, deceitful woman" (*unselige Betrügerin,* Arnim 1997, 71) uses her doppelganger looks insidiously to her advantage because it is the only thing she has to offer. In *The Seduction of the Occult and the Rise of the Fantastic Tale* (2003), Dorothea von Mücke describes the golem woman fittingly: "She is mere surface, mere looks, mere appearance, made of clay and of borrowed thoughts; she has no flesh, no blood, nor a desire and will of her own" (209). By highlighting the ultimate victory of the real Bella over the golem, Arnim seemingly alludes to the triumph of the Romantic principle over rationalism, nature over science, and the organic over the machine. From the moment of creation to the moment of destruction, Arnim's artificial bride is an utterly negative, monstrous, and treacherous creature.

The Golem in American Media

To this day, the trope of the artificial bride prevails in popular Western literature and film, although in significantly altered form, as discussed in the examples of *The Stepford Wives.* Having lost nothing of its fascination and relevance, the motif of the golem bride reemerges in the 1997 episode "Kaddish" (season 4, ep. 15) of Chris Carter's television series *The X-Files.*[23] Interestingly, the episode reverses the gender roles of the theme, revolving around a golem bridegroom instead of a bride, and adds new twists to the supernatural creature. Most importantly, the golem figure is recontextualized in terms of a heartfelt love story that connotes the golem figure positively. In this episode, a Hasidic Jewish man, Isaac Luria (Harrison Coe), dies from an anti-Semitic attack in Brooklyn, New York. After his fiancée, Ariel Luria (Justine Muceli), resurrects his dead body in the form of a golem created from mud, Isaac takes revenge and kills the neo-Nazis who murdered him. But despite the golem's vengeful action, the tropes of Romance and true love are the central focus of the episode. Indeed, Isaac is not portrayed as the "abomination" and "monster" that he is supposed to be according to Kenneth Ungar (David Wohl), a scholar from the Judaica Archives consulted by FBI agent Fox Mulder (David Duchovny) during his investigation:

KENNETH UNGAR: Truth. Emet means truth. See, Mr. Mulder, therein lies the paradox . . . because the danger of the truth is contained in the word Golem itself. Which means matter without form, body without soul.

FOX MULDER: So the Golem is an imperfect creation?

KENNETH UNGAR: Oh, kind of a monster, really. Unable to speak or feel anything but the most primitive of emotions. In legends, it runs amok. It has to be destroyed by its creator.

The "golem expert" Ungar leads Mulder (and the viewers) to believe that the supernatural creature is a dangerous, mute dummy that does not possess a soul and is unable to feel true love. But it soon becomes clear that the producer and writer of the episode, Howard Gordon, took certain liberties with the golem legend. The resurrected golem is not a shapeless form but resembles a doppelganger-zombie, an undead look-alike of Isaac. Because the golem creature is a physical reflection of Ariel's true love, a facsimile of the original relationship still exists. The fact that she resurrects her fiancé makes it clear that Ariel has not yet overcome Isaac's death. She holds on to the body, if not the soul, of the love of her life, falling prey to the illusion that she can still be with Isaac and continue the relationship.

In the final scenes of the episode, Mulder and Dana Scully (Gillian Anderson) arrive at the synagogue, where Ariel, dressed in a white wedding gown, and her artificial bridegroom perform a Jewish wedding ritual. After Ariel recites the wedding vow, "I am to my beloved as my beloved is to me," golem Isaac puts an elaborate, communal wedding ring on her finger. In a *Romeo and Juliet*–like moment that reiterates the issues of true love, death, and resurrection, Ariel kisses Isaac's hand and declares her affections once more with the words "I loved you." Realizing that she must put aside the fantasy of being able to preserve their love relationship, a crying Ariel rubs the Hebrew letters off the golem's hand. While she recites the Kaddish, the Hebrew prayer for the dead, the creature slowly returns to dust. Thus, Ariel not only ends the deceptive psychological illusion that she can maintain a romantic relationship with Isaac, she also destroys the physical deception personified by the golem itself. This haunting and emotional scene invites viewers to connect with Ariel and Isaac as star-crossed lovers and to empathize with their tragic fate. At the same time, the fact that Isaac is supposedly a soulless golem who cannot feel true love is called into question. The golem figure in "Kaddish" is not primarily about avenging a murder or righting a wrong but rather about holding on to something beloved that seems to be lost forever. This desire to hold on to something loved is exemplified also in Ariel's wedding ring, which was saved by a Holocaust survivor who hid it from the Nazis. In an interview, Gordon states that Ariel's flaw is related to her "loving [Isaac] too much, not being able to let go, because of the cruelty and injustice of what she suffered" (Vitaris 1997, 39). Ariel's motivations for creating the golem are first and foremost driven by love and romantic desire. For Gordon, the story was essentially worth telling because of the love theme behind it (Vitaris 1997, 39). Although the golem takes revenge on his killers and runs amok, he is ultimately a creation of love, which sheds a positive light on the golem figure.

The trope of the artificial bride and bridegroom resurfaces also during a wedding scene in the popular animated sitcom *The Simpsons* (1989–present) that imbues the golem figure with comedic characteristics, self-determination, and a sense of agency. The 2006 Halloween Special "Treehouse of Horror XVII" (season 18, ep. 4) features a male and a female golem in the segment "You Gotta Know When to Golem." The segment parodies Paul Wegener's *Golem* series of German expressionistic silent films (1915–29). Paul Wegener, who was fascinated by fairy tales and the

Romantic, not only directed and acted in his own films based on fairy tales, folklore, and legends, he also designed his golem stories in a fairy-tale fashion, as cautionary pieces with a moral message (Giesen and Storm 2012, 3). In the episode of *The Simpsons*, Bart finds the Golem of Prague in Krusty the Clown's prop museum. Krusty tells Bart that in the seventeenth century, the golem was sculpted out of clay by a powerful rabbi and would obey any command written on a scroll and placed in his mouth. Although the golem ostensibly was created to protect Jewish villages, he would obey any scroll placed in his mouth, evil or good. He has been passed down through many generations and now works for Krusty, primarily by killing with a shotgun anyone who interrupts or criticizes Krusty's show. Bart steals the golem and uses him as a servant to carry out his bidding: beating up the bullies at his school, spinning Principal Skinner up and down like a yo-yo until his body splits in two, and becoming Bart's personal barber. Lisa thinks that the golem does not like hurting people and feeds him a note reading: "Speak." Now that he is given the ability to talk, the golem reveals that he is a decent being who feels guilty about being used to commit heinous acts. To make him feel better, the Simpsons create a female golem out of Play-Doh for lifelong companionship.

This episode of *The Simpsons* is particularly noteworthy because the figure of the monstrous golem as voiceless killing machine and soulless servant is spoofed, morally scrutinized, and endowed with human character traits. When the golem is first introduced, Bart asks Krusty "What's that monster?" and Krusty replies "It's the Golem of Prague, legendary defender of the Jewish people, like Alan Dershowitz, but with a conscience." Thus, from the very beginning, the episode hints at the fact that the golem is more than just a mindless dummy. Further, the episode uses parody and comic relief to demystify the golem as a supernatural creature and magically animated anthropomorphic being. When the golem is about to speak for the first time, he first roars, then coughs, and then regurgitates excessive scrolls, one of which reads: "Kill the Czar." Next, he cracks a joke, calling it

Jewish humor. Lisa explores the theological dimension of the golem's nature, whether he is indeed a soulless monster or a sentient being, by asking the golem: "Do you feel bad about what you did?" The golem replies with a sense of agency: "Of course I feel bad . . . I feel so guilty! I've mangled and maimed thirty-seven people and I told a telemarketer I was busy when I wasn't!" By confirming that he regrets his deeds and by his self-realization "I am not a good man," the golem, who physically bears a striking resemblance to Wegener's golem impersonation, makes it clear that he has a bad conscience and thus presumably a soul. To help the golem overcome his depressive state of mind, Bart, Lisa, and Marge create a colorful Play-Doh companion for him. The golem's free will, self-determination, and protecting nature are revealed when he prevents Homer from killing the female golem, crying "No! What are you, nuts? She was made for me." In a final scene, the golem, wearing a *kippah*, marries his new companion in a traditional Jewish ceremony including a wedding canopy and the breaking of a glass.

Although many contemporary television series (e.g., *Supernatural* [2005–present], *Grimm* [2011–17], *Gargoyles* [1994–97], and *Extreme Ghostbusters* [1997]) frame the golem within the context of Jewish legend, drawing on the notion of the golem as a miraculous protector of the innocent, the

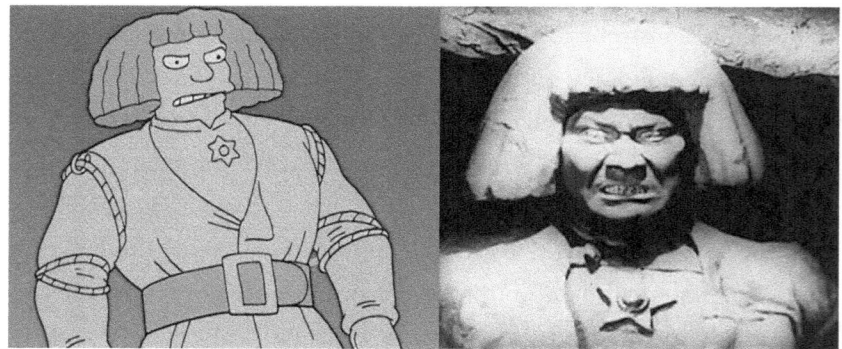

The golem in *The Simpsons* 2006 episode "Treehouse of Horror XVII" is a parody of Paul Wegener's golem representation in his German expressionistic silent films (1915–29).

series *Sleepy Hollow* adds a layer of voodoo magic to the supernatural mix. In this regard, the creature featured in the 2013 episode "Golem" (season 1, ep. 10), who protects twelve-year-old Jeremy Crane (Braden Fitzgerald), the son of the protagonist, Ichabod Crane (Tom Mison), cannot be seen as a villain or entirely negative character. In the episode, which is set in the eighteenth century, young Jeremy needs a protector because the head of the war orphanage where he lives, a sadistic priest who intends to beat the evil out of the boy, abuses him physically. The golem that comes to Jeremy's rescue, however, is not a clay monster, and the episode's explanation for the creature's existence is taken almost completely out of the mythological context of Jewish folklore. Instead, the golem appears first in the form of a little voodoo-like doll given to Jeremy by his mother. After Jeremy has suffered through several beatings by the abusive priest, his blood drips on the doll and turns it into an animated, towering golem. The awakened monster is a manifestation of Jeremy's rage, grief, and pain. Looking like the hand-made doll with stitched-up eyes and mouth, the golem kills the priest in an instant and serves as Jeremy's protector from that moment on.

At first glance, the golem is a monstrous and mindless creature, but the narrative soon reveals that the golem has a soft, caring side as well. This positive character trait is emphasized when the supernatural figure gently strokes Jeremy's face after the priest's beatings. The gesture humanizes the golem to some degree by depicting him as a compassionate, sympathetic being, which subverts the one-dimensionality of the character. Clearly, this golem is more than just an evil monster. In the twenty-first century, Jeremy's father, Ichabod, attempts to determine the origin of the "monster," who, by the means of magic, is still animate in the same time period as Ichabod. Looking for an explanation of the creature's origin, Ichabod reads Psalm 139 in the Bible: "And your eyes did see my substance being yet unformed"—a reference in both the Bible and the Judaic Talmud to an enchanted being made from inanimate matter—"like the first son of God, born of mud." He concludes that the "monster" is a golem, a creature imbued with its creator's most ardent passions. At the end of the episode, the golem takes revenge on four razor-teethed, evil witches who once put a hex on Jeremy's heart to stop it from beating. He then goes on a rampage at a carnival, where Ichabod is able to stop him by stabbing the creature's chest with a dagger-sized piece of mirror covered in Ichabod's own blood. Since Jeremy's blood gave the golem life, only his blood (or the blood of his father) can end it. But in the moment of final struggle, the creature becomes humanized once more through dialog and gestures.

In an emotionally charged scene, Ichabod bonds with the creature and the heartfelt scene invites viewers to do the same. Ichabod expresses to the golem his gratitude for protecting his son, calling the golem Jeremy's "only friend, his guardian, and in many ways a father." Ichabod tells the golem that he does not have to continue his rampage because Jeremy is gone and his protection of Jeremy is no longer needed. There is a moment of reflection during which the golem lowers his head, seemingly considering standing down. But, incapable of letting go, the golem lunges at Ichabod, who has no choice but to kill the creature. The pitiable being drops to the ground with a howl-like groan that tapers off into a doggish whimper. Ichabod takes the golem's hand into his own, saying, "You've endured enough pain. Bear it no more. My son, be at peace." At that moment, the supernatural being transforms back into Jeremy's doll. Because the golem essentially symbolizes a part of Jeremy, he must be understood as more than just a wicked monster or artificial, emotionless dummy. Indeed, the golem embodies several positively coded personae, representing a friend, a protector, and a father to Jeremy, and also indirectly "a son" to Ichabod. The sentimental ending touched viewers, such as Sandra Gonzalez, who wrote in a recap of the episode: "Now, can someone explain why I was crying OVER A MONSTER?!" (Gonzalez). Gonzalez's reaction to the scene makes clear that the golem in *Sleepy Hollow*, albeit an artificial creature, is a character with which to empathize.

Just like the "monstrous" golem is a gargantuan look-alike of Jeremy's doll, so are Hoffmann's and Arnim's artificial, puppet-like women, Dörtje and golem Bella, tied to the theme of the mysterious or magical doppel-ganger in German Romantic literature. Since the Romantic writers enjoyed working in the realm of the supernatural, basing their fairy tales on fantastic creatures, occultism, the "night side" of life, irrational forces, dreams, and the unconscious, it is not difficult to imagine why their signature trope of the doppelganger quickly reduplicated itself in the literature of German Roman-ticism. As S. T. Joshi has noted, "The German Romantics began a trend that continues even today, as the imaginative nature of the doppelgänger motif lends itself to science fiction, horror, and fantasy" (2007, 190). Therefore, this chapter continues with an analysis of how contemporary media prod-ucts of American popular culture reinterpret and reframe the supernatural creature of the double portrayed in German Romantic fairy tales.

The Doppelganger in German Fairy Tales

Although manifestations of doubles and the concept of doubling in litera-ture may be traced back much further than the early nineteenth century, Hoffmann and his fellow Romantic Jean Paul are well known for having introduced the German word "doppelgänger" into world literature. In his novel *Siebenkäs* (1796), Paul first defined the doppelganger in a footnote as "Leute, die sich selber sehen" ("people who see themselves") (239). In their German dictionary *Deutsches Wörterbuch* (1860), the Brothers Grimm noted, "doppelgänger, auch wol doppeltgänger, m. jemand von dem man wähnt er könne sich zu gleicher zeit an zwei verschiedenen orten zeigen" ("double-goer, also possibly doubled-goer, someone of whom one imagines he could show himself at the same time at two dif-ferent places") (1263). Particularly interesting is the change of perspective in the two explanations: whereas Paul's definition refers to the internal or subjective point of view of an individual who experiences a self-reflecting encounter, the Grimms' definition emphasizes the external or objective viewpoint of someone who believes that another person can be at two places at once.

For my examination of the double in German Romantic fairy tales and American popular culture, I find Otto Rank's more comprehensive definition in his landmark study *Der Doppelgänger* (1925) most suitable because it comprises the terminologies of both Paul and the Grimms. The Austrian psychoanalyst and close colleague of Freud differentiates two modes of treatment of the doppelganger trope: the first form, in which the self visually separates itself from the individual and appears in mirror images and shadows; and the second form, in which the double appears as physical person, bearing an external resemblance to someone else. Rank distinguishes between doppelganger appearances as follows: "The modes of treatment of this subject which we have so far considered—in which the uncanny double is clearly an independent and visible cleavage of the ego (shadow, reflection)—are different from those actual figures of the double who confront each other as real and physical persons of unusual external similarity, and whose paths cross" (1971, 12). In other words, the doppelganger is an uncanny motif comprised of two distinct types: first, the split personality or dark, monstrous, devilish half of the protagonist, which may act as a physical manifestation of a dissociated part of the self; second, the identical double of a protagonist who is either a victim of an identity theft perpetrated by a mimicking supernatural presence or subject to a paranoid hallucination. As examples of the former definition of the double, Rank cites the literary fairy tales "Peter Schlemihls wundersame Geschichte" ("Peter Schlemihl's Miraculous Story," 1814) by Chamisso, "Die Geschichte vom verlornen Spiegelbild" ("The Story of the Lost Reflection," 1815) by Hoffmann, and "Skyggen" ("The Shadow," 1847) by Andersen. As examples of the latter definition of the double, Rank names Hoffmann's novels and stories *Die Elixiere des Teufels* (*The Devil's Elixirs*, 1815), *Die Doppeltgänger* (*The Doubles*, 1821), and *Lebens-Ansichten des Katers Murr* (*The Life and Opinions of the Tomcat Murr*, 1819–21).

In Western and Russian folklore and literature of the nineteenth and twentieth century, the doppelganger is a look-alike or ghostly counterpart of a living person who is often portrayed as a harbinger of bad luck. Seeing a friend's or relative's doppelganger portends illness or danger, while seeing one's own doppelganger is said to be an omen of death.[24] Because the double is deeply rooted in the tradition of the figure of the devilish or Mephistophelean Other (an expression of the soul-body dichotomy and man's dualistic tendencies toward good and evil), encountering the double is generally perceived to be a negative and uncanny experience. Already Veronica Schanoes remarked that the role of the double in literature, folklore, and the psyche is a static one; "it is inherently threatening, inherently destabilizing, an irruption by definition" (2015, 201). Based on Rank's study of the double, in his essay "The Uncanny" Freud ties the antagonistic, psychodynamic development of the doppelganger idea to the human soul. He notes that the double was originally a creature of primary narcissism and thus an insurance against the destruction of the self (1917-19, 235).

According to Freud, the double was nothing else than a belief in the immortal soul, which, in Rank's words, "energetically denies the power of death" (1971, 84). To put it another way, the notion of the double was initially a positive coping mechanism against the fear of mortality, and the invention of doubling served as preservation against extinction. But when the phase of primary narcissism in the mind of the child as in that of primitive man was left behind, for Freud, the idea of the double took on a different aspect and changed from the assurance of immortality to become "the uncanny harbinger of death" (Freud [1919] 2003, 142). Therefore, Freud categorizes the doppelganger along with other inherently uncanny things, for instance, when there is intellectual uncertainty whether an object is alive or not and when an inanimate object becomes too much like an animate one or vice versa: "The double has become an object of terror, just as the gods become demons after the collapse of their cult" (143). Uncanny is also that which is supposed to remain hidden but comes to light instead, and the double externalizes that aspect of the individual.

In literature, the fantastic creature of the doppelganger embodies that which is already innate but concealed in the protagonist, one of the most prominent examples being Robert Louis Stevenson's novel *Strange Case of Dr. Jekyll and Mr. Hyde* (1886). There is usually only one way for the protagonist to free herself or himself of the menacing "evil twin," namely, through murder. But killing the doppelganger oftentimes results in the death of the protagonist as well, although there are exceptions. Schanoes notes: "It [the double] negates us while it duplicates us; this dynamic is often reflected in literature by having a character's double destroy his life through irreparably ruinous behavior while simultaneously acting out the character's own repressed desires" (2015, 204). In this sense, the protagonists carry the antagonists within them, recalling Goethe's famous quote "Zwei Seelen wohnen, ach! in meiner Brust/Die eine will sich von der andern trennen" (Two souls, alas, reside within my breast/And each withdraws from and repels its brother). The quote demonstrates that the protagonist Dr. Heinrich Faust in *Faust: Der Tragödie erster Teil* (*Faust: The First Part of the Tragedy*, 1808) was only too aware of his divided nature. Goethe's magnum opus *Faust* is a great parable of the divided soul or the "two souls," which stand for "the shattering, sometimes frightening image of two forces—call them Heaven and Hell—that made unresolvable claims upon man's life, thoughts, and actions" (Ewen 2004, 241). Based on the historical legend of German alchemist and magician Dr. Johann Georg Faustus (ca. 1480–1541), the tragic play features the sinister Other, or dark side of the self, personified in the demon Mephistopheles on one side and the hero Dr. Faust, a scholar and physician, on the other. Goethe's drama treats the leering tempter Mephistopheles as a "projection" of Faust's inchoate moral turpitude and as Faust's evil doppelganger.

Absorbed into the psyche of German Romanticism, the concept of the "two souls" or man's struggle between light and darkness, good and evil, God and Satan, became manifest in the figure of the doppelganger, the symbol of human self-division. Doppelgangers as objects of existential fear, ego dissociation, fragmentation, and identity loss can be traced back to the rediscovery of the unconscious. As Joel Black has pointed out, "it was during the Romantic period that the role and range of unconscious operations in human life and artistic creation became widely recognized" (2000, 130). Especially the Dark Romantics were interested in exploring the mind's "night side," and therefore the question of their own self gained in significance. This preoccupation with the self triggered an identity crisis of the individual, which could lead, in extreme cases, to the separation of the self. The motif of the double as visual expression of the separated self, its disruption and desperation, is a central theme in a wide variety of German Romantic literary works, notably the texts by Hoffman as the classic creator of the double-projection. Besides "The Sandman," some of his other literary fairy tales and narratives that portray doppelgangers and deserve mentioning here are "Ritter Gluck" ("Knight Gluck," 1809), "Don Juan" (1813), "Ignaz Denner" (1817), "Das steinerne Herz" ("The Stone Heart," 1817), "Die Brautwahl" ("The Choice of a Bride," 1819), "Prinzessin Brambilla" ("Princess Brambilla," 1820), and "Signor Formica" (1820).

In *Kunstmärchen* of the Romantic period, the supernatural creature of the doppelganger appears in a variety of different shapes, including shadows (Chamisso's "Peter Schlemihl's Miraculous Story," 1814), mirrors (Hoffmann's "The Story of the Lost Reflection"), statues and dolls (Eichendorff's "Das Marmorbild" ["The Marble Statue," 1819]; Arnim's "Melück Maria Blainville," 1812), and the golem figure (Arnim's "Isabella of Egypt," 1812). However, regardless of the shape, size, or manner in which the doppelganger surfaces in German fairy tales, it remains an inherently uncanny, negative, threatening, destabilizing, and ominous phenomenon. Chamisso's "Peter Schlemihl" serves as a primary example in this case, which Rank ascribed to the split personality type of the doppelganger. The tale is one of the few German *Kunstmärchen* besides Hoffmann's "The Golden Pot" and Fouqué's "Undine" that could assert itself as world literature (Wührl 2003, 149). "Peter Schlemihl" tends to be remembered above all for its tropes of the shadow bargain and societal alienation. In the story, the protagonist, Schlemihl, sells his shadow in a moment of naïveté to a "gray stranger"—the devil—in exchange for a sack of gold coins that always fills up again. Soon Schlemihl comes to realize the social price for the immoral trade with the "gray stranger" since a man without a shadow is shunned by human societies. Mina, the woman he loves, rejects him, and he himself becomes involved in guilt. Yet when the devil wants to return Schlemihl's shadow to him in exchange for his soul, Schlemihl—who is as his Hebrew name implies "a friend of God"—rejects the proposal and throws the bottomless gold sack into an abyss. With this action he cuts his last ties to the devil. Finally, he seeks refuge in his studies of nature. Aided by a pair of magical seven-league boots bought at a country fair, Schlemihl travels all over the world in scientific exploration, leading a life that is solitary yet compatible with his true self.

In this fairy tale, the shadow does not represent Schlemihl's soul but rather a negatively connoted part of his identity. Interestingly, it is not the presence but the absence of Schlemihl's shadow-doppelganger, literally his dark half, that draws attention to the motif's adverse symbolism. Without his shadow, Schlemihl becomes an outsider of society and, despite his incredible wealth, is shunned by the people, who are now suspicious of his shadowless state and repulsed by him. By selling his shadow to the devil, Schlemihl loses his outward appearance and reputation as a respected bourgeois citizen. But the society is portrayed negatively, as reputable members with proper shadows are dishonest and immoral or inhumane. Thus, the shadow becomes synonymous with illusory values and corrupted morals. Although the shadowless protagonist continues to live, or rather to exist, he is robbed of his old identity and therefore takes on a new identity when he is mistaken for Count Peter. Schlemihl hides behind his newly adopted identity, and by wearing this "mask" he attempts to disguise the fact that he does not have a shadow. The division of Schlemihl's self into Count Peter and his shadow, or rather the confrontation of this split, leads to Schlemihl's process of self-awareness and consciousness. Although Schlemihl matures and eventually comes to terms with his personality in his later life, he never gets his shadow back. There is no reunion of Schlemihl and the shadow-doppelganger, no joining of the self and the Other. The fact that Schlemihl can still live a fulfilling life without his shadow is understandable because of the shadow's ambivalent meaning in the tale. On the one hand, the shadow is a cipher for the accepted bourgeois norms and values, which are presented in a questionable if not ridiculous light. By selling his shadow, Schlemihl frees himself of all societal constraints and, although isolated, can happily pursue his scientific goals in botany. On the other hand, the shadow can be understood as a type of warning or harbinger of demise: if one sells one's shadow to the devil, one might eventually also lose the soul (Derjanecz 2003, 37). Since Schlemihl does not commit to a "Faustian deal," such as Goethe's Dr. Faust, who trades his soul for omniscience, Chamisso's hero is able to save his soul and thus his life.

The relationship between Schlemihl and his shadow, or rather the absence of an interaction with a personified doppelganger, contradicts the assumption that the Other self is always represented as an autonomous and active entity in fairy tales. This fact needs to be taken into consideration when taking into account Gerald Bär's assertion:

> As (palpable) personified projections of the self, doppelgangers can gain various degrees of distinctive features and autonomy. Being identified as the "other," they haunt and challenge the protagonist's internalized image of himself. The result of this externalized inner action is usually either the acceptance of the rejected (self-knowledge) or (self-) destruction. (2007, 92)

Indeed, the encounter with one's double oftentimes culminates in self-destruction, mentally and physically, since the purpose of the personality as irreplaceable individual is gone. But as is evident in Hoffmann's "The Sandman," self-destruction and madness are not necessarily tied to a projection of the self but can be linked to an encounter with another person's double as well. The protagonist Nathanael does not face his own self in the form of an uncanny double vision but conflates in his mind the barometer-seller Giuseppe Coppola, the obnoxious lawyer Coppelius, and the evil Sandman figure. Although the automaton Olimpia incites Nathanael's madness, it is at the sight of Coppelius toward the end of the literary fairy tale that the protagonist leaps over the railing of the tower to his death. The tale demonstrates that the notion of the haunting double is not always equivalent to seeing the Other self. However, confronting the doppelganger of another person can raise similar doubts about one's healthy state of mind as when coming across one's mirror image. At the beginning, one might attempt to find a logical explanation for the double visions, as does Nathanael when he expresses his suspicion that Coppelius simply masqueraded as Coppola. In a letter to his friend Lothair he writes about Coppola: "If I tell you, my dear friend, that the barometer-dealer was the accursed Coppelius himself. . . . He was dressed differently, but the figure and features of Coppelius are too deeply imprinted in my mind, for an error in this respect to be possible." In summary, the doppelganger is wedded with destruction, death, darkness, deception, and drag in German fairy tales.

In *Symbolik des Märchens* (*Symbolism of the Fairy Tale*, 1952–57), a three-volume work that draws on Jungian archetypes to discuss self-realization within fairy tales, Hedwig von Beit sees the doppelganger of the hero in the masqueraded and deceitful figure of the servant. Influenced by the work of Marie-Louise von Franz, Beit takes a deep psychological approach and identifies the princess's servant maid in the Grimms' tale "The Goose Girl" to be the shadow or dark self of the princess. In this tale, a chambermaid usurps the position of a princess in order to marry a prince. After the queen sends off her daughter and a servant maid to a distant kingdom where the princely bridegroom awaits, the false servant maid forces the princess to take off her own royal clothing and put on the chambermaid's shabby clothes instead. This motif is known in Stith Thompson's motif index of folklore literature as motif K1810.1. *Disguise by putting on clothes (carrying accoutrements) of certain person.* The princess then has to take an oath and swear "under the open heaven that she would not say one word of this to anyone at the royal court. If she had not taken this oath, she would have been killed on the spot." Since the servant maid threatens to murder the princess, the masqueraded doppelganger embodies a destructive, annihilating persona. Upon arriving in the distant kingdom, the prince mistakes the servant maid for the princess and takes her into the castle while the true princess tends to the geese in the field.[25] The identity theft is ultimately revealed and the impostor bride tricked by the king into proclaiming her own punishment. Whether the servant double represents in fact the dark side of the princess, which she needs to overcome in order to mature from dependent girl to independent woman, is of secondary importance here. What matters is that the servant, shadow, or doppelganger is coded negatively as liar, fraud, and impostor, and tied to impersonation and masquerade.

The Grimms' fairy tale also evokes Wilhelm Hauff's Orientalist *Kunstmärchen* "The Story of the False Prince," in which the ambitious tailor Labakan attempts to break through the societal order by impersonating royalty. However, this doppelganger is less menacing in his deceptive approach than the chambermaid in "The Goose Girl." Disguised as Prince Omar, the tailor arrives at the sultan's palace and competes with the true heir to the throne in an identity-revealing contest. When Labakan has to choose between two magical boxes with the inscriptions "Honor and Fame" and "Fortune and Riches," he decides on the latter and finds a needle and thread instead of a crown. Without punishment, the usurper then returns to his original profession of tailoring.

Besides "The Goose Girl," Walter Pape recognizes in *Enzyklopädie des Märchens* (1981) the Grimms' fairy tale "Ferdinand the Faithful and Ferdinand the Unfaithful" for its close connection to the doppelganger trope. "Ferdinand the Faithful and Ferdinand the Unfaithful" is a tale about a young man, Ferdinand, and his disloyal companion, Ferdinand the Unfaithful. In an attempt to do away with Ferdinand, the unfaithful travel companion suggests to the king that he send Ferdinand the Faithful to rescue the king's love from giants. After Ferdinand successfully rescues the princess, she marries the king although she cannot stand his facial disfigurement. One day, the new queen claims she can cut off someone's head and put it back on again. Ferdinand the Unfaithful suggests she should try her trick on Ferdinand the Faithful. The queen cuts off his head and puts it back on again. Then the king volunteers for the trick and she cuts off his head. The queen then pretends she cannot put the king's head back on the body and marries Ferdinand the Faithful. Although there is no masquerading or identity theft in this tale, Ferdinand the Unfaithful can still be interpreted as the doppelganger, alter ego, or "evil twin" of Ferdinand the Faithful. The names of the characters already imply this relationship of doubling.

Evoking the concept of the shadow double, the malignant companion follows the protagonist wherever he goes, first into an inn and later to the king's court. The tale links Ferdinand the Unfaithful early on with bad luck, dark magic, and the power to read other people's thoughts: "Now it was unfortunate that Ferdinand the Unfaithful knew everything that another person had ever thought and everything he was about to do; he knew it by means of all kinds of wicked arts." The tale contains a variation of Stith Thompson's motif K1931.3 *Impostors kill hero* since the disloyal companion plots to have Ferdinand the Faithful killed and for the brief moment of the hero's beheading the sinister Other succeeds. Instead of murdering Ferdinand the Faithful himself, the evil double makes insidious recommendations first to the king, hoping that Ferdinand the Faithful will perish on his perilous journey to the giants, and later to the queen, scheming for Ferdinand to die by beheading. Therefore, the tale ciphers the doppelganger not only as wicked creature but also as a lethal threat to the hero figure. By portraying the double adversely to the core in their tales "The Goose Girl" and "Ferdinand the Faithful and Ferdinand the Unfaithful," the Grimms' negative representation of the double resembles the double in the works of Hoffmann, Chamisso, Arnim, and other Romantic writers of German literary fairy tales. Whereas in nineteenth-century tales the double manifests time and again as uncanny, threatening creature, twenty-first-century texts have taken different, innovative approaches to representations of the double. The following section scrutinizes two popular fairy-tale-inspired television series that aired within the past decade, *Grimm* (2011–17) and *Once Upon a Time* (*OUaT*) (2011–18), and the world-famous British-American film series *Harry Potter* (2001–11) based on the *Harry Potter* novels by author J. K. Rowling. The corpus is limited to these media productions because of their close ties to the fairy tale and fairy-tale tropes, their popularity, and their recentness.

The Doppelganger in American Media

Today, about two centuries after the period of German Romanticism, the motif of the doppelganger pervades North American media productions on the small and silver screens. Viewers of *Grimm*, *Once Upon a Time*, and *Harry Potter* will be especially familiar with the trope of the double in a variety of different forms—for example, as legendary Wesen (fantastic beings), menacing fear spirits, soul-stealing shadows, magically transformed look-alikes, or supernatural crossbreeds. But how exactly is the doppelganger portrayed these days via television and motion pictures in popular culture? How does the doppelganger in contemporary American media compare to the dark Other, the uncanny and negatively coded alter ego depicted in eighteenth-century German fairy tales? Does the notion of the deceptive harbinger of death still exist, and if so in what form? What particularly interests me in *Grimm*, *OUaT*, and the *Harry Potter* series are the ways in which these different stories reshape the double in intriguing and diverse ways. Whereas NBC's supernatural police series *Grimm* follows in the footsteps of the Brothers Grimm by taking a particularly grim and dark approach to the representation of the double, the Disney-owned ABC show *OUaT* adds Disneyfied "happily ever after" endings to the episodes featuring doubles, and the *Harry Potter* films frame the appearance of the double primarily in comedic and humorous contexts.

Perhaps most closely aligned to the tradition of German Romantic *Kunstmärchen*—after all, the show features a direct quote from Hoffman's "The Sandman"—and the uncanny depiction of the doppelganger is NBC's fairy-tale procedural *Grimm*. As previously established, encounters with doppelgangers always raise the issue of identity. Monika Schmitz-Emans analyzes the Other in Hoffmann's novel *The Devil's Elixirs*, noting that "the experience of losing identity and self-control are almost necessarily connected to outbursts of madness and raving" (2008, 163). Indeed, as we know from Nathanael's tragic fate in "The Sandman," seeing the double of oneself or a stranger can trigger insanity, especially if the sightings are repetitive and within a short period of time. This leitmotif can also be found in the *Grimm* episode "Cry Luison" (IV, 5), where a woman is driven to madness by four look-alikes who are in fact quadruplets. Unaware that her husband and his three brothers are so-called Luison Wesen, wolf-like creatures from South America, Ava Diaz (Jacqueline Obradors) believes that a stalking wolf monster haunts her. Although the wolf doppelgangers pretend to be kind, Ava knows they are lying and trying to kill her. Since nobody believes Ava's story about a wolf creature chasing her everywhere she goes, Dr. Bern (Karla Mason) diagnoses the woman with severe mental illness and prescribes her several combinations of anti-psychotics. One night, the Luison doubles drive Ava out of her house in fear. Horrified by her sightings, Ava gets into her car, and after accidentally hitting someone she crashes the car and is hospitalized.

This episode draws heavily on the topos of the eerie doppelganger and infuses the motif with supernatural elements by portraying the quadruplets as fantastic Wesen creatures. Ava believes she is losing her mind not only because she sees a talking wolf—a fact that sounds irrational on its own—but also because that creature appears to be in many different places at once, including the rooms in her house and the backseat of her car. The episode's focus on framing repetitive sightings of the doppelganger as a cause for insanity, following in the footsteps of Hoffmann's "The Sandman" and *The Devil's Elixirs*, perpetuates the notion of the negatively coded Other.

The double also manifests in *Grimm* in the form of mixed identities through magical transformation. Contrary to the shadow doppelganger representing the repressed and hidden "night side" of the self, the doppelgangers in the episodes "Goodnight, Sweet Grimm" (season 2, ep. 22), "Blond Ambition" (season 3, ep. 22), and "Highway of Tears" (season 4, ep. 6) are the result of a magic potion used to switch identities for a temporary period of time. Instead of broaching the theme of split identities, these episodes center on inverted identities and the trope of the double as an agent of deception. In "Goodnight, Sweet Grimm," the Hexenbiest (a witch-like Wesen that resembles a zombie) Frau Pech (Mary McDonald-Lewis) brews a doppelganger potion. After consuming it, she turns into a facsimile of the Hexenbiest Adalind Schade (Claire Coffee), while Adalind turns into a facsimile of Frau Pech. After Frau Pech is killed because her deception is perceived, the magic potion wears off and the respective bodies revert to their former selves. In the episode "Blond Ambition," Adalind inhales the vapors of a *Verfluchte Zwillingsschwester potion* (Damned Twin Sister Potion) and turns into Juliette Silverton (Bitsie Tulloch), the girlfriend of the series' hero, Nick Burkhardt (David Giuntoli). In her newly disguised form, the Hexenbiest Adalind deceives Nick and has intercourse with him to the catastrophic effect that Nick loses his powers to differentiate between Wesen and humans.

The motif of transformation for the purpose of seduction has a long tradition in folklore, as highlighted in Stith Thompson's motif index of folk literature: D658.3.1. *Transformation to seduce man* and K1911 *The false bride; an impostor takes wife's place without detection*. The *Grimm* episode not only shares commonalities with the Grimms' fairy tale "The Goose Girl" in its depiction of a false bride/betrothed/girlfriend, but is also reminiscent of the ancient Greek myth of Amphitryon in which Amphitryon's wife Alcmene is seduced and impregnated by Zeus, who assumes the shape of her husband. In "Highway of Tears," Juliette uses the same magic potion as Adalind to transform herself into a doppelganger. Looking like Adalind, Juliette has intercourse with Nick and afterward experiences sharp physical pains before the potion wears off. The three episodes of *Grimm* thus code the identity-thieving doppelganger negatively and tie the trope of the double to deceit, disempowerment, sexual infidelity, pain, and death. Whereas *Grimm* ties the doppelganger to motifs of trauma, psychosis, and visual deception, Disney's *OUaT* uses the double as a physical adversary and foil that the heroes need to defeat to bring about a "happily ever after." In the Disneyfied approach, doubles are strongly linked with people's personal identities. They either represent the dark side of the self that needs to be overcome for the sake of goodness or they are depicted as vessels of human souls, expressed in the form of shadows, which are essential for the survival of the physical body. *OUaT*'s foregrounding of defeating the sinister double to emphasize happy endings corresponds to the show's formulaic, overarching tenor of good always triumphing over evil.

In some ways, the show *OUaT* itself is a doubling of characters who live in two worlds: a "Land Without Magic," also known as the fictional town of present-day Storybrooke, Maine (seasons 1–6) or Seattle, Washington (season 7), and an enchanted, magical land of different fairy-tale realms. The popular television series, created by Edward Kitsis and Adam Horowitz, is a postmodern fairy-tale mash-up that first aired on October 23, 2011. It draws on innovative retellings of fairy stories written by well-known authors and on related genres, from the Grimms, Lewis Carroll, L. Frank Baum, J. M. Barrie, and Carlo Collodi to the *Arabian Nights*, Greek mythology, the Arthurian cycle, and science fiction.

Featuring mostly Disney-inspired characters, the show thrives on the tensions between the Disney canon and the creators' reimaginings thereof. *OUaT* follows various fairy-tale characters who were transported to "our world" and robbed of their original memories by a powerful curse. Although the two worlds feature the same cast, the characters take on different identities and appearances based on who they are representing in the stories. The enchanted land, for instance, is reigned over by the evil queen (Lana Parrilla) from "Snow White," who also controls the town of Storybrooke as Mayor Regina Mills and in the seventh season plays the bartender Roni. Another lead character of the show, Rumplestiltskin[26] (Robert Carlyle), is also known as the Crocodile from J. M. Barrie's *Peter Pan* (1911) and Beast from the fairy tale "Beauty and the Beast." In Storybrooke, Rumplestiltskin is Mr. Gold, a cunning pawnshop owner, and in Seattle, his counterpart is the mysterious Detective Weaver. In other words, the notion of the double is already built into the very structure of the series.

During my research, I found that Gerald Bär's statement "the doppelgänger represents the repressed feelings of the protagonist, unfulfilled wishes or fears of a personified 'alter ego'" holds true especially for the episode "The Tower" of *OUaT* (season 3, ep. 14) (2007, 91). This episode, which is particularly poignant in its use of the doppelganger, features so-called doppelganger fear spirits, paranormal doubles of live-action characters in the show. When a person in the story seeks nightroot, a plant that removes fear, this person is faced with a doppelganger who personifies the character's worst fears. Doppelganger fear spirits are tall, hooded, uncanny creatures that not only possess superhuman strength but are also capable of magic. In the episode, the princess Rapunzel (Alexandra Metz) is trapped for many years in a large tower after searching for the plant nightroot to remove her fears of becoming queen. David Nolan (alias Prince Charming, played by Josh Dallas), who also searches for the plant because he fears the responsibilities of fatherhood, climbs Rapunzel's tower and helps the young woman to face her fears. When the fear spirit appears in the tower to steal Rapunzel's courage, looking like her exact double, it becomes clear that the princess is only scared of herself. In a struggle with David, the fear spirit double dangles outside the tower, holding on to Rapunzel's hair. To cast off her fear once and for all, Rapunzel slices off her long hair and the creature falls to its death. In Storybrooke, David faces his own doppelganger. He is taunted by the fear spirit double before stabbing and killing his alter ego with his sword. Only by facing, accepting, and overcoming their fears, Rapunzel's fear of becoming queen and David's fear of being a father, can the two characters defeat their menacing doppelgangers. A noticeable difference between the fear spirits and most doubles in German fairy tales is that the fear spirits are from the outset creatures of supernatural origin with magical powers that supersede the human powers of the protagonists. They are much more "hands-on" in the sense that they engage in physical combats with the protagonists. The fear spirits attack their victims not only physically but also psychologically by belittling and derogating their opponents verbally. In contrast to Schlemihl's passive doppelganger shadow, which has to obey its "lawful owner" the devil and is thus under external control, the fear spirits are active, self-controlled, manipulative creatures whose sole purpose is to kill the people whose fears they reflect.

The shadows in Seasons Two and Three of *OUaT are also life threatening*. The shadows are shadow people that emulate the human bodies to which they belong. When the shadows are ripped from their bodies, all that is left behind are the corpses of the shadows' previous owners. The shadows are mysterious, dark beings with gleaming eyes. Although they can fly through the air, most shadows are trapped in Dark Hollow in Neverland, the darkest spot on the entire island. Peter Pan's shadow, voiced by Marilyn Manson and known as "The Shadow," plays a special role in the series. The executive producers, Eddy Kitsis and Adam Horowitz, casted Manson because they wanted someone with the vocal ability to make the audience's skin crawl (Neumyer). While Pan uses the sinister creature to carry out his bidding, the show clarifies in Season Three that The Shadow was first a separate being, Neverland's only resident, before it became a part of Pan. The boy was once a grown-up known as Malcolm (Stephen Lord), the father of Rumplestiltskin. Malcolm plays down the nature of The Shadow to his son: "It's not a monster, Rumple. It's a friend; a part of the island. And, after

I do what it told me, it will become a part of me too" (season 3, ep. 8). As a villain in the show, Pan enlists The Shadow to enter the open windows of sleeping children in the "real world" and kidnap unsuspecting boys, flying them to Neverland.

In contrast to Schlemihl's shadow and the doppelganger fear spirits, the shadow people in Seasons Two and Three of *OUaT* appear to embody the soul of a person, since the process of separating the shadow from its owner results in a dead body. In "Peter Schlemihl," the shadow is a part of the protagonist's identity but an omissible part that Schlemihl can exist without. His shadow represents the illusory values of a negatively portrayed bourgeois society, and because of this circumstance Schlemihl is in fact better off without his shadow. In *OUaT*, the uncanny doppelganger fear spirits are also a part of the protagonists' identities but an adversary, destructive, and life-threatening part that the protagonists need to overcome by killing their look-alikes in order to survive themselves. The shadow people, in comparison, are vessels of human souls. When the shadow people rip the shadows from people's bodies, the shadow's former hosts become lifeless, collapse, and fall down dead. However, this process can be reversed. In "Going Home" the destruction of The Shadow saves the Blue Fairy/Mother Superior (Keegan Connor Tracy) from death because her own shadow is returned to her (season 3, ep. 11). In sum, it is safe to say that *OUaT* depicts the doppelganger as an uncanny, dangerous, and malignant Other, but also as a supernatural creature that is defeated time and again by the heroes in the story. Whereas doppelgangers in nineteenth-century *Kunstmärchen*, such as Hoffmann's "The Sandman" or Andersen's "The Shadow" (1847), often-times cause the protagonist's demise, *OUaT*, being a product of the Disney-ABC Television Group, emphasizes happy endings and the triumph of good over evil.

In stark contrast to the image of the uncanny and negatively coded Other, the British-American film series *Harry Potter* puts a comedic twist on the motif of the doppelganger induced by magical transformation. By associating the idea of the double with comedy and humor, the popular film series moves beyond the one-sided portrayal of the terrifying alter ego in German fairy tales as well as the traumatizing depiction of *Grimm* and the Disneyfied representation of *OUaT*. At the same time, *Harry Potter* uses comic relief to demystify the encounter between the self and the Other self and features humorous scenes with multiple doubles interacting among themselves. Thanks to the powers of the Polyjuice Potion, which allows a person to assume the physical appearance of another living being, doppelganger transformations occur rather frequently throughout the film series. The magical transformation effect of the Polyjuice Potion is not unlike the effect of the *Verfluchte Zwillingsschwester Potion* in *Grimm*. In *Harry Potter and the Chamber of Secrets* (2002), the second installment of the series, Harry Potter (Daniel Radcliffe) and Ron Weasley (Rupert Grint) use the Polyjuice Potion for the first time to change into Draco Malfoy's (Tom Felton's) sidekicks Vincent Crabbe (Jamie Waylett) and Gregory Goyle (Joshua Herdman). Thanks to the technologically enhanced special effects, the process of transformation is visible to the viewer. Harry's bubbling skin and distorting features turn into an entertaining spectacle, which is more pronounced in the films than in the books. Hermione Granger (Emma Watson), who accidentally mistook cat hair for human hair in her potion, transfigures into a cross-species, semi-girl and semi-cat. Her sight causes Moaning Myrtle (Shirley Henderson), a ghost haunting the girl's bathroom at Hogwarts, to laugh out loud, while Ron remarks jokingly: "Look at your tail."

Polyjuice Potion is also used in *Harry Potter and the Goblet of Fire* (2005) by Barty Crouch Jr. (David Tennant) and in *Harry Potter and the Half-Blood Prince* (2009) by Crabbe and Goyle to allow them to magically transform into doppelgangers. Finally, the potion is used extensively in *Harry Potter and the Deathly Hallows: Part 1* (2010). In one scene, Alastor "Mad-Eye" Moody (Brendan Gleeson) creates six replicas of Harry as camouflage strategy to confuse the Death Eaters (a group of dark wizards and witches following Lord Voldemort) who are trying to capture Harry.

The scene depicting the transfigurations of the six characters—Hermione, Ron, Fleur Delacour (Clémence Poésy), Fred and George Weasley (James and Oliver Phelps), and Mundungus Fletcher (Andy Linden)—is designed to be humorous due to its visual effects. Body parts shrink and grow with the help of computer-generated imagery while the actors make funny facial expressions to mimic the metamorphic process. Characteristic features are mixed for comedic effect during the transformation, such as Hermione's delicate face with Harry's bushy eyebrows. The fact that the doppelgangers maintain the voices and clothes of the original characters contributes to the humorous act. For example, one Harry double wears a blue dress while another double wears a suit and tie and yet another wears a women's jeans jacket. Harry and his doppelgangers then have to swap their clothes for matching outfits to complete the picture of perfect look-alikes. This entertaining scene is complemented by some hilarious remarks by the characters. Fleur-Harry who is shown wearing a bra, says in her French accent (with the real Harry standing right next to her) "Bill, look away; I'm 'ideous!" The Weasley-Twins-Harrys exclaim excitedly at the same time, "Wow, we're identical!" and Hermione-Harry declares in a schoolmasterly, female tone, "Harry, your eyesight really is awful."

Other amusing doppelganger transmutations occur when Harry, Ron, and Hermione use the Polyjuice Potion to infiltrate the Ministry of Magic incognito by impersonating three employees of high rank, and when Hermione uses the potion to enter Gringotts Wizarding Bank disguised as Bellatrix Lestrange (Helena Bonham Carter). In these very tense moments of deception, the film resorts to comic relief as the young wizards act rather clumsy in their roles as doppelgangers. For example, it is comical to hear the trio's whiny voices come from their older doubles, the Ministry of Magic workers. They awkwardly walk around the Ministry, making goofy attempts to act casual and blend in with the other wizards. In the background of this scene, we find official Ministry propaganda posters, wanted signs, and pictures of wizards being ruthlessly intimidated. Juxtaposing these dramatic, political aspects of the scene with comedic elements serves the purpose of releasing built-up tensions. Another example of comic relief occurs at the suspense-ful moment when the trio tries to sneak out of the Ministry undetected, attempting to save Mary Cattermole (Kate Fleetwood), a witch on trial at the Ministry, along the way. Suddenly, Mary throws her arms around Ron's neck and kisses him passionately, thinking that he is her husband, Reginald Cattermole (Steffan Rhodri). In this instant, Ron reverts to his normal self just as an underwear-clad Reginald makes an appearance. While Mary is mortified, Ron has only enough time to say apologetically "Long story. Nice meeting you!" before the three young wizards have to make a run for it.

By framing the doppelganger in a comedic context, the *Harry Potter* films subvert the unilateral German fairy-tale tradition of the uncanny, for-bidding, destructive, and destabilizing Other. The doppelganger is no longer an agent of evil and death, and its negative connotation is reversed and takes on a positive signification. The act of deception, which we also see in *Grimm* and to some degree in *OUaT*, functions as an act of protection because the double is no longer the antagonist but an ally and the spectator continues to root for "the good guys" even when they are in magical disguise. At the same time, the nature of the doppelganger is demystified in the *Harry Potter* film scenes that emphasize the transformation process triggered by the Polyjuice Potion as a comical spectacle. To sum up, we can see differences in the treatment of the double, ranging from the uncanny, threatening, and demonic Other in the tradition of German Romanticism to postmodern recastings of the doppelganger as external, adverse agents of deception and psychological trauma in *Grimm*. In *OUaT*, the double embodies fear; it is an essential, dark part of the self that needs to be "defeated" but is also linked to the human soul and cannot exist without the body. Finally, the *Harry Potter* films resort to the doppelganger motif for comic relief and to create humor-istic scenes that entertain audiences. Here the double takes on a positive, subversive connotation as a form of protective magical masquerade that helps the heroes of the story to succeed in their endeavors.

Conclusion

There is a strong presence of supernatural creatures in the form of automatons, golems, and doppelgangers in today's American fairy-tale films and television series, even though we might not always recognize them as such at first glance. In Disney's popular animated film *Frozen* (2013), for example, the protagonist, Elsa, creates two artificial snow creatures, Marshmallow and Olaf, which are, in effect, types of golems. Marshmallow is Elsa's personal protector and acts as a security guard to the North Mountain, keeping intruders away from her ice palace. Just as the small, cute, happy, and playful snowman, Olaf, represents Elsa's childlike persona, the enormous, icy Marshmallow born from Elsa's powers appears to represent her desire to be left alone as well as her feelings of anger and desperation. Both creatures represent distinctive parts of Elsa's self, but it is solely Marshmallow who embodies the monstrous, threatening Other. Although Marshmallow is a hulking behemoth of a snowman possessing immense physical strengths, he can easily be outsmarted, as shown in a scene where he is chasing the other characters Kristoff and Anna. Like a golem, the snow beast is without a clear, consistent shape. His joints are comprised of ice rather than sticks, and his fingers are made from rounded icicles resembling sharp knives. When he gets enraged, Marshmallow's eye sockets light up demonically and ice spikes protrude from multiple parts of his body, especially from his back similar to the quills of a porcupine or hedgehog. His appearance is extremely scary and he shouts only the two phrases "Go away!" and "Don't come back!" throughout the film, making him an almost mute character. In many ways, Marshmallow resembles a mindless servant, a soulless creature, and ruthless protector—all characteristics of a traditional golem. However, in a post-credits scene, he is shown in a very different light. On his return to the ice palace, a battle weary, pitiful Marshmallow hobbles across the room and stumbles over Elsa's old tiara. Uncertain, the snow monster looks around the room to ensure that no one is watching, smiles happily into the camera, and lets out a relieved sigh after placing the tiara on his head. The snowman retracts his threatening spikes and a light glow appears above his head. This scene demonstrates that Marshmallow has a very soft, likable, and infantile side to him that sharply contrasts with the trope of the golem as monstrous, emotionless creature.

This chapter has demonstrated the ways in which the uncanny, menacing Other prevailing in German fairy tales of the Romantic period is reinterpreted, undermined, and subverted in contemporary American television series and fairy-tale-inspired films. Automatons, golems, and doppelgangers have a long tradition of negative valence, especially in the literary works of the German Dark Romantics. German fairy tales depict the eerie, threatening Other as a one-dimensional adversary and opponent, commonly tied to detrimental topoi, such as madness, death, destruction, deceit, and weirdness. But postmodern North American popular culture reimagines these particular fantastic creatures in a very different light, endowing them with positive character traits, humanizing the monstrous, and metamorphosing scary supernatural figures into sympathetic beings that allow for viewer identification. Fairy-tale-infused American media productions increasingly frame the Other in emotionally charged or comedic contexts, thereby radically challenging our notion of the Other. Differently put, the Other appears no longer uncanny, or rather, the fear of the Other—at least certain types of Others and forms of Otherness—has "softened" in the twenty-first century. This development is symptomatic of a broader shift in popular culture that refrains from casting the Other as evil and threatening monster to be avoided, repressed, destroyed, or hidden. Instead, contemporary media productions focus on the commonalities shared by the self and the Other, the human viewer and the supernatural character, transforming the Other into a character to which audiences may relate. Thus, the supernatural creature becomes a character that the viewer can accept, comprehend, identify with, and perhaps consider as a reflected part of the self. Already in 2005 Susan Bruce pointed to a similar recognition with regard to ghosts as supernatural, scary Other: "Ghosts, one might remark, appear to be experiencing not only a comeback, but also some kind of shift or change in what they mean to us: where classically they have scared us . . . we have been encouraged more recently, both in fiction and in theory, to grieve for them instead" (23). However, there is more to this trend than solely commiserating with the Other.

In the majority of films and television series that I analyzed, it is not the supernatural creatures that are portrayed as the real monsters or villains but human beings instead: the sadistic priest who beats the boy Jeremy in *Sleepy Hollow*; the anti-Semitic attackers of Isaac Luria in *The X-Files*; Prince Hans Westergaard in *Frozen,* who battles Marshmallow and changes from Prince Charming to become the main antagonist in the film; the small-minded, suburban townspeople who set out to kill Edward in *Edward Scissorhands*; the patriarchal men driven by male chauvinism in *The Stepford Wives*; the brutal, anti-mecha fanatics in *A.I.*; and so forth. Viewers of these productions are oftentimes led to believe that the supernatural figure is the villain at first, or rather, the audience is conditioned to fear the uncanny Other before the narrative discloses that the automaton, golem, or doppelganger is really a misunderstood creature or victim, deserving the empathy of the spectators. We are confronted with the fact that the supernatural creature is not the monstrosity but that the monstrousness lies with us, as human beings, with our communities, neighbors, families, and ourselves. This recognition forces us to reconsider the relation between selves and others and also raises the question of identity. Spectators are compelled to take a closer look at their own character traits, especially their "dark side," and to reflect upon their own feelings in relation to the portrayed Other. By blurring the boundaries between the self and the Other, contemporary reimaginings of supernatural creatures in American fairy-tale film and TV shows impel us toward a revision of fundamental dichotomies, such as evil and good, supernatural and natural, fantastic and real, animate and inanimate, abnormal and normal, and uncanny and familiar.

Because today's North American media productions reinterpret supernatural fairy-tale figures in new and innovative ways, encouraging viewers to sympathize with fantastic creatures and to recognize "the monster" within the members of society as well as within themselves, it becomes evident sthat the membrane between the self and the Other is a highly permeable one. But also the boundaries between various types of supernatural species, all of which can be considered different incarnations of the Other, have become fragile and easily traversable. Hybrid species—e.g., doppelganger automatons, doppelganger vampires, zombie golems, human witches, werewolf wizards, and the like—are on the rise, upsetting the comfortable, familiar distinctions between them. Furthermore, television shows and fairy-tale-imbued films reverse the uncanny elements of the Other by interspersing the trope with humoristic elements, as seen in *The Stepford Wives* (2004) and *Harry Potter*, or by tying the theme a priori to the genre of comedy, as in *The Simpsons*. This reinvention of the uncanny Other in postmodern American pop culture, of course, is not limited to the automaton, golem, and doppelganger, but concerns a wide variety of supernatural beings. Hence, this book centers on the wider palette of fantastic characters, comprised of evil queens and witches, monsters, beasts and wolves, and dwarfs.

By reading media productions as cultural artifacts of society, we can gain a deeper understanding into how Americans view the uncanny Other, as radically heterogeneous stranger or foreigner, today. The fact that supernatural creatures formerly imagined to be threatening, terrifying, and weird are now stripped of their monstrosity, cast in a favorable, forgiving role, and anthropomorphized as emotional beings that invite audience empathy indicates a novel trend of development directly linked to the fairy-tale genre. This paradigmatic shift in the representation of classic fairy-tale and fantasy figures gains transparency in view of a world where the forces of globalization move us closer together by breaking down cultural barriers and creating cross-cultural mosaics everywhere. Part of the phenomenon of globalization is an increased multicultural awareness in the twentieth and twenty-first centuries in America. This type of multiculturalism and acceptance of diversity did not exist in the early nineteenth century, when German nationalistic sentiments emerged as a strong force after Napoleon conquered many of the independent German states, kingdoms, and principalities in 1807. Due to the influences of globalization, we now live at a time of accelerated contact and mixing between different cultures, whether through travel, trade, communication, sports, or the media. In this postmodern climate, North American pop culture, including fairy-tale-inspired films and television shows, propagates the fact that difference does not equal monstrosity or danger. Indeed, alterity and fantastic Otherness are promoted as alluring rather than terrifying. The cultural significance of the Other in fairy-tale texts and fantastic narratives appears in a new light: what used to be alien, outlandish, and strange has become familiar, normal, and customary. What used to be ominous, sinister, and detestable has been demystified, trivialized, and made more appealing. And obviously, this "makeover" of the supernatural creature sells, be it in the form of popular literature, film, television, online media, or theme parks. In addition, fantasy-themed costume conventions, dressing-up parties, and masquerade events, where fans mimic their favorite supernatural character, are shooting out of the ground like mushrooms. Very pointedly put, the undesirable has become desirable in North American popular culture, and this phenomenon deserves further exploration in the following chapters.

2

EVIL QUEENS AND WITCHES

Mischievous Villains or Misunderstood Victims?

"There are no heroes and there are no villains. There are just opposing points of view. That's all history is . . . the viciously long battle between world views."[1]

—Peter J. Tomasi

"We always vilify what we don't understand."[2]

—Nenia Campbell, *Horrorscape*

"Far more often [than asking the question 'Is it true?'] they [children] have asked me: 'Was he good? Was he wicked?' That is, they were far more concerned to get the Right side and the Wrong side clear. For that is a question equally important in History and in Faerie."

—J. R. R. Tolkien, *Tolkien on Fairy-stories*

In 2010, I watched a performance of the Broadway production *Wicked: The Untold Story of the Witches of Oz* at the Apollo Victoria Theatre in London. The musical, based on Gregory Maguire's best-selling novel *Wicked: The Life and Times of the Wicked Witch of the West* (1995), which, in turn, is a retelling of L. Frank Baum's classic 1900 story *The Wonderful Wizard of Oz* and its 1939 film adaptation *The Wizard of Oz*, is told from the perspective of the witches of the Land of Oz. It was during this performance that I first pondered more deeply upon the growing trend of highlighting villains' backstories in fairy-tale retellings in contemporary North American pop culture. *Wicked* tells the behind-the-scenes story of how young Elphaba, the smart, talented, headstrong, but, due to her emerald green skin, misunderstood outcast befriends Galinda—who becomes Glinda—the beautiful, ambitious, and very popular blonde. The tale revolves around these two unlikely friends and how they grew up to become the infamous rivals better known as the Wicked Witch of the West and the Good Witch of the North. The plot of the musical continues to follow Elphaba's tragic life journey, focusing on her thoughts, trials, tribulations, meaningful relationships, and ultimate descent into wickedness. When Elphaba uncovers corruption in her land, she is given a choice to accept the status quo or be exiled. Instead of returning to the community that rejected her, she makes bad decisions that, while fueled by good intentions, eventually lead to her downfall. On February 14, 2016, *Wicked* presented its performance number 5,124, making it one of Broadway's longest-running shows (Gans 2016).

What is the secret of *Wicked*'s long-lasting popular appeal? One key factor contributing to the musical's popularity appears to be Elphaba's powerful background story, which presents the audience with a creative and drastic twist on the traditional villain figure, here the young Wicked Witch. In fact, besides her green skin, Elphaba's sympathetic character bears very little resemblance to the classic Hollywood portrayal of the horrifying Wicked Witch played by Margaret Hamilton. The stage production is based on Gregory Maguire's revisionist novel *Wicked: The Life and Times of the Wicked Witch of the West* (1995) and his "brilliant idea to take this hated figure and tell things from her point of view" (Buckley 2004). Hated, yes, but do we not love to hate villains? After all, what is evil can also be fascinating and alluring to us. Fairy-tale antagonists and villains in pop culture who flaunt their moral corruption still intrigue us more than they repulse us. What would Harry Potter be without Voldemort? Luke Skywalker without Darth Vader?

Peter Pan without Hook? As psychologist Roy Baumeister explained in his influential book *Evil: Inside Human Violence and Cruelty* (2001):

> Villains survive in popular entertainments because people still like to see them—in some important way, they do correspond to how people see the world. Indeed, the very fact that villains endure in popular entertainments despite being discredited by high literature, theology, and psychology is a testimony to how strong the appetite for them is. . . . They speak to a deeply rooted preference for understanding evil in certain ways. (64)

Admittedly, not all stories feature villains, and heroic feats are not always preceded by a villainous attack. Popular films, such as *Forrest Gump* (1994), Disney's *Brave* (2012), and *The Martian* (2015), or classic fairy tales, such as the Grimms' "The Seven Ravens" (ATU[3] 451) and "The Twelve Dancing Princesses" (ATU 306) come to mind. But the larger the villain looms, the more impressive is the triumphant heroine or hero. According to Neil Sinyard, Alfred Hitchcock proclaimed once, "the stronger the villain, the stronger the picture," emphasizing the appeal of a fully fleshed-out villain to the audience (1988, 94).

Oftentimes the villain functions as the catalyst for the action that unfolds in the story and plot, whereas the heroine or hero takes on the reactive role. In other words, villains provide the forces against which heroines and heroes strive. In *Morphology of the Folktale* ([1928] 1968), folklorist Vladimir Propp identifies the villain as one of the seven *dramatis personae*. These standard figures also include the donor, the helper, the princess and her father, the dispatcher, the hero, and the false hero.[4] Each of the *dramatis personae* controls various functions, and a function is understood as "an act of a character, defined from the point of view of its significance for the course of the action" (21). The functions in turn, logically join together into "spheres of action," which correspond to their respective performers (79). The principal functions that fall into a villain's sphere of action are categorized by villainy, struggle, and pursuit or chase:

> Villainy: a story-initiating villainy, where the villain caused harm to the hero or his family ("VIII: The villain causes harm or injury to a member of a family," 30)
>
> Struggle: a conflict between the hero and the villain, either a fight or competition ("XVI: The hero and the villain join in direct combat," 51)
>
> Pursuit/Chase: a pursuit of the hero after he defeated the villain or obtained the object of his quest ("XXI: The hero is pursued," 56)

The villain(s), whose "role is to disturb the peace of a happy family, to cause some form of misfortune, damage, or harm," may be a dragon, a devil, bandits, merchants, an evil princess, a stepmother, an old hag, a witch, or the like (27, 91).

Propp's *dramatis personae* or archetypes, such as the villain, loom large in classic folk and fairy tales, such as the Grimms' *Kinder- und Hausmärchen* (*Children's and Household Tales*, 1812). The wicked witches, evil queens, robbers, and other villains we encounter in these stories significantly lack character depth. The miscreants are evil to the core, but the tales rarely give explanations about the roots of this viciousness. Because the questions of why, how, and when the villains became malignant in the first place remain largely unanswered, these basic character types offer the reader little attraction or fascination. The same could be said about the archetypal representation of the Wicked Witch of the West in the novel and film versions of *The Wizard of Oz*. Indeed, the Wicked Witch remains a static and flat character throughout the story. The situation is quite different, however, with regard to an increasing number of depictions of fairy-tale villains in postmodern adaptations, such as, for example, in the musical *Wicked*, in the television series *Once Upon a Time* (*OUaT*) (2011–18), or in the film *Maleficent* (2014). In these fairy-tale recastings, villains take center stage, and their captivating personal histories are crucial for mass audience appeal.

Postmodern fairy-tale retellings in North American film, television, and theater twist, distort, and subvert the classic, archetypal portrayal of villains as they appear in German folk and fairy tales. These redesigned villains in present-day pop culture are intriguing to audiences because the evildoers are developed with interesting background stories and equipped with a wide palette of different personality traits. Fairy-tale-inspired reimaginings not only reconsider the nature of villainy by turning antagonists to protagonists, they also refrain from repeating the Grimms' black-and-white, dark-and-light, and evil-and-good dualisms. Today's remodeled villains are no longer simply bad or "black" but have turned into more complex characters tinged with "gray." In fact, they might display attributes traditionally associated with heroism, such as courage, selflessness, caring, and forgiveness, or might alternate between positive and negative roles throughout the narrative. Readers and spectators gravitate toward these intricate figures because many villains are nowadays presented as desirable and "cool."

From their attractive costumes and stunning looks to their demeanor and supernatural abilities, fantastic evildoers in popular culture exert a strong, fascinating allure. Hence, children and adults alike crave the newly designed fantasy villains as they appear in a variety of genres and media, such as in film and television, cartoons, animation, comics, theater productions, video games, graphic novels, illustrations, and so forth. In his chapter "The Aesthetic of Evil," Daniel Forbes describes his childhood captivation with the Darth Vader and Imperial Stormtrooper action figures as follows:

[T]he bad guys were the ones that I found the most fascinating and desirable. Part of the reason why, if you had asked me back then, was that I found these characters cool. And they really *looked* cool—much cooler than any of the heroes. . . . Even now as an adult I continue to find them very appealing—and, when they're at their best, very intriguing. (2011, 13)

Similar reactions can be found among the fans of various fairy-tale villains, popularized in Western culture predominantly through the Disney franchise. Lis, a fan of the Disney-inspired role-playing video game *Kingdom Hearts* (Square Enix 2002) commented online: "I love to fight Maleficent in Kingdom Hearts, she's so . . . centered . . . her evil personality is so cool it's almost good! Also, evil Disney queens are a lot cooler than poor innocent princesses" (Lis 2012). The drawing power of postmodern villains has not gone unnoticed in fairy-tale scholarship. In an interview about the popularity of the evil queen in today's film retellings, renowned fairy-tale scholar Jack Zipes remarked, "As a figure, she [the evil queen] is much more fascinating than this dumb, innocent, naive Snow White, so why not focus on this figure who is tragic in many ways?" (Berkowitz 2012).

The exploration of a villain's background can make the character more interesting to an audience, on the one hand, and contribute to demystifying the villain, on the other hand. All of a sudden, the villain is no longer shrouded in complete mystery but her or his actions become comprehensible. A difficult childhood, a traumatic experience in the past, unjust treatment by others, the loss of a loved one, or a combination of these "trigger events" can help explain why a character chooses to follow the path of darkness rather than light. We might not only learn more about the powerful motivation driving a villain's actions but even endorse these actions to some extent. Such insights into a villain's personal history allow us, the listeners, viewers, and readers of the story, to empathize with the character because she or he becomes a figure with which to identify. If we can relate to a villain on a personal level based on that villain's unique and in many cases disturbing backstory, we are more inclined to feel sympathy for the villain as a misunderstood victim of society and social misfit. Further, fairy-tale villains can evoke compassion because they are imperfect individuals whose own mistakes oftentimes lead to their downfall. As Leon Z. Surmelian limns, "The villain becomes the tragic hero and people sympathize with him. When the end comes, he is not hated and arouses the pity and fear which provide the tragic pleasure in the poetics of movie plots and their counterparts in magazines and books" (1968, 152). At the same time, we may identify with certain character flaws of supernatural antagonists—for instance, lying, cheating, selfishness, jealousy, vengefulness, or over-confidence—because we recognize similar faults in others and ourselves. Differently put, character flaws can contribute to humanizing villains because evildoers who are imperfect appear more "like us," given that the average person is not morally and ethically perfect.

This chapter concentrates first and foremost on postmodern depictions of the evil queen based on the Grimms' fairy tale "Schneewittchen" ("Snow White"). Because the queen in Disney's first full-length animated version, *Snow White and the Seven Dwarfs* (1937), "has become in popular consciousness a dominant visual embodiment of this villainous character," the chapter includes this cinematic adaptation at the beginning of its analysis (Aldred 2016, 842). Since the past decades have seen a significant number of "Snow White" recastings in film and television, this chapter's investigation is limited to those fairy-tale retellings that I consider most crucial for proving my argument. To further narrow the scope of media adaptations from which to choose, the chapter focuses primarily on productions of the recent past decades, including *Snow White: A Tale of Terror* (1997), *Once Upon a Time* (2011–18), *Mirror Mirror* (2012), *Snow White and the Huntsman* (2012), and *The Huntsman: Winter's War* (2016). The selection of these particular adaptations is also determined by my wish to include in the analysis a wide variety of different subgenres of fantasy, from horror (*Snow White: A Tale of Terror*) to comedy (*Mirror Mirror*) and from action (*Snow White and The Huntsman, The Hunstman: Winter's War*) to drama (*Once Upon a Time*).

The Grimms' "Snow White"

It is well known in fairy-tale scholarship that the Grimms' *Kinder- und Hausmärchen* edition of 1812/1815 introduces Snow White's biological mother as the queen who turns evil, driven by her jealousy of her daughter's beauty. In all following editions the birth mother is replaced with a wicked stepmother. This drastic change from natural parent to stepparent occurs not only in the fairy tale "Snow White" but also in many other tales throughout the collection. Fairy-tale scholars have offered different explanations for this literary device, which can be ascribed mostly to Wilhelm Grimm, since the younger brother was responsible for the bulk of the revisions and imprinted his own narrative voice in the stories. Zipes and Vanessa Joosen, among other scholars, have argued that "the Grimms held motherhood sacred," and it was therefore their intention to preserve this idealized image of the good mother (Zipes [1999] 2013, xxiv). The Grimms' literary device of replacing the good (usually dead) mother with the evil stepmother not only reinforces "the ideology of the nuclear family" (Joosen 2014, 94) but also, from Bruno Bettelheim's psychoanalytical perspective, "helps the child not to be devastated by experiencing the mother as evil" (1976, 69). Furthermore, the Grimms may have used this literary device to reflect the common circumstances of their time, when young stepmothers replaced mothers who had died in childbirth. By exchanging birth mothers with stepmothers and eliminating sexual references and profanities in their stories, the Brothers adhered to the public tastes of their time, which called for a more child-friendly version of the tales. Historically, the shift of the different mother types is significant because it demonstrates a slow transition from the originally targeted audience of middle-class adults to the new target audience of children.

Because the stepmother represents the "alien intruder who disturbs the harmony among blood relatives," her presence in most German fairy tales is connoted negatively as the antithesis of the heroine (Tatar 1985, 33). At the same time, the maternal role of the (step)mother and the monarchal role of the queen conflate into one sinister figure in all seven "Snow White" versions published by the Brothers Grimm. Diametrically opposed to the all-good, innocent heroine of the story, the queen remains synonymous with the term "evil" and thus corresponds to the Grimms' black-and-white pattern. Vanity and jealousy lie at the root of the queen's maleficent actions and feelings of hatred toward her stepdaughter. Although the queen herself is a beautiful woman, her attractiveness fades in comparison with that of the seven-year-old Snow White, a much younger rival in beauty. The Grimms describe the queen as proud and arrogant but do not offer any information as to the character's personal background.[5] Why did the queen become so focused on beauty in the first place? Was she always evil? Interestingly, the fairy tale does not mention any tensions between the antagonist and protagonist up until the moment when Snow White's beauty starts blossoming. In fact, for the first six years of her life, nothing happens to Snow White. The passing of time and the process of aging are crucial factors in the tale because the queen feels threatened by her stepchild only once Snow White's beauty supersedes her own. Ultimately, it is a battle against time, which the aging (step)mother is destined to lose against her (step)daughter. The queen's repetitive question, "Mirror, mirror, on the wall, who in this land is fairest of all?" is set up for competition. Her adult anxieties of aging have been interpreted by scholars, such as Roger Sale and Maria Nikolajeva, as an expression of her fears of losing sexual power and of being replaced by a younger woman (Sale 1979, 42; Nikolajeva 2005, 155).

The queen's experience of fear is, in fact, supported by the tale's text and presents the driving force behind the queen's extreme emotional reaction. As soon as she learns from her magic mirror that Snow White is "a thousand times" fairer than she, which inevitably implies that she is a thousand times uglier than Snow White, the queen is "shocked" and turns "yellow and green with envy." From that exact moment on, the queen feels such hatred for Snow White that whenever she sees the girl, "her heart . . . [turns] over inside her body." However, Sandra M. Gilbert and Susan Gubar have claimed that the queen's hatred of Snow White already exists "before the looking glass has provided an obvious reason for hatred" because Snow White represents "the ideal of renunciation," free of the queen's consuming mirror-madness (Gilbert and Gubar 1979, 38). The evil queen relies on the mirror's judgment because she knows that the mirror always speaks the truth. Her daily ritual of self-absorption, the obsessive questioning of the mirror every morning, is not merely an act of narcissism but a sign of her weakness and insecurity. It is through the looking glass, so it seems, that the queen defines her entire identity and self-worth; a definition as superficial as the reflective surface of the mirror. If the queen were a self-confident, independent woman, she would not need the confirmation of the mirror, which Gilbert and Gubar, among other feminists, identify as an embodiment of the otherwise absent king. The mirror's voice, according to Gilbert and Gubar, is the "patriarchal voice of judgment" that rules the queen's self-evaluation, since in the tale's patriarchal society, a woman's social value emanates from her beauty (38). It must be duly noted, though, that the tale never explicitly states the gender of the mirror and that the German word "der Spiegel" (the mirror), with its masculine article "der," should not be used to draw conclusions about the gender of the mirror either.

Whether the mirror is interpreted as the male gaze of a patriarchal culture, a grotesque maternal body, the inner, schizophrenic female voice of the queen herself, or, as suggested by Bettelheim, the daughter, it clearly has power over the queen and orchestrates her life (Bettelheim 1976, 207). As Zipes elucidates, "if the queen had disregarded the mirror instead of gazing into it and becoming absorbed by it, her life might not have ended so tragically" (2011, 116). But obsessions, such as the queen's compulsive behavior, are hard to break, and the relationship of the queen to her magic mirror appears to be an addictive, pathological one. Also morbid is her lethal jealousy of Snow White, which culminates in her atrocious demand to have the girl murdered and her cannibalistic desire to devour Snow White's vital organs, her lungs and liver, salted and cooked. This cannibalistic wish to consume one's enemy is far more intimate than other forms of domination or possession.

Bettelheim, among other theorists, has analyzed the queen's cannibalistic desires and concluded that the queen is "arrested on the oral incorporative stage" (1976, 206–7). "The queen, jealous of Snow White's beauty, wanted to incorporate Snow White's attractiveness, as symbolized by her internal organs" (207). In other words, the (step)mother hopes that by consuming her (step)daughter's body parts, she will absorb Snow White's youth, beauty, and sexual power, and thus rejuvenate herself to become once more the fairest, most desirable woman in the land. Surprisingly, the wicked queen has no intention of consuming Snow White's heart, one of the body's most important and central organs and one with symbolic character. However, if the queen truly believes that one acquires the power and characteristics of what one eats, then the tale suggests that she seeks only outer but no inner transformation. Following this train of thought, the incorporation of Snow White's "innocent heart" (*unschuldiges Herz*) would undoubtedly transform the queen's "envious heart" (*neidisches Herz*) and thus change her identity from what Gilbert and Gubar have coined a "monster-woman" to an "angel-woman" (1979, 36). The wicked queen therefore chooses deliberately to remain a vicious, evil person to the core with a heart full of pride, envy, and arrogance. When the huntsman brings to her the lungs and liver of a young boar, the queen eats the organs, believing that she is consuming the liver and lungs of her (step)daughter. Gilbert and Gubar have interpreted the queen's eating of the wild boar's organs symbolically by stating, "she devours her own beastly rage, and becomes (of course) even more enraged" (39). The (step)mother's evil desires and actions are that much more horrifying because the crimes are not only attempted murder and cannibalism, they are attempted child murder and cannibalism of a child's body parts. This type of threefold transgression is not uncommon in fairy tales, and places the queen in close proximity to other fairy-tale monsters, such as, for example, the witch in "Hansel and Gretel."

Another theorist, Shuli Barzilai, however, reconsiders the queen's attempt to incorporate Snow White and interprets the text passage as "a refusal to relinquish the daughter" (1990, 531). For Barzilai, the queen is identical to the biological mother whose wish is "to take the daughter back into herself, to recreate the condition in which her creation was the very flesh of her own flesh" (531). Barzilai's argument foregrounds the mother's role as a creator whose artistic vision of a child "as white as snow, as red as blood, and as black as ebony" preceded Snow White's creation. Indeed, the queen's beauty is not, as Sale suggests, the regent's "only one power" (1979, 43). Already Gilbert and Gubar have observed that the queen is more than a beautiful and maleficent woman but a "plotter, a plot-maker, a schemer, a witch, an artist, an impersonator, a woman of almost infinite creative energy, witty, wily, and self-absorbed as all artists traditionally are" (1979, 38–39). Needless to say that this list could be expanded further, since the queen is also determined, persistent, clever, cunning, resourceful, gifted, and convincing, with a talent for acting and rhetorical skills. Her creative and magical powers enable her to pursue Snow White on her own without the help of the huntsman and, after the first failed murder attempt, make three more attempts on Snow White's life.

When the magic mirror reveals to the queen that Snow White is still alive and resides with the seven dwarfs behind the seven mountains, the queen is terrified. The crafty villainess devises a second scheme to kill Snow White, which substantiates that the desire and plan to eliminate her (step)daughter were not an ad-hoc, impulsive decision sparked by a momentary loss of reason but a rationally calculated maneuver. After coloring her face and disguising herself as an old peddler woman, the queen approaches the house of the dwarfs to offer Snow White a bodice lace "that was braided from colorful silk." Preying on the princess's own narcissistic desires, the queen uses her ruse to tie Snow White's bodice so quickly and hard that the young girl cannot breathe and falls to the floor unconscious. As is well known, this second murder attempt by the evil queen ultimately fails, as do the following attempts with a poisoned comb and a poisoned apple. Snow White is intrigued by the lace and comb, objects of adornment that would make her appear more beautiful, more mature, and sexually attractive. Hence, the queen's assassination attempts can be read symbolically as the (step)mother's efforts to prevent the transition of her (step)daughter from childhood to puberty. The temptation of the apple as an object of seduction also fits into that line of thought. This argument follows in Barzilai's footsteps in seeing the queen as an artist who wants to keep a hold on her creation or as a biological mother who does not want to be separated from her daughter. This separation anxiety might stem from the fact that the daughter is approaching the age of puberty and will soon become an adolescent. In fact, for some scholars, such as Bettelheim, "the laces suggest the pubescent princess's wish to be sexually desirable" (Cornfeld 2014, 129). Bettelheim goes even one step further by asserting that Snow White's "collapsing unconscious symbolizes that she became overwhelmed by the conflict between her sexual desires and her anxiety about them" (1976, 212).

The lace, the comb, and the apple, on the other hand, also represent objects of motherly nurture and care that the abandoned, exiled (step)daughter is lacking but may long for. After all, dressing, grooming, and nourishing are the essential tasks a mother usually does for her child. Because Snow White has neither her biological mother nor her stepmother left to care for her, she desires a substitute, a maternal figure to fill the vacuum. Thus, instead of Snow White's interest in the objects displaying a wish to enter the stage of puberty, her desire for the objects may simply reflect Snow White's yearning for a motherly touch and parental care. The queen, in turn, might not pry on Snow White's interest in beautification but on her obvious need for parental care. On the first visit, the "old woman" indeed acts like a reproaching mother, concerned about the proper looks of her daughter: "'Child,' said the old woman, 'what a fright you look; come, I will lace you properly for once.' Snow White had no suspicion, but stood before her, and let herself be laced with the new laces." On her second visit, the disguised queen once again implies that Snow White is not well taken care of and lacks an experienced, motherly guide to teach her proper appearance: "After they had agreed on the purchase, the old woman said, 'Now I will comb you properly for once.' Poor little Snow White had no suspicion, and let the old woman do as she pleased." Finally, on the third visit, the queen attempts to win Snow White's trust as a mother would convince a child, by setting an example: "'Are you afraid of poison?' asked the old woman. 'Look, I'll cut the apple in two. You eat the red half, and I shall eat the white half. . . . Snow White longed for the beautiful apple, and when she saw that the peasant woman was eating part of it she could no longer resist, and she stuck her hand out and took the poisoned half." Furthermore, Snow White's childish naïveté, befitting a seven-year-old girl, is reflected in her decision to allow an apparent stranger to enter her privacy and approach her physically.

In the middle of the tale "Snow White," the text discloses that the queen uses her creative powers for evil by the means of witchcraft, merging her monarchal and maternal roles with a magical one, namely, that of the wicked witch. Thanks to her knowledge in the "art of witchcraft," the queen fabricates first the poisoned comb and then the poisoned apple. The fact that she is able to make an apple "so artfully" that only one half, the red cheek, is poisoned, highlights that the queen is a truly skilled master in the art of witchery. But the Grimms do not offer any background information as to how the queen learned witchcraft in the first place, whether she was born with these powers, or how her magical abilities relate to her wonder-ful looking glass. Was the queen always evil or did the magic corrupt her over time to commit evil deeds? How far do her powers stretch and what are her limitations? The text sheds light, however, on the extent to which the evil queen is willing to go in order to reach her goal of killing Snow White. Driven by her pathological envy of the princess's beauty, the queen shouts angrily after the third failed murder attempt: "Snow White shall die . . . even if it costs me my life!" At this point, the text already foreshadows the demise of the villainess, almost as if the evil queen cursed her own destiny in a self-fulfilling prophecy. The queen thus paves the way for her expectation to become reality, to be specific, for Snow White's death to come with the price of her own downfall. Ironically, the queen's morbid prediction only comes true after Snow White's resurrection from the dead.

At the end of the tale, the evil regent is invited to a wedding, puts on her fine clothes, and consults her magic mirror as usual. Unexpectedly, the looking glass informs the queen about a younger queen in the land who is once more "a thousand times fairer" than she. After an initial wave of anger and cursing, the queen is overcome with tremendous fear, which leaves the maleficent woman in a perplexed and restless state: "she became so frightened, so frightened, that she did not know what to do. At first she did not want to go to the wedding, but she found no peace." Despite all of her efforts, the aging queen finds herself again threatened by a younger, more beautiful woman who can supplant her. Although she is indecisive about whether or not to attend the festivity, the queen's envy and curiosity to see this new and younger rival in beauty for herself wins the upper hand in the end. When the queen realizes that she is attending the royal wedding of her (step)daughter, who is alive and well, the (step)mother experiences nothing short of a panic attack: "[T]errorized, she could only stand there without moving." For her punishment, the queen is then forced to dance in hot iron slippers until she dies, evoking the medieval burnings and brandings of women accused of witchcraft.

As is common for the Grimms' fairy tales, the villains are severely punished for being purely bad antagonists, oftentimes with public humiliation, mutilation, or death, whereas the all-good heroes and heroines are rewarded mostly with materialistic goods or a higher societal status. Since the Grimms compiled their collection with the pedagogical mission in mind of presenting their readers, a dualistic audience of children and adults, with an "educational manual" (*Erziehungsbuch*), this clear separation between good and evil characters runs like a leitmotiv through the tales (Grimm and Grimm 1815, VIII). The simplistic, black-and-white pattern also reinforces the embedded morals and augments the tales' happy endings, such as Snow White's ascent as new queen and triumph over her wicked (step)mother. Much has been said in scholarship about the medieval-style, gruesome death penalty of the evil queen. Bettelheim interprets the "fiery red shoes" psychoanalytically as symbolic of "untrammeled sexual jealousy," which, as it "tries to ruin others, destroys itself" (1976, 214). Further, he draws a comparison between the evil queen and the witch from "Hansel and Gretel," since both women are punished for their cannibalistic desires by fire (214). Cornfeld notes that the queen's beauty "literally goes up in smoke," and therefore hypothesizes that the hot iron shoes may "serve as a reminder that youthful beauty does not last forever, and that attempting to stay young too long can result in fast burnout" (2014, 130). Cornfeld also observes that it is a communal rather than an individual justice surrounding the queen's death, given that it is not one specific character who passes judgment and forces the queen into the slippers but rather an anonymous, communal action: "Then they put a pair of iron shoes into burning coals. They were brought forth with tongs and placed before her [the queen]. She was forced to step into the red-hot shoes and dance until she fell down dead."

Justice plays a pivotal role in the Grimms' fairy-tale world in which the severity of the queen's punishment corresponds to the magnitude of her committed crimes. Grizzly penalties for the wicked, including physical pain and torture, are the order of the day in the stories. From the first time Jacob and Wilhelm Grimm wrote down "Snow White" in 1810, in a collection known today as *Ölenberg manuscript* (*Ölenberger Handschrift*), to their final publication of the tale in 1857, the penalty of the evil queen's death dance has remained the same. Despite the fact that the Grimms, in particular Wilhelm, significantly reworked and sanitized their tales after the 1812/1815 edition by eliminating profanities, adding Christian prayers, replacing mothers with stepmothers, and purging the stories of sexual references, lurid punishments escaped censorship. It appears the Grimms deemed harsh corporal punishments for villains to be not only appropriate but necessary elements of their stories. In her groundbreaking historical-psychological study *The Hard Facts of the Grimms' Fairy Tales* (1987), literary scholar Tatar illuminates that "The Grimms only occasionally took advantage of opportunities to tone down descriptions of brutal punishments visited on villains" and that "[w]hen they did, it was often at the behest of a friend or colleague rather than of their own volition" (5). But in most literary and cinematic adaptations of "Snow White" in the twentieth and twenty-first centuries, the evil queen no longer dances herself to death in red-hot shoes. Instead, she simply vanishes, is banished, or dies by some disastrous, accidental stroke of fate resembling a godly punishment. According to fairy-tale expert Zipes, one main reason for this drastic change in contemporary adaptations is the fear in popular culture that the queen's death dance "might damage the souls of putative innocent child readers/viewers" (2011, 116). Probably the best-known adaptation of "Snow White" in cinema with such a radical alteration is Disney's animated feature-length fairy-tale film *Snow White and the Seven Dwarfs,* whose portrayal of the evil queen has predominantly shaped people's imagination of the villainess.

Walt Disney's *Snow White and the Seven Dwarfs*

On December 22, 1936, Walt Disney asserted in the story meeting for his company's first feature film, *Snow White and the Seven Dwarfs,* that, "In our version of the story we follow the story very closely. We have put in certain twists to make it more logical, more convincing and easy to swallow" (Davis 2014, 7). The Disneyfied portrayal of the evil queen (sometimes referred to as Queen Grimhilde), however, differs significantly from the Grimms' version in several key aspects. The film opens with a storybook text informing the audience that the queen, here Snow White's vain and wicked stepmother, feared that someday the princess's beauty would surpass her own and so she dressed her in rags and forced her to work as a scullery maid. This beginning, reminiscent of the fairy tale "Cinderella," insinuates that the queen feels threatened by Snow White's beauty and seeks to control it long before the magic mirror proclaims the stepdaughter to be the fairest one of all. Snow White, no longer a child but an adolescent girl, is juxtaposed with a mature woman who is not only icily beautiful but also alluringly sexy. From her black, open face, balaclava-like headpiece to her carefully pedicured, long fingernails and orange-yellow high-heel pumps, this queen's looks add to her role as seductress. Her pale skin, green eyes, and serene, Marlene Dietrich–esque face are accentuated by makeup with rouge, blood-red lipstick, purple eye shadow, and seemingly penciled-on, extremely arched eyebrows. The queen's skintight purple gown and red rope belt tied around her waist emphasize her feminine, slender figure. Apparently, Walt Disney's animators followed his instructions to the letter when he explained his vision of the antagonist: "The Queen/Witch should be a mixture of Lady Macbeth and the Big Bad Wolf. Her beauty is sinister, mature, plenty of curves" (Pickard 1978, 244).

Based on the queen's slinky appearance and her commanding demeanor—she forces Snow White into servitude and humiliating tasks far below the royal status of a princess—the cinematic portrayal of the queen evokes that of a mistress and dominatrix. The character's sexual association with dominatrix, a Latin term that literally translates to "female ruler," is strengthened by her relationship with her servant in the magic mirror she calls "slave." Before introducing Snow White, the film first depicts the evil queen (voiced by Lucille La Verne) approaching her oversized looking glass with the words: "Slave in the magic mirror, come from the farthest space, through wind and darkness I summon thee. Speak! Let me see thy face." The queen's slave in the looking glass, an imprisoned spirit resembling a theatrical mask with hollow eye sockets, has a male voice and addresses her submissively with the words "my queen." Instead of a whip, the queen possesses a scepter that rests, as a reminder of her power, beside her elevated throne, which is appropriately decorated with a relief of a peacock to reflect her vanity. It is here where she orders her subject, the faithful huntsman, to kill Snow White. At his attempt to protest, the queen leaps off her throne in a dominating posture with one raised arm to silence him and threatens to punish him should he fail. As proof of his deed, the hunter is supposed to bring the queen Snow White's heart in a small chest.

The switch from lungs and liver in the Grimms' tale to the heart in the Disney version is matched by the elimination of the queen's cannibalistic desires. The film leaves the viewer in the dark about what the queen intends to do with Snow White's heart, but there is no indication that she wishes to consume it. Interestingly, when the queen receives what she believes to be her stepdaughter's heart, she initially places the word of the huntsman above that of the mirror. When the mirror tells the queen that Snow White dwells in the cottage of the dwarfs, the queen objects by presenting the chest to the looking glass with the words: "Snow White lies dead in the forest. The huntsman has brought me proof. Behold, her heart." The queen's reaction suggests that she is less trusting of the mirror than in the literary version because she obviously doubts his omniscience. This challenging of the mirror's statement that Snow White is still alive indicates a more individualistic, empowered queen who is less dependent on the mirror than in the Grimms' text. Indeed, the power balance between the queen and her magic mirror appears to be reversed in the Disney film, with the queen holding more power and control over the mirror than vice versa. Not only does the queen dominate her slave in the looking glass and force him into her services, she is also able to control nature's elements. When she first summons the spirit in the mirror, she is surrounded by wind, thunder, and lightning, followed by flaring flames and smoke in the mirror. Later, the queen conjures up a blast of wind and a thunderbolt as ingredients for her transformation spell.

As in the Grimms' tale, the evil queen, in her undisguised form, never interacts with Snow White directly. But whereas the Grimms' variant offers no tangible references that link the two female figures as sexual competitors seeking male attention, the Disney version introduces a love triangle element between the queen, the prince, and Snow White. This significant change to the story takes place early on in the film. Snow White's singing voice and her beautiful looks capture the attention of a dashing prince who happens to ride by the castle courtyard where Snow White is scrubbing the stairs. It is love at first sight for the prince, who approaches Snow White in her ragged attire at the wishing well. In a *Romeo and Juliet*–like scene that is witnessed by the queen from a window high above, the prince serenades Snow White briefly at her balcony, professing that his heart is hers alone. Filled with indignation that the charming prince so fervently pursues her stepdaughter, the disgruntled queen energetically draws the curtains of her windows. The scene manifests that the queen is not only jealous of Snow White's beauty but also of her femininity and power of attracting the opposite sex. Hence, much more explicitly than the Grimm version, the Disney film suggests the queen's fear of being replaced by a younger woman whose sex appeal is greater than her own.

Besides her character-defining vanity and jealousy of Snow White, the queen's macabre sense of humor is a new personal trait added by the Disney production. Her grim humor comes to the fore when the beautiful queen magically changes her physical appearance into that of an old and ugly witch. Rather than merely masquerading as an old peddler's woman, like in the Grimms' tale, the queen has the powerful ability to transform herself into a hag with warts, bulgy eyes, and a crooked nose.[6] After creating the poisoned apple in her laboratory, the witch offers the deadly fruit to her pet raven with the words "Have a bite?" Terrified, the raven flaps wildly, trying to escape, and backs away, causing the witch to cackle maliciously. The old hag makes another cruel joke when she walks through her skull-and-bone-filled dungeon and passes by the skeleton of a prisoner reaching for a pitcher. Accompanied by sardonic laughter, the wicked witch cries, "Thirsty? Have a drink!" and kicks the pitcher toward the skeleton, which crumbles into pieces. Although the film endows the queen with a black sense of humor, other characteristics, such as the scope of her cunningness, artistry, creativity, and ingenuity, fall short in comparison with the Grimm version. Instead of attempting to kill Snow White herself using three different disguises and resorting to three different approaches, the queen in the Disney film deploys just a single plan. Her creation, the wholly poisoned apple, however, lacks the artistry of the apple in the Grimms' tale, which consists of only one poisoned half.

Whereas the relationship between the child Snow White and the disguised evil queen in the Grimms' version is framed by an underlying mother-daughter trope, the Disney adaptation hints at a grandmother-grandchild relationship instead. When the horrid witch arrives at the dwarfs' cottage to tempt Snow White with her poisoned apple, the birds of the woods attack her in order to save the princess from the "Sleeping Death" curse. Unsuspecting, Snow White, however, shoos the birds away and scolds them: "Shame on you, frightening a poor old lady." In this scene, Snow White takes on the role of protector and caregiver, helping the apparently old woman by holding and comforting her with the words: "There, there. I'm sorry." It is because of Snow White's caring nature that the hag decides spontaneously to play the role of an ailing grandmother who is unwell, feigning cardiac chest pains: "Oh! My heart! Oh, my . . . My poor heart. Take me into the house and let me rest. A drink of water, please." After Snow White fetches a chair and a glass of water for her, the witch continues, "And because you've been so good to poor old granny, I'll share a secret with you." She tricks Snow White by making her believe that the apple is no ordinary fruit but a magic wishing apple and by appealing to the enamored princess's desire of being with her prince. Although much older than her literary counterpart, Disney's Snow White naïvely buys into the witch's promise that after only one bite of the apple all her dreams will come true. Grimms' Snow White, in contrast, undergoes a learning process of not allowing strangers into the house and ultimately becomes suspicious of the offered apple being poisonous. Striking is the fact that the queen in the Grimm version is much more cunning and sophisticated in her approach to murdering Snow White than in the Disney version. By utilizing a bodice lace, a poisoned comb, and a semi-poisoned apple as murder weapons, the Grimms' evil queen demonstrates far greater ingenuity and skill than Disney's evil queen, who simply lies about her apple possessing magical properties.

The queen's demise at the end of the animated adaptation deserves special attention since the antagonist's punishment departs significantly from the Grimms' version. The death of Disney's evil queen occurs offscreen and is, in fact, less gruesome than the literary torture scene. Instead of being forced to dance in hot iron slippers at Snow White's wedding, the queen—still transformed as an old hag—is chased by the furious dwarfs up a mountain and toward a rocky cliff. When she finds herself trapped at the end of the cliff, the witch tries to kill the dwarfs by crushing them with a massive boulder nearby. Suddenly, a bolt of lightning strikes the cliff and the hag falls to her death. The boulder tumbles down after her, presumably smashing her body into pieces. Two vultures then fly down the cliff to devour her remains, confirming her demise to the viewer. Amy Davis suggests that Disney's changes, in particular the alteration of the queen's death, were made to comply with the so-called Hays Code (2014, 8). According to the first of the General Principles listed in the Motion Picture Production Code of 1930 (a.k.a. the Hays Code): "No picture shall be produced that will lower the moral standards of those who see it. Hence the sympathy of the audience should never be thrown to the side of crime, wrongdoing, evil or sin" (Davis 2014, 8–9). Because of the code, the Grimms' description of the queen's grizzly death dance would have been banned and replaced by a less violent, accidental, or godly punishment for the villainess. The fact that a flash of lightning leads to the queen's death is ironic, considering that the film portrays her earlier in the story as being capable of controlling nature's elements through magic.

Remarkably, the queen in the Grimms' tale dies in all her beauty and sumptuous gowns, whereas Disney's queen dies in her transformed hag appearance, which Heidi Breuer refers to as the hag's final and therefore "true form" (2009, 114). As is common for fairy-tale villains and witches, her outside looks reflect her inner ugliness, rotten moral character, and grotesque monstrosity. Breuer describes such revelation of a foul core hidden behind the veneer of beauty as the "Snow White factor," although it might be more fitting to call it the "Evil Queen factor" (114). In her hag guise, Disney's evil queen does indeed look wicked and becomes recognizable as such for the viewer. How does this circumstance affect her function as evildoer in the film? A villain who can be easily identified to be vicious based on appearance is less threatening than a villain who seems to be harmless and good but very unexpectedly does something horrific, such as Prince Hans in Disney's *Frozen* (2013). Walt Disney himself described the transmogrification of the queen into a sinister crone as a "Jekyll and Hyde thing," but failed to realize that the good side of the personality, "Mr. Jekyll," is missing, since the queen consists of only two sinister "Mr. Hydes" (Tatar 1992, 232). In both forms, her beautiful appearance that conceals her wicked core, and her ugly double, the queen represents a genuinely disturbing and maleficent figure.

Another significant alteration made by Disney concerns the prominent status of the queen as antagonistic fairy-tale character embedded in a narrative that foregrounds her own rise and fall. From the first five minutes of the film when the villainess takes center stage in the dialog with her magic mirror, to her terrifying transformation in the middle, to the dramatic moment of her death at the end, the evil queen occupies about fifteen minutes of screen time packed with action and suspense that propel the story. In many ways, *Snow White and the Seven Dwarfs* could be considered the queen's film in which Snow White merely plays the role of accidental heroine. Although Disney does not offer a lengthy background story that explains the queen's evil nature and origin, the depth of her "'history' is represented in the length of time it takes to absorb her image" (Rushkoff 1996, 57). With her panache in voice, gestures, and clothing, her majestic composure, band collar, and long-flowing cape, the vengeful, diva-like queen "steals the show" from an inconspicuous Snow White. We may identify with the simply drawn protagonist Snow White but it is the powerful visuals of the detailed drawn antagonist that hold great fascination for the viewer. This is perhaps not surprising since "the animators of the Disney film preferred to draw the evil queen because she was more real and complex as a woman, more erotic, and driven to desperate acts by her magic mirror" (Zipes 2011, 115). Whether consciously or unconsciously, Disney's animated production thus laid the cornerstone for a series of contemporary "Snow White" reimaginings that prioritize the queen's personal narrative and illuminate her character in unprecedented and intriguing ways.

Michael Cohn's *Snow White: A Tale of Terror*

Who is the queen? What is the source of her evilness? What are her internal drives, her desires, fears, needs, and wants? Michael Cohn's *Snow White: A Tale of Terror* (1997), featuring Sigourney Weaver in the role of wicked step-mother Lady Claudia Hoffman, addresses these questions in a quasi-queen-centric narrative. In this Gothic-influenced horror television film, the villainess is portrayed primarily as a tragic but also sympathetic character who is driven into monstrous madness after losing a baby. In her excellent chapter "A Dark Story Retold," Andrea Wright hypothesizes that the fascination with characters such as Claudia might derive from "the destruction of women's image as protectors and nurturers that is so disturbing and yet intriguing" (2014, 229). The film explores the tropes commonly associated with the Grimms' "Snow White"—for instance, the representation of beauty, gender roles, family relationships, and the process of aging—but interweaves these themes with elements of horror to "dramatize psychological conflict" (Tiffin 2016, 948). A veritable antithesis of the Disney version, Cohn's dark, live-action fairy-tale film also touches on novel aspects, such as miscarriage and stillbirth, infertility, and the jealousy of a stepchild, while emphasizing the darker psychological underpinnings of the Grimms' version.

After losing his pregnant wife in a horrific carriage accident, Count Frederick Hoffman (Sam Neill) saves his baby daughter by performing a caesarian section. He raises his daughter, Lilli (Taryn Davis/Monica Keena), for several years on his own until he decides to remarry the beautiful noblewoman Claudia Alvise. Although Lilli is afraid that her new step-mother might not love her, it is Lilli's jealousy that complicates the rela-tionship between the two women initially. At their first encounter, the noblewoman exhibits a friendly, motherly demeanor toward her stepdaugh-ter and even passes on the moral values of responsibility and loving care for others by gifting Lilli a Rottweiler puppy with the words "Treat him well and he will always be faithful." The young girl, approximately seven years of age, perceives her new stepmother as an intruder and is jealous of her father's devotion to her. After arriving late to the formal greeting of the new lady of the house, Lilli shows more interest in a caterpillar than in Claudia. The first tension arises when Lilli secretly watches her father and stepmother in a passionate embrace. When Claudia notices the little girl, she stares back at Lilli and places her hand on the back of Frederick's head, signaling con-sciously or unconsciously that he belongs to her now. Claudia truly loves her soon-to-be husband, as she openly admits to her brother, Gustav (Miroslav Táborský). Her statement "he will love me," however, implies that although Frederick is infatuated with his betrothed, he does not yet love her. To win Frederick's heart, the new countess inevitably has to compete with Lilli, who is already loved dearly by her father.

Until the moment of the Hoffman wedding, Claudia shows no obvious malice toward her independent, hardheaded stepdaughter or vice versa. But the situation changes when Lilli is supposed to bless the union of the wed-ding couple by pouring holy water over their conjugal bed and splashes it into Claudia's face instead. Her actions forebode that the union between her father and stepmother will be an unfortunate one. Contrary to the Grimms' fairy tale, the difficult relationship between the two women in the movie is instigated by Lilli, a.k.a. Snow White, and not by her stepmother. After nine long years have passed, the countess is finally with child, and thanks to the pregnancy she appears more radiant and beautiful than ever before. While she sits in front of a mirror inherited by her mother, she rubs her belly softly, speaking in a soothing voice to her unborn child: "Your blood mingles with mine. You grow stronger with every beat of my heart. And I seem to grow more beautiful with each beat of yours." Claudia depends on her baby not only for social reasons, to satisfy Frederick's desire for a male heir, but also to uphold her beauty. Unlike the evil queen in the Grimms' "Snow White," the countess is depicted as neither particularly vain nor jealous of Lilli, who has become the likeness of her dead mother. The two women clash over a simple dress that belonged to Claudia when she was a girl and that Lilli is supposed to wear to a dance. Lilli rebuffs the dress because she feels too old for it. The friction between them arises because Claudia still considers Lilli to be a child instead of a maturing woman. The stepmother's desire to establish a good rapport with her rebellious stepdaughter appears wholehearted when she pulls Lilli aside to ask her: "Lilli, why must we struggle so?" Although the noblewoman attempts to fulfill her maternal role, Lilli's rejection of her makes clear that she has failed.

On the evening of the ball, Lilli arrives late in a fancy white dress with a fur neckline that once belonged to her dead mother. The attention of the audience and her father shifts immediately from the spectacle of Claudia's vocal performance to the young woman. Lilli thus literally steals the show from her stepmother so that Claudia stops singing without applause. She watches, crestfallen, how Frederick laughingly approves of Lilli's appearance and asks his daughter to dance with him. While father and daughter spin happily around on the dance floor and the music grows louder, the countess experiences dizziness, collapses, and goes into early labor, delivering a stillborn boy. After Dr. Peter Gutenberg (David Conrad) informs Frederick that his wife can never have children again, neither Frederick nor Lilli are shown to comfort the suffering woman in her hour of need. The countess's tragic fate evokes great compassion and empathy in the viewer. Desperately stricken with grief, Claudia sends away the nurses and seeks consolation by clasping her mother's mirror, which is encased in an ornate cabinet. She stares at the reflection of her distraught, exhausted face in the mirror and attempts to restore her looks by frantically putting lotion all over her face as a form of coping mechanism. Once more the film ties Claudia's baby and the loss thereof directly to her beauty. When the noblewoman realizes that she cannot "fix herself" with facial cream, she smears it across the mirror, distorting her reflection. By analogy, Cohn's adaptation distorts the traditional portrayal of the evil queen and her desire to be the "fairest one of all." Claudia's first and foremost desires are to be a mother and to be loved by her husband. Ultimately, as Wright aptly puts it, "Claudia's failure to be the perfect wife and mother drives her to psychosis and murder" (2014, 236).

The film's depiction of Claudia's character is striking because it negates the classic notion of the queen in the Grimms' "Snow White" as a woman who is vile from the outset. Weaver stated about her role: "It was vitally important to me to make it clear that Claudia and Frederick are madly in love at the beginning and that's what Lilli resents. Then when she changes from perfect wife into the worthless mother of a stillborn child, that's when she looks hideous in the mirror and blames Lilli for everything. . . . The key to Claudia is that she starts out as normal as the rest of us. She isn't evil" (Jones 1997b, 28). Yet, it is not really the countess who blames Lilli but an evil spirit in the magic mirror, which seduces the noblewoman into believing that she has enemies who envy her beauty. On the night she loses her baby, Claudia cries, drowned in tears, "Why is this happening to me?" and the mirror answers by calling her name with soft, repetitive whispers. The distressed woman sees the mirror image of her tear-stained, tired face, which suddenly turns into the likeness of her previous radiant and beautiful self. "Your face is perfection," the mirror reassures her. "Is it?" Claudia asks in disbelief. "I will always tell you the truth. They have always envied you," the mirror claims. The countess asks, confused, "They?" And the spirit in the mirror replies, "Your enemies." Again Claudia asks, perplexed, "Who?" before the scene in the film changes.

Gradually, the mirror's image takes possession of Claudia and drives her into murder and madness. The mirror, of course, can be interpreted in several different ways, as has been done with the mirror in the Grimms'

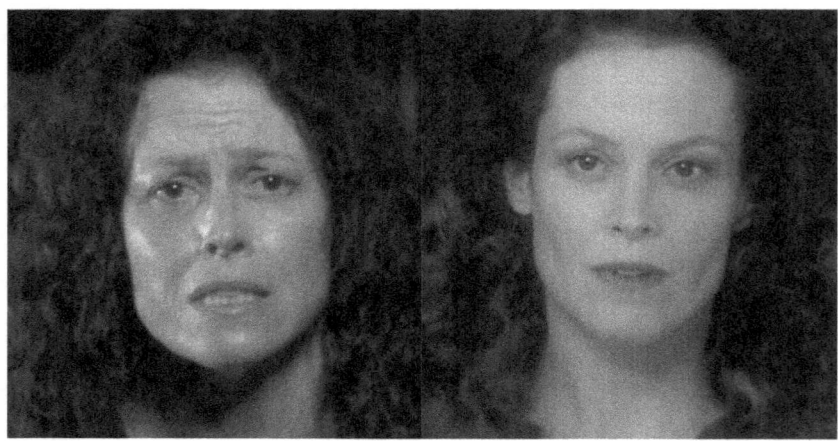

Lady Claudia (Sigourney Weaver) speaks with her evil-spirited mirror image in *Snow White: A Tale of Terror* (1997).

"Snow White." For instance, it could represent a fragment of Claudia's own psyche, a schizophrenic voice in her head, or the ghostly vestige of her dead mother. In any case, the female voice of the mirror links femininity with dark, dangerous, and "unholy" magic. The mirror once belonged to Claudia's mother, who, according to the film script, was "dabbling in witchcraft" (Jones 1997b, 28). This explains Claudia's affinity for paganism and the ancient arts in juxtaposition with Frederick's pious conviction as devout Christian. In an early scene, the noblewoman burns the feathers of a small bird's wing over a candle and then strokes them gently over her pregnant belly, talking to her unborn infant about "casting the runes" for nine years. Under the manipulating influence of the mirror spirit, Claudia's magic powers eventually grow so that she can carry out her crimes by the means of witchcraft. As per her orders, Gustav tries to kill Lilli, but when she escapes him he brings his sister the heart of a pig instead. Claudia orders him to put the remaining body parts into a stew, which she later devours with great gusto and satisfaction. After the mirror informs her of Gustav's betrayal, Claudia bewitches her brother into having horrific hallucinations, and he commits suicide. Then, she attempts to murder Lilli herself by collapsing a mine to crush her to death, and when that fails by conjuring up a storm that knocks down the trees close to Lilli's hiding place in the woods.

The magic powers of the corrupted countess significantly exceed the powers of the evil queen in the Grimm and Disney versions. Claudia turns her servants over time into zombie-like beings, controls the forces of nature, teleports, and uses her telepathic abilities to force animals into her service. This augmentation of witchery makes Claudia a more threatening, unpredictable, and terrifying villain than her predecessors in the literary and animated variants. In stark contrast, however, Cohn's embodiment of the evil queen is linked neither to artistry nor to a high degree of creative ingenuity, for that matter. Everything the countess does is carefully orchestrated, controlled, and plotted by the mirror's malevolent spirit. Although the mysterious spirit appears only within the magic mirror, there are many other mirrors in the castle and Claudia's bedchamber that appear to further amplify the spirit's influence on the countess. When Claudia first arrives at her new home, she gazes into a round mirror hanging in the hallway, which distorts her face grotesquely and warps the image of her body form in such a way that she looks pregnant. The scene can be interpreted as a foretelling of Claudia's future, her desired pregnancy on the one hand and the hideous monster she will become on the other. Not only does Claudia's character change over time by taking on ghastly features, she also undergoes a physical transformation as part of her plan to kill Lilli. But, unlike the evil queen in the Grimms' tale and Disney's adaptation of "Snow White," the noblewoman is heavily reliant on the powers of the magic mirror, her mother's legacy, to disguise herself. This dependence on the looking glass makes her persona a weak simulacrum of the classic evil queen. Evoking a maternal figure, the mirror's spirit promises Claudia reassuringly, "Don't be afraid. I'll take care of you," while Claudia undergoes an audibly agonizing metamorphosis under her bedsheets. What emerges visibly for the viewer after the transmogrification process is the old, shriveled hand of an ugly hag clasping a poisoned, crimson apple.

The poisoned apple in *Snow White: A Tale of Terror* is not a testament to Claudia's artistic nature or creative wits but rather an indication of the mirror's hold over her. The countess offers her own "flesh and blood," her brother's eviscerated heart, to be magically turned into the deadly fruit. Paradoxically, the mirror's spirit as representation of the dark arts, witchcraft, and the magical Otherworld alludes to man's fall from God's grace in the Book of Genesis by saying to Claudia: "You must become like the serpent; the serpent's fruit is what you need." The mirror thus ties the poisoned apple to temptation and sin in the Christian sense and Claudia to the biblical incarnation of Satan, who used the serpent as a garment in order to seduce Eve. Throughout the film, the trope of seduction also coalesces with that of sexuality. Bewitched by the mirror, Claudia turns into a sinful woman with adulterous and incestuous desires. She seduces Lilli's betrothed, Dr. Gutenberg, alluring him into kissing her, and also approaches her brother Gustav inappropriately with a voluptuous kiss. Because the mirror's spirit tells Claudia that she can resurrect her dead infant with the seed and blood from Frederick, the femme fatale forces a nightly sexual encounter on her husband. For Frederick, whose recovery from the injuries of a riding accident is hindered, as the film suggests, by Claudia's gradual poisoning of him, the sexual act is a mixture of pleasure and pain. Parallel to Claudia's beguiling agency growing in power, the three men in the narrative, Frederick, Gustav, and Dr. Gutenberg, become more and more helpless and feeble under her authority.

When Claudia seduces Lilli into taking a bite from the poisoned apple, she uses the strategy of first establishing a grandmother-granddaughter trust relationship, evoking the approach of the evil queen in the Disney version. Transformed into an old woman and leaning heavily on a walking staff, she pretends to be concerned about Lilli being alone in the woods at night and warns her of wild beasts and other creatures inhabiting the forest. After offering Lilli the cursed apple for good luck, the crone sits down next to her, involving the young woman in a conversation about her "boyfriend," with whom Lilli wants to share the apple. "I was young once. I had many boyfriends," the hag says to communicate a sense of empathic understanding and to bond with Lilli over the allegedly shared experience of being in love. "So tell me, what's he like?" the crone inquires, and after Lilli's description she continues, "And you love him, don't you? You can tell me, your old granny," stroking Lilli's cheek softly. Claudia preys on Lilli's need for a close confidant and her need to feel understood by another woman. By referring to them as "two ladies on the road together," the crone alludes to a close relationship between Lilli and her, metaphorically suggesting that the two women are on the same path of life, "that will unavoidably involve aging and disappointment" (Wright 2014, 241).

Ironically, the unfit stepmother and grandmother in disguise ultimately reaches her goal of being the mother of her son, but the magically resurrected infant also causes her doom. In the film's final scenes, Lilli finds Claudia in her bedchamber cradling her newly revived but weak baby. The two women engage in a physical fight for survival, resulting in accidentally setting the room alight. As she endeavors to strangle Lilli to death with her bare hands, Claudia's protective maternal instinct takes over when she hears her baby's cry from her bed that caught on fire. After Lilli realizes the source of her stepmother's strength and weakness, she drives a dagger through the ornate-looking glass, and Claudia suffers the consequences as if stabbed directly into the heart. In horror, the countess watches herself age rapidly in the shattering mirror, which explodes, firing shards into her face and body. Stepping backward into the flames, Claudia begins to burn, and her desperate swirls are evocative of the evil queen's death dance in fiery slippers in the Grimms' tale. When the bed collapses on her, the witch burns to death, perpetuating the traditional punishment for fairy-tale witches.

Despite this classic death for witches, Cohn's adaptation modifies the portrayal of the evil queen in a dramatic fashion, imposing realistic details on the character, which the Brothers Grimm outlined in a poetic but simple black-and-white manner. The film's reinvented evil queen has a name and a family history, feels true love for her husband, desires motherhood, and, most importantly, is not malicious from the outset. According to producer Tom Engelman, the reason Claudia does not get along with her stepdaughter is because Lilli never tries to make an effort. "From the moment she arrived in the household, Claudia has sought Lilli's approval and has had it thrown in her face" (Jones 1997a, 26). What sends Claudia over the edge is the pivotal event of her miscarriage, a traumatic experience that leaves her hurt, broken, and most likely feeling worthless in her societal role as woman and wife expected to produce a male heir. In many ways Claudia thus represents a tragic, misunderstood character who either becomes the victim of a supernatural entity taking control of her desperate plight or suffers under the influence of her mad alter ego and hallucinations. Alternatively, Claudia tries to become one with her witch-mother and, in order to live up to her expectations, strives to "carry out her mother's designs" (Zipes 2011, 125). If *A Tale of Terror,* with its Gothic tropes and horrific framing, is the antithesis of the lighthearted Disney version, then surely Tarsem Singh's *Mirror Mirror,* with its comedic characters, emphasis on irony, and essential lack of realism due to theatrical sets and minimalist style, can be seen as the antithesis of Cohn's grim adaptation.

Tarsem Singh's *Mirror Mirror*

Mirror, mirror on the wall, who is the funniest evil queen of them all? This, or a similar device might have been the guiding motto for Tarsem Singh's Bollywood-tinged, live-action "Snow White" adaptation *Mirror Mirror* (2012). With regard to the evolution of the evil queen—for example, her different characterizations in American film and literature since the Grimms' "Snow White"—Singh's portrayal of the wicked stepmother Clementianna (Julia Roberts) stands out for two main reasons: first, she is comical, and second, her narration frames the story. The film opens with Clementianna's retelling of the classic "Snow White" tale, interspersed with sardonic remarks leading the viewer to believe that this is really a story about her and not Snow White (Lily Collins). During her introduction of the narrative, Clementianna's voice-over changes unexpectedly from third-person narrator to first-person narrator with the illusory effect of providing the audience with a personal, firsthand, and thus more authentic perspective of the events: "This queen was the most beautiful woman in the world. She was intelligent and strong. And just to clarify, she was me. And this is my story. Not hers." In Clementianna's variant of the tale, Snow White was given "the most pretentious name" her parents could excogitate, and the people in the happy kingdom danced and sang day and night because "apparently, no one had a job back then." Her sense of humor, albeit malicious and cynical, makes Clementianna a likable character and allows viewers to connect with the queen positively on an emotional level. Significantly, the queen's name is a derivative from the Latin name Clemens or Clementius, meaning "merciful" and "gentle."

The queen's comedic lines endow her character with a tongue-in-cheek wickedness, although there seems to be more to the figure than meets the eye. Her beautiful appearance conceals a grotesque creature within, as the animated opening of the film suggests when her shadow mutates into a large, hunchbacked monstrosity with claw-like hands. The visual images of the prologue contradict the text of Clementianna's voice-over claiming that "Bewitched by my beauty, the king begged me to marry him. I was everything to him: the stars, the moon." As to be expected from a villainess, Clementianna is coldhearted, vain, and selfish. However, compared to other classic embodiments of the evil queen, including Disney's portrayal of Queen Grimhilde, Clementianna comes across as a cartoonish buffoon. Director Singh has highlighted about her character: "She's not evil; she's just insecure . . . about beauty, about things that are passing her by, and now she wants to have power" (Bibbiani 2011). Naturally, the queen's greatest worry and source of insecurity is tied to her beauty and the fact that she gets more "crinkles," Clementianna's euphemism for her facial "wrinkles." Driven by her inferiority complex vis-à-vis Snow White, the queen bullies the princess on her eighteenth birthday by telling her "there is something about you that's just so incredibly . . . irritating. I don't know what it is. The slumped shoulders. The hair, that voice . . . Mm! I know what it is—I think it is the hair. I hate your hair." To compensate for her lack of confidence, Clementianna wears ostentatious regal clothing, surrounds herself with materialistic pomp, indulges in baroque-style splendor, and hosts opulent balls at the castle. Nevertheless, her horrible actions speak for themselves, revealing the queen's dark and bad nature: firstly, she puts a spell on the king that turns him into a fierce beast that inhabits the woods near the kingdom; secondly, she burdens her subjects with outrageous taxes, forcing them to starve; and thirdly, she attempts to kill Snow White and the dwarfs several times.

Similar to Disney's and Cohn's adaptations, the queen is the true show stealer of this postmodern persiflage. The powerful stepmother is the catalyst to the most amusing moments and has a complexity and entertainment value that exceeds that of all nonvillains, including the protagonist Snow White. More "bitch" than witch, Clementianna confines Snow White to the castle for the majority of her youth. It is not until she turns eighteen that Snow White rebels, escapes the castle grounds, and has her first encounter with Prince Andrew Alcott (Armie Hammer) in the woods. Annoyed by the prince's attraction to Snow White, Clementianna cracks jokes about the princess's beauty to cover up her own shortcomings:

PRINCE: I think she's the most beautiful woman in the whole world.

QUEEN: Agree to disagree. Let's leave it at that.

PRINCE: But do you know her? Ivory skin, black hair . . .

QUEEN: Her hair is not black, it's raven, and she's eighteen years old, and her skin has never seen the sun, so of course it's good.

Although Clementianna despises the beauty of Snow White, vanity and jealousy are not the main reasons for the queen's treacherous plan to kill her, as in the Grimms' tale. In fact, in the film Clementianna never poses the fundamental question "Who is the fairest one of all?" Rather, the queen feels threatened by Snow White's direct challenge of her authority to rule the kingdom. Clementianna fears for her position of power, not because the stepdaughter grows fairer than the stepmother but because Snow White grows into an autonomous, responsible, and brave young woman ready to embrace her royal inheritance. Upon witnessing the oppressive rule of her stepmother firsthand, Snow White confronts her boldly: "You have no right to rule the way you do. And technically, I'm the rightful leader of this kingdom." This is the particular moment when the queen realizes that Snow White is no longer under her control and therefore she now represents "a threat to everything," as Clementianna remarks in the following scene.

The casting of A-list Hollywood actress and "Pretty Woman" Julia Roberts in the role of the queen may be seen as a metacommentary on the Hollywood edict that proclaims women of a certain age are less desirable and empowered than their younger counterparts. Further, the film employs the character of the evil queen to critique contemporary society's standards of beauty and obsession with beauty regimes to achieve physical "perfection." In one scene that emphasizes the ugliness of beauty's upkeep, Clementianna undergoes a strange, repulsive, and nauseating beautification treatment involving facials made of bird droppings, squirming maggots in her belly button and ears, fish nibbling on her fingertips, a serpent slithering across her body, bees stinging her lips to make them puffy, and other disgusting skin treatments using snails and scorpions. The queen undergoes the ridiculous beauty enhancements in the hope of catching the affections of Prince Alcott. However, she woos the upright prince primarily for practical rather than for personal reasons. Although Clementianna is not immune to the dashing looks of the prince, as is evident in several scenes where he appears shirtless in front of the queen, she pursues him with financial interests in mind. A marriage with the wealthy prince would ensure the bankrupt queen her continuous reign and lavish lifestyle. Clementianna's passion for chess games, and her mastery thereof, indicates that she is a highly strategic thinker and that the handsome prince is nothing but a "pawn" in her game for power.

The film subverts traditional gender and fairy-tale roles by reversing Snow White's role as passive princess with that of an active fighter and rescuer and by portraying the queen exercising absolute control over the two most powerful men in the story, the king and the prince. After magically transforming the king into a beast, Clementianna uses two moon charm necklaces to force the monster into doing her bidding until Snow White heroically breaks the spell by cutting off the beast's necklace. To bring the honorable Prince Alcott to heel and gain his consent in marriage, the queen wants to manipulate him with a love potion. When she accidentally gives the prince a Puppy Love Potion instead, Clementianna literally becomes Prince Alcott's "master," giving him commands such as "get off," "sit," and "fetch." Contrary to the Grimms' tale, in this story it is Snow White who rescues the enchanted prince from the rather humiliating spell with a kiss after she kidnaps him from the queen's wedding. Clementianna's expression, "my bridegroom was stolen," rather than "kidnapped" or "taken hostage," objectifies the prince by suggesting that he is a piece of valuable property owned by the queen. Although the film clearly manifests Clementianna's dominance over powerful men, it also reveals the boundaries of her regal authority. Because the queen cannot keep the thieving dwarfs at bay, the gentry declare her unfit to rule the kingdom and decide to depose her.

Clementianna's power ultimately derives from her magic mirror, which, in fact consists of several mirrors within what appears to be a different realm. Behind a locked door in her bedroom stands a large looking glass, and after Clementianna recites the words "Mirror, mirror, on the wall" the surface of the glass becomes a liquid portal. As she steps through the liquid, the queen resurfaces from an ocean or huge lake in the other realm, where two large wooden huts stand on a dock. In the first hut is a room filled with mirrors, and Clementianna consults with the reflection of herself in them. The mirror queen is a younger version of Clementianna who offers advice but also cautions her that magic always comes with a price. Most importantly, the mirror queen possesses the magic Clementianna needs for her evil deeds. In one scene the mirror queen, for example, is supposed to punish Clementianna's manservant, Brighton (Nathan Lane), for disobeying her command to kill Snow White.

QUEEN: And I want Brighton dead, too.

MIRROR: Don't overreact. Kill Brighton and you'll be without your executive bootlicker.

QUEEN: That's a very good point. But he has to be punished for lying to me. Do something terrible to him. Use your magic!

MIRROR: You'll pay the price . . .

QUEEN: I know! I'll pay the price for using magic! I've got it! Now punish him!

Sharing Clementianna's sense of humor, the mirror queen metamorphoses Brighton into a cockroach with a snap of her fingers. Later on, it is the mirror queen who uses her powers to create two gigantic wooden puppets in the forest, attempting to kill Snow White and the dwarves. As puppeteer, she sits in her hut in the other realm and pulls the strings of two marionettes, evoking voodoo magic. By cutting the strings of the colossal puppet doubles, Snow White is able to break the spell in the end.

What is the relationship between the queen and the magic mirror? What does the mirror realm represent? According to film director Singh, Clementianna is "outsourcing" her wickedness by creating an imaginary alter ego in her mind:

[I]f she looks into the mirror . . . she enters the landscape, which is a mindscape, and in there is a house, inside which are many mirrors, and in those mirrors she just talks to herself. So basically, it's like all those nasty people that'll always do what they want to do, but they hear voices, or [say] people told them. So it's actually just her talking to herself. She's just bad, but wants to outsource the evil and say "That thing told me." (Bibbiani 2011)

Assuming that the mirror queen is a part of Clementianna's personality, one could argue that the wicked stepmother is suffering from a psychiatric illness affecting her mental faculties, such as a narcissistic personality disorder (NPD). Eve Caligor, Kenneth Levy, and Frank Yeomans defined NPD in the *American Journal of Psychiatry* as "characterized by a pervasive pattern of grandiosity (in fantasy or behavior), need for admiration, entitlement, and lack of empathy" (2015, 416). Moreover, they determined that core psychological features of the disorder include "vulnerable self-esteem" and "feelings of inferiority" (416). At close examination, Clementianna exhibits several of the key criteria for NPD as identified by Caligor, Levy, and Yeomans: She has a grandiose sense of self-importance; is preoccupied with fantasies of unlimited power and beauty; requires excessive admiration; s interpersonally exploitative; lacks empathy; is often envious of others or believes that others are envious of her; and shows arrogant, haughty behaviors and attitudes (418). But could NPD explain Clementianna's desire to kill Snow White? In their article, Caligor, Levy, and Yeomans cite the case of "Ms. D," a forty-four-year-old single woman suffering from NPD. She threatens to kill either her therapist or herself, should he interfere with her ability to receive disability benefits by "working the system" (415). In the film, Prince Alcott's faithful valet and confidant, Charles Renbock (Robert Emms), alludes to the queen's mental state by claiming that she "radiates crazy" and, more specifically, the "good old-fashioned, plain, traditional psycho crazy." It is therefore conceivable that Clementianna is a misunderstood victim of NPD and that the queen's ill behavior and criminal acts can be explained through the lens of psychiatry.

As in the Grimms' tale, Clementianna attempts to kill Snow White four times in different ways. First, she orders her manservant Brighton to murder her stepdaughter in the woods by feeding her to the beast. But in contrast to the evil queen in the Grimm, Disney, and Cohn versions, Clementianna does not gain pleasure from seeing or eating Snow White's organs. When Brighton brings her the liver, kidneys, and spleen, among other assorted parts, of the alleged murder victim, the queen simply remarks, "That's disgusting." This queen is neither a cannibalistic witch nor a cunning villainess. The fact that she simply buys into Brighton's lie that he disposed of Snow White without asking for any proof makes her a gullible character. Second, Clementianna's alter ego magically animates gigantic string puppets to slay Snow White. Third, the queen orders the beast to slaughter her stepdaughter in the forest. Fourth, Clementianna tempts Snow White with a poisoned apple at the end of the film. Interestingly, this scene represents one of the most significant departures from the Brothers Grimm fairy tale, because instead of Snow White, Clementianna eats the cursed apple. Further, the queen does not disguise herself but turns into an old hag as a consequence for using magic. At Snow White's wedding celebration, the crone offers her the apple as a gift "for good fortune to the fairest of them all." However, Snow White sees through Clementianna's plot and cuts off a slice from the apple with the words "age before beauty." As the queen must eat from her own poisoned fruit, the mirror queen declares that it was Snow White's story, after all, and the looking glasses in the other realm as well as the mirror portal in the castle shatter into pieces. Under the eyes of the wedding party, Clementianna's figure slowly degenerates and disappears into nothingness.

To sum up, *Mirror Mirror* sheds a positive light on the queen by portraying her as a funny, dazzling, entertaining, but insecure character whose criminal actions might be symptomatic of an untreated psychiatric disorder represented by the mirror world. This subverts the traditional notion that the narcissistic queen is evil by design. Clementianna's punishment, her rapid aging and her dissolution, is, in fact, self-inflicted and could therefore be read as suicide. Instead of eating a slice from the poisoned apple, the queen could have asked for Snow White's mercy and awaited her individual judgment. But the queen's decision to willingly poison herself complicates her character and makes her fate tragic rather than just. By framing the diegesis with a prologue and epilogue narrated by the queen, the film not only invites the audience to empathize with Clementianna's character but also places her center stage. Although the mirror queen asserts in the end that it was Snow White's story all along, it remains paradoxically the queen's film because Roberts's Hollywood star power in playing Clementianna outshines Collins's performance of Snow White. Collins had initially auditioned to play Snow White in *Snow White and the Huntsman*, which opened two months after *Mirror Mirror* in 2012, but lost the role to Kristen Stewart. Directed by Rupert Sanders, the former film is everything that Singh's burlesque adaptation is not: a dark, gritty, epic adventure fantasy film with a Joan of Arc–like, armor-clad action heroine (Kristen Stewart) as Snow White and a vampiric, misandrist Queen Ravenna played by the glamorous South African–born Hollywood actress Charlize Theron. In 2016, Cedric Nicolas-Troyan's *The Hunstman: Winter's War* aired in American movie theaters, adding the character of Freya (Emily Blunt) to the narrative. Both a prequel and sequel to *Snow White and the Huntsman*, Troyan's film fuses the tales of the Grimms' "Snow White" with Hans Christian Andersen's "The Snow Queen," creating an unorthodox fairy-tale concoction.

Rupert Sanders's Snow White and the Huntsman and Cedric Nicolas-Troyan's The Huntsman: Winter's War

Sanders's representation of the evil queen in *Snow White and the Huntsman* stands out for its powerful and provocative feminist edge, on the one hand, and for its novel treatment of the vanity motif, on the other. In particular, the film reinvents the queen as a femme fatale who is power hungry and brutal beyond measure, while at the same time exploring her backstory as a victim of male exploitation and violence. Her name, Ravenna, derived from the Middle English "raven," potentially alludes to the pet raven of Disney's evil queen and is befitting of her magical ability to transform into a flock of ravens.[7] At the beginning of the live-action adaptation, Ravenna appears disguised as a prisoner of war. King Magnus (Noah Huntley) finds her dirty, barefoot, and chained in a small wagon after defeating a phantom army of demonic glass soldiers conjured by the villainess. Her preference for masquerade to deceive others evokes the Grimms' evil queen, who disguises herself three times to delude Snow White. Beguiled by her beauty, King Magnus "rescues" the enchantress, takes her to his castle, and marries her. Upon meeting Snow White, a child of approximately ten years, the queen continues her pretense by simulating empathy and a sense of caring for her new stepdaughter:

YOUNG SNOW WHITE: You're so beautiful.

QUEEN RAVENNA: That's kind, child. Especially when it's said that yours is the face of true beauty in this kingdom. This all must be difficult for you. I too lost my mother when I was a young girl. I can never take your mother's place, ever. But I feel that you and I are bound. I feel it there, your heart.

Because Ravenna tells the truth about the shared experience of tragically losing her mother early in life, her feigned sympathy is that much viler. The fact that Ravenna refers to Snow White's heart instead of her own contradicts the notion that she has feelings in her own heart, which raises the question of whether she has a heart at all.

After the coronation, the sorceress shows her true face on the night of her wedding with King Magnus. During the foreplay in bed, Ravenna's misandrous attitude comes to the fore as she discloses in an angry voice that she suffered from gendered violence and abuse in the past. The timing of this revelation and her choice of phrasing strongly suggest that Ravenna became a rape victim, which explains her general hatred toward men: "I was ruined by a king like you once. I replaced his queen. An old woman. And in time I too would have been replaced. Men use women. They ruin us and when they are finished with us they toss us to the dogs like scraps." As she talks about men's exploitation of women, a poisoned glass of wine she gave King Magnus before the sexual encounter takes effect and he begins to suffocate. Ravenna stabs the king to death with a dagger, declaring that she will first take his life and then take his throne. Then, the queen unlocks the castle gates for her Dark Army and her brother, Finn (Sam Spurell), to gain entry and take over the castle. Ravenna's ruse proves that her character is extremely cunning, insidious, strategic, and ruthless. Contrary to other portrayals of the evil queen, Ravenna is not driven by her desire to assert her femininity and regal position against female competitors but to take revenge on the opposite sex while fighting against the predominant patriarchal system. Her campaign of vengeance, to vanquish kings and ravage their kingdoms, is a personal vendetta in retaliation for her own suffering caused by powerful men.

Although the Grimms' evil queen is known for being wicked and murderous, Sanders's portrayal of the character takes a new dimension, as Ravenna is nothing short of a mass murderer. After the enchantress takes control of the castle, she orders her army to kill all remaining prisoners, including men, women, and children. The only reason why she spares Snow White is because "her royal blood may be of value." Thus, she not only thirsts for the blood of kings but the merciless queen seeks to eliminate all those who might represent an obstacle to her reign of terror, which is so poisonous that even nature turns on itself and the land becomes bare. And yet, Ravenna is not without humanizing emotions and gestures, which complicates her character and challenges the idea of a purely evil villainess. When her brother is dying at the hands of Eric the Huntsman (Chris Hemsworth), Ravenna feels the pain physically as well. Although the siblings are miles apart, they are bound by Ravenna's magic, which sustains Finn's life. Upon realizing that she cannot save her younger brother from death because it would most likely mean her own demise, Ravenna genuinely weeps for Finn and asks him for forgiveness. In another scene, the visibly aged queen sheds tears in front of a mirror as she recalls the memories of a traumatic childhood event. The flashback in the film reveals crucial information about Ravenna's magical origin, family history, and source of power. When a king and his armed horsemen raid her home village, Ravenna's mother, a sorceress, tells her daughter that only her beauty can save her. She cuts Ravenna's hand with a knife so that her blood drips into a bowl of milk, reminiscent of the beginning of the Grimms' "Snow White" with its trope of red blood on white snow. Ravenna drinks the milk while her mother casts a spell that will keep her daughter young and beautiful. The girl is told that the enchantment will make her beauty her power and protection, but Ravenna's mother also warns her that the spell can be broken by "fairest blood." The soldiers forcibly separate the children from their crying mother, who screams out to Ravenna, "Avenge us!" The end of the flashback depicts the king riding away with Ravenna on his horse, presumably abducting her for sexual exploitation, given her extraordinary beauty.

The spell Ravenna's mother placed on her daughter gave her the ability to preserve her youth and beauty, on the one hand, but turned her into a vampiric monster, on the other hand. Since magic in this story comes at a lofty price, for every life there must be a death and for every gain there must be a loss. Ravenna's dilemma is that her power fades with time and "the expense grows," as she admits to Finn. Much like a vampire, Ravenna is cursed to "suck" the youth from young women, and the number of her victims from whom she needs to steal beauty and youth is increasing. In the film, Ravenna absorbs the beauty from a girl named Greta by lifting her up by the throat and draining her youth through her opened mouth until Greta's appearance rapidly ages to that of an old woman. This power has enabled Ravenna to live already "twenty lives," a fact she prides herself with, which makes her 800 to 1,500 years old and almost immortal. However, in order for Ravenna to cheat death time and again, she needs to continuously incorporate the life energy of others, which makes her drive to remain "the fairest of them all" a struggle for survival. This significantly distorts the vanity motif known from the Grimms' portrayal of the evil queen whose jealousy of Snow White's beauty triggers her desire to eliminate her stepdaughter. It is not Ravenna's vanity but her mother's spell and with it the power she gained that corrupted her to do evil and become a parasitic, beauty-sucking creature. In addition, the queen's tragic background, the exploitation, violence, and disappointment she experienced at the hands of men in her life, did the rest to turn Ravenna into a man-hater and misanthrope. Her statement "I will give this wretched world, the queen it deserves," demonstrates that she blames not just men but the whole of mankind for her personal hardship and misery.

Sanders's screen incarnation of the evil queen possesses magical abilities that are mightier and therefore more threatening than most of her predecessors' witchery in Western literature and media. The range of Ravenna's "magic tricks" makes for fascinating visual spectacles, such as her superhuman strength and her powers of regeneration, healing, youth absorption, and shapeshifting. Furthermore, the sorceress is in control of a black substance known as "Dark Fay," which in its liquid form can morph to tendrils with razor-sharp talons and points, and she has the ability to consort with the omniscient, clairvoyant entity that resides within her magic mirror. The always-truthful mirror man, a gold-covered figure with a male voice (Christopher Obi), is visible to only Ravenna and serves several functions in the story. First, he provides Ravenna with food for thought by critically questioning her actions. After the queen has usurped King Magnus's castle and sovereignty, she consults the mirror man, who observes, "Yet another kingdom falls to your glory. Is there no end to your power and beauty?" Second, the mirror appears to be a major power source for Ravenna's magic. In one scene, the weakening queen dissolves into Dark Fay and reaches out with her arm toward the mirror in search of help. In the next moment,

Ravenna's power is fully restored, suggesting that the mirror healed her. Third, he warns the enchantress that Snow White's innocence and beauty might be her undoing as well as her salvation. The mirror man counsels the queen, "Take her [Snow White's] heart in your hand and you shall never again need to consume youth. You shall never again weaken or age." Thus, the mirror entity promises Ravenna nothing less than immortality. It is this incentive of never having to grow old and die that fuels Ravenna's desire to kill her stepdaughter rather than a competition for beauty or male affection.

Underneath Ravenna's evilness lie her gerascophobia and death anxiety, her fear of aging and perishing. Disguised as Snow White's childhood friend William (Sam Claflin), Ravenna tricks her stepdaughter into eating the poisoned apple. After shapeshifting back into her own form, an aging Ravenna bends over Snow White's paralyzed body, raising a dagger with the reproachful words "You don't even realize how lucky you are never to know what it is to grow old." Because it is impossible for Ravenna to come to terms with her own mortality, she resorts to magic and desperate, malfeasant measures to circumvent the inevitable. Director Sanders stated about the character:

> It was very important that we didn't have a terrible cut-out villain. We had someone who was doing evil things from a fear and weakness. I think it is important that you do sympathize with her to a degree, but also really understand why she is the person she's become because she wasn't born evil. It was a journey for her to become evil. (Aquino 2012)

By endowing Ravenna with a unique and dramatic backstory, Sanders demonstrates that the antagonist is a victim of her own fears and phobias as well as her traumatic childhood experiences.

The construction of Ravenna's character invites viewers' sympathy to a certain extent because of her tragic background but discourages it at the same time. A scene in which the queen takes a Cleopatra-like milk bath, perhaps in allusion to the enchanted milk she drank as a child to gain power, reveals that Ravenna grew up with her siblings in poverty. She asks her brother if he remembers when they were children and begging for scraps. Based on the queen's humble beginnings, her figure is designed to elicit compassion and empathy in the viewer. Despite having experienced famine for herself, however, Ravenna does little to alleviate the hunger of the starving peasants below her window who struggle with one another to drink and contain the milk that pours from an outside faucet. Although the queen considers this milk spout to be a "kind" gesture on her part, the scene emphasizes her oppressive rule and thus effectively demotivates feelings of sympathy for her character. The following scene visually complements Ravenna's distorted understanding of "kindness" and contorted self-perception of being merciful. After the queen submerges herself in her baptismal font of a bathtub still wearing her crown, she resurfaces covered completely in the milky substance, resembling a marble statue of the Virgin Mary or "Mother of Mercy." The candles and church-like window in the background add to the religious connotation of the image. Ravenna's white coat, a stark contrast to her otherwise sable appearance in the film, is paradoxical due to its symbolism of purity and innocence. It appears as if she is attempting to conceal her

Ravenna (Charlize Theron) evokes the Virgin Mary after a milk bath in a scene of *Snow White and the Huntsman* (2012).

darkness within under a layer "as white as snow." Further, the milk invokes the nurturing quality of motherhood that the queen has foregone in favor of herself. The sorceress is, in fact, neither a kind and caring mother, nor stepmother, nor "Queen Mother."

In Nicolas-Troyan's *The Huntsman: Winter's War*, motherhood and Ravenna's relation to her younger sister Freya play a pivotal role. The film opens with a prequel story of Ravenna killing a king she seduced into marriage during a chess match. As she compares herself to "a humble pawn" who can bring down kingdoms, the chess game signifies Ravenna's talent for strategic thinking and tactical scheming, a trait she shares with the queen in *Mirror Mirror*. The scene foregrounds Ravenna's cruel passion for "playing" with her victims first before destroying them. She also plays chess with Freya, but although Ravenna is the stronger player, she usually lets her younger sister win. She does so presumably out of love for her "weaker" sister, who has not yet discovered her magical abilities, which all women of their family line possess. Calling Freya her "weakness," Ravenna appears to truly care and look out for her in a sisterly fashion. When Ravenna discovers that her sister is not only in love with Andrew, the Duke of Blackwood (Colin Morgan), but also carries his child although the duke is already promised to another, Ravenna attempts to prepare Freya for the duke's rejection of her and the baby. Her concern, "I'm not being cruel. I simply wish to protect you," sounds sincere. However, Freya is convinced that the duke will break off the sealed engagement and stand behind her, their love, and the offspring of their illicit affair. Her remark, "You know much, Ravenna. But you do not know all," shows that she does not trust in her older sister's ability to predict the future when it comes to matters of true love. And yet, the omniscient narrator of the film implies that Ravenna's projection was correct and her concern, albeit perhaps harsh, justified: "Freya did not believe her sister. For love blinds even the clearest eye."

Despite being a cruel villainess, Ravenna is capable of love and of caring for her younger siblings, Finn and Freya, an aspect that humanizes her character and allows viewers to connect with her on that affective level. But the queen remains a tragic figure with regard to romantic love, because she has experienced only disappointment and betrayal in her past relationships with men, as certain quotes in Sanders's *Snow White and the Huntsman* suggest. When Ravenna faces a young and handsome captive in her throne room, she states scornfully, "There was a time I would have lost my heart to a face like yours. And you, no doubt, would have broken it." In another scene, Ravenna, disguised as William, says to Snow White, "You see child? Love always betrays us" after her stepdaughter has taken a bite from the poisoned apple. The quotes insinuate that the queen has indeed entered love relationships with men after her traumatic childhood events of abduction and presumably sexual violation by a ruthless king. Ravenna's negative attitude toward love and her erosion of confidence in men's faithfulness can be understood in light of her past experiences. From her point of view, love is a weakness and one is stronger without it. Rather than being jealous of any woman whose beauty surpasses her own, as in the case of the Grimms' evil queen, Ravenna is jealous of the fact that her "inferior" sister has what she was denied in life: Freya is pregnant with a baby girl fathered by a man she truly loves. Toward the end of Nicolas-Troyan's *The Huntsman: Winter's War*, Ravenna confesses angrily to her sister, "Did you not think I wanted a child? Did you not think I wanted love? But these things . . . were not meant for me." Ravenna's personally disturbing and hurtful experiences as well as her mother's wicked spell, which condemns Ravenna to extinguish beautiful women for self-preservation, were all contributing factors throughout her life that made her malicious.

On her path to evilness, the mirror represents another curse in Ravenna's life. The entity in the mirror serves as an oracle to inform the queen about anyone who is or will be a threat to her beauty spell. Without the mirror man's influence as her seer whose foretelling is taken as the truth by the queen, it is questionable whether Ravenna would have committed the atrocious acts she did. Interestingly, she never doubts the mirror, although the golden, circular dish is inscribed with runes that read, "The age can be wicked to those who walk alone. When I look into the mirror, I see myself as I might become." The mysterious epigraph indicates that the looking glass shows only a potential future of what might be and not what will be. When the mirror man predicts that Freya's daughter will one day grow to be more beautiful than Ravenna, the queen believes she has only one choice to save herself and that is to kill her niece. At first, Ravenna struggles with the mirror's foretelling, but the mirror entity emphasizes that he is merely a servant under her command, making no demands himself:

QUEEN RAVENNA: You cannot ask such a thing of me.
MIRROR: I ask nothing. I am but a reflection. And you . . . you have already decided.

Instead of murdering the child herself, Ravenna bewitches Andrew to set the baby's crib on fire. Under the assumption that her lover is responsible for the death of their daughter, Freya destroys him with her long-suppressed ice powers in a grief-fueled rage. The ice queen thus becomes the victim of her sister's intrigue, and it is because of Ravenna's machination that Freya's faith in love dies. In many ways, Freya's agony evokes Lady Claudia's suffering after her miscarriage in Cohn's adaptation; both tragic events are designed to elicit the viewer's sympathy.

Following in her sister's footsteps, Freya becomes a coldhearted, ruthless, and powerful queen who denies others the love that she lost, sharing Ravenna's view that love only causes pain. Despite distancing herself from emotions after being consumed by grief, Freya's desire for motherhood, oddly enough, still exists but takes on a perverse form. The sorceress orders the children of her kingdom to be kidnapped and brought to her castle, where they are trained in the arts of combat. Ironically, Freya thus repeats her own childhood trauma: the forceful separation of children from their parents. The ice queen exploits the boys and girls by using them to raise an army of huntsmen willing to fight for her. By teaching them not to love, Freya is convinced that she is giving these children an incomparably precious gift: freedom and salvation from ever experiencing the inevitable sorrows of a broken heart. The fact that Freya refers to the grown-up huntsmen as her "children" in the film reflects her desperate attempt to fill the gap left behind by her daughter's death. The story of *Winter's War* continues by leaping seven years into the future after Snow White seemingly defeated and killed Ravenna. Just as power-hungry as her sister, Freya gets ahold of the magic mirror, but instead of the mirror man, the new slave in the mirror is a resurrected Ravenna, who preserved her spirit in the looking glass before she took her last breath. Hence, Nicolas-Troyan's adaptation reconstructs the classic archetype of the evil queen by fusing it with the magic mirror and its powers, effectively anthropomorphizing a mystical object and gendering it female.

Although Ravenna has become the entity within the magic mirror, she is still able to form a body and leave the actual looking glass, in contrast to the other mirror spirits previously discussed in this chapter. By not being physically confined to her golden sanctuary, the evil queen is free to continue her dominion alongside her sister. Despite some rivalry among the sisters for authority of rule, Ravenna saves Freya's life from a deadly arrow shot by Eric the Huntsman, showing that she still cares about her sister's well-being. Because Freya summoned her sister from the magic mirror, Ravenna is bound to tell Freya the truth about her daughter's death. After learning about her sister's betrayal, Freya is disillusioned and appalled, telling Ravenna that she loved her daughter as well as her. In the fight that follows, Ravenna wants to demonstrate that she is the stronger one of the two for not giving in to "cheap sentiments" such as love, and she injures Freya before attacking the huntsmen. To protect her "children," Freya hugs her sister in a deadly embrace, forcing Ravenna to fatally wound her own sister. The different approaches to murdering one another, Freya's embrace versus Ravenna's impaling of her sister with Dark Fay, can be interpreted symbolically as a gesture of forgiveness versus a gesture of aggression. In the dramatic ending, Freya uses her remaining ice powers to help Eric destroy the golden mirror and thus Ravenna's spirit, whose materialized form shatters into pieces. Before Freya succumbs to her wounds, she has a vision of her younger self as a mother, smiling and cradling her baby next to the crib. As she dies, Freya witnesses the true love between two of her warriors, Eric and Sara (Jessica Chastain), and marvels at how lucky the couple is.

Nicolas-Troyan's adaptation shows the demise of two "evil" queens, both victims of tragic events, but whereas Ravenna's powers irreversibly corrupted her over time, Freya's love persevered and triumphed in the end. Both women are heavily influenced by the powers of the magic mirror, which is negatively connotated because it harbors dark forces. In his visually spectacular film, Nicolas-Troyan challenges the notion that the magic mirror represents a patriarchal voice of judgment by portraying Queen Ravenna as the new entity in the looking glass. She becomes the "curse" that befalls anyone who possesses it, including Queen Snow White, who falls mysteriously ill before ordering the object to be taken away. Still, the mirror maintains its function of judgement because, once summoned out of the mirror, Ravenna judges Freya by condemning her "weakness." Despite straying from the path of goodness, the ice queen ultimately redeems herself by protecting her "children" from Ravenna's fury and by ridding the world of her wickedness. The fact that she sees the image of her daughter in her final moments highlights that although Freya could not save her daughter, she could preserve the love for her and hold on to that treasured moment of motherhood. The tropes of motherhood and true love are also fundamental concepts tied to the personal development of villainess Regina Mills (Lana Parrilla), a.k.a. the evil queen, in ABC's television series *Once Upon a Time (OUaT)*.

Edward Kitsis's and Adam Horowitz's *Once Upon A Time*

The fantasy-drama series *OUaT* has succeeded commercially, as "it was one of the most popular debut dramas among adults eighteen to forty-nine years old in 2011" (Hay and Baxter 2014, 316). The live-action show is a fairy-tale medley that resonates with North American viewers because it draws upon the widely popular Disney films, the type of fairy-tale reimaginings most familiar to its audience. The basic framework of *OUaT* is to interweave fairy tales with today's reality, continuously blending fantastical elements with realist settings. Disney-, Grimm-, and non-Grimm-inspired fairy-tale figures, such as Prince Charming, Snow White, Rumpelstiltskin, Belle, and Robin Hood oscillate between magical realms and Storybrooke, a fictional seaside town in contemporary Maine, United States. This approach of magic realism serves to make the well-known fantasy figures who have been transplanted to a modern locale more relatable to the audiences. The series relocates the evil queen, for instance, from her palace in the fictional world of the Enchanted Forest to a mansion in small-town Storybrooke. There she lives as stern mayor Regina Mills, pursuing a regular job and earning a living to support her adopted son, Henry (Jared S. Gilmore).

By fleshing out the traditional fairy-tale characters with elaborate backstories and complex personalities, the television series humanizes the supernatural figures so that viewers may identify with them. In their new environs, the characters resemble everyday people with mundane problems, such as custody battles, financial hardships, tense relationship issues, family dramas, parental abandonment, and unwed motherhood, to name but a few. Hay and Baxter note, "Because *OUaT* has multiple episodes to explore and thus humanize these Disney fairy-tale characters, the show dives into their relationships, revealing romantic ties deeper than love at first sight and explaining classic antipathies as more than an aging stepmother's jealousy of her younger, fairer stepdaughter" (319). Indeed, the series complicates the character of the evil queen in unprecedented ways, making her a fan favorite, according to internet voting and fan websites, where she has been crowned one of the most interesting, best-developed villains and most popular characters of the show (Suvannasankha 2016). Significantly, Kitsis and Horowitz twist and embellish plotlines to create innovative fairy-tale retellings and rigorously transform the roles of familiar fairy-tale protagonists and antagonists, essentially reversing the classic roles of heroes and villains. Thus, the character of the evil queen in *OUaT* evolves over the course of six seasons, between the years 2011 and 2017, from iconic villainess to redeemed heroine.

In the narrative of the show, the evil queen Regina has cursed all creatures of the Enchanted Forest, casting them out of the magical reality to the disenchanted human world. The dark curse condemns the fairy-tale characters, including Snow White (Ginnifer Goodwin), a.k.a. Mary Margaret Blanchard, her husband, Prince Charming (Josh Dallas), a.k.a. David Nolan, and Rumpelstiltskin (Robert Carlyle), a.k.a. Mr. Gold, among many others, to a truncated, dreary existence without memory of their past identities. As mayor of Storybrooke, Regina, whose name means "queen," maintains power over the fairy-tale figures, trapped not only physically behind the borders of the town but also in a bubble of stagnant time (the clock tower is stuck at 8:15). Through flashbacks that connect the world of the magical past with the bleak present, viewers learn that Snow White and Prince Charming saved their infant, who grows up to become Emma Swan (Jennifer Morrison), from the curse by transporting her through a magic wardrobe into the "real world." Twenty-eight years later, Emma's life as a bail bonds person drastically changes when she meets Henry, the now ten-year-old son she gave up for adoption at birth. The boy attempts to convince Snow White's daughter of her royal parentage and her destiny to save the fairy-tale people by breaking the curse and thus restoring the characters' lost memories. Following Henry's plea for help, Emma drives her son back to Storybrooke, where she encounters his adoptive mother, Regina. The grande dame of witchy villains not only controls the city but also manipulates the lives of the fairy-tale characters' contemporary counterparts, who have taken on different identities with ordinary occupations: Snow White is a sweet, sensitive, and timid elementary school teacher—the very cliché of "goodness"—and hospital volunteer; Rumpelstiltskin owns a pawnshop and deals in antiquities; Prince Charming works at an animal shelter after being a comatose patient at the hospital; Red Riding Hood (Meghan Ory), a.k.a. Ruby, waits tables at Granny's Diner; and so forth.

In the first season of *OUaT*, Henry provides a source of both conflict and common interest between his biological mother, Emma, and his adoptive mother, Regina. As the story unfolds, flashbacks reveal that Regina adopted Henry because she felt devoid of emotion and hoped a baby would fill the emptiness in her heart. Although she struggles with her new parental role at first, she grows into it and becomes a caring and loving mother. Hence, Kitsis and Horowitz portray the evil queen's devotion and aspiration to be a good parent as one of her redeeming virtues, contesting the imagination that the fairy-tale witch and loving motherhood are opposing concepts. Upon encountering Emma, Regina's motherly protective instincts take over as she fears Henry's biological mother may want to claim custody of the child. Because she is afraid of losing her son, she threatens Emma fiercely in the pilot episode:

REGINA: Miss Swan, you made a decision ten years ago. And in the last decade, while you've been . . . well, who knows what you've been doing. I've changed every diaper. Soothed every fever. Endured every tantrum. You may have given birth to him, but he is my son.

EMMA: I was not . . .

REGINA: No! You don't get to speak. You don't get to do anything. You gave up that right when you tossed him away. Do you know what a closed adoption is? It's what you asked for. You have no legal right to Henry and you're going to be held to that. So, I suggest you get in your car, and you leave this town. Because if you don't, I will destroy you if it is the last thing I do. Goodbye, Miss Swan.

The show plays with viewers' expectations by radically departing from the Grimms' or Disney's construction of the queen as pure diabolic miscreant and by deliberately juxtaposing the maleficent, egoistic, and ruthless fairy-tale character with a tender, affectionate, and caring mother figure. Yet,

Regina remains authoritative, dictatorial, and manipulative in her political position as mayor, which is ironically a public office held by someone elected to represent the town's citizens and to serve in the community's interest. Her totalitarian "rule" of Storybrooke turns her municipal function into a farce. Albeit not a perfect mother, Regina works very hard at having a good mother-son relationship. For those viewers questioning Regina's feelings toward Henry, given her coldhearted alter ego, a dialogue between the two mothers zooms in on the crux of the matter:

EMMA: Do you love him?
REGINA: Excuse me?
EMMA: Henry. Do you love him?
REGINA: Of course I love him.

Baxter and Hay point out that Regina's motherhood humanizes her in ways that allow fans to relate to the character despite her otherwise evil nature. They quote a fan commenting: "I like Regina, too. I'm really loving the humanity that's being brought to these traditionally evil characters. And I can't wait to find out more of EQ's [evil queen's] back story" (2014, 325).

By illuminating the background of the fairy-tale figures, including the villains, the series transforms them into multifaceted and dynamic characters with whom the audience can identify as human beings, seeing them as people rather than formulaic personas. For their show, Kitsis and Horowitz strove to make the character of the evil queen realistic and three-dimensional by telling the "true" story behind her upbringing and the tragic events that led to her defection from goodness. As in the case of Sanders's fabrication of Queen Ravenna, a trigger event in Regina's past changed her personality for the worse, eventually making a killing monster out of her. In the episode "The Stable Boy" (season 1, ep. 18), at a time before evil blackened her soul, good-hearted Princess Regina saves the young Princess Snow White (Bailee Madison) from a rogue horse. Based on her heroic deed, one could assert that Regina was a heroine before she became a villainess. Snow White's father, King Leopold (Richard Schiff), expresses his gratitude and proposes to Regina, unaware that she is in love with her riding instructor and the family's stable boy, Daniel (Noah Bean). After Snow White accidentally witnesses Regina and Daniel share a passionate kiss, she promises Regina to keep their secret safe. On the night Regina and Daniel want to elope together, Regina's cruel and controlling mother, Cora (Barbara Hershey), intervenes and kills Daniel by magically ripping out his heart. In front of Regina's eyes, her mother crushes her lover's heart to ensure Regina's marriage to the king. In desperation, Regina picks up Daniel's dead body, crying "Mother, why have you done this?" Cora defends her action by telling her she is doing what is best for Regina to ensure her "happy ending."

In a video interview posted on YouTube, actress Lana Parrilla states that the scene portrays a significant turning point in Regina's character because her heart breaks after witnessing the murder of her true love. "When there is a trauma in one's life, I think something happens to the brain, and I think that's what has happened to Regina. Something just switched and she slowly starts to become this evil queen" ("Once Upon a Time" 2012). The episode "The Stable Boy" continues with Regina's discovery that the child, Snow White, had broken her promise and divulged Regina's secret relationship with Daniel to Cora. Although a loving and warm bond existed between Regina and Snow White before the tragic event, Regina now grows cold and vengeful of her stepdaughter, vowing to destroy Snow White. This important episode discloses the root cause of Regina's hatred toward Snow White, whose broken promise resulted in the death of Regina's fiancé and sentenced her to a loveless marriage with the much older King Leopold. Despite her later evil actions, fans of *OUaT* have expressed sympathy for Regina on social media websites and online platforms, not least because she is the victim of a scheming maternal figure. Since Cora was taught that love is a weakness, she passes on that conviction to her daughter, her credo that the possession of power is the most important thing in life. With her rotten ideology of grabbing power at all cost, Cora is able to successfully corrupt Regina's mind and lure her into darkness over time. Many fan reactions suggest that losing a loved one evokes in the viewer a strong sense of compassion for the show's miscreants, in particular for the leading villains, Regina and Rumpelstiltskin. Fan "adevilishdiva" wrote in an online forum, "Yes, I do feel sorry for Regina. As it is stated many times 'Evil is not born. It's made.' She wasn't evil until she lost her love. Snow White made that evil spark to life within Regina when she betrayed her secret and created that metaphorical snowball that ruined EQ's [evil queen's] life" (adevilishdiva 2012). Another fan posted in a different forum, "Both of them were never evil to begin with and they have reasons for doing what they did. I sympathize with both Rumpel and Regina" (Greenhill and Rudy 2014, 313).

OUaT challenges the fairy-tale conventions of absolute dichotomies, such as good and evil, right and wrong, just and unjust, and so forth, by highlighting the backstories and versatile personalities of each character. This emphasis of the show caters to audiences who not only prefer to watch nuanced rather than polarized protagonists but also find it easier to relate to multifaceted characters with a detailed personal history rather than archetypal fairy-tale figures. However, if the evil queen is truly a victim of her past traumas and evokes viewers' empathy because her evilness was not innate, how does that change our understanding of a fairy-tale happy ending? Should the audience cheer or feel sympathy at the character's impending destruction or punishment? What are the implications when villains, such as Regina, possess redeeming and humanizing qualities that allow viewers to identify with them? Season One portrays Queen Regina as a strong, bold, and confident woman, but the pain and hurt she feels over her past shine through her facade every now and then. In the Enchanted Forest, it appears as if she uses her powerful magic to shield herself against any feelings of sadness or remorse. In Storybrooke, Regina masks as the town's draconic mayor, whose facial features always seem in control, never betraying her hidden emotions. And yet, in the final episode of the first season, "A Land without Magic," Regina's true sentiments come to the fore when she genuinely grieves for Henry, who collapsed after eating the poisoned apple turnover intended for Emma. When Regina realizes that she cannot help Henry and that she might have lost him forever, she sincerely mourns for her son. After Emma breaks the curse and wakes up Henry from his "death sleep," Regina affirms to Henry that she loves him, no matter what he might think or other people might tell him. Regina's motherly devotion to her son and her open display of emotions starkly resonated with followers of the show and evoked strong feelings of compassion for the evil queen. Kee Leichtle, a male fan of the series, commented, "Can anyone join me on feeling bad for Regina in today's epic finale? Well the show did it. They made me feel sorry for the villains. It honestly broke my heart when Regina was crying when Henry temporarily died and when she was crying on his pillow. . . . I never thought I'd be showing sympathy for villains lol" (beekee404 2012). Two female fans responded, "Yes. I cried over poor Gina. I've always felt so sorry for her. She's not really evil. She's just scared" (loYol 2012); "OMG I was almost crying, when she [Regina] told him [Henry] she loved him no matter what anyone said. Holding the pillow crying. My poor poor Gina, why can't you just be happy?" (Zanhar1 2012). A Facebook website titled "I feel bad for Regina aka Evil Queen" with 2,530 likes by followers of the show in 2016 indicates just how much this episode elicited fans' empathy for the villainess.

The fans' comments prove three central aspects: first, that these fans do not perceive Regina as a truly or completely evil person; second, that they empathize with Regina and other villains as humanized characters; and third, that they wish for the villains to have happy endings. A right to happiness is also what the villains of the show claim for themselves in Season Four. In her secret vault, Regina faces the author, Isaac Heller (Patrick Fischler), of the *Once Upon a Time* book, a magical item in the show containing the life stories and future developments of all fairy-tale characters, and demands that he change her destiny as villain. At this point in the show, Regina is madly in love with Robin Hood (Sean Maguire), and she hopes that the author is able to rewrite her story in the book so that she may live happily ever after. Isaac admits to her that of all the characters, she "really gets screwed over the most," an implicit justification for the audience that if anyone deserves a chance for happiness it is Regina. At the same time, the author has second thoughts about revising her figure as villainess, which he thinks of as enthralling: "It's a shame. I mean, writing a happy ending for the evil queen . . . well . . . you've always been a favorite of mine. Very clear goals, plus totally damaged personality, with a self-destructive streak. A recipe for compelling . . ." (4, 21). Thus, it can be argued that Isaac's dilemma echoes the voice of those viewers who love to watch Parrilla play one of the show's most popular and intriguing villains on the one hand but who want to see her character find true love and happiness on the other.

The creators of *OUaT* fundamentally destabilize the negative conception of the Grimms' evil queen by turning her into a positive character as the series evolves and characters' personalities develop. In an unprecedented manner for fairy-tale adaptations on television, Kitsis and Horowitz endow the evil queen with a strong desire to renounce her wicked ways and take the path toward redemption. After spending several episodes atoning for past sins, the archetypical villainess emerges as savior and heroine in Seasons Four and Five of the show, exhibiting a radical about-face from her first appearance in the show as Madam Mayor. Tired of not getting her happy ending and for the sake of her son Henry, Regina decides to leave the darkness behind her and work very hard at becoming a better person. However, her attempts to shake off her reputation as "monster" are frequently undermined by the show's plotlines. For instance, Robin Hood's formerly dead wife, Maid Marian (Christie Laing), returns through a magic time portal in Season Four, taking away Regina's happiness and chance at a blissful love relationship with Robin. Although Regina steps into the hero role by saving Marian's life, the selfless act leaves her without the prospects of a happily ever after with her lover. Her character thus changes from that of a traumatized villain to that of a pitiable hero, and her dramatic journey from malignity to benignity reflects the postmodern perspective of the evil queen as a misunderstood victim worthy of at least partial redemption.

Conclusion

North American fairy-tale adaptations in popular culture exhibit the trend of recasting well-known villains, such as the evil queen from the Grimms' fairy tale "Snow White," by elucidating the antagonists' backstories and by framing the antagonists as pitiable victims of past traumas and disturbing experiences. The postmodern representation of the evil queen in media and stage productions, for instance, is set apart from the Grimms' embodiment of the fantastic figure through a complex personality and personal history, putting into question the character's evil nature and origins. Many contemporary retellings of the fairy tale significantly alter, distort, and recreate the queen's image, depicting her not as the villainous Other, wicked witch, and monstrous woman but as a realistic, tragic, and sometimes likable character, inviting viewer identification and sympathy. Indeed, we, as viewers of such a film, television show, or theater performance, may identify and empathize with the antagonist because we recognize some part of ourselves or of people close to us in the fairy-tale character and thus establish a personal connection, which elicits an emotional response in return. When a fictional fabrication such as the evil queen is humanized as a three-dimensional persona with positive attributes and depth of character, audiences may root for her because they find her intriguing, charismatic, easy to relate to, or worthy of redemption. Based on the hypothesis that villains are made and not born, it is conceivable that they can be "ummade" as well. As exemplified in this chapter, postmodern American fairy-tale adaptations defy the antithetical conception of all-good heroes versus all-bad villains and challenge the principle of absolute villainy. By exploring the queen's past, for instance, the retellings highlight that there is a dramatic root cause for the character's wickedness and establish that the queen was not evil from the outset.

Further, today's reimaginings of the fairy tale "Snow White" manifest not only that villains are misunderstood individuals capable of changing for the better but that they possess the potential of becoming tomorrow's heroes.

The concept of equipping fairy-tale characters with elaborate backstories, portraying them as realistic, everyday people instead of archetypal sketches typical for fairy tales, and transplanting them to real-life settings resonates with American audiences. The long-arc television serial *OUaT*, for instance, attracts a loyal fan base willing to invest significant amounts of time to watch the complex backstories of the characters unfold over several seasons. The level of identification among fan-based communities, as Hay and Baxter point out, has reached "new horizons" through fan fiction, as well as new media platforms, including *OUaT* online forums and official Facebook pages (2014, 325–26). As an example, they emphasize how the evil queen Regina inspires identification among fans who do not necessarily relate the fairy-tale figure only to themselves but compare her to other people in their lives, for example, "mothers, exes, girlfriends, mothers-in-law, and even teachers" (327). Regina, as this chapter has demonstrated, is only one example of the latest wave of screen reincarnations of the iconic wicked witch. Indeed, the "evil queen" stereotype has undergone a noteworthy progression in North American pop culture, from Disney's adaptation of the Grimms' coldhearted, cannibalistic, monstrous female villain in its animated feature film from 1937 to a character colored in all shades of gray with a wide range of emotions, moral principles, and personal values, strengths and weaknesses of character, and a varied palette of personality traits, much more in tune with perceptions of modern femininity. Whereas traditional fairy-tale villains are known for being driven predominantly by their desire for power or for committing criminal acts simply for the sake of their own evilness, today's recastings of the evil queen construct her as an exploited, misconceived, and sometimes rehabilitated figure. Whether we look at the embodiments of Lady Claudia, Clementianna, or Ravenna as evil queen, nearly all of these characters' atrocious deeds are severely misguided. However, despite their cruel behavior, viewers may empathize with these representations of the evil queen based on the roots of legitimate motivation that guide the characters' development. In stark contrast, it is less likely that the Grimms' one-dimensional antagonist from "Snow White" invokes in the reader of the tale a feeling of sympathy similar to the loyal viewer's emotional investment in the multifaceted figure of the evil queen Regina on television.

There are plenty of rotten apples and black sheep in our society who may have tragic personal narratives that explain their apparent malevolence; they may have positive qualities, like Clementianna's sense of humor or Regina's fierce and protective mothering. America's news coverage tends to paint the world as a grim battleground of good versus evil forces—of heroes versus villains—propagating a worldview that is as black and white as the interior design of Regina's office in Storybrooke. The real world, however, does not follow this simplistic division. The fast-paced, globally connected, digital age in which we live allows us to access information more easily than ever before and to consult different sources of old and new media. Although some news reports and television shows thrive on sensationalism and the magnification of negative events, others offer serious analyses and discussions of why tragic events take place. What leads today's villains and perpetrators to act in such horrific and socially unacceptable ways? Remarkably, as of January 1, 2016, there were 55 women and 2,888 men on death row in the United States (DPIC 2016). What drove these women and men into crime and what are their background stories? The villains in today's fairy-tale and fantasy adaptations kill numerous innocents, but few of them receive punishments for their criminal activities. Instead, viewers root for the reimagined evil queen and popular fantastic antiheros, such as Wade Wilson in *Deadpool* (2016) and the dangerous criminals in the film *Suicide Squad* (2016). What does that say about society's notion of villainy in real-life versus fictional narratives? Surely, the current trend of humanizing fairy-tale villains through their personal narratives, and the evolution of the character of the evil queen in particular, is an indicator that our basic understanding of "evilness" has changed due to rejecting the concept of evil as a universal principle and absolute truth.

This trend of revealing the "true story" about villains' backgrounds, which thrives on the tensions between the classic fairy-tale canon and novel retellings, is by no means limited to the character of the Grimms' evil queen. The dark fantasy film *Maleficent* (2014), featuring Angelina Jolie in the role of the powerful fairy Maleficent, serves as a prominent example beyond the corpus of "Snow White." Inspired by Charles Perrault's classic tale "La Belle au bois dormant" ("The Beauty Sleeping in the Wood"), the Grimms' "Dornröschen" ("Little Briar Rose"), and Disney's 1959 animated film *Sleeping Beauty*, the production *Maleficent* redefines yet another traditionally villainous fairy-tale character by means of a powerful and tragic backstory. *Maleficent* takes an exceptional feminist approach to reinterpreting the fairy tale by recounting the narrative from the perspective of the eponymous antagonist, portraying her conflicted relationship with Sleeping Beauty, also known as Princess Aurora (Elle Fanning), and King Stefan (Sharlto Copley), the ruler over a corrupt kingdom. Similar to many characterizations of the evil queen in contemporary fairy-tale adaptations, the horned and winged fairy in Disney's live-action production starts out as an innocent, kindhearted, and loving figure. Her eventual turn to the dark side is triggered by a traumatic event in her adolescence involving love, betrayal, and metaphorical rape.

The film begins with the voice-over of an elderly Aurora, who narrates Maleficent's backstory of how the young fairy grew up in the magical and idyllic forest realm of the Moors. One day, the girl fairy befriends the human peasant boy Stefan and they become playmates. Over time, the two "most unlikely of friends" fall in love, and on her sixteenth birthday, Stefan gives

Maleficent the gift of "true love's kiss." As the years go by, however, Stefan's love is overshadowed by his greed for power. His ambitions pull him away from Maleficent and toward the temptations of the human kingdom. Maleficent has risen to become the protector of the Moors, defending the peaceful natural realm from the attacks of the aggressive neighboring human kingdom. When the dying king announces that the person who kills the "winged creature" will become heir to his throne and marry his only daughter, Stefan returns to the Moors to visit Maleficent. After drugging her with a sleeping drink, he violates her physically by cutting the wings off her body with silver chains as evidence of her death. This scene, a metaphor for rape and sexual abuse, represents the traumatic experience that changes the good-natured, happy spirit into a sinister, bitter, and vengeful fairy. Overwhelmed by pain and Stefan's betrayal, Maleficent declares herself Queen of the Moors, which she transforms into a dark kingdom. In an interview, lead actress Jolie confirmed that the core of the film "is abuse, and how the abused then have a choice of abusing others or overcoming and remaining loving, open people" (Holmes 2014).

Maleficent's background story evokes the tragic childhood experience of Queen Ravenna and how her hostility toward men fueled her desire for revenge. Whereas *Snow White and the Huntsman* does not highlight Ravenna's direful past in more than a brief flashback, *Maleficent* foregrounds the symbolic rape of the fantastic figure. When Maleficent wakes up on the day following the assault, her cries of anguish pierce the air and her facial features reflect the horrific realization of what has happened to her. The powerful scene resonates strongly with viewers, such as Corrina Lawson, who describes the scene in an online blog as "a moment of such cruelty that it takes your breath away" (2014). By ripping off her wings, Stefan not only robs the fairy of power and freedom, he also destroys her hope and faith in the goodness of the world. The physical mutilation and "castration" of the female body by male force encourages the audience to feel sympathy and outrage for the victim. However, unlike Ravenna's personal revenge campaign following her traumatic encounter with men, Maleficent's ongoing journey after her disfigurement is less about revenge and madness than it is about women's recovery from abuse. Initially driven by her thirst for vengeance on Stefan, the fairy attends the christening of King Stefan's daughter Aurora uninvited. Maleficent curses the infant princess to fall into a sleep like death on her sixteenth birthday after pricking her finger on the spindle of a spinning wheel. The spell can be broken only by true love's kiss, but since the fairy no longer believes in love she is confident that Aurora will sleep forever. Against her expectations, Maleficent becomes fond of the little princess as she watches her from afar growing older. Underneath her veneer of anger, the fairy begins to feel love for the girl she calls fondly "beastie"; for the girl who is not afraid of her and who thinks of Maleficent as her "fairy godmother." Her interaction with Aurora reveals a genuine affection for the princess, and as the bond between them becomes stronger, Maleficent takes on motherly tasks, such as tucking Aurora in at night.

Reminiscent of Regina's role as Henry's stepmother in *OUaT*, motherhood humanizes Maleficent and demonstrates that evilness can be remedied through the principle of love. Touched by Aurora's kindness and innocence that melts the fairy's hardened heart, Maleficent unsuccessfully attempts to revoke her own wicked spell. When the curse takes its course and Aurora falls asleep, it is not the prince who awakes the sleeping beauty but Maleficent's kiss on Aurora's forehead that breaks the spell, proving that the fairy's motherly tenderness is indeed true love. With this feminist twist of the fairy tale, the producers of *Maleficent* play with the expectations of those viewers who anticipate the princess will be saved by a man. The figure of Maleficent thus conflates the two archetypical fairy-tale identities of villain and hero. At first glance, the trend of humanizing evil female villains such as Maleficent or the archetypal wicked stepmother extraordinaire in adaptions of "Snow White" through the redemptive powers of motherhood appears to be positive. At second glance, however, the trend domesticates these active and independent women by defining them through their identities as mothers, circumscribing the female empowerment the novel fairy-tale adaptations promise.

Whereas contemporary fairy-tale films and television shows, such as *OUaT* or *Maleficent*, displace women's dependence on matrimonial romance and male rescue, on the one hand, they isolate and marginalize female villains, on the other hand, by linking their redemptive potential to their roles as caregivers and nurturers. As Jackie Pinkowitz observed in 2014,

> the redemption of "evil" women through motherhood ultimately works to strip Regina and especially Maleficent of much of their potential complexity and the transformative possibilities of their "villainous" femininity. Furthermore, it reveals their "evil-ness" to have been merely the product of thwarted heterosexual love; their true nature, as caring, virtuous, and maternal women, becomes revealed and (re)asserted through their selfless acts as mothers.

Lady Claudia in Cohn's *Snow White: A Tale of Terror* and Freya in Nicolas-Troyan's *The Huntsman: Winter's War* are also centrally defined by their roles as mothers. In their motherhood-as-redemption motifs, contemporary fairy-tale reimaginings in North American popular culture further reinscribe what Susan Douglas and Meredith Michaels refer to as the "new momism" of the early twenty-first century, a myth that insists that "no woman is truly complete or fulfilled unless she has kids, that women remain the best primary caretakers of children, and that to be a remotely decent mother, a woman has to devote her entire physical, psychological, and emotional, and intellectual being, 24/7, to her children" (2004, 4). Thus, instead of perpetuating the traditional notion of the villainous fairy-tale stepmother, postmodern retellings present audiences with highly romanticized images of rehabilitated "new moms" whose motherly devotion and love for children leads them back from the path of darkness to the path of light. Whereas the concept of redemption for mischievous villains is appealing to many viewers because it offers the sense of hope people may crave in real life, the popular trend of foregrounding motherhood as the only imaginable approach to redemption and salvation for women remains unsettling.

3

Taming the Monstrous Other

Representations of the Rehabilitated Big Bad Beast in American Media

"See! Sweet and sound she sleeps in granny's bed,
between the paws of the tender wolf."

—Angela Carter, *The Bloody Chamber and Other Stories* (1979)

"All stories are about wolves. All worth repeating, that is.
Anything else is sentimental drivel. . . . There's escaping
from the wolves, fighting the wolves, capturing the wolves,
taming the wolves. Being thrown to the wolves, or throwing
others to the wolves so the wolves will eat them instead of you.
Running with the wolf pack. Turning into a wolf. Best of all,
turning into the head wolf. No other decent stories exist."

—Margaret Atwood, *The Blind Assassin* (2000)[1]

O f all the creatures and critters that roam, crawl, wiggle, leap, flutter, fly, and swim through the world of the fairy tale, two different kinds of beasts stand out: the enchanted, superficial ones whose marvelous animal guises conceal their true human forms for a temporary period of time and those creatures who are beastly by nature. Of the first group, popular animal bridegrooms in the shape of a frog, a hedgehog, or a bear come to mind that we find in the Grimms' tales "Der Froschkönig" ("The Frog King, or Iron Heinrich"), "Hans mein Igel" ("Hans My Hedgehog") and "Schneeweisschen und Rosenrot" ("Snow White and Rose Red"). Of the second group, the most prominent example in the Grimms' collection is probably that of "Rotkäppchen" ("Little Red Cap"), followed by "Der Wolf und die sieben jungen Geißlein" ("The Wolf and the Seven Young Kids"). Commonly known in North America as the Big Bad Wolf, this fairy-tale beast, in particular, may seem so familiar that it hardly requires an introduction. And yet, this chapter offers a (re)reading of the tales featuring this generic archetype of a menacing predatory antagonist to demonstrate that the Grimms' fairy tales are not only dark but also feature beasts that represent the terrifying, harrowing, and life-threatening Other. North American pop culture has inverted this archetypal image of the dangerous, scary, bad wolf as manifestation of the uncanny, negatively connoted Other into a supernatural creature that is not primarily Otherized or "monstrified" but portrayed in a positive light, either as rehabilitated, appealing, sexy, and likable werewolf figure or as funny, infantilized, anthropomorphized "good" wolf.

Many postmodern fairy-tale retellings replace the Big Bad Wolf with a humanized werewolf figure to allow for viewer identification and to demonstrate that the Other can be embraced and accepted as part of the self, rather than feared. In fact, a number of fairy-tale adaptations and fantasy stories today celebrate the concept of Otherness, of being different, especially when Otherized characters differ from humans in a supernatural way. Examples of fictional creatures, such as the vampires and werewolves in Catherine Hardwicke's *The Twilight Saga* (2008–2012) based on Stephenie Meyer's novel series (2005–2008) or Marvel Comics' X-Men, featuring the mutant Wolverine, come to mind. In stark contrast to the Grimms' fairy tales, contemporary reimaginings tie fantastic transformations and physical mutations to the creation of romanticized Others, beautified beasts, and marvelous monsters who are superior in skills and appearance compared to the average human. Hence, these romanticized Others are craved and worshiped as superheroes or heroines, and their attributes fetishized by North America's consumerist society. By comparison, the process of bodily transformation and metamorphosis from human into beast, the animalistic Other, occurs in the Grimms' tales predominantly as a form of punishment or as a fateful result of an evil enchantment.

German fairy tales code human-animal transformations negatively and portray magical mutations of human body parts into animalistic extremities as disadvantageous. Examples range from animal bridegroom tales, such as the Grimms' "The Frog King, or Iron Heinrich," in which a wicked witch once turned a prince into a frog, and "Snow White and Rose Red," in which an evil dwarf bewitched a prince to run about the forest as a savage bear; to tales of fateful wishes, such as "Die Sieben Raben" ("The Seven Ravens"), in which a father's thoughtless wish turns his sons into ravens; to tales that center on the violation of an interdiction, such as Wilhelm Hauff's "Die Geschichte von Kalif Storch" ("The Story of the Caliph Stork," 1825), in which a malicious magician tricks a Caliph and his Grand Vizier into becoming storks. In Hauff's fairy tale "Die Geschichte von dem kleinen Muck" ("The Story of Little Mook," 1825), the hero and trickster figure Little Mook uses magic figs to punish an ungrateful king and his royal household with the growth of donkey ears. Also in the Grimms' tale "Der Krautesel" ("The Donkey Cabbage"), human-animal transformation serves as a means for corporal punishment and chastisement. In this story, a huntsman transforms, by means of magic cabbages, three women into donkeys who then have to endure daily beatings by a miller. Whereas some animal bridegrooms in the Grimms' tales can choose to take off their beastly skin, for instance, in "Hans My Hedgehog" and "Das Eselein" ("The Little Donkey"), other animal spouses are magically cursed to oscillate between their human and beast form, such as in "Das singende, springende Löweneckerchen" ("The Singing, Springing Lark"), until the spell is broken. The latter tale, which features a lion as animal bridegroom, represents the Grimm version that relates most closely to Gabrielle-Suzanne Barbot de Villeneuve's eighteenth-century fairy

tale "La Belle et la Bête." In 1756, Jeanne-Marie Leprince de Beaumont published a shorter variant of "La Belle et la Bête," which has been popularized
by Disney with its animated adaptation *Beauty and the Beast* (1991).

The trope of the monstrous husband evokes the mythical tale of "Cupid
and Psyche," a tale written by Roman author Lucius Apuleius in the satirical
novel *Metamorphoses* (or *The Golden Ass*). This variant of the tale type cycle
known as The Search for the Lost Husband (ATU 425) is linked to both
ATU 425A, The Animal as Bridegroom, and ATU 425 B, Son of the Witch.
As noted by Virginia E. Swain, the emphasis of this tale lies on the transgression of the beautiful girl, Psyche (2016, 108). Fated to become the bride
of a horrid, serpentlike, winged creature, the youngest of three daughters
is transported to a marvelous palace where invisible attendants tend to her
every need. Venus's son, Cupid, visits her at night and makes her his wife
but does not reveal his true identity. Psyche gradually learns to look forward to his visits, though he always departs before dawn and forbids her to
look upon him, and soon she becomes pregnant. Envious of the splendor in
which Psyche lives, her sisters suggest that Psyche's husband is a wild beast
who will soon devour her and her child. Spurred on by her two wicked sisters, Psyche intends to kill the monster. Equipped with a dagger and a lamp,
Psyche breaks the taboo and gazes upon her husband while he sleeps, only to
discover that he is the winged god of love and the most beautiful creature she
has ever seen. When a drop of lamp oil awakens him, Cupid disappears and
Psyche must undergo several trials imposed on her by Venus, including a
quest to the underworld, before she becomes immortal and receives Jupiter's
consent to be united with Cupid in marriage as equals.

It is easy to see a kinship between the mythical tale of "Cupid and Psyche," Beaumont's "Beauty and the Beast," and the Grimms' "The Singing,
Springing Lark." All three tales feature a young woman who goes to live
with a supernatural or enchanted groom, followed by the groom's departure because of the violation of a prohibition. The bride is either questing
for her groom or performing specific tasks to regain his love before their

ultimate reunion. Unlike the story of "Cupid and Psyche," however, the tales "Beauty and the Beast" and "The Singing, Springing Lark" center less on the transgression or breaking of an interdiction than on the enchantment of the beastly bridegroom, the deliverance from that bewitchment, and the retransformation from animal into human being. Both Beast in the French version and the lion in the German are princes imprisoned in their beastly bodies. However, their brute appearance and behavior are only a superficial veneer. At first glance, the beasts in these tales are savage, scary, and unforgiving and display a predatory killer instinct. In Beaumont's tale, Beast threatens the trespassing father who picked a rose for his youngest daughter, Beauty: "You shall die for this mistake; I give you but a quarter of an hour to prepare yourself, and say your prayers."[2] In the Grimms' tale, the lion roars "until the leaves on the trees trembled" and cries at the trespassing father, "I will eat up anyone who tries to steal my singing, springing lark!" Both fathers narrowly escape death only by promising their youngest daughter to the animal.

At second glance, however, the animal bridegrooms win the love of the young women who come to live with them, proving that they are not as ferocious and wild as they first appear. Beaumont's Beauty tells Beast: "There are many men who make worse monsters than you, and I prefer you, notwithstanding your looks, to those who under the semblance of men hide false, corrupt, and ungrateful hearts." In "The Singing, Springing Lark," the lion receives his new bride kindly and she lives happily with him at his castle, considering herself to be well off. The young woman loves her animal groom so much that she spends seven years searching the world for him without rest in the hope to redeem him. Although the "monstrous" husbands turn out to be not as savage as they look, both tales code the beast form or supernatural Other negatively and make the retransformation of the bewitched princes from animals to human beings a necessary element for the protagonists' happy endings. Remarkably, the corpus of the Grimms' tales follows this notion of branding beastly Otherness as negative,

unfavorable, adverse, and disreputable. A quick survey of enchanted individuals, most of which are, in fact, male, in the Grimms' collection manifests
that the fantastic beasts they shape-shift into are predominantly ferocious,
unsightly, or revolting, such as lions, bears, hedgehogs, donkeys, ravens,
frogs, and snakes. Much rarer are bewitched men and boys taking the shapes
of beautiful, gentle, and tame creatures, such as deer and doves, for example,
in the Grimms' "Brüderchen und Schwesterchen" ("Brother and Sister") and
"The Singing, Springing Lark." But even in these tamed beast forms, the animal Other functions as a detrimental consequence and influence following
the transgression of a prohibition.

Whereas human-animal metamorphoses engender temporary and
superficial bestiality in the Grimms' tales, the monstrosity of animalistic,
magically induced "masquerade" fades in comparison to those creatures
whose bestiality is innate. Hence, veritable beasts such as the wolf in "Little Red Riding Hood" (ATU 333) appear that much more threatening and
dangerous than any character in a marvelous animal disguise. The Grimms'
version of the tale, as is well known today among "Grimm scholars," was told
to the brothers between 1811 and 1812 by the sisters Jeanette and Marie Has-
senpflug. Both were educated women of partly French Huguenot ancestry.
In addition, the Grimms' were familiar with Ludwig Tieck's verse play *Leben
und Tod des kleinen Rotkäppchens* (*The Life and Death of Little Red Riding
Hood*, 1800) and Charles Perrault's 1697 French variant "Le Petit Chaperon
rouge" (Zipes 1983, 14). In Tieck's play, Little Red Riding Hood (LRRH) does
not survive. Neither does the wolf who gobbles her up to take revenge on
her father for killing his beloved mate, a she-wolf. The tragic ending echoes
Perrault's preceding tale. Perrault, a member of the *haute bourgeoisie* and
salon regular, wrote his literary tales for a readership of children and adults
of the upper educated classes. Presumably influenced by French folklore
on werewolves and "uncivilized" oral folk narrations of "Little Red Riding
Hood" containing cannibalism, Perrault penned his "refined" bourgeois version (Zipes 1984, 4).[3] "Le Petit Chaperon rouge" is a cautionary tale about

vanity, power, and seduction, containing clever sexual innuendos and tragic elements as the wolf devours LRRH without resurrection in the end. Metaphorically, the wolf represents a predatory male whose victim is blamed by Perrault in the tale's moral for causing her own rape. His warning is that children, especially young, pretty, well-bred, nice girls, should never listen to strangers, for if they should do so, they might get eaten by a wolf: "I say wolf, for all wolves are not of the same kind. There are some with winning ways, not loud, nor bitter, or angry, who are tame, good-natured, and pleasant and follow young ladies right into their homes, right into their alcoves. But alas for those who do not know that of all the wolves the docile ones are those who are most dangerous" (Zipes 1984, 71).

Perrault's literary version was too carnal, gruesome, and tragic for the Grimms' taste. Therefore, their story "Little Red Cap" features a proper little girl whose modest behavior corresponds to the emerging *Biedermeier* values of the time. The Grimms avoided any sexual references and, most importantly, endowed the fairy tale with a happy ending. After the wolf has devoured the grandmother and the girl, a hunter rescues both from the wolf's belly. What follows is a motif borrowed from the folk tale "The Wolf and the Seven Kids." The wolf's empty belly is filled with large stones, which eventually kill the beast as the wolf jumps up and tries to escape. Another alteration by the Grimms is the addition of a second, anticlimactic story of "Little Red Cap" in which the girl and her grandmother outwit the wolf without the help of a male rescuer. The moralistic tale that resembles a coda or epilogue demonstrates that the two women have learned their lesson and can defeat the beast by themselves. This time, Little Red Cap does not stray from the path after her encounter with the wolf and walks directly to granny's house, where both women barricade the door. The lurking wolf climbs up onto the roof of the house, but thanks to the old woman's ingenuity, the beast ends up falling into a trough of water and drowning.

The Grimms' sanitized, more optimistic fairy tale "Little Red Cap" appears to be the version with which most people in today's Western culture are familiar. Indeed, the characters popularized in North America under the names Little Red Riding Hood and the Big Bad Wolf resurface in countless reincarnations in books, magazines, comics, advertisements, and films, and on television, the internet, and social media websites, and influence numerous consumer products, such as toys, clothing, games, and other merchandise. This chapter focuses on depictions of the Grimms' fairy-tale wolf in postmodern retellings based on "Little Red Cap" and adaptations thereof. To lay the foundation for analysis, the chapter begins with a socio-historical contextualization of the wolf in the Grimms' *Märchen* followed by a hermeneutic reading of the wolf's function as prototypical predator and antagonist. Then the figure of the Big Bad Wolf in North American mainstream pop culture is examined. To narrow the scope of study, the chapter scrutinizes only fairy-tale reimaginings inspired by "Little Red Cap" since the early twenty-first century, including revisionist fairy-tale films and television series, a comic book series, and a video game. Specifically, the chapter concentrates on representations of the wolf as they emerge in the character Monroe in NBC's *Grimm* (2011–17), the figure of Ruby/Red in ABC's *Once Upon a Time* (2011–18), the protagonist Valerie and her lover Peter in Catherine Hardwicke's *Red Riding Hood* (2011), the tritagonist Wolf W. Wolf in *Hoodwinked!* (2005), and Bigby Wolf in Bill Willingham's *Fables* comic book series (2002–15) and the spin-off video game *The Wolf Among Us* (2013–14).[4]

"Little Red Cap" (1812–57)

Since the publications of Perrault and the Brothers Grimm, scholars have interpreted "Little Red Riding Hood" in an astonishing number of different ways, from Freudian approaches as a tale representing the Ego overcome by the Id, to seasonal mythology as an allegorical tale of spring conquering winter, and solar theory, which manifests the wolf as the night swallowing up the light of LRRH, to the personification of Good triumphing over Evil. From a structural perspective, as Catherine Orenstein has pointed out, the "plot is powerfully simple. Opposites collide—good and evil, beast and human, male and female" (2002, 4). This clash between polar opposites, between what I interpret to be the known self and the unknown Other, creates strong antithetical tensions in the narrative. According to Bruno Bettelheim, the image of a charming, naïve, "innocent" girl devoured by a wild, cunning wolf "impresses itself indelibly on the mind" (1976 166). Perhaps this collision of contrasting characters is precisely what makes this particular tale so appealing to many. In fact, "Little Red Riding Hood," viewed through the roseate lenses of the Brothers Grimm, is one of the most widely read, well-recognized, and popular fairy tales in the world (Zipes 2000, 302; Bettelheim 1976, 167; Beckett 2016, 585). Whereas in Perrault's version the wolf embodies the role of a rapist, a predatory male, and a sexual seducer, the wolf in the Grimms' "Little Red Cap" is a beastly creature of nature, epitomizing wilderness and the untamed animalistic Other. His function in the tale is mainly a pedagogical one, since he incarnates the direful consequence, corporal punishment, for the girl's transgressions in the story.

"Little Red Cap" begins with the background information of how a young girl received a little cap of red velvet from her grandmother, who loved her most dearly. Because the cap suited the child so well, she was henceforth called Little Red Cap or *Rotkäppchen*. The German diminutive *Käppchen* (Little Cap), first introduced in Tieck's 1800 play, contributes to the infantilization and thus desexualization of the child protagonist. Interestingly, though, Ludwig Emil Grimm, who chose to illustrate "Little Red Cap" as one of his seven copper engravings for the *Kleine Ausgabe* (Little Edition) of 1825, drew an image of a pubescent girl, whose body has already developed breasts. In his copper engraving, Little Red Cap wears a traditional feminine dress, including bodice, blouse, full skirt, and apron, resembling an Austrian or Bavarian dirndl. *Dirndl* is a diminutive form of the dated word *Dirn(e)* for "girl," which the Brothers Grimm used in their first sentence of the fairy tale: "Es war einmal eine kleine süße Dirne" (Once upon a time there was a little sweet girl).[5] The little red cap or bonnet is barely visible in Ludwig Grimm's illustration, which depicts the girl in her grandmother's idyllic, *Biedermeier*-style house as she pulls back the curtain of the bed in which the wolf lies wearing her grandmother's sleeping cap.

The red color of the girl's headpiece, already mentioned by Perrault, has traditionally been associated with sin, sensuality, menstruation, witchery, and the devil, but has also been tied by Wilhelm Grimm directly to the supernatural of Germanic mythology and elves (Zipes [1983] 1993, 26; Uther 2013, 66–67). In the Grimms' personal copy of *Irische Elfenmärchen* (Irish Elf Tales, 1825), Wilhelm remarked in a side note: "also the traditional costume of the little red cap, in Perrault le petit chaperon rouge, may originally be something elvish" (Uther 2013, 66–67). Zipes sees in the doting grandmother's present of the red cap a reference to the child's "spoiled nature" and, in one of Walter Crane's 1875 book drawings, the British illustrator complemented the girl's "devilish" red garment with a wolf in sheepskin, a biblical reference to the devil (Zipes [1983] 1993, 26). Scholars have also pointed to Christian motifs in the bottle of wine and piece of cake, evoking Christian Communion, given to Little Red Cap in a basket by her mother to deliver to the house of the ailing grandmother. The Grimms' variant of Little Red Cap and her grandmother emerging from the belly of the beast echoes the biblical story of Jonah emerging from the belly of the whale (Tatar [2004] 2012, 152). Although the Grimms do not directly link the wolf to the devil, the hunter in their sixth and seventh editions of the tale (published in 1850 and 1857, respectively) refers to the beast as *"alter Sünder"* or "old sinner," aligning the wolf with satanic forces and flagitious behavior. The "sinful" color of the little girl's red cap thus parallels the "sinful" attributes of wolf.

Little Red Cap's transgression is rooted in the breaking of the verbal commitment to her mother, who instructs her daughter to walk properly without leaving the path. The mother's instructions concerning obedience, caution, and general manners reflect the Grimms' spirit of using their *Children's and Household Tales* as *Erziehungsbuch* or educational manual, as stated in the preface to the volume of 1815. In the Grimms' final edition of 1857, the mother cautions Little Red Cap:

> "Set out before it gets hot, and when you get out there, be nice and walk properly and don't stray from the path, otherwise you will fall and break the glass, and the grandmother will have nothing. And when you go into her room, don't forget to say good morning, and don't peep into every corner beforehand." "I will do everything just right," said Little Red Cap to her mother, and gave her hand on it.

Little Red Cap promises her mother to follow the instructions and creates a binding "contract" between the two by shaking her hand. Without the interference of the wolf on the way, who entices the child into breaking the parental obedience deal, Little Red Cap most likely would have kept her agreement. The wolf thus embodies not only a seducer but also a cunning schemer, disruptive figure, and powerful agent of annihilation.

At their first encounter in the woods, Little Red Cap is not afraid of the wolf because she "did not know what a wicked animal he was." This pivotal moment has captured the imagination of many illustrators and painters over the years. Among the most famous and influential engravings of "Little Red Riding Hood" are the works by Gustave Doré, Walter Crane, and Arthur Rackham, whose illustrations continue to influence current artists (Beckett 2016, 589). In several depictions, the wolf is personified as a man, walking on two legs and dressed as a wanderer with a hiking staff and hat (Walter Crane, 1866), as a gentleman with a top hat, cane, and monocle (ca. 1890), or as a soldier (ca. 1880). Johnny Depp's appearance as The Wolf in Disney's 2014 musical fantasy film *Into the Woods* wearing a lupine zoot suit accessorized with a tie, a hat, wooly boots, and a mustache, is reminiscent of those early illustrations. Whereas these "men-wolves," who oftentimes present an appetent tongue, sexualize the encounter with the girl in the woods, other imaginings portray the wolf as a beast of nature without personifying attributes. As Zipes has highlighted, the meeting with the wolf is generally depicted "more like a tête-à-tête than a dangerous encounter," amplified by the fact that the facial expression of Little Red Hood rarely shows any trace of fear ([1983] 1993, 39). Perhaps the most memorable engraving of the scene is the one of 1883 by prolific French illustrator Doré, which accompanied Perrault's fairy tales when they were republished in 1867. His powerful illustration shows a disproportionately imposing wolf turning his back to the viewer and blocking the wooded path. His eyes look down into the big eyes of a girl whose plumb bare arms suggest, as Sandra Beckett noted, that the girl must be very young because "she still has some of her baby fat" (2004, 2). LRRH, appearing dwarfed by the enormous, hairy monster, seems to be intrigued by the wolf's acquaintance rather than afraid of it. Her gaze is without fear and has a faint seductive, submissive, somewhat defiant undertone. Because of the intimacy between the wolf and the girl, whose bodies seem to touch each other as if in a close, rotating dance, the excluded beholder is reduced to a voyeuristic position. Zipes has interpreted Doré's sexually charged engraving as a portrayal of LRRH's desire for the wolf and thus "as a desire for the Other" (1987, 243).

Although the wolf typifies the monstrous, ominous, foreign Other, Little Red Cap does not recognize him as such. In her childish naïveté, Little Red Cap is not in the least suspicious of the wolf's inquisitive demeanor nor of the fact that he already knows her name. After a polite exchange of greetings, the wolf interrogates the girl with a total of five questions. The first three questions concern the child's destination, the contents of her basket, and the location of her grandmother's house. Little Red Cap's willing answers reveal not only the poor health condition of her grandmother to the wolf but also the fact that she lives only fifteen minutes away. Based on this information, the wolf realizes that he must devise a cunning strategy in order to eat them both, the grandmother and Little Red Cap: "This young tender thing is a tasty morsel, which will taste even better than the old one.

You must be sly, so you can catch them both." One may wonder, however, why the wolf finds it necessary to contrive a complex plan to begin with if he could have simply gobbled up Little Red Cap first and then moved on to devour the grandmother. We can find an explanation for the Grimms' apparently illogical construction of the tale by going back to Perrault's version of 1697. Here, the wolf does not dare to eat the girl because of some woodcutters working nearby in the forest.[6] Hence, the wolf's sly scheme is more than a greedy course of action but in effect a cautionary approach to self-preservation. Instead of pouncing on Little Red Cap out in the open of the forest where he runs the risk of being discovered, interrupted, or caught by hunters, wood choppers, or anyone who would kill a wolf on sight, the lupine antagonist plays it safe by being patient. Once *inside* a protective environment, the domestic space of grandmother's house, the wolf can commit his double murder, or symbolic double rape, *outside* of the public eye. The only way for the wolf to achieve this goal is to eat the grandmother first and then wait for Little Red Cap to arrive. Proper timing and planning, ironically both skills highly valued in German culture to the present day, are essential factors for the wolf's strategy to succeed.

Because the wolf wants to gain time, he lures Little Red Cap off the path by pointing out the delights nature has to offer: "Little Red Cap, just look at the beautiful flowers that are everywhere. Why don't you take a look around? I believe you aren't listening at all to how lovely the little birds are singing? You are walking along as though you were on your way to school and it is such fun to dwell in the woods." The wolf insidiously and strategically beguiles Little Red Cap into indulging in nature's sensual pleasures. It is only after the conversation with the wolf that the little girl "opens her eyes" and seems to truly notice the beauty of her surroundings for the first time. This moment of awakening goes hand in hand with Little Red Cap's desire to stray from the path to pick flowers for her grandmother. Although the child's intention of cheering her grandmother up with a flower bouquet is amiable, Little Red Cap's transgression of the agreement with her mother cannot go unpunished as the story unfolds. Little Red Cap's punishment is to become the victim of the conniving wolf who seduced the girl in the first place.

In scholarship, the figure of the wolf has been associated with male sexuality and deception as well as with the symbolic representation of natural urges and social nonconformity. The link between wolf and masculinity already existed in an oral variant of "Little Red Riding Hood," presumably told by peasants in France's Old Regime, long before the Grimms and Perrault penned their tales (Beckett 2016, 586; Orenstein 2002, 5). In this early folktale entitled "The Story of Grandmother" and recorded by French folklorist Paul Delarue in 1885, a girl encounters a *bzou*, or werewolf, the etymological equivalent to "man-wolf"[7] (Zipes [1983] 1993, 67). The werewolf first invites the girl to a cannibalistic meal (she unknowingly consumes the flesh and blood of her grandmother), then to perform a lengthy striptease for him, and finally, when she is naked, to share the bed with him. The Grimms, however, purged their "Rotkäppchen" of any sexual innuendos and werewolf references. Rather than a sexual male predator, the wolf in their version allegorizes a strange and unknown element, a foreign and mysterious Other, in Little Red Cap's environment. Because the child lacks experience, she is unable to cope with the uncanny Other, maneuvers herself into a most terrible situation, and needs saving in the end by an adult *Jäger* (hunter), a male authority figure and protector in control of nature's beasts.[8]

The reason why Little Red Cap does not recognize the wolf as a life-threatening, monstrous Other is not only her lack of experience concerning beasts but also because the wolf appears to her in the middle of the woods, a sylvan space of unknown dimensions to the child. The Other is "at home" in the enchanted woods, a place that can be as mysterious, frightening, and dark, or as alluring and fascinating, as the supernatural creature that inhabits it. Fairy-tale characters can get lost in the woods, find refuge, or experience an adventure. The woods are the home of witches and thieves but also the realm of the huntsman and fantastic beings. In the Grimms' universe of wonder tales, the forest is a place of both magical encounters and threatening danger, as well as a locale of liminality and transformation.[9] Because Little Red Cap has not yet explored the woods, she does not know the nature of the wolf. However, once Little Red Cap enters the intimate, domestic space of her grandmother's house, the wild, untamed Other is out of place. In these surroundings, the wolf has to hide his Otherness through masquerade. After the beast has gobbled up the grandmother, he disguises himself as the old woman by putting on her dress and bonnet. Despite the attempt to conceal his identity as the dangerous Other, Little Red Cap can sense that something foreign and uncanny has invaded the private sphere. This sensation of something *unheimlich* (uncanny) and strange inside the *Heim* (home) causes the girl to be fearful: "She walked into the parlor, and everything looked so strange that she thought, 'Oh, my God, why am I so afraid? I usually like it at grandmother's.'"

Due to the wolf's intrusion, the house of the grandmother has changed for Little Red Cap from a familiar place that is *heimisch, heimlich* (homelike) to a place that is *unheimlich* or a *locus suspectus*, to use Sigmund Freud's Latin equivalent ([1919] 2003, 125). In volume 10 of the Grimms' dictionary, the word *heimlich* is defined, inter alia, as "opposition to foreign" and with reference to animals as "opposition to wild" (1854–1971, 874). Further, a person who feels *heimlich* is "free from fear" (1854–1971, 874). From the idea of "homelike," "belonging to the house," the further idea is developed of something withdrawn from the eyes of others, something concealed or secret, and this idea is expanded in many ways (1854–1971, 875). The wolf does not belong to the house of the grandmother and conceals himself to appear friendly and familiar to Little Red Cap. The level of uncanniness for the girl rises with every new discovery of estrangement about her "grandmother's" physical features. As Freud has highlighted, the "uncanny" is that class of the terrifying that "goes back to what was once well known and had long been familiar" ([1919] 2003, 124). Because the old woman is someone long known and very familiar to Little Red Cap, the changes in "her" appearance increasingly alienate the child:

Then she went to the bed and pulled back the curtains. Grandmother was lying there with her cap pulled down over her face and looking very strange.

"Oh, grandmother, what big ears you have!"

"All the better to hear you with."

"Oh, grandmother, what big eyes you have!"

"All the better to see you with."

"Oh, grandmother, what big hands you have!"

"All the better to grab you with!"

"But, grandmother, what a horribly big mouth (*Maul*)[10] you have!"

"All the better to eat you with!"

Little Red Cap's climactic reactions to the physical alterations build up from surprise and bewilderment about the grandmother's strange looks to the girl's appalled recognition that the old woman is, in fact, a beast. This recognition becomes slowly apparent when Little Red Cap's phrasing changes slightly from "Oh, grandmother" to "But, grandmother," indicating the girl's doubts and objection to what she is being told. Further, and even more importantly, Little Red Cap refers in her last exclamation specifically to a big *Maul* instead of a big *Mund*, the former denoting the mouth of an animal in German, the latter the mouth of a human being. This uncanny moment of recognition, that the Other has infiltrated the intimate space and impersonated her grandmother, causes Little Red Cap's angst. The girl's horror about the size of the "mouth" also conveys her fear of the beast and confrontation with the Other.

Remarkably, Little Red Cap invokes the senses of hearing, sight, touch, and taste, leaving out the sense of smell, a wolf's most developed sense and greatest asset. Naturally, the human sense of smell is feeble compared to that of dogs and wolves. The omission of olfaction in Little Red Cap's list highlights the girl's initial expectation of encountering a human being rather than an animal in the bed. At the moment of the wolf's exposure—his last sentence, "All the better to eat you with!" only confirms the unmasking dis-covery already made by the child—the ravenous beast gulps down Little Red Cap, climbs back into bed, and falls asleep. Scholars have interpreted this scene as a symbolic death of Little Red Cap, followed by her "rebirth" to a higher plane of existence, thanks to the patriarchal protection of a male rescuer and father figure (Tatar [2004] 2012, 152; Bettelheim 1976, 179–80). The heroic function of the hunter who comes to the rescue of the two female victims might not be a surprise, given that "Little Red Riding Hood" is pri-marily a male creation and projection. The loud snores of the napping wolf attract the attention of a huntsman who happens to pass by. The huntsman, a figure in charge of controlling the wild beasts within the forest, has been searching for the "sinful" wolf for a long time. In what Bettelheim calls a "Caesarean section," the *Jäger* cuts open the sleeping wolf's belly with a pair of scissors, liberating the fearful girl and the old woman (1976, 177). Little Red Cap and her grandmother both emerge alive and unharmed out of the wolf's stomach, thereby restoring the tale's archetypal patterns.

In the Grimms' fairy-tale world of absolute dichotomies, the attempt of the monstrous, animal, savage Other to merge with the normal, human, civilized self and thereby collapse the constitutive categories is bound to be only temporary. Thus, the wolf's incorporation of Little Red Cap, which blurs the boundaries between self and Other—and by extension good and evil, domestic and foreign—must be relativized in the end to uphold the binary structure of opposites underlying the Grimms' tales. Since the pun-ishment of villains is a near staple of the *Children's and Household Tales*, the wolf in "Little Red Cap" is doomed. As retaliation for the wolf's actions, Little Red Cap fetches some large stones and, together with her granny and the hunter, they fill the wolf's empty belly with rocks. When the wolf awak-ens and attempts to run away, the stones are so heavy that he immediately falls down dead. Once the wolf is killed, the huntsman skins the wolf and goes home with the pelt. The wolf skin thus becomes the hunter's trophy and reward for his heroic deed of saving Little Red Cap and the grandmother alive. Whereas the wolf's gruesome death is the punishment for his "mortal sin" of gluttony and seducing the protagonist, Little Red Cap's atonement for her disobedience is her frightening experience of getting swallowed up by the hairy beast and her temporary death in the wolf's dark abdomen.

The Brothers Grimm, both skilled jurists and sons of a district judge (*Amtmann*), "regarded their work as part of a social effort to foster a sense of justice among the German people" (Zipes [1987] 2003, xxviii). Indeed, the concept of justice remained a pivotal constant throughout the revisions of their tales and a fundamental aspect of their imagined happy endings. Furthermore, there is some indication that the Grimms changed the French-inspired version of "Little Red Riding Hood" to their variant "Little Red Cap" with a political agenda in mind. Already Tieck's tragedy replaced the fashionable *chaperon rouge* with a simple *rote Mütze* (red hat), which the seven-year-old protagonist received as a Christmas gift from her grandmother. Hans-Wolf Jäger has argued that Tieck's and the Grimms' use of the name *Rotkäppchen* can be read as a reference to the red Phrygian caps (*bonnet rouge*) worn by the Jacobins in honor of the French Revolution. Since the Grimms collected their tales at a time when French troops occupied the city of Kassel and the Rhineland, "Little Red Cap" may be interpreted as a commentary on the French invasion force on German soil during the Napoleonic Wars. From an anti-French perspective, the wolf symbolizes the French oppressor, a foreign, intruding Other, who destroys the virtues of Germany but could also represent a metaphor for the temptations of the revolution to liberate the German youth (Zipes 1983, 17). Jäger points to the fact that the Grimms understood Tieck's play upon the red cap and the wolf: "One can reasonably assume that the Grimms, who specifically mention Tieck's fairy tale play in their annotations to their own version, must have understood the allusions to 'red cap' and 'wolf' as referring to Jacobins, Frenchmen, and revolutionaries" (1989, 112). Jäger also emphasizes that the image of the wolf was applied to foreign rule as represented by Napoleon in other parts of early-nineteenth-century German literature. Kleist's "Hermannsschlacht" (The Battle of the Teutonburg Forest) of 1808, for instance, calls the invader the "wolf from the banks of Tiber" and in his 1809 "Germania an ihre Kinder" (Germania to her children), Kleist instigates a fight against the French, drawing on the idea of the wolf hunt (98).

The potentially political connotation of the wolf as French intruder and oppressor adds another layer of negativity to this archetypical antagonist, portrayed by Perrault and the Grimms as the great corrupter, rapist, monster, and Other. Although the image of the "bad" wolf is still present in contemporary fairy-tale retellings and media adaptations, many reimaginings of the European hypotexts feature the wolf and LRRH in a drastically different light. The Anglo-American literature of the twentieth century gave rise to a number of remarkable recastings of the traditional "Little Red Riding Hood" plot, most notably feminist and pseudofeminist updates. From Angela Carter's complex, multilayered tales "The Werewolf" and "The Company of Wolves" (1979) and Tanith Lee's dark, Gothic tale "Wolfland" (1983) to Roald Dahl's witty, satirical poem "Little Red Riding Hood and the Wolf" (1982), these revisionist hypertexts subvert the classic fairy-tale roles by empowering the heroine or challenging the wolf's status as the true beast of the story. Orenstein notes, "Some of these revisions just give the heroine a change of clothes. Others transform her entirely into a she-wolf—or bitch" (2002, 163). In several recastings, for instance Dahl's poem or Stephen Sondheim's Broadway musical *Into the Woods* (1986), it is not the hunter but the empowered heroine who skins the wolf, either herself or together with her grandmother. In the following sections I will demonstrate that increasingly since the beginning of the twenty-first century, the focus of "Little Red Riding Hood" media adaptations in the United States appears to have shifted away from the idea of the big bad beast and toward a more diversified, moderated, and also trivialized notion of lupine agency within the narrative. Because of the large number of different media adaptations, I decided to narrow my selection down to *Grimm* and *Once Upon a Time* (*OUaT*), two fairy-tale drama television series whose longevity of at least six seasons are a testament to their popularity.

Grimm (2011–17)

In North America today, many fairy-tale-inspired television series and films draw on the Grimms' "Little Red Cap" but replace the monstrous Other with a wolfish character or werewolf figure that is primarily good-natured, funny, and likable rather than threatening, gluttonous, and bestial. Through the allocation of leading roles and supporting roles, *Grimm* and *OUaT* prioritize positive portrayals of the wolf over negative portrayals. In *Grimm*, the positively depicted character Monroe (Silas Weir Mitchell) is a reformed "Blutbad" (bloodbath), or rather "Wi(e)der-Blutbad"[11] (again/against bloodbath). As one of the main characters of the show and sidekick to lead actor Nick Burkhardt (David Giuntoli), his role as human-lupine Wesen (being) features much more prominently than any antagonistic Blutbad creature in a supporting role. The show depicts Monroe as the "wolf-man" from next door who enjoys a quiet life in his suburban bachelor pad and abstains from killing humans. In one of his first encounters with Nick, Monroe blames the Grimms for the poor image of his species:

MONROE: Look, I don't want any more trouble, okay? I'm not that kind of *blutbad*. I
    don't kill anymore, I haven't in years.
NICK: Wait. What did you say you were?
MONROE: *Blutbad*. Vulgarized by your ancestors as "the big bad wolf."

Although NBC's fairy-tale-tinged crime procedural takes place in Portland, Oregon, the apparently real world is a magic realist space in which the fantastic is presented as an integral part of the human world. Nick is a descendant of the Brothers Grimm and inherited their special powers of being able to identify the supernatural Wesen, animal-like fantasy creatures partially based on fairy-tale characters. Thanks to his Grimm ancestry, Nick can use his special gift to detect the animalistic and/or monstrous faces of the Wesen who masquerade as humans so that they may live and work among them incognito. Moreover, as a person with Grimm blood, Nick possesses the unparalleled power to fight rogue Wesen to maintain harmony in society.

A closer examination of the supernatural creatures in *Grimm* reveals that they bear little resemblance to the traditional European fairy-tale characters and their Disneyfied reincarnations familiar to the series' North American viewership. Indeed, the show counteracts most audience expectations by alienating the classic fairy-tale figures in drastic but innovative ways. As I have elucidated in my chapter "Getting Real With Fairy Tales" in *Channeling Wonder* (2014), the Wesen are not what they seem on three different levels. First, their appearance is visually deceptive. Whenever the fantastic beasts experience strong emotions, for example, they lose control of their "human masks" and briefly reveal their true identity to Nick and thus to the audience. Second comes a subversion of the traditional fairy-tale character, as some Wesen are sly inversions of their classic predecessors. A fairy-tale figure expected to be friendly, harmless, beautiful, or cute may be represented as aggressive, ugly, and ferocious. In the episode "Happily Ever Aftermath" (season 1, ep. 20), for instance, an attractive, blonde woman embodying Cinderella turns into a bloodthirsty "Murciélago," a monstrous bat with glowing red eyes and vicious rows of teeth. The Three Little Pigs transform into murderous, wild boars with giant tusks and the Three Bears become savage hunters who chase after their human prey resembling Goldilocks in a rite-of-passage ritual. In contrast, a fairy-tale figure commonly thought of as fearsome, threatening, and ominous may be quite the opposite, such as Monroe the Blutbad. Third, the majority of the Wesen's German names are linguistically contorted. The German compounds exist neither in the Grimms' fairy tales nor generally in the German language—for example,

The episode "Happily Ever Aftermath" (2012) of the television series *Grimm* (2011–17) depicts Cinderella as a supernatural creature or Wesen who can shape-shift into a bestial monster bat called "Murciélago."

"Spinnetod" (spider death), "Seltenvogel" (rare bird), "Jägerbär" (hunter bear), "Bauerschwein" (farmer pig), "Hundjäger" (dog hunter), "Eisbiber" (ice beaver), and "Hexenbiest" (witch beast), among others.

NBC's *Grimm* undermines the Grimms' absolute dichotomies of good versus evil by presenting the audience with a wide spectrum of diverse supernatural creatures, whose personalities can significantly fluctuate within a certain species. This high level of diversity suggests that the show challenges, to some degree, stereotypical notions of the Other and the Grimms' clichéd generalizations of heroes and villains, or of all-innocent characters and all-brute monsters. Although in the magic realist world of *Grimm* many fantastic creatures still conform to the nature of their species—for example, the mouse-like Wesen "Maushertz" (mouse heart) are typically harmless and shy, whereas the lion-like Wesen "Löwen" (lion) are incredibly strong, fast, aggressive, competitive, and violent—these creatures are not necessarily defined by their species on a personal level. Exemplary of this independency from one's hereditary predisposition are the Blutbad Monroe and, to a certain extent, the Hexenbiest Adalind Schade (Claire Coffee), both members of the main cast. Adalind, who starts out as one of the show's perpetually mischievous Wesen, is on a character-defining roller coaster throughout the series. From her evil beginnings as wicked witch, to seeking redemption and siding with the good guys, Adalind eventually takes on the persona of a reformed villainess. After temporarily losing her powers, the rehabilitated witch falls in love with the hero, Nick, and becomes the mother of his child. The series portrays Monroe, on the other hand, from the outset as a positive character. Despite his savage Blutbad nature, Monroe epitomizes a friendly, charming, nonthreatening, and comic Other.

One could argue that Monroe has managed to tame the wild beast within by consciously shaking off the shackles of monstrosity biologically inscribed upon his body. As the viewers learn in the pilot episode, Blutbaden are not werewolves but rather wolfish creatures who can control their ability to shape-shift, the so-called *woge* (a powerful wave), between human and supernatural, animalistic form. All Wesen are liminal—that is, they display two states of existence within one physical body. Since the *woge* is impulse driven and often triggered by emotions, at times it can be difficult for Wesen to keep their human facade intact. Outside elements may also cause some Wesen to transmogrify. For example, the full moon can give Blutbaden an increased desire to *woge*. Even for Wieder Blutbaden, such as Monroe, it is difficult to control this desire and therefore they prefer to stay at home on nights of the full moon (season 2, ep. 3). Hence, *Grimm* draws on specific tropes of werewolves and lycanthropy in its creative design of certain Wesen. The episode "Lycanthropia" divulges that Lycanthropia is a rare genetic disease that mutates the DNA of a Blutbaden (season 5, ep. 14). The Lycanthrope Wesen, who are the basis for the werewolf myth, are driven temporarily insane during the three nights of the full moon each month. Another allusion to werewolf lore in the show is the use of wolfsbane, a plant reputed to repel werewolves. In the pilot episode, the protagonists Nick, his homicide partner Hank (Russell Hornsby), and Monroe rub wolfsbane on their skin to prevent a criminal Blutbad from detecting their scent.

The pilot episode opens with a quote of the Grimms' 1812 "Little Red Cap," thereby establishing a direct intertextual link with the German fairy tale: "The wolf thought to himself, what a tender young creature. What a nice plump mouthful." The trope of "Little Red Cap" resurfaces several times throughout the episode, although with great liberties. The beginning of the episode shows how a female college student, dressed in a red hooded sweatshirt, goes for a jog through the woods. She stops when she discovers a porcelain Hummel figurine (named after the German Franciscan Sister Maria Innocentia Hummel) on the path. The little figure can be interpreted as a symbol of childhood, innocence, and fragility, which "the wolf" uses to lure or distract his victim.[12] As the young woman picks up the figurine, a vicious Blutbad attacks her by dragging her off the path. Off camera, he then kills the screaming student in order to feed on her. The second victim of the criminal Blutbad is a little girl between the ages of six and eight years who is on her way to her grandfather's house after school. The girl, named Robin Howell (her first name and her initials are evocative of Red Riding Hood), also wears a red hoodie. The killer Wesen, who works as a postman in his human form, follows the girl when she deviates from the route set down by her mother to take a shortcut across a wooded park. The postman Blutbad abducts Robin by putting her in a sack and then imprisons her in a secret basement of his house in the woods. His "trophies" in the closet, all red sweatshirts and hoodies, reveal that he is a serial killer. Reminiscent of the witch in the Grimms' "Hansel and Gretel," the perpetrator confines Robin with the intention to fatten her up for a few days with chicken potpies. Twice the girl begs to go home and twice the abductor tells her that she *is* home, recalling the Freudian principle of the *unheimlich* and the notion of a home that is, in fact, an uncanny, terrifying place.

The episode plays with viewers' expectations by leading them to believe that Monroe is the "Big Bad Wolf" after Nick sees Monroe for the first time *woge* into a bestial-looking Blutbad. Because of Monroe's Otherness, his Wesen nature, Nick immediately assumes that Monroe, who happens to live in the neighborhood of the crime scene, must be the killer. Using comic relief, the episode then debunks Nick's misconception in a scene when Monroe, fully morphed, jumps through the window of his house to tackle Nick. "You shouldn't have come back!" Monroe says in a threatening manner but suddenly retracts and adds with an amused chuckle: "Okay, okay, okay, lighten up, I'm just making a point. Come on. Let's grab a brew. And by the way, you're paying for that window." Monroe invites Nick into his house for a drink, telling him that stories about the Wesen-hunting Grimms "scared the hell" out of him when he was a child. Firstly, the scene enlightens viewers about stereotypical perceptions of the Other and, secondly, it stresses that monstrosity is a subjective concept and matter of perspective, as for Blutbaden the Grimms are the true monsters.

MONROE: You people started profiling us over 200 years ago. But as you can see I am not that big, and I am done with the bad thing.

NICK: Well, how do you . . . ?

MONROE: How do I stay good? Through a strict regimen of diet, drugs and Pilates. I'm a reformed Blutbad. A Wieder Blutbad. It's a different church altogether.

NICK: Wait, you guys go to church?

MONROE: Sure. Don't you?

As it turns out, Monroe has not only eschewed his old life of hunting and killing in favor of a more peaceful existence, he is also "Mr. Nice Guy" who plays the cello, has an extensive collection of knitwear, and has a penchant for gourmet coffee, picnics, and Christmas celebrations. Furthermore, he is willing to help Nick with his police investigation to find the kidnapped girl. Thanks to Monroe's excellent sense of smell and tracking skills, he is able to lead Nick to the killer's house in the woods. Whereas in "Little Red Cap" a hunter detects the wolf, the police detectives Nick and Hank hunt down the murderous Blutbad. Hank ends up shooting the postman to death and Nick rescues Robin from the beast's basement rather than from the beast's belly.

Throughout the series, Monroe becomes a trusted member of Nick's circle of friends, assists him in solving crimes, and functions as a consultant with his knowledge pertaining to creatures of the Wesen world.

Monroe is a fan-favorite character for his very human and humorous cultural and domestic pursuits. According to an online poll titled "Who is your Favorite Character on Grimm?" of the fan website "grimmforum.com," 33.96% of the show's followers voted for Monroe, making his character the winner in this category.[13] Viewers connect with Monroe's character primarily on the basis of his funny and likable personality: "Monroe. He's hilarious and really livens the show up" (the-epic-prince, 03-12-2013); "I quite simply love Monroe . . . he's funny, awkward, smart, sarcastic, and engaging. If I knew a real-life Monroe, I would be in love with him" (busyizzy, 11-24-2014); "I have to say that Monroe is my favorite. He's the funniest character on the show!!!! He makes me laugh with tears every time!! A blutbaden and a vegan?? Very nice!!" (ioannaza, 02-01-2014). On a different website, fan "Wickett6029" writes, "Hands down, it's Monroe. . . . Monroe is the easy-going, eager-to-please, likeable guy you always hope to find in real life" and fan "TheBakercist" agrees, "He's just so likable. He goes out of his way to help his friends any way he can, no matter the cost" (reddit.com, 06-26-2015).[14] The online comments demonstrate that viewers relate to Monroe on a very personal level. They see him as more than a supernatural creature; they see him as a person.

The way in which *Grimm* humanizes fairy-tale characters, and especially the wolf from "Little Red Cap," resonates with audiences. In an online interview with Mitchell, the actor playing Monroe emphasizes that his character inspires viewer identification:

> I think in a lot of ways, Monroe is like an audience surrogate. . . . I feel like the humanity of Monroe is what's interesting about him. Although he's descendant of Blutbad, I feel like a lot of reactions to the world around [Monroe] are the reactions that normal people in the world would

have. . . . I think there's meant to be, in the writing, a relatability. I really think there's a humanity and a truthfulness to Monroe's experience that people in the audience, if they were in [Monroe's] shoes, they would have similar responses to this madness. (Mitchell 2015)

Viewers relate not only to *Grimm*'s approach of humanizing Otherness that appears monstrous, but also to the show's reality of magic realism in which fairy-tale characters face real-life struggles, such as family and relationship issues. By highlighting Monroe's interracial marriage to Rosalee Calvert (Bree Turner), who is a friendly fox-like Wesen called Fuchsbau (fox hole), *Grimm* challenges normative perspectives on same-race marriages and brings discriminatory stereotyping into keen focus. The episodes "The Wild Hunt" (season 3, ep. 12) and "Revelation" (season 3, ep. 13), for example, deal with how Monroe's Blutbad mother and father, both strong believers in a "natural law" of nonmiscegenation, are coming to terms with their son's love for a Fuchsbau Wesen. Mitchell explains:

When you get to Monroe and Rosalee, I would say absolutely that relationship is founded on real stuff and what real people go through. Because the show is meant to be about real life. . . . I do think that the Monroe-Rosalee interspecies thing and their struggles with [Monroe's] parents is totally meant to be real. That's absolutely what it's about. It's just that on *Grimm* you see it through a different lens. (Mitchell 2015)

David Greenwalt and Jim Kouf, the writers and producers of *Grimm*, revealed in an interview that they wanted to achieve a tone of reality where "the emotions feel real and the problems—at least the emotional problems—are real" (Farr 2015, 32). The writers point to the fact that Monroe, in a way, is more human than the human characters because "he is fighting his inner demons so forcefully" (Greenwalt and Kouf 2012). According to Greenwalt and Kouf, the show's entire concept is rooted in the notion of an anthropomorphized

Big Bad Wolf whose humane, charming personality topples viewers' expectations about the traditional fairy-tale villain:

> It all came from the idea that the Big Bad Wolf in the fairy tale speaks, so if the Big Bad Wolf can speak, there must be something human about him. . . . We wanted to explain him in the first episode, but we didn't want this particular one, Monroe, to be bad. We wanted that to be a twist; you think the [villain] is him, and then it turns out it's not. That's where we discovered the show, writing that scene, and all of a sudden Monroe started to talk. . . . And he was funny. (Farr 2015, 28–29)

Grimm exemplifies, as do other North American postmodern adaptations of classic fairy-tale monsters, that the balance is shifting away from a one-sided, archetypical portrayal of Otherness toward a more nuanced, many-faced Other. Already the pilot episode of the show debunks any biases of those viewers who paint fairy-tale creatures with the same broad brush. By removing the Grimmian lens through which a particular magical character becomes readily recognizable and identifiable, these retellings convey to the audience that appearances can be just as illusive as names and ancestries. At the same time, Monroe's character suggests that Otherness does not equal evilness. Although Blutbaden generally appear scary and threatening on the outside, the fantastic divergence of their Wesen form from human beings is no indication as to a Blutbad's inner disposition. Along the lines of the metaphorical phrase "don't judge a book by its cover," a fitting complement to the show could be, "don't judge a fairy-tale creature by its appearance and reputation."

Once Upon a Time (2011–18)

In 1975, American literary critic and Marxist political theorist Fredric Jameson declared the concept of evil to be at one with the category of Otherness itself. He noted, "evil characterizes whatever is radically different from me, whatever by virtue of precisely that difference seems to constitute a very real and urgent threat to my existence" (140). Jameson refers to figures—for instance, individuals speaking different languages and following different customs—in which the fundamental identity of the representative of the Other is visible. The point, as Jameson highlights in his article, "is not that in such figures the Other is feared because he [*or she*] is evil; rather he [*or she*] is evil because he [*or she*] is Other, alien, different, strange, unclean, and unfamiliar" (140). This view supports the notion that certain classic fairy-tale figures, such as the wolf in the story of "Little Red Riding Hood," are portrayed as evil *because* they are different. Further, Jameson's statement raises the question of whether those fairy-tale characters in question are depicted as villainous *because* they are outsiders of society. Indeed, many of the Grimms' fairy-tale villains appear in the roles of social outcasts or as shunned, segregated beings with an existence in isolation: the wolf is a creature dwelling in the woods who is hunted by the *Jäger*; the witch in "Hansel and Gretel" lives secluded in the forest far away from other humans; the thirteenth fairy or wise woman in "Sleeping Beauty" is excluded from the royal festivities; Rumpelstiltskin resides like a hermit in a little house at a place far behind "a high mountain at the end of the forest, where the fox and the hare bid each other good night"; and so forth. Following this train of thought, perhaps the wolf seeks to take revenge on humans for being hunted by them. The witch's cannibalistic desires and attempt to burn Gretel in the oven could be fueled by personal motivations of revenge on a society that condemns, tortures, and burns witches. The thirteenth fairy in "Sleeping Beauty" might not have cursed the princess if she had not been treated as an outcast and social misfit. The reason that Rumpelstiltskin asks for the child of the miller's daughter might be rooted in the fact that he is an odd looking, lonely creature seeking companionship, and children are, as is well known, less judgmental than adults.

Instead of a single wolf, the episode "Child of the Moon" (season 2, ep. 7) in ABC's *OUaT* features an entire wolf pack that lives in a secret den in the Enchanted Forest due to its animosity toward humans and vice versa. Inspired by the Grimms' "Little Red Cap," the episode tells the story of Ruby Lucas's (Meghan Ory's) past life and how she came to terms with being a werewolf. The character is referred to as Ruby in Storybrooke and is more commonly known as Little Red Riding Hood or simply Red in the magical realm of the Enchanted Forest. Contrary to most oral and written versions of the ATU 333 tale, Red was raised by her grandmother in a small village in the Enchanted Forest and was unknowingly plagued by a curse that transformed her into a wolf with every full moon. To prevent her from turning into a monstrous wolf, her grandmother, a.k.a. Granny (Beverley Elliott), gave her an enchanted red cloak to wear. Before learning about her true nature, Red loses control as a werewolf and unintentionally kills her own boyfriend, Peter ("Red-Handed" [season 1, ep. 15]). Driven by her shame at being a "monster" and her fear of not being able to control the beast within, Red runs away to escape a hunting party in the episode "Child of the Moon." She encounters Quinn (Ben Hollingsworth), a fellow werewolf, who brings Red to his pack, a small community of werewolves living in a subterranean hiding place in the woods. The pack's leader, Anita (Annabeth Gish), is revealed to be Red's mother. Anita tells Red that she can teach her to learn control by accepting her Otherness, the wolf, as a part of herself. Red, who no longer wants to be afraid of her lupine disposition, accepts her mother's proposition and remains with the pack.

Interestingly, the wolfish hideout is an outlandish locale that reinforces the trope of Otherness by means of its Middle-Eastern décor. The den is decorated with colorful Oriental rugs, Moroccan coffee tables, pillows, lanterns, lavish drapes, and other accessories that evoke the exoticism of the *Arabian Nights*. According to Quinn, the lair used to be the grand hall of a castle, until it sunk underground. The burning fires, incense lamps, and candles in the room add to its mystic atmosphere. It is a place where Red feels at home, being among her own kind. Her mother's appearance, dressed in a long, feathery gown complemented by a pair of feather earrings, further highlights the peregrine ambience of the wolf den. The exotic domicile of the werewolves thus reflects their own outlandish Otherness. Because these lupine people are different, they live as society's outcasts in isolation, hidden from human eyes. As such they are reminiscent of the classic historical "misfits," including freedom fighters, political opponents, dissidents, ethnic, sexual, and religious minorities, and other marginal communities who follow different norms and customs of society. Their misanthropist convictions are deeply rooted in the belief that humans vilify the werewolf because they do not understand the werewolf's nature, recalling Jameson's statement cited above. In the past, humans have hunted and killed werewolves, which, in turn, has radicalized the pack in its views about humans.

The episode debunks the notion of the traditional fairy-tale wolf as purely evil villain and challenges the viewer's understanding of monstrosity. At their first encounter in the den, Anita explains to her daughter: "Humans want us to believe we're the monsters. The moment you believe them, that's when you become one. . . . So many of us spent so much of our life suppressing the wolf. They have no idea how to control it. They just need help. Help embracing their true nature. The only way you will ever control the wolf is by accepting it as a part of you" (season 2, ep. 7). Similar to Monroe in *Grimm*, Red needs to learn how to tame the wild beast within by exercising control over her primal side. Ever since she was thirteen years old, Red has suppressed her Otherness by wearing the enchanted red cloak, but, following Anita's request, she lets go of this "safety cover" and takes off the cloak. No longer perceiving lycanthrope as a hostile force invading her body, Red willingly adopts the she-wolf inside her and runs freely with her pack through the woods. In the morning, Red remembers the entire experience and is no longer afraid of her supernatural Other half. As she is coming to terms with her new identity, however, her friend Snow White (Ginnifer Goodwin) arrives unexpectedly at the hideout. When Quinn attacks her, mistaking her for a hunter, Red rushes to protect her friend, asserting that she is innocent.

RED: No! Don't! She's not here to hurt us!

QUINN: What other reason do humans have for entering our den? (season 2, ep. 7)

From Quinn's perspective, the true monsters are the humans who hunt and kill the werewolves. As if to confirm his radicalized viewpoint, Quinn is fatally wounded by an arrow fired suddenly by a henchman of the Queen who followed Snow White to the hideout. The Queen's guards enter the den and are rapidly taken out by the pack, but a grieving Anita blames Snow White for Quinn's death and asks Red to kill her friend.

Based on Anita's extreme reaction and cruel request, the viewer learns that Red's mother is as much of a monster as the hunter who kills the were-wolf. Anita declares: "Wherever humans go, death follows. The only way to stop them, is to kill them first" (season 2, ep. 7). Although Anita con-siders herself to have mastered her brutish nature, her prejudiced hatred for humans makes Anita a different kind of beast. When Red is unwilling to carry out the barbaric deed, Anita prepares to do it herself, having Snow White tied up against a pillar and transforming into a wolf to feast on her. To save her friend from death, Red morphs into a wolf as well and lunges at her mother, causing Anita to be accidentally impaled. Red mourns her mother's tragic death and apologizes, emphasizing to her that she is not a murderer. The scene illustrates that the fairy-tale wolves in the show *OUaT* cannot be lumped together as one archetype but must be looked at on an individual basis. Whereas her grandmother wanted Red to suppress her inner wolf, her mother expected Red to be more wolf than human. In the end, Red discovers that it is alright to be both, the human and the wolf, and that she must find a way to balance the two forms so that one species does not take precedence over the other.

A second story line in "Child of the Moon" foregrounds how the percep-tion of evilness and the fear of malignity are interconnected with Otherness. Bearing Jameson's statements in mind, the episode portrays the challenges Ruby faces in Storybrooke for being different from the rest of the town's residents. For twenty-eight years the town was under the Dark Curse cast by the Evil Queen, a.k.a. Regina Mills (Lana Parrilla), which stripped the fairy-tale characters from the Enchanted Forest of their past life memories and trapped them without magic in Storybrooke, Maine. Now that the savior, Emma Swan (Jennifer Morrison), has broken the curse, Ruby remembers her werewolf nature and tragic backstory. Afraid of being "a bit rusty" for not having turned in twenty-eight years, Ruby and her grandmother take precautions by building a cage for Ruby where she may spend the night of the first full moon. Although she was previously able to control her Otherness, Ruby fears what might happen when she turns. Because she does not want to take any chances of hurting someone, Ruby asks her grandmother to lock her up overnight in the freezer of Granny's Diner. On the following day, Granny finds the freezer torn to shreds, and Ruby wakes up after a blackout in the middle of the woods. Tormented by her own doubts, Ruby worries that her wild, Other half may have done something monstrous. Her suspicions appear confirmed when Ruby, her grandmother, and the town's Sheriff, David Nolan, a.k.a. Prince Charming (Josh Dallas), find the dead body of Ruby's friend Billy (Jarod Joseph) at the docks. Convinced of her guilt Ruby screams in horror: "It was the wolf! It was me!" David's insistence that "It had to be something else" meets with Ruby's denial, "No, I did this! We both know it" (season 2, ep. 7).

In the Storybrooke story line of the episode, Ruby undergoes a significant identity crisis because she believes that being a monstrosity is at the core of her being. Given that she is a werewolf and thus different from all other inhabitants of the town, Ruby assumes that she must have killed Billy and that her inner beast has won the upper hand over her human side. Based on this conviction, Ruby seeks to atone for her "evil" deeds by delivering herself to the wrath of the townspeople. In a conversation with her friend Belle (Emilie de Ravin), Ruby reveals that she thinks she deserves to be punished by death to make amends for her past actions:

RUBY: I am a monster. And that's why I need to make sure I don't ever hurt anyone again. . . . The mob wants a wolf, I'm going to give them one. I need to pay for all I've done.

BELLE: And they'll kill you!

RUBY: Isn't that what I deserve?

Ruby's plan to give herself up to the citizens of Storybrooke is tantamount to a suicidal act. She considers herself to be a threat to society and believes the townspeople's fear of her to be justified. Although there is no evidence that ties the young woman to Billy's death, most inhabitants of the town, including Ruby, simply presume that she is the killer. Thus, the episode sheds a critical light on prejudice and bias against Otherness, which is rooted in blind or irrational fear of the unknown, the strange, and the alien. Such a fear, especially when associated with the domain of perceived Otherness, is generally described as xenophobic.

Peter Schuck has defined the term "xenophobia" as "an undifferentiated fear of foreigners or strangers as such" (1998, 5). He suggests that sources of xenophobia may be congenital and therefore reflect "some deeply embedded, universal feature of human psychology and identity by which individuals seek to distance themselves from those whom they define as 'others' or 'strangers'" (5). Further, Gerard Delanty and Peter Millward have argued that fear differs from anxiety in that fear is based on an external threat to the self whereas anxiety "seems to be without an object" (2007, 144). They continue to argue that contemporary racist discourses reflect a connection between anxiety and fear of the Other (144). Although Ruby cannot be considered a foreigner, she is, after all, a member of the fairy-tale community in both realms, the magical Enchanted Forest as well as the nonmagical Storybrooke, the townspeople nevertheless view her as an outsider. Their fear and anxiety of Ruby's Otherness find expression in what can be interpreted as a racist attitude. The leader of the riotous mob, Albert Spencer, a.k.a. King George (Alan Dale), objectifies Ruby by referring to her as a "thing," thereby stripping her of her human identity. When David promises Ruby that he will find whoever killed Billy, Albert answers: "You already have. That thing. That she-wolf. . . . Hand that over to me, and let the town decide her fate" (season 2, ep. 7). Albert, who represents the voice of the radicalized people in town, refrains from calling Ruby by her name and degrades her from person to animal and property. His intimidating remark to David, "This town is bigger than you think. I start telling people that you're putting their lives in danger," evokes xenophobic rhetoric and propaganda about the perceived threat originating from foreigners.

Whereas in the Grimms' fairy tale "Little Red Cap" the wolf becomes the target of only a single *Jäger*, an entire mob of angry people chase after Ruby in what is reminiscent of a witch hunt. Spurred on by their leader, Albert's followers gather around him in front of the sheriff's station, where he incites the crowd to hatred and violence in the form of ruthless self-administered justice. His diatribe, "We won't cower in fear of this creature any longer! We know who she is, we know where she's hiding. So why is she still alive?" is met with the crowd's cheers in agreement. Albert's rhetorical question, "How many more people have to die . . . ?" not only draws on the fear of the townspeople but also fuels it by suggesting that their lives are in direct danger as long as the wolf exists. Armed with burning torches, baseball bats, pitchforks, rifles, and other weapons, the people have formed a systematic lynch mob, which intends to take justice into its own hands. At first the mob storms the sheriff's station in the hope of finding Ruby locked up in one of the jail cells. But the jail cells turn out to be empty and so the "hunters" roam the streets of Storybrooke until they find Ruby transformed into a wolf and corner her in a backyard with dumpsters. Albert tries to shoot the wolf dead but Granny intervenes just in time and shoots the gun out of his hand with her crossbow. David, who represents the law of the town as sheriff, manages to gain the crowd's attention and deescalates the situation by uncovering the truth about Billy's death. He clarifies that Albert killed Billy in cold blood and hid the evidence along with Ruby's magical red cloak in the trunk of his car. By making the murder look like it was done by a wolf, Albert tried to frame Ruby for Billy's death. In conformity with the Grimms' fairy tales, the episode thus broaches the issue of justice and ensures that righteousness triumphs over blatant injustice in the end. However, unlike in the traditional stories, where villainy is met with severe penalties, Albert, by comparison, receives a very mild form of punishment when David punches him in the face and knocks him to the ground.

On the basis of Ruby's positively drawn character in *OUaT*, the episode critiques ignorant prejudging of the Other and centers on the message of tolerance within the complexities of subjectivity and the self-Other dyad. After exposing the true murderer and appeasing the mob, David addresses the wolf directly. He reassures Ruby that she is not a beast, since Albert did the horrific killing: "Don't let him trick you into thinking you're a monster" (season 2, ep. 7). David reminds Ruby that despite her monstrous looks, she is good on the inside and that she is in control of the wolf. He then throws the enchanted red hood over Ruby, transforming her back into a human being. At the end of the episode, a rehabilitated, self-confident Ruby offers emotional encouragement and support to David, who is facing problems of his own. Now that Ruby has accepted her inner wolf anew, she enjoys her animalistic side by deciding to go for a run under the full moon. Brittany Warman has pointed out that although *OUaT* is not the first adaptation of the fairy tale to make LRRH herself a werewolf, "it is perhaps the most popular and wide-reaching one to do so," besides the other major contender, *The Company of Wolves* (1984) based on Angela Carter's short stories (Warman 2016, 101). Although the character of LRRH colliding with the archetype of the wolf is not frequently seen in either oral or written versions of the traditional fairy tale, there is a twenty-first-century cinematic production in North American popular culture that does make use of this idea: Catherine Hardwicke's *Red Riding Hood*.[15]

Red Riding Hood (2011)

Fairy-tale scholars Pauline Greenhill and Steven Kohm have referred to the film *Red Riding Hood* as "teensploitation/werewolfsploitation," thus drawing attention to its exploitative, sensationalist, and lurid nature (2013, 89). To get a better understanding of how these terms relate to Hardwicke's production, it is helpful to consider the definition of the terms first. Merriam-Webster's Collegiate Dictionary defines "teensploitation" as "the exploitation of teen-agers by producers of teen-oriented films."[16] The genre, which was first labeled in 1982, has also been described by Maureen Callahan as "movies about teenagers made for teenagers but watched by everybody" (1999, 64), emphasizing its wide popular appeal beyond youth. The plots of such movies usually revolve around rebellious youngsters tearing at the moral fabric of society and struggling to navigate through life's challenges, including sex, drugs, alcohol, and crime. For these commonly low-budget teensploitation films and television shows, "filmmakers assemble a delirious barrage of beasts, road trips, shower scenes, drinking games, pillow fights, pot smoking, superbabes, and raging house parties . . ." (Callahan 1999, 64). Although teensploitation films have been a staple of North American cinema since as early as the 1940s and 1950s—as, for example, with Gene Fowler's *I Was a Teenage Werewolf*, a 1957 horror film starring Michael Landon as a troubled teenager—recent decades have seen an increasing trend of romance-loaded, at times schmaltzy teen films based on fairy-tale retellings. Examples range from *Ella Enchanted* (2004), *A Cinderella Story* (2004), and *Beastly* (2011) to *Jack the Giant Slayer* (2013) and Disney Channel's television film *Descendants* (2015). Other fairy-tale adaptations on the silver screen, such as *The Brothers Grimm* (2005), *Snow White and the Huntsman* (2012), and *Hansel & Gretel: Witch Hunters* (2013), which thrive on action, violent combat, and spectacle, may be described as rooted in "teensploitation" due to their audience appeal. As David Gritten stressed in his review of *Hansel & Gretel: Witch Hunters* for the *Telegraph* (2013): "Here is a film that knows its target audience: boys in their late teens with a taste for gore, violence, exploding bullets and shape-shifting special effects."

Greenhill and Kohm's use of the term "werewolfsploitation" is a neologism that has, up to this date, no clear definition in scholarship. Therefore, I derive from the more common expression "exploitation films" that werewolfsploitation refers to films that attempt to succeed financially by exploiting the trope of the werewolf. This form of exploitation happens when a film promises its audience the shocking spectacle of lurid, horrific, gory, or sexuality-infused tales of werewolves. A popular, albeit romanticized example of werewolfsploitation that comes to mind is *The Twilight Saga* film series based on Stephenie Meyer's novels. The five romance fantasy films feature the character of Jacob Black (Taylor Lautner), whose role as sexy, caring, and protective werewolf is famous among young adults of today's consumer culture. The notion of the attractive, affectionate werewolf radically undermines the imagination of the wolf as sexually aggressive male and evil rapist. Already Angela Carter's werewolf stories in *The Bloody Chamber and Other Stories* (1979) break with the tradition of portraying the woman as a victim of lupine violence. At the end of Carter's tale "The Company of Wolves," a subversive recasting of LRRH, the wolf is no longer the "carnivore incarnate" but a "tender wolf," and the girl representing Red Riding Hood contentedly falls asleep in his arms (118). At the same time, the story is one of female empowerment: "Since her fear did her no good, she ceased to be afraid . . . she freely gave the kiss she owed him . . . she knew she was nobody's meat" (220). In the narrative, the female protagonist actively seeks out the company of the wolf, is confident in her own sexuality, and thus robs the wolf of his power, essentially "taming" him. This clear break with the conventions of the traditional fairy tale à la Grimm or Perrault increases the effect of a reformulation and reassessment of the monstrous Other.

Since Catherine Hardwicke moved on from directing the first *Twilight* adaptation in 2008 to *Red Riding Hood* in 2011, it is perhaps not surprising that both films draw on similar Gothic fairy-tale elements, including dark forests and spaces, bestiality, bodily mutilation and dismemberment, death, and murder. *Red Riding Hood* begins with a voice-over narrated by protagonist Valerie (Amanda Seyfried) alias Red Riding Hood; hence the story is told from the interior perspective of an adolescent female. Hardwicke's approach evokes the fairy-tale storytelling format, on one hand, and promotes intimacy with the viewers on the other. Valerie, a headstrong teenage girl, lives with her parents, Cesaire (Billy Burke) and Suzette (Virginia Madsen), and older sister, Lucie (Alexandria Maillot), in the medieval village of Daggerhorn, which has long been savaged by a werewolf. Valerie's romantic interest is her childhood friend, the woodcutter Peter (Shiloh Fernandez), but her parents have arranged for Valerie to marry the wealthy Henry Lazar (Max Irons). Unwilling to lose each other, Valerie and Peter are planning to run away together when they learn that Lucie has been killed by the werewolf. Hungry for revenge, the townspeople call on Father Solomon (Gary Oldman), a world-renowned werewolf hunter, to help them kill the beast. Following scapegoating dynamics, the tyrannical Solomon turns neighbor against neighbor by propagating that the werewolf must be one of the town's inhabitants. Valerie, who discovers that she can communicate with the wolf telepathically, is stigmatized and persecuted as a witch. After Henry and Peter join forces to help Valerie escape, she suspects that the werewolf could be someone she loves. Finally, she learns that the werewolf terrorizing the village is her father, Cesaire. In a moment of rage about his wife's infidelity he had murdered his illegitimate daughter, Lucie, and tried to connect with Valerie because she shares his genetic ability of lycanthrope. Before Peter can kill the werewolf, he is bitten and is thus cursed to become a werewolf himself. Before Peter departs in order to learn how to control his lupine impulses, Peter and Valerie consummate their relationship. Eventually, after many months, Peter returns to Valerie, who is seen holding a baby, which is her baby with Peter.

Hardwicke's cinematic adaptation conflates elements of classic fairy-tale versions of LRRH and the Grimms' "The Wolf and the Seven Young

Kids" with popular lycan-lore. The plot parallels Perrault's story in that the film is fraught with sexual innuendo, underlining the sexual awakening of an attractive young woman and the transition from childhood to adult womanhood. The film references the Grimms' version in which the mother cautions Little Red Cap to be obedient: "My mother always told me, 'Don't talk to strangers. Go get water and come straight home.' I tried to be a good girl and do what she said. . . . Believe me, I tried." Already the narrative introduction to the film foreshadows Peter's fate of becoming a werewolf, since he is identified as "the seducer" who encourages Valerie to "stray from the path." Valerie's voice-over explains: "I know good girls aren't supposed to hunt rabbits or go into the woods alone. But since we were kids, [Peter] always had a way of making me wanna break the rules." Other characteristic symbols and references to the traditional tale include Valerie's obligatory red cloak, her lonely grandmother living in the woods, and the distinctive dialog between the girl and the "old woman" in one of Valerie's nightmarish dreams:

> "Grandmother, what big eyes you have."
> "The better to see you with, my dear."
> "Grandmother, what big ears you have."
> "The better to hear you with, my dear."
> "What big teeth you have."
> "The better to eat you with, my dear."

Valerie is not the naïve, little girl from the Grimms' version but a young, alert woman who is suspicious of the people in her surroundings. She shows initiative by visiting her grandmother to find out whether or not she is the werewolf and later actively tries to kill Peter when she (wrongly) suspects him. The film's move beyond gender norms, however, is limited, in that Valerie cannot kill the wolf, Cesaire, on her own but only with Peter's help. The woodcutter Peter thus also represents the *Jäger* and savior of Red Riding

Hood. Together they cut open Cesaire's belly, fill it with rocks, sew it back together, and then dump the body in a lake, evoking the wolf's drowning in "The Wolf and the Seven Young Kids."

Red Riding Hood portrays the antagonistic lycanthrope as a ferocious beast and monster, about twice the size of an ordinary wolf, with intimidating yellow eyes, pitch-black fur, and a snarling muzzle filled with sharp fangs. This supernatural creature not only possesses super strength, speed, and agility but also heightened senses because the werewolf can see, hear, and smell better than humans even when shape-shifted to human form. Bryan Senn notes that the attempts of the terrified villagers to appease the beast with sacrifices of livestock recall "the time when early man not only feared the predator but turned that terror into veneration, making the beasts that preyed upon them into deities—creatures to be feared but also to be appeased" (2017, 183). In comparison with the classic fairy-tale wolf, *Red Riding Hood* elevates the werewolf to a preternatural being endowed with demonic powers. The fact, that the werewolf cannot walk on "holy ground," can be hurt by silver, has a contagious bite, and appears only at night ties the creature to the medieval belief of lycanthrope as expression of witchcraft and satanic forces. Hardwicke highlighted in an interview that the beastly creature in *Red Riding Hood* varies greatly from the teen-friendly wolves in the *Twilight* films: "Our wolf is different. . . . He only comes out at night, so you don't see him in the day, and he's ferocious; he is not like the good guy you can go up and pet" (Senn 2017, 184). And yet the question arises whether the werewolf is the true villain in the story. Determined to discover the wolf's human identity at all costs, Father Solomon's ruthless character emerges as a dangerous beast that is, perhaps, even more threatening to the townspeople and their community than the werewolf.

The figure of the despotic werewolf-hunter Solomon, for whom the end justifies the means, adds a political layer to Hardwicke's cinematic fairy-tale retelling. In his merciless approach to exposing the lupine perpetrator, Solomon resorts to aggressive tactics of torture, denunciation, fear, deprivation, intimidation, and public humiliation. Reminiscent of a Nazi hunting for Jews, Solomon tramples on the villagers' human rights and freedoms ("Your homes will be searched, your secrets brought to light") and incites them against each other by sowing the seeds of discord. Under his tyrannical influence on the town, neighbors suspect neighbors, friends mistrust friends, and Valerie doubts her own grandmother as well as her true love, Peter. Contrary to his name, which evokes "peace" and "wisdom," Solomon's blind arrogance and pride have abysmal consequences for the village, culminating in the torture and death of the young autistic man, Claude (Cole Heppell). Solomon tosses him into a large, elephant-shaped, brazen bull with a fire burning beneath its belly as punishment for his alleged studies of the dark arts. Senn elucidates on the politically charged subtext of the scene, "Here Solomon almost becomes worse than the Wolf, the cure turning out worse than the disease. Such as metaphor solidifies when seen through the fear-clouded lens of the post-9/11 climate" (2017, 184). Indeed, Hardwicke sees the paranoia among the villagers that creeps in when Solomon begins his werewolf hunt in a political context: "When Gary Oldman [Solomon] arrives he's almost like Homeland Security, 'Turn in your friends if you see anything suspicious'" (Keegan 2010). The currency and relevance of *Red Riding Hood*'s subliminal criticism of American politics become evident when seen in the light of the immigration ban ordered by President Donald Trump in early 2017.

Hardwicke neither romanticizes lycanthropy in *Red Riding Hood*, as it may appear in the *Twilight* films, nor does she establish that werewolves are evil creatures by design. Rather, it depends on the character traits of the person carrying the werewolf gene whether she or he becomes a monster or not. For the genetic carrier, lycanthropy can represent either a gift or a curse. Because Valerie unknowingly inherited the werewolf gene, she possesses the ability to telepathically converse with her lupine father. Hardwicke thus conflates the positively coded figure of the fairy-tale heroine LRRH with the negatively coded antagonist of the wolf, thereby unsettling the boundaries between self and Other. Whereas Cesaire believes his condition is a gift and tries to convince his daughter to accept it, Valerie rejects his offer, seeing her father as a diabolical person:

CESAIRE: It's a gift. It's a gift my father gave to me that now I can give to you. I'm stronger than he was, you'll be even stronger than me. Think about it. We will be invincible.

VALERIE: There must be a God, because you're the devil.

Cesaire turns out to be a monster not because he is a werewolf but because he is a power-hungry, revengeful, bitter alcoholic. The film implies that Cesaire, consumed by his lust for power, eventually killed his own father, perhaps to get rid of competition and take over his territory. Presumably because he had difficulty earning enough money and felt disrespected, Cesaire fell into drinking. Although he repeatedly states that he loved his family, he kills Lucie in a rage when he finds out that she is not his daughter, murders his own mother to protect his secret identity, and claws his wife's face in revenge for her betrayal.

Similar to *Grimm* and *OUaT*, Hardwicke's fairy-tale adaptation *Red Riding Hood* exemplifies that lycanthropy alone does not make a monster and that the beastly Other can indeed be controlled and "tamed." In his struggle with Cesaire, Peter is bitten and thus contracts the werewolf magic. However, because Peter is a good-hearted, brave man who is in love with Valerie, he does not turn into a bloodthirsty, ferocious werewolf like Cesaire. At the end of the film, Peter departs in order to learn how to tame his inner beast, vowing to return only when he's able to ensure Valerie's safety. The fact that Peter does return some time later proves that he has gained full control of his werewolf nature. Peter arrives at Grandmother's cabin in the woods, where Valerie now lives, on the night of a full moon. Valerie hears Peter growl, turns around, and sees him in his wolf form. She smiles at the creature because she recognizes her true love and knows that he is a threat neither to her nor to the baby she holds in her arms. Since the film suggests that the werewolf gene is hereditary, the baby, as Peter's firstborn, most likely inherited the magic, leaving the viewer to speculate on whether the future generation of the fairy-tale wolf will embrace or reject its Otherness.

In academic scholarship, *Red Riding Hood* has not only been criticized for its werewolfsploitation (Greenhill and Kohm 2013) and lack of "feminist impulse" (Sue Short 2015, 150) but also been cited as an example of how contemporary filmmakers hype their fairy-tale productions by using mass media to exploit the general public's interest in fairy tales. Most notably, Jack Zipes bemoans the fact that Hardwicke's film omits any hints that LRRH "is a serious and complicated tale about rape," pedophilia, and manners (2015b, 214). Hardwicke, he condemns, "is all about hype, herself, and the spectacle" (2015b, 216). In his critique, Zipes claims that *Red Riding Hood*'s "theme-park sets, stereotyped characters, and father-turned-werewolf gave rise to a ridiculous, convoluted plot that bored audiences" (2015b, 216). Although the cultural value of Hardwicke's film is certainly debatable, whether it is a shallow product that will not last, as Zipes argues, his criticism concerning the media hyping of fairy tales appears justified. In today's consumer-oriented culture, individual filmmakers, production companies, and large corporations, such as Disney, generate profit-driven paratexts, especially via multimedia platforms, including radio, film, television, and the internet, to market specific fairy-tale adaptations to the masses. The hyping of new fairy-tale reimaginings as extraordinary achievements, whether in the form of television series, films, books, musicals, or other products, "cheapen the meaning" of the Grimms' fairy tales, according to Zipes (2015b, 213). Also questionable is Disney's approach of infantilizing certain fairy-tale characters to appeal to a child audience. Besides *Red Riding Hood*, Zipes touches on *Hoodwinked Too! Hood vs. Evil* (2011) as another example of an overhyped fairy-tale film. This computer-animated film is a sequel to the 2005 *Hoodwinked!*, which retells LRRH as a police investigation, using flashbacks to show multiple characters' points of view. Following in the footsteps of the animated *Shrek* films (the first two parts were released in 2001 and 2004, respectively), which feature a mash-up of infantilized, comedic fairy-tale characters, *Hoodwinked!* presents its spectators with a similar type of humorous fairy-tale parody, turning away from the well-known archetype of the Big Bad Wolf.

Hoodwinked! (2005)

Structurally inspired by nonlinear crime dramas, such as *Rashômon* (1950), *Pulp Fiction* (1994), *Run Lola Run* (1998), and *Memento* (2000), *Hoodwinked* is an action-comedy that targets an audience of young and adult viewers alike. Director and cowriter Cory Edwards approached *Hoodwinked!* as a cop story, only with little critters in the woods. Popular cartoons and comedic characters from shows such as *Bugs Bunny, Road Runner, Rocky and Bullwinkle,* and *The Muppets* have all served as inspirations for the film. To differentiate the production from the previously released, fairy-tale-themed *Shrek* films, Edwards explained in an interview, the world of *Hoodwinked!* is one without magic, wizards, or fairies (Goodman 2006). And yet, the crime drama unfolds in a fantastic reality where animals are anthropomorphized, live double lives, and coexist, more or less harmonically, with people. Further, there are several marvelous moments in the film that recall traditional fairy-tale dynamics. A prominent example is the close relationship between the heroine and the birds in the forest, which come to her aid whenever needed. In one scene, Red Puckett (Anne Hathaway), a.k.a. LRRH, uses her red hood, which turns out to be carried by flying hummingbirds, as a ruse to distract the wolf chasing after her. In a different scene, hummingbirds are lifting up Red on her bicycle to help her safely cross a river in the woods.

The film begins with Red's discovery of the Big Bad Wolf in disguise as Granny. At that moment, her grandmother, all tied up, jumps out of the closet and an axe-wielding woodsman bursts through the window, startling everyone. The police arrive at the scene and begin to investigate the case, interrogating everyone involved in the incident. Red begins by explaining that she was delivering goodies for her grandmother and that in the attempt to save her Granny's recipes from the so-called Goodie Bandit she came across a very interrogative wolf. Although the wolf went after her, she managed to escape and eventually reached her Granny's house, where the wolf already waited in ambush. As the criminal investigator, Detective Nicky Flippers (David Ogden Stiers), turns to the wolf, Wolf W. Wolf (Patrick Warburton) reveals that he is an investigative reporter. In his search for the true identity of the Goodie Bandit he believed that Red and Granny were the culprits. He went undercover in an attempt to get to the bottom of the mystery, hoping to question the girl and her grandmother and to find incriminating evidence. In the following interrogations, Kirk the Woodsman (Jim Belushi) is revealed to be an aspiring actor whose bursting through the window was a mere accident, and Granny Puckett (Glenn Close) is exposed as an extreme sports enthusiast who participated in a ski race earlier that day. An accident with her parachute left her all tied up in her own closet. Detective Flippers determines that the true Goody Bandit is the bunny Boingo (Andy Dick), who was present in all stories told. However, Boingo already got his hands on Granny's recipes and fled to his secret hideout at a cable car station. Red, Wolf, Granny, and the Woodsman join forces to bring down the criminal and his evil henchmen. Later on, the Woodsman has a successful career as a member of a yodeling troupe, and Red, Granny, the Wolf, and his sidekick, Twitchy (Cory Edwards), a hyperactive squirrel, are enlisted by the police investigator to join a crime-solving organization called the Happily Ever After Agency.

The presence of the Woodsman in *Hoodwinked!* and the happy ending for the lead protagonists suggests that the story of Red Puckett is very loosely based on the Grimms' version of LRRH. The filmmakers, however, decided to design their characters in opposition to their Grimmian templates. Hence, the weak old grandmother turns into an action hero who does extreme sports, and the savior figure, the patriarchal woodsman, turns into a "big child" who does not know how to tie his own shoes. As one of the filmmakers, Preston Stutzman, explained: "We didn't want to make her [Red Riding Hood] boring, or too innocent, or always in distress, so we gave her a sort of James Dean quality. She just wants to get out of town, go find her way" (Goodman 2006). Because the filmmakers intended the film to be about surprises and secret lives, they gave the Grimms' lupine villain a dramatic makeover as well and decided that he should be one of the good guys. Another filmmaker, Todd Edwards, had the idea of endowing Wolf W. Wolf with a dry, deadpan humor based on the *Los Angeles Times* reporter Irwin M. "Fletch" Fletcher, a character played by Chevy Chase in the comedy action-thriller *Fletch* (1985). Similar to the outfit sported by Chevy Chase, Wolf wears a Lakers jersey and a faded blue hoodie, giving his character a relaxed, casual, and easygoing dimension, which contradicts with the wolf's image as wild animal. The parallels to Fletch do not stop at Wolf's wardrobe and his job as investigative reporter. Like the hero of the '80s classic comedy who is known for his phenomenal abilities as improvisational actor, assuming zany false identities to help gain information, so does Wolf take on numerous disguises in *Hoodwinked!* His ingenuity comes to the fore when he masquerades as Granny Puckett, a Turkish aristocrat with moustache, monocle, and fez, a chef, an African American basketball player, Health Inspector Rick Shaw, a sheep, and a building inspector. Because of his low-key nature, Edwards paired Wolf with his foil, Twitchy the squirrel, who is very fast and upbeat.

Hoodwinked! debunks the viewer's assumption of the Big Bad Wolf by portraying him as neither bad nor big. Instead, Wolf's personality could be described as uncouth and blunt but not without a certain amount of amusing charm. His sarcasm and witty remarks in the film $A=\pi r2$ a main source of comic relief. On the one hand, Wolf is smart and resourceful when things go wrong, but on the other hand, he is portrayed as being slightly clumsy at times. When he chases after Red in the woods, for instance, he stumbles over a tree trunk and, gasping for air, falls to the ground in a very unathletic manner. He then continues racing after the red coat in front of him until he runs over the edge of a cliff and plunges into a river. Although Wolf might seem rough on the outside, he is essentially good on the inside, with his heart in the right place. In contrast to most literary versions of LRRH, Wolf means no harm to Red and simply follows her through the woods because she is his lead suspect, and he tries to get as much information from her as possible. In one scene, a series of events leads to the point where Red feels threatened by Wolf. She mistakes the growling of his empty stomach for an aggressive, menacing growl and thinks he is about to attack her when his tail accidentally gets stuck in the winding sprockets of a camera, causing him to scream at her ferociously.

Those audience members who only know the Grimms' version of ATU 333 might be surprised by the way *Hoodwinked!* destabilizes the traditional roles of predator and victim in the following scene. When Wolf catches up to Red in the woods, it becomes apparent that he is physically inferior to the self-confident, feisty girl. In a sudden act of what she thinks to be self-defense, Red first uses a spray bottle of "Wolf Away" to temporarily blind her opponent and then beats him up severely with some very impressive karate skills. A short interception of the scene shows the viewer a picture of Red in her martial arts uniform that reads "Red Puckett: Forest Regional Karate Champion." Clearly, the anthropomorphized, tamed "beast" is no match for this emancipated, powerful, postmodern heroine who knows how to make quite a fool of the wolf. The film further accentuates the jarring juxtaposition between the subdued wolf and the fierce girl, between the "tamed Other" and the "wild self," by having Detective Flippers interrupt Wolf's narration of the events with the sneering rhetorical question "So you really took a beating . . . from a little girl?" The fact that the classic villain is recast in the role of innocent victim or perhaps misunderstood character encourages audiences to reflect on the ways in which *Hoodwinked!* subverts traditional fairy-tale dynamics of ATU 333. The frequent interruptions by the criminal investigator also serve to remind viewers that they are watching a story from a specific character's retrospective point of view, "subtly problematizing the nature of truth itself" (Greenhill and Kohm 2013, 96).

On the whole, the film portrays Wolf's character as courageous, clever, analytic, creative, determined, and also courteous at times. Most importantly, though, he is the intellectual mastermind behind the mission to rescue Red from the hands of Boingo and his malicious henchmen. First, Wolf has the ingenious idea to give Twitchy some coffee so that the hyperactive squirrel is fast enough to catch up with the police and inform them that they are going the wrong way to catch the Goodie Bandit. Then, Wolf shares his plan with Granny and Kirk the Woodsman on how to bring down the criminals. Although the rescue mission of Red is a team effort, Wolf's actions and ideas as team leader make him stand out. He thus fulfills the role of the Grimms' helpful *Jäger*, the male protector who saves LRRH. Because Wolf has a talent for masquerade and impersonation, he disguises himself as a building inspector and instructs Kirk to dress up as one of Boingo's accomplices. Like a mentor, Wolf also provides reassuring guidance to the aspiring actor in a motivational pep talk: "You're an actor, right? So this is your big part. This is the role of a lifetime. Make them believe in you. Don't act like an evil henchman, be an evil henchman. Got it?" When the Woodsman fails in his performance, however, Wolf takes over by posing as building inspector to save the situation and manages to distract Boingo. It seems only fitting that the positively coded wolf-turned-rescuer joins the police force at the end of the film, along with Red and Granny, to help hunt down villains.

Because Wolf is a fairy-tale hero rather than a villain, one might be tempted to assume that there is nothing wolfish—that is, nothing animalistic or wild—left to his character's nature. Moreover, since all anthropomorphized animals in the reimagined fairy-tale universe of *Hoodwinked* either talk, sing, behave, or dress as humans do, it appears that the filmmakers have stripped the critters completely of their primal attributes. However, one scene where Wolf goes undercover as a sheep in disguise reveals that he still possesses primal instincts that hark back to the Grimms' predatory antagonist. In a conversation with one of his informants, a sheep named Woolworth (Chazz Palminteri), Wolf reminds the perky ungulate of the predator-prey relationship between them by stressing, "You're looking pretty tasty." He then returns to his companion, Twitchy, with the words, "Those sheep made me hungry. After this, we're grabbing a bite." What seems to be a rather insignificant scene in the film is, in effect, a crucial detail regarding Wolf's character, which demonstrates, firstly, that he is a carnivore with an appetite for sheep and, secondly, that he is able to control his natural urges. Thus, the importance of exercising control over the lupine drives connects the animated, infantilized, comedic wolf with the lycanthropes previously analyzed in this chapter, from Monroe in *Grimm* and Red in *OUaT* to Peter in *Red Riding Hood*. This suggests that the tamed, monstrous Other in contemporary North American popular culture is inevitably linked to self-discipline exercised by the "beast" through intrinsic motivation rather than extrinsic forces or influences.

Whereas in the Grimms' tales magical Otherness can be rehabilitated only through physical transformation triggered by a "normal" member of society, fairy-tale retellings today focus primarily on the mental attitude or personality of the individual Other rather than physical looks. Besides *Hoodwinked!*, a prime example is the animated *Shrek* film series, which "elevates beastliness and monstrosity into a position of moral superiority" (Tatar 2015, 4). These films subvert the traditional role of the monstrous Other, here the socially inept green ogre, Shrek (Mike Myers), as villain by recasting him in the role of hero. Against fairy-tale conventions and Disney's gender paradigms, Princess Fiona (Cameron Diaz) magically transforms into an ogress instead of a human being, reminding the viewer that the perception of beauty remains in the eye of the beholder. DreamWorks' *Shrek* thus undermines any expectations established by classic tales, including "The Frog King" and "Beauty and the Beast," and invites reconsiderations about the binary oppositions good/evil, beauty/ugly, normal/abnormal, and self/Other. Contrary to the Grimmian model of enchantment and disenchantment, Fiona's external transformation is triggered by the monstrous Other when Shrek gives her true love's kiss. The magical power of the kiss turns Fiona permanently into her real self, which is her ogre nature. Shrek's transformation, on the other hand, is an internal one as he changes gradually from a grumpy, reclusive grouch to a life-embracing, happy, family-oriented ogre who is beloved among the local villagers.

In the postmodern fairy-tale realms of *Shrek* or *Hoodwinked!*, Otherness is either accepted or rejected not based on appearance but based on character. Following *Shrek*'s approach of character reversal, the Big Bad Wolf, belittled in the films as "Wolfie" (Aron Warner), represents a good fairy-tale figure. Like Shrek, he lives in the swamp, a place of exile for outsiders of society, ever since LRRH sold him to the military. Hence, from the outset, his background story marks him as a victim rather than a perpetrator. Interestingly, Wolfie shares many characteristics with Wolf W. Wolf from *Hoodwinked!*, being a laid-back, funny, calm, and mature creature with a passion for masquerade. He helps the other protagonists to defeat the evil Fairy Godmother in *Shrek 2* and helps to save Shrek from being killed by disguising himself as a bear. Thus, in many ways he exhibits the same heroic and bold traits as his investigative, crime-solving "successor." However, the two wolf characters differ somewhat in comedic tone, design, and trivialization. The makers of *Shrek 2* (2004) even charged one particular bed scene of Wolfie with odd sexual innuendo or overtones. When Prince Charming enters the chamber in the tower where Princess Fiona was imprisoned, he pulls back the gossamer curtains to find Wolfie in her bed instead. Dressed in grandmother's pink nightgown and nightcap, the Big Bad Wolf is reading a magazine called "Pork Illustrated." Most adult viewers will recognize this magazine, alluding to "Sports Illustrated," as a special magazine for wolves. Subtitled "Bacon in the Sun," the cover shows a female pig, wearing a red

Shrek 2 (2004) trivializes the Big Bad Wolf as "Wolfie" (Aron Warner) and endows the character with odd sexual innuendo.

bikini and posing at a tropical beach, an image that parodies the sexualized female athletes on the cover of "Sports Illustrated." Next to Wolfie lies an open snack bag of bacon-flavored, hot and spicy, fried pork rinds. The image conflates the wolf's natural desire as a carnivore with his sexual appetite for, bizarrely, female pigs.

As the writer-director of *Hoodwinked!*, Edwards strived for a different style of humor than *Shrek*, choosing to create a film that is less cynical and less of a fairy-tale satire. On his personal website, Edwards dissociates the characters and comedic tone of *Hoodwinked!* from the fairy-tale parodies of the *Shrek* films: "We went to great lengths to distance our film from Shrek's humor. . . . I would hope that *Hoodwinked!* and its sequels will be seen as trying to do something genuine with its characters, rather than look for the next joke at the expense of innocence. . . . I'd like to think that Red and her friends are teaching your kids some uncynical, real lessons" (coryedwards 2007). Edwards shares the view of James Poniewozik, who discusses the dangers of a culture where fairy-tale parodies are being substituted for the classic fairy tales:

There is something a little sad about kids growing up in a culture where their fairy tales come pre-satirized, the skepticism, critique and revision having been done for them by the mama birds of Hollywood. Isn't irony supposed to derive from having something to rebel against? . . . Isn't there room for an original, nonparodic fairy story that's earnest without being cloying, that's enlightened without saying wonder is for suckers? (Poniewozik 2007)

Although Edwards does not want to see *Hoodwinked!* lumped in with *Shrek*, both films present their audiences with a trivialized, infantilized, and belittled form of Otherness. In fact, the films reduce the entire art form of the fairy tale to trivial amusement and entertainment with little depth. Poniewozik points out that today's world of fairy tales is "parodied, ironized, meta-fictionalized, politically adjusted and pop-culture saturated" in the attempt to appeal to the socially progressive grownups who chaperone their children's trips to the movie theaters. Traditional fairy tales, he argues, are boring to the parents, the Generation X, not their children. This is the reason why contemporary filmmakers tweak their fairy-tale retellings by adding inside jokes to which their adult audiences can relate (Poniewozik 2007). Indeed, adult fans of *Hoodwinked!* praise the film for its witty jokes, clever script, and hilarious punch lines, which in their eyes make up for the low-budget animation. One fan commented: "This is a very fast paced movie that plays to the two levels successful animated films play to: The kids are entertained, but so are the parents. There are zingers that . . . will only catch the attention of the adults in the house, but don't detract from kids' enjoyment. But some will get all generations to laugh" (BillyGoat3 2005). Another fan praised Wolf's comedic effect in particular: "The highlight though is Patrick Warburton as the Wolf. He is blessed with some of the best lines of dialogue ([Nicky Flippers] 'What do you do?' [Wolf] 'I'm a shepherd') and his storyline is by far and away the movie's milestone. Warburton is perfectly cast as the sarcastic canine and effortlessly steals the entire film" (ExpendableMan 2007).

The postmodern pop culture industry in North America increasingly instrumentalizes the idea of the monstrous Other for its entertainment purposes by recasting the classic fairy-tale beast (e.g., the wolf, ogre, troll, dragon) as an agent of foolishness, a buffoon, in a carnivalesque world. A closer look at the script of *Hoodwinked!* reveals that Wolf's comedy ranges from simple word puns (Raccoon Jerry: "What did you say your name was?" The Wolf: "Shaw. Rick Shaw. Came in from Japan.") to jokes tailored specifically to adult audiences (Nicky Flippers: "So! Mr. Wolf . . . May I call you Wolf?" The Wolf: "You can call me Sheila. I like long walks and fresh flowers"). Other humorous dialogues rely heavily on the viewer's knowledge of the fairy-tale hypotext of LRRH:

RED PUCKETT: [Red encounters the Wolf, wearing a plastic Granny mask and apron and using a falsetto voice] Who are you?

THE WOLF: I'm your grandma.

RED PUCKETT: Your face looks really weird, granny.

THE WOLF: I've been sick, I . . . uh . . .

RED PUCKETT: Your mouth doesn't move when you talk.

THE WOLF: Plastic surgery. Grandma's had a little work done . . .

RED PUCKETT: Whoa, what big hands you have.

THE WOLF: Oh! All the better to scratch my back with.

RED PUCKETT: And what big ears you have . . .

THE WOLF: All the better to hear your . . . many criticisms. Old people just have big ears, dear.

RED PUCKETT: And Granny . . . what big eyes you have!

THE WOLF: Are we just gonna sit around here and talk about how big I'm getting?

THE WOLF: You came here for a reason, didn't you? So tell old Granny what you've got in the basket.

RED PUCKETT: Ugh! Granny! What bad breath you have!

[The Wolf takes off the mask; Red screams and backs away]

RED PUCKETT: You again! What do I have to do, get a restraining order?

Although *Hoodwinked!* received varied critical reviews, the film was a commercial success, earning over $150 million worldwide with a budget of less than $8 million, making it the most profitable animated film of its time (Amidi 2009). The sequel that followed in 2011, *Hoodwinked Too! Hood vs. Evil*, however, was a financial failure that elicited very negative reviews. The sequel portrays Wolf as an unlikely hero who is much more clumsy and foolhardy than in the prequel. Wolf's overconfidence impedes police operations and his jealousy of Red's secret combat training drives a wedge in their friendship and work as partners. It is not until much later in the story that Wolf's heroic attributes resurface. After saving Red, the two overcome their differences and save the day together.

Fables (2002–15), *The Wolf Among Us* (2013–14)

As one might expect, the rehabilitated fairy-tale wolf has not only found its way into the landscapes of American television and film but also into the world of comic books and video games. One of the most prominent examples is *Fables*, Bill Willingham's series of comics and winner of fourteen Eisner Awards. For thirteen years, the series was published monthly by DC Comics' imprint Vertigo, a line intended for a mature readership that in the past has included well-known comics for adults, such as Neil Gaiman's *Sandman* (1988–96) and Grant Morrison's *Invisibles* (1994–2000). Besides the twenty-two collected volumes of Willingham's completed comic book series *Fables*, multiple spin-offs exist that expand the series' universe, including *Fables: 1001 Nights of Snowfall* (2006), *Jack of Fables* (2006–11), *The Literals* (2009), *Peter and Max: A Fables Novel* (2009), *Cinderella: From Fabletown with Love* (2009–10), *Cinderella: Fables are Forever* (2011), *Fables: Werewolves of the Heartland* (2012), *Fairest* (2012–15), and five episodes of the video game *The Wolf Among Us*. Adam Zolkover has identified *Fables* as a form of fairy-tale pastiche, a "postmodernist blending of elements from a variety of loci within fairy-tale discourse that serves at once as commentary, play, and a fairy tale in its own right" (2008, 41). Illustrated by different artists (Mark Buckingham, Steve Leialoha, Michael Allred, Andrew Pepoy, D'Israeli, Gene Ha, Joelle Jones, Barry Kitson, and David Lapham, among many others), *Fables* is yet another example of how fairy-tale characters continue to be meaningful in today's pop culture and how the Grimms' fairy-tale wolf pervades contemporary American media in rehabilitated, redeemed form.

The premise of *Fables* is that a savage, mysterious, and powerful creature known only as the Adversary conquered the Homelands, the fabled lands of legends and fairy tales, and all of the infamous inhabitants of folklore were forced into exile. The magical creatures, who call themselves Fables, consist of various characters from fairy tales, legend, myth, nursery rhymes, and children's literature. They range from classic protagonists of *Märchen* (e.g., Snow White, Cinderella, Red Riding Hood, Rose Red, the Witch, and Prince Charming) to other fantasy and imaginary figures, including Baba Yaga, Mowgli, King Cole, C. S. Lewis's lion Aslan, Frank Baum's flying monkeys, Lewis Carroll's Alice and the white rabbit, and Cervantes's Don Quixote and Sancho Panza. Disguised among the normal citizens, the non-Fables or "Mundies" of modern-day New York (mundane humans, akin to "muggles" in the *Harry Potter* series), these fantastic characters have created their own peaceful and secret society, a hidden enclave, within an exclusive luxury apartment building called Fabletown. As evoked by the title of the first volume, *Legends in Exile*, the Fables are refugees, trying to live alongside each other in their new home, New York City, referred to as a "dreary mundane place: the one world the Adversary seemed to take no interest in" (Willingham 2002, 84). The Fables established the General Amnesty, in which all previous crimes, debts, and grievances are pardoned and will not be brought up again. Based on this peaceful agreement, all Fables can have a fresh start in their new home, whether they were villains or heroes in their past lives.

The first volume series opens with an apparent murder case of the party girl Rose-Red. Her sister, the deputy mayor of Fabletown, Snow White, helps the town's sheriff, Bigby Wolf, the reformed and pardoned Big Bad Wolf, determine who the killer is. The main suspects are Rose's boyfriend, Jack of Fables, and Rose's ex-lover and notorious bride-killer, Bluebeard, who claims to have been engaged to Rose. Although Bigby and Snow White manage to solve the crime case with the help of Snow White's ex-husband, Prince Charming, there are many more cases to solve, battles to fight, dangers to overcome, and adventures waiting for the Fables throughout the entire series. Ultimately, the Adversary is revealed to be the cold, ruthless, and calculating Geppetto, the creator of Pinocchio and other wooden puppets turned soldiers. As one of the series' main antagonists, Geppetto's desire to increase the power of his empire results in the devastation of the Homelands, causing the deaths of hundreds of Fables. In the following war between Fabletown and the Adversary's armies, the combined forces of Fabletown defeat Geppetto's mighty Empire. Despite his antagonistic actions, Geppetto is offered the General Amnesty in the end, the key civilizing institution of Fabletown, which he accepts and thus becomes a citizen of Fabletown himself.

Many scholars from various disciplines have written on *Fables*, most notably Neta Gordon (a literary scholar), Cristina Bacchilega (a fairy-tale scholar), Rebecca-Anne C. Do Rozario (a fairy-tale and children's literature scholar), Mark C. Hill (a popular culture and film studies scholar), Wilson Koh (a popular culture and media studies scholar), Karin Kukkonen (a comic books and cognitive studies scholar), Laurie Taylor (a digital humanities scholar), Adam Zolkover (a folklorist), and Jason Marc Harris (a literary scholar and creative writer). These scholars have focused on the portrayal of identity, social roles, and race, explored the representation of gender, analyzed the series in connection with globalization, examined *Fables'* approach to genre mixing, and drawn attention to the way *Fables* alludes to certain political, economic, and world events—for instance, the portrayal of war. Of particular interest to me for the purpose of this book is the representation of Bigby Wolf's character as rehabilitated and pardoned fairy-tale beast and monstrous Other. I am especially intrigued by Bigby's origin story, his character's generic crossovers, and how his backstory leads up to his personal path of redemption and roles as hero, sheriff, and loving family man. How strongly is *Fables'* lupine creature linked to his literary, fairy-tale "predecessors"? How does Bigby manifest his heroism? How does the Big Bad Wolf find redemption and how does he come to terms with his wolfish identity?

In *Fables*, we see the fairy-tale wolf reincarnated in multiple personas, representing the main hero, the protector of justice and law in Fabletown, a beastly warrior in the war with the Adversary, and Snow White's devoted husband and father of their cubs. The eleventh volume, *War and Pieces*, describes Bigby in the "Who's Who in Fabletown" section as "a monster and a brute, but a reformed one, now on the side of the angels" (Willingham 2008, 6). Indeed, Bigby's past is a horrific one that portrays him as a revenge-driven, monstrous mass murderer. Through Willingham's expansions of the character's backstory, the reader learns that Bigby had a difficult childhood as one of seven pups born to the deity known as the North Wind and the white she-wolf Winter. Since he was the runt son, his brothers mockingly called him "Big Bad Wolf" and, in short, "Bigby." Bigby hated his father for leaving his family, and when his mother died early he could not protect her corpse from scavengers. It was then that Bigby vowed to kill something bigger every day until he was "bigger and stronger than anything" (Willingham 2006a, 77). He started with a fat grasshopper, then a mouse, followed by a raccoon, a boar, and finally he went after the Three Little Pigs. His first human kills were LRRH and her grandmother, but because "there was magic in them" they survived his attack (Willingham 2006a, 79). The backstory "The Runt" not only links Bigby directly to fairy tales, but two panels that portray a huntsman who, after rescuing LRRH and her grandmother, sows heavy rocks into the wolf's body tie Bigby's character explicitly to the Grimms' version of "LRRH" (Willingham 2006a, 79). Despite this clear Grimmian reference, however, Bigby's "masculinity and heroism are just as much related to werewolf legends as to a range of 'mythic' narratives, including that of the underdog, the cowboy outlaw, the World War II American soldier, and the Bogart-like detective" (Bacchilega 2014, 157). Hence, besides the Grimmian inspiration, Bigby's character conflates a panoply of narrative threads, from mythology and werewolf lore to the English fable of the "Three Little Pigs" (1840s), Sergei Prokofiev's musical fairy tale "Peter and the Wolf" (1936), to conceptions of America and of vigilantism, power, and justice.

As the son of the mythical deity the North Wind, Bigby is, in effect, a demigod equipped with a wide array of supernatural powers. Already his nature as a Fable makes him almost immortal. However, as a lycanthrope demigod who can transform back and forth between his animal and human form at will, Bigby also possesses superhuman strengths, durability, and speed, enhanced senses, and incredible wind powers inherited from his father. Harris called Bigby's mythic origin story "a masterstroke of improvisational mythmaking by Willingham; the character's desire to become a legendary monster and the power of gusty wolfish breaths makes perfect sense via this hereditary etiology" (2016, 186). Whether due to his father's godlike nature or due to his personal oath, Bigby grew larger than any other wolf, devoured whole armies, one by one, and destroyed entire towns. He then decided to hunt down his father, the North Wind, but failed since he was no match for the deity. From that moment on, Bigby made a second oath to bury the thought of his parents and to forever walk and terrorize the world alone. Bigby's endless thirst for blood and pitiless killings truly portray him as a horrific monster, one without any feelings of remorse or guilt. As Bigby stated to Boy Blue in the afterlife: "I had no trouble being a monster. I *loved* it, in fact, and would have been perfectly content to grow ever more monstrous, day by day" (Willingham 2014, 111).

Whether a traumatized victim of his unfortunate childhood and of his damaged father-son relationship or a severely flawed character struggling with an identity crisis, Bigby's terrible acts appear inexpiable. How can such a monster be redeemed or tamed? Willingham's answer to rehabilitating the Big Bad Beast follows traditional fairy-tale conventions: through "true love." As the army of the Adversary starts to encroach into the great wolf's territory, Bigby frees a chain gang of prisoners containing Snow White and her sister Rose Red and leads them to the gate between the Homelands and the Mundy world. After meeting Snow White, Bigby takes his first step toward his redemption and reformation from his evil ways. He narrates to Boy Blue, "Then I ran across Snow . . . and I was overthrown. Instantly. From that moment on, anything short of being with her would have been misery" (Willingham 2014, 111). Bigby eventually follows Snow White into the human world, but because of his monstrous past, many years pass before the Fables are ready to trust him. Bigby dedicates his new life to protecting his fellow Fables as the sheriff of Fabletown, demonstrating that he is a firm believer in the law and due process. In his capacity as sheriff and commanding advisor against the forces of the Adversary, Bigby's heroic attributes come to the fore. His budding heroism merges with his growing degree of civilization, visually manifested in the human shape that Bigby must maintain while living in Fabletown to blend in with the mundane environment. His path to redemption is therefore inextricably linked to his civil role as public servant of the Fabletown community and his adherence to the rules of the General Amnesty, which connects personal autonomy with communal responsibility.

Willingham imbues his lupine creature with a conservative, highly masculine profile that adds to Bigby's heroic aura. As Harris noted, "Bigby channels well-known icons of masculinity from the comic-book world of super-superheroes and the cinematic genre of noir hard-boiled detectives: Wolverine and Sam Spade" (2016, 188). Indeed, Bigby wears the habitual beige trench coat, his face is covered in a constant five o'clock shadow, and he perpetually holds a cigarette in his hand, evoking the archetypal hard-boiled private detective epitomized by Humphrey Bogart. Moreover, Bigby's well-muscled body combined with his shaggy hair and the scowl on his hirsute face is reminiscent of Hugh Jackman's performances as Marvel Comics' character Wolverine in the *X-Men* film series. Similar to Wolverine, who can be seen fighting as a soldier in the American Civil War, both World Wars, and the Vietnam War in *X-Men Origins: Wolverine* (2009), Bigby's masculinity and heroism are further emphasized, even glorified, through military conflict. In the "War Stories" arc, Bigby is depicted as an American soldier, fighting for the righteous cause against the Nazis in World War II. Arguing that this arc "invokes the cultural memory of the masculine hero-soldier in a war worth fighting," Mark C. Hill laments the fact that neither courage, nor duty, nor the righteousness of the American cause are questioned (2009, 186). Embedded in part two of "War Stories," however, is the question of monstrosity/Otherness versus evilness. In the story, evil Nazi scientists are trying to reanimate Frankenstein's monster in the hope that it can be of use to the "fatherland" (Willingham 2005, 55).

Bigby manifests his heroism by shape-shifting from his human form into his bestial nature to fight as an American Werewolf against the resurrected Frankenstein monster. Clearly marked by the *Reichsadler* (Imperial Eagle) Nazi tattoo on the back of his head, the undead golem monstrosity appears to personify the force of the German enemy. What follows is an impressive clash between the two creatures, who, although they are fighting as enemies, are united by their shared Otherness. Bigby emerges as the eventual winner by beheading his opponent but soon discovers that the Frankenstein monster was simply bait designed to lure him into a devious Nazi trap. Bigby finally manages to escape but he does not leave without the "war souvenir" of the creature's severed head (Willingham 2005, 71). The ending of the narrative illustrates that despite its monstrous appearance and Nazi tattoo, Frankenstein's creation is not hostile at all. In fact, the two "monsters" are now portrayed as friends. Bigby keeps his buddy "Frankie" in a cushioned birdcage in his business office and shows concern about his well-being. Frankie, in return, calls Bigby amicably "Biggs" and has made friendships with other Fables as well. The war story serves as a manifesto for the subversiveness of the series, challenging readers' imagination of classic monsters and fairy-tale creatures as evil beings.

With the civilizing institution of the General Amnesty, the diverse Fabletown community is founded on values that encourage personal redemption narratives, such as the Big Bad Wolf's successful rehabilitation journey. But it is not the political decree itself, as Harris observed, that allows traditionally destructive and wicked characters—e.g., Bigby, Bluebeard, Frau Totenkinder (a.k.a. the witch of "Hansel and Gretel")—to peacefully coexist with positively coded Fables, such as, for example, Snow White. Rather, "free will is the bridge that Willingham indicates makes a personal transformation convincing" (Harris, 187). The General Amnesty, however, helps to establish the political framework conditions and environment that allow for such a personal transformation to burgeon. *Fables* suggests, according to Neta Gordon, "that redemption requires acts of reimagination and reinterpretation, whereby one's actions in the past must be generally accepted as stages along a journey" (2016, 56). In Bigby's case, his personal path to redemption is a difficult one, interspersed with multiple opportunities to revert back to the dark side of his wolfish identity. In an interview with the creators of the comic book series, Mark Buckingham and Bill Willingham confirm that despite Bigby's rehabilitation, his monstrous Otherness was never completely absent:

BUCKINGHAM: In a way, Bigby started out in the series as a bad guy but his fascination with Snow is what triggered the turning point. He wanted to protect her. And he accepted the things that were offered to him in order for him to become the champion of Fabletown. . . . In his origin story, there is a darker side to his character. But the monster was always there, potentially. There was always a chance that he could fall.

WILLINGHAM: . . . At his core, Bigby is a monster. The civilized Bigby is a shell around him, the purpose of which is to keep the monster from getting out. But sometimes, shells break. (Renaud 2015)

The creators of *Fables* reveal in this interview that Bigby, similar to Monroe in *Grimm*, Red in *OUaT*, Peter in *Red Riding Hood* and Wolf W. Wolf in *Hoodwinked*, needs to keep his beastly nature constantly in check to peacefully coexist with humans or other fantastic creatures in a community. It is the only way for the fairy-tale wolf, the lupine Other, to find redemption and forgiveness. In fact, *Fables* indicates that any evil committed can be forgiven and that any villain is worthy of redemption. In *1001 Nights of Snowfall*, Snow White, among other Fables, temporarily takes over the fictional landscape of the *Arabian Nights*. As the ambassador of Fabletown, the fairy-tale heroine travels to the far-away palace of King Shahryar with the political mission of gaining support from the Arabian Fable worlds in the fight against the Adversary and his legions. To appease the wicked Sultan, who is deeply disillusioned with women after his wife's betrayal and has already killed a thousand virgins, Snow White takes on the role of Shahrazad. She tells the tyrannical ruler stories in the hope that they will have a therapeutic effect by curing him of his misogynistic wrath. In "The Runt," Snow White narrates the backstory of Bigby's horrid past and his atrocious acts that followed, to point out to the Sultan that "even the great wolf's many offenses could be forgiven in time. He is now a trusted and loyal member of our community in exile, and no citizen of Fabletown fears him any longer. . . . The wolf is reformed in full" (Willingham 2006a, 85). Hence, thanks to the General Amnesty of the Fabletown community, any villain or criminal can have a fresh start and can enter the compact "with newly cleansed hands" (85). As stated earlier, this stipulation even applies to the mighty Adversary, the embodiment of ultimate villainy, who is granted amnesty for his past crimes as a citizen of Fabletown.

On October 11, 2013, Telltale Games released worldwide the first of a five-episode interactive mystery graphic adventure video game called *The Wolf Among Us*, which in turn has provided impetus for a printed and digitalized adaption of the game's narrative in comic book form. The video game, which is set as a prequel to the comic book series in the year 1986 (nearly twenty years before the events in *Fables*), is played from the third-person perspective of the protagonist Bigby Wolf, who must investigate the murder of Faith, a woman later identified as a Fable from the Grimms' "Allerleihrauh" and Charles Perrault's "Donkeyskin." As in the comic book series, Bigby is a street detective and the sheriff of Fabletown. The player navigates through the mystery story from Bigby's point of view, solves puzzles, follows clues, unlocks secrets, and chooses dialog options during conversations. The player's decisions on the narrative choices will have either a positive or a negative effect on how other characters view Bigby, and their perceptions will influence future events in the story. This decision-making power that rests with the player about making Bigby more or less violent, honest, or compassionate along his investigative journey determines the character's level of virtuousness and integrity to a greater or lesser degree. Still, the video game features the rehabilitated Big Bad Wolf in the role of the archetypical hero from the very outset of the narrative. Here, Bigby heroically saves the prostitute Faith from the Woodsman, a drunken, obscene, and brutish reincarnation of the Grimms' *Jäger*. In a rage, the Woodsman slaps Faith across her face before Bigby can intervene, and knocks him to the ground. The video game narrative and dialog drastically subvert the traditional fairy-tale roles, depicting the Woodsman as the aggressive beast and Bigby as the savior:

WOODSMAN: I'm the woodsman you whore. I saved Little Red Riding Hood from this monster. I cut this fucker open and filled his belly full of stones! And threw him in the fucking river! That's who the fuck I am, you stupid bitch!

BIGBY: I said be nice or you wait outside! (He throws himself, together with the Woodsman, out of the apartment's window)

As the fight continues on the street, the Woodsman tries to force Bigby to transform into a wolf by strangling him: "I know you are fucking in there. Come on out, you fucking dog. I'll put you out of your misery. You fucking mongrel. You ignorant fuck. Come on out, wolf." Faith comes to Bigby's aid but the Woodsman eventually escapes. Before Faith departs, she tells Bigby that he is not as bad as everyone says he is. It is problematic, though, that the trope of violence done to women, including female injuries and abuse leading to the deaths of these women, is often used as a plot device in comic books and video games to stir the male hero into action and to heighten the hero's masculinity (Robbins 2010, 216, cited in Gordon 2016, 182).

Conclusion

Ever since the 1960s and 1970s, numerous writers, such as Janosch, Tomi Ungerer, Philippe Dumas and Boris Moissard, Angela Carter, and many others, have "renovated" fairy tales by creating highly innovative tales that reverse and subvert traditional fairy-tale roles. These revisionist rewritings call into question the deceptively simple design of classic fairy-tale characters, their functions in the texts, and the tales' general aesthetics. Many retellings, from Ungerer's "Little Red Riding Hood" in *A Storybook* (1974), a story that ends with the happy marriage of a lonely, aristocratic wolf to a homely LRRH, to Dumas's *Contes à l'envers* (Upside Down Tales), "a book in which recycled red riding hoods terrorize the wolf and drive him out of town," set the trend for rehabilitating the lupine villain (Malarte-Feldman 2016, 5). Sandra Beckett has already demonstrated in *Recycling Red Riding Hood* (2002) how Dumas and Moissard demystified in their tale "Le Petit Chaperon Bleu Marine" ("Little Navy Blue Riding Hood," 1977) the powerful and mythic fear of the wolf by reconstructing the animal as a mirrored, good character (2002, 107–16). What began as a minor trend in the latter half of the twentieth century in the field of Anglo-European literature has become a major approach to retellings of LRRH in today's North American media culture. Indeed, the archetypical villainous fairy-tale wolf emerges in the twenty-first century most notably as a positively charged figure. This transformation in character presentation stretches beyond the simplistic exchange of the dichotomous labels "good" and "bad." Contemporary reimaginings of the wolf in *Märchen*-inspired adaptations are, firstly, rooted in elaborate, personal backstories; secondly, not restricted to male bodies; thirdly, presented as heroic, likeable, comedic, and infantilized characters; fourthly, merged with werewolf lore and other mythologies; and lastly, "tamed" Others who exercise control over their animalistic side to live a civil life.

The lasting power of particular fairy-tale characters and the tales they inhabit lies in their potential to be reworked and retold in endless ways. Hence, the reason why creatures such as the Big Bad Wolf continue to endure and resonate with audiences is precisely the fact that classic fairy-tale figures are mere templates of the imagination that leave a lot of room for interpretation. Because fairy tales give us very little information about the individual characters, may it be the wolf, the witch, or the princess, these archetypes lend themselves to adaptation and revision. According to Adam Zolkover, the effectiveness of Willingham's *Fables* lies in the fact that fairy-tale characters are used in new and innovative ways to create fresh, compelling stories by reinterpreting traditional fairy-tale texts. Willingham and his creative partners do so by modifying, distorting, and integrating folklore in their work: "they play with it and parody it; and ultimately they transform it, coming out with a multivalent response to the fairy-tale genre . . . treating the genre with a subversive, parodic laughter" (2008, 40). Besides the literary genre, film, television, video games, and the internet increasingly make use of this concept of fairy-tale parody and subversion, from children's and family shows to popular adult entertainment. Aside from the most prominent examples already discussed in this chapter, mentions of LRRH-themed parodies and subversions of the tale in contemporary North American popular culture are too frequent too enumerate them all. Further examples include, for instance, episodes of *Sesame Street* (1969–present), the animated sitcom *Family Guy* (1999–present), the anime web series *RWBY* (2013–present), the fashion doll franchise *Ever After High* and its eponymous spin-off web series (2013–present), numerous television commercials (e.g., by brands such as Volvo, Glaxo Smith Kline, Adidas, Chanel No5, Honey Nut Cheerios, etc.), music videos, and a Google Doodle.

In 2001, *Sesame Street* featured an episode with a segment called "Musical Fairy Tales" that spoofed the story of "LRRH." In this particular parody, the wolf is a harmless, friendly creature that loves to sing. When LRRH enters her grandmother's house, she comments on the wolf's facial features:

LRRH: "Granny, what big eyes you have."
WOLF: "All the better to see you with, my dear"
LRRH: "Granny, what big ears you have."
WOLF: "All the better to hear you with, my dear."
LRRH: "And Granny, what big . . ."
WOLF: "Hold it, hold it. This is silly."
LRRH: "Hm? Oh, you mean it's silly to pretend that you're my granny when you're obviously a wolf."
WOLF: "No. I mean it's silly for us to talk about this when we can sing about it."

The wolf and LRRH join in singing the duet "One Fine Face" before they leave the house together to play bingo with Grandma. In 2014, the episode "Grimm Job" (season 12, ep. 10) of the show *Family Guy* depicts a woodsman with a chainsaw violently slaughtering the wolf and exposing the remains of Grandma before rushing onto the next house. Red wonders if the woodsman was really the fairy-tale's hero or just a lunatic going from house to house killing people. In *Ever After High*, the Big Bad Wolf, or Mr. Badwolf, married LRRH and has two teenage daughters, Cerise Hood and Ramona Badwolf. The lycanthrope teaches General Villainy at Ever After High, a high school in the form of a castle opened by the Brothers Grimm where the next generation of the fairy-tale characters learns to live their legacy. On December 20, 2014, Google featured a Doodle of "LRRH" in celebration of the two-hundredth anniversary of the Grimms' fairy tales. In a comic book format, the viewers could pan through the story themselves, which featured an alternative ending of the traditional tale. When the woodsman comes to the rescue, he finds a knitted thread hanging out of the sleeping wolf's mouth. Another panel depicts the grandmother knitting inside the wolf's tummy and a sorrowful LRRH sitting beside her. By pulling the knitted thread, the woodsman yanks the two women out of the wolf's belly unharmed.

It is conspicuous that the rehabilitated, reformed fairy-tale wolf in particular has been featured in a wide range of postmodern adaptations of "LRRH" and has thus also gained widespread currency in North American pop culture. This "cleansed" reinvention and renewal of a classic villainous archetype signifies that a shift of paradigm is in course toward the cele- bration of Otherness, difference, monstrosity, abnormality, and deviance. Today's fairy-tale adaptations emancipate the animal, the beast, the monster, the traditional "other than" the human, from the category of pejorative dif- ference by portraying Otherness in a more positive light. The fairy-tale wolf has shaken off its biologically inscribed and culturally reinforced shackles of monstrosity as he rarely represents a fearsome beast in today's "LRRH" adaptations. At the same time, postmodern fairy-tale retellings call for a rethinking of the Other, the anomalous, and the monstrous, by humanizing and trivializing the fairy-tale wolf in manifold ways. Viewers can identify with supernatural characters, such as Monroe in *Grimm* or Ruby/Red in *OUaT*, because they are friendly, anthropomorphized fairy-tale wolves that invite viewers' empathy. These are characters audiences can relate to because they appear realistic by working ordinary jobs (Monroe is a clock maker, Ruby/Red is a waitress), facing real-life problems, struggling with family relationships, and pursuing romantic relationships. Whether the wolfish reincarnations are designed to make audiences laugh or cry or simply empa- thize with them, viewers are encouraged to recognize a part of themselves in the postmodern fairy-tale wolf and thus embrace the Other without hav- ing to fear it. This shift of balance in the concept of Otherness in our society, I believe, is reflective of current societal perceptions and social attitudes toward the larger dimensions of race, ethnicity, culture, language, gender, sexual orientation, age, disability, class status, and religious and spiritual orientation.

Lastly, one might wonder why turning to the "minor" genre of the fairy tale appears appropriate to trace societal changes in the perceptions of Otherness that is taking place at present. Rosi Braidotti made a fitting remark in this context, and although her quote is a reference to the science-fiction genre it certainly applies to the fairy-tale genre as well. Braidotti noted that the "low culture" genre is "mercifully free of grandiose pretensions—of the aesthetic or cognitive kind—and thus ends up being a more accurate and honest depiction of contemporary culture than other, more self-consciously 'representational' genres (such as the documentary, for instance)" (2002, 182). Fairy tales, reinterpretations thereof, and fairy-tale-inspired adaptations in popular culture are the ideal breeding grounds to explore the representation of supernatural creatures. Just like fairy tales are the looking glass of society and the cultural signifiers of a country at a particular time, so do the fantastic beings within these stories serve as mirror images in which people can (re)discover, to a greater or lesser degree, aspects of themselves. The more we can identify with the fantastic Other and encounter positive portrayals of Otherness in postmodern fairy-tale retellings, the better we will be able to relate to Others in our society and thus to create community.

4

DWARFS, DIVERSITY, AND DEFORMATION

From Fairy-Tale Imps to Rumpelstiltskin Reloaded

"What did you think of *Snowwhite and the vii Dwarfs*? . . . The worst thing of all was the vulgarity of the winking dove at the beginning, and the next worst the faces of the dwarfs. Dwarfs ought to be ugly of course, but not in that way."

—C. S. Lewis in a letter to A. K. Hamilton (1939)[1]

"And what about you? You must be some kind of beardless dwarf?"
"I'm not a dwarf! I'm a girl. And actually I'm tallest in my class."

—*The Chronicles of Narnia: The Lion, the Witch and the Wardrobe* (2005)[2]

In December 2013, my husband gave me for Christmas a LEGO set called "The Unexpected Gathering," which is based on the film adaptations of J. R. R. Tolkien's novel *The Hobbit, or There and Back Again* (1937). To my delight, the model of Bag End, Bilbo Baggins's hobbit hole, came with six miniature figures, including the hobbit Bilbo Baggins, the wizard Gandalf the Grey, and the dwarfs (or dwarves) Balin, Dwalin, Bombur, and Bofur, all with assorted weapons. As is common for LEGO toy figures, they all have the exact same size, disregarding the fact that humans, dwarfs, and hobbits in Tolkien's fantasy world are of different physical heights. In the *Hobbit* film series (2012–14), directed by Peter Jackson, all three species are played by average-sized actors who appear feet shorter than they are in real life, thanks to techniques of trick photography and scale models. My LEGO toy set, however, featuring a mini-human, a mini-hobbit, and several mini-dwarfs, makes the different body types indistinguishable. The erasure of the most significant physical differences of the three races reveals how much fantastic creatures are defined by their different body sizes as part of their identity. Besides their small size, dwarfs in mythology, folklore, and fantasy are usually recognized by their long beards and old age, but so are wizards. Without his wizard hat, the Gandalf toy figurine could easily pass for a dwarf. Hobbits or Halflings, in turn, stand out for their lack of beards, short, curly hair, and slightly pointed, elvish ears. Tolkien excogitated this diminutive, humanoid race as a separate "branch" of humans, also referred to as "little people" in his novels (Schneidewind 2007, 66). However, somebody unfamiliar with the Tolkien universe might refer to "hobbits" as "dwarfs" or associate them with dwarfs rather than with little people, given their physical shortness. At the same time, Jackson's *Hobbit* trilogy portrays thirteen unique dwarf characters of different personalities and looks, challenging the stereotypical folkloric prototype. The film adaptations evoke the questions if the traditional character traits of the dwarf archetype found in fairy tales and fantastic stories, such as short body height, old age, and long beard, still hold true in the twenty-first century? How are fairy-tale dwarfs in today's pop culture portrayed and identified? What is the relationship between the presentation of fairy-tale dwarfs in contemporary media and our perception of deformation, disability, and diversity?

Postmodern American media does not bifurcate the Grimm-inspired fairy-tale dwarfs into good and bad characters, but rather emphasizes the diversity of dwarfs' personalities and celebrates the potency of dwarfs' physicality. Today's fairy-tale retellings subvert the notion of the long-bearded, old, ugly, wealth-obsessed midget and propagate an image of humanized, heterogeneous dwarfs to whom viewers can relate. Departing from the idea of fairy-tale imps as deformed, emasculated, infantilized, asexual people, contemporary films and television shows increasingly draw on regular-height actors to portray traditional fairy-tale dwarfs in multifaceted and, at times, sexually charged roles. Such roles are not limited to the Grimmian model of the mean-spirited demon and benevolent helper figure but range from feisty bandits, freedom fighters, and social outcasts to troubled family figures, enamored suitors, sexual partners, magical seers, sacrificial saviors, political usurpers, wedding crashers, anti-heroes, and many more. The subversion of the "classic" dwarf conception as physically misshapen in relation to human society and the heterogeneity in the portrayal of this supernatural creature may be indicative of a societal shift against disability bias and "ableism." Ableism (sometimes also termed "disableism") is discrimination and social prejudice against people with disabilities. It refers to "ideas, practices, institutions, and social relations that presume able-bodiedness, and by so doing, construct persons with disabilities as marginalized, oppressed, and largely invisible 'others'" (Chouinard 1997, 380).

Tolkien, who is commonly celebrated as the father of modern fantasy, drew inspiration for his fantastic stories and creatures from Old English literature, Germanic mythologies, and Norse sagas, including the *Völsunga saga*, the *Hervarar saga*, the *Poetic Edda*, the *Prose Edda* (*Snorri's Edda*), and the *Nibelungenlied*. From these sources, Tolkien's dwarfs take their characteristic affinity with mining, metalworking, crafting, and avarice. European fairy tales and legends, in particular the writings of the Brothers Grimm, have also influenced his high-fantasy works *The Hobbit*, *The Lord of the Rings* (1954), and *The Silmarillion* (1977). In fact, Tolkien was not only familiar with the Grimms' fairy tales and their depiction of dwarfs but also considered them reference points to his own imaginings. As Maria Raffaella Benvenuto noted, "A number of motifs from the Grimms's fairy-tales can be recognized in Tolkien's work, especially in *The Hobbit*. . . . Tolkien probably derived some elements of the Dwarves's character and behavior from the tales of 'Schneewittchen' ['Snow-white,' also from 1812] and 'Schneeweisschen und Rosenrot' ['Snow-white and Rose-red,' from the 1837 edition]" (2007, 236). Benvenuto's assumptions about the close connection to the Grimms' fairy tales and their direct impact on Tolkien's construction of his dwarfs can be further supported with a quote from Tolkien's personal correspondence. In a letter written on December 16, 1937, Tolkien said of *The Hobbit*: "Mr. Baggins began as a comic tale among conventional and inconsistent Grimm's fairy-tale dwarves, and got drawn into the edge of it" ([1981] 2014, 26).

Although Tolkien first conceived his dwarfs as evil beings in *The Book of Lost Tales* (published posthumously in two volumes in 1983 and 1984), he endowed them with some comedic and bumbling characteristics in *The Hobbit* and portrayed them generally as honorable and serious-minded. Still, they maintained some negative traits, such as being greedy for gold, stubborn, secretive, easily offended, extremely proud, vengeful, and occasionally officious. A short and stocky race, they took great pride in their thick, luxuriant beards, which they tucked into their belts. For *The Lord of the Rings*, Tolkien devised the fictional language Khuzdul as a secretive language spoken by the dwarfs, which he based on the Semitic languages and the influence of Hebrew phonology. In a letter dated December 8, 1955, Tolkien elucidated his understanding of the connection between dwarfs and Jews: "I do think of the 'Dwarves' like Jews: at once native and alien in their habitations, speaking the languages of the country, but with an accent due to their own private tongue" ([1981] 2014, 229). The question of a direct influence of Richard Wagner's opera cycle *Der Ring des Nibelungen* (The Ring of the Nibelung) on Tolkien's work is debated by critics. The plot revolves around a magic ring that grants the power to rule the world. The ring is forged by the Nibelung dwarf Alberich, the main antagonist driving events, from gold he stole from the *Rheintöchter* (Rhine daughters), three water-nymphs, in the river Rhine. A popular illustration by Arthur Rackham dated around 1910 depicts the Rhine maidens as they reject the advances of Alberich. Rackham depicts the chief of the Nibelung race of dwarfs as an ugly, hairy, wild-looking dwarf with a long, dark mane, beard, and eyebrows above a hooked nose. A different illustration by Rackham of 1910 depicts Alberich as a tyrannical ruler who enjoys cracking the whip over his subjects carrying gold and silver treasures.

In Germanic mythology, Alberich is the king of a lineage of elves and dwarfs, an equivalent to the dwarf Andavari in Norse mythology who has the magical ability to transform himself into a fish at will. The name "Alberich" is a compound of the Old High German word *Alb-*, meaning *Elb* (elf) or "nature spirit," and–*rich/rîh/rik*, meaning "ruler" or "king." The Middle High German legend *Ortnit* speaks of the dwarf "Elberich," who uses his magical powers to assist the hero Ortnit, the king of Lombardy, to court and marry the daughter of a heathen king (Simrock 1864, 450).[3] In the variation of "Auberon/Oberon," the name is also associated with the king of the fairies in the thirteenth-century French epic poem (*chanson de geste*) *Huon of Bordeaux*, the Arthurian legends, William Shakespeare's *A Midsummer Night's Dream* (1595/96), Christoph Martin Wieland's epic poem *Oberon* (1780), and many other historical works (Petzold [1990] 2003, 18). Jacob Grimm elaborated on the close affiliation between the two supernatural species, dwarfs and elves, in his treatise *Deutsche Mythologie* (German Mythology) published in 1835.[4] He pointed out that in the *Prose Edda*, compiled by Icelandic scholar Snorri Sturluson around the year 1220, a differentiation is made between the light elf or white elf (liosâlfar) and the dark elf (döckâlfar) or black elf (svartâlfar). This distinction became necessary because the two classes of creatures got mixed up and confounded. Whereas the white elves, who live in the heavenly Álfheim (home of the elves), are brighter than the sun, the dark elves are blacker than pitch and live underground. For Snorri, the dark/black elves are synonymous with the dwarfs (dvergar) who dwell in Svartâlfaheim (Grimm [1887] 2004, 445).

Contrary to Snorri's duality of light elves and dwarfs (dark/black elves), Grimm postulated the hypothesis of a tripartite division between light elves, dark elves, and black elves in Norse mythology. However, Grimm's hypothesis is complicated by the fact that Snorri described the dark elves (and not the black elves) as pitch-black ("döckâlfar eru svartari en bik"), essentially merging the two classes. Therefore, Grimm pronounced Snorri's statement fallacious and argued that dwarfs are associated with grey, brown, and pale colors rather than with black in certain folkloric traditions. According to his hypothesis, the light elves live in heaven, the dark elves in hel, the heathen hades, and the black elves in Svartâlfaheim ([1887] 2004, 445). It is noteworthy that Grimm's claim has been met with scholarly criticism, such as Tolkien scholar Tom Shippey's remark, "Snorri can be trusted, then, when he says something Grimm is prepared to accept, but has to be ruled out when his statement is unwelcome" (2004, 8). Although Jacob Grimm's approach to Snorri's division of elves and dwarfs might be questionable, his detailed descriptions of the dwarf's characteristics are significant for analyzing the supernatural creature in the Grimms' fairy tales.

In *Deutsche Mythologie*, Grimm provides illuminating information about the age, personality, physical appearance, and body height of dwarfs in German and European folklore. He details that man and dwarves age differently, "Whereas man grows but slowly, not attaining his full stature till after his fifteenth year . . . ; the dwarf is already grown up in the third year of his life, and a greybeard in the seventh" ([1887] 2004, 448). Dwarfs may attain the stature of a four-year-old child or appear much smaller, sometimes only a thumb long (a dwarfish figure by stature appears in "Thumbling" KHM 37; "Thumbling's Travels" KHM 45). Grimm emphasizes the deformed corporal form and ugliness of the dwarf (or elf) but also highlights the creature's keen mind in comparison with men and giants: "All elves are imagined as small and tiny, but the *light* ones as well-formed and symmetrical, the *black* as ugly and misshapen" ([1887] 2004, 449). "By so much of bodily size and strength a man surpasses the elf or dwarf, he falls short of the giant; on the other hand, the race of elves and dwarfs has a livelier intellect and subtler sense than that of men, and in these points again the giants fall far below mankind" (518). Often color-coded, the dwarf appears in the fairy tales as "gray manikin" (e.g., "Die Bienenkönigin" ["The Queen Bee"], KHM 62; "Die goldene Gans" ["The Golden Goose"], KHM 64), as dwarf with an "ashen-gray face" and "fiery red eyes" (e.g., "Schneeweißchen und Rosenrot" ["Snow White and Rose Red"], KHM 161), as "little white manikin" (e.g., "Hurleburlebutz," KHM 66 in the 1812 edition), or as "little black manikin" (e.g., "Der König vom goldenen Berg" ["The King of the Golden Mountain"], KHM 92; "Das blaue Licht" ["The Blue Light"], KHM 116). Grimm continues, "the dwarf adds to his repulsive hue an ill-shaped body, a humped back, and coarse clothing" ([1887] 2004, 449). The disabled and distorted body of the dwarf also exhibits sometimes deformed feet, such as geese or duck feet (450).[5]

The generic name *Zwerg* (dwarf) in German folktales, fairy tales, and sagas is frequently substituted for alternative designations alluding to the creature's space of living or activity, such as *Erdmännchen/-männlein* (earth manikins), *Bergmännchen/-lein* (mountain manikins), *Waldmännchen/-männlein* (forest manikins), *Unterirdische* (subterraneans), *Haulemännerchen/-männlein* (hauling manikins), and its physique, such as *Kröppel* (cripples), *Kielkröpfe* (thick necks, goiters), *Dickköpfe* (thick heads), *Spitzbärte* (goatees), *Graumännchen/-männlein* (gray manikins), *Däumlinge* (thumblings), *Fingerlinge* (fingerlings), *kleines Volk* (little people), and so forth. Grimm also identifies *Wechselbälger* (changelings) as unsightly dwarf children. "They [dwarfs] abstract well-shaped children from the cradle, and substitute their own ugly ones, or even themselves. . . . The motive of the exchange seems to be, that elves are anxious to improve their breed by means of the human child, which they design to keep among them, and for which they give up one of their own" (468). In their fairy tale "Die Wichtelmänner" ("The Elves," KHM 39) the Grimms describe dwarfs with the euphemistic term *Wichtelmänner*, which translates to wights, brownies, or elves.[6] The third part of this Hessian tale tells of a mother whose child was taken from the cradle by elves and swapped with a changeling. The creature has a thick head and staring eyes and does nothing but eat and drink. When the change-ling sees how the woman boils water over the fire in eggshells, the *Klotzkopf* (blockhead) cries out: "Well, I am as old as the Westerwald, but I never saw anything boiled in eggshells" (469). This makes the changeling laugh, and a band of elves appears to return the rightful child.

It must be emphasized, however, that changelings in fairy tales and legends are described as deformed, disabled, or sickly in relation to human families, although they are presumably ordinary dwarf children or dwarfs. Hence, it is only from the perspective of a human that the dwarf may seem misshapen and ugly, when in fact the fantastic creature would pass as "nor-mal" among his own kind, where everyone else is also of very small stature. Ann Schmiesing observantly remarks, "While human prejudice against them might at times manifest itself in portrayals of dwarfs as mischievous, devious, malevolent, physically misshapen, and agents of disease, they are 'deformed' principally in relation to human society" (2014, 153). A similar argument can be made about other supernatural creatures and their stereo-typical ugliness or deformation in fairy tales and folklore, such as the old, cannibalistic witch, commonly portrayed with warts, a crooked nose, a pointed chin, and a hunched back. Although the perception of beautiful and ugly aesthetics is entirely subjective, the Grimms endowed their fairy tales with an absolute system of black-and-white dualisms, suggesting beauty to be synonymous with goodness and health whereas ugliness equates with evilness and disease. Following this overly simplistic dichotomy, the Grimms' tales portray normality versus abnormality and ability versus dis-ability in accordance with the moralities and zeitgeist of their times.

In the Grimms' fairy tales, dwarfs are ambivalent beings because they are either devious, ghastly, crude, and wicked or they are friendly, support-ive, caring, and consultative. Jacob Grimm states, "When, in legends and fairy tales, dwarfs appear singly among men, they are sage counselors and helpful, but also apt to fire up and take offence" ([1887] 2004, 471). Their function in the tales can be of rewarding or punishing nature for the protagonists. Although Simon Gilmour acknowledges the creature's ambivalence, he claims that the notion of the sinister dwarf features more prominently in the Grimms' tales than the benevolent dwarf (1993, 10). This chapter focuses on the prominent characteristic features of the dwarf in German Romantic fairy tales and examines how North American fairy-tale retellings in contemporary popular culture reinterpret the stereotypical image of the old, long-bearded, ugly, and deformed dwarf. The scope of analysis includes only those media productions that are directly and intertextually linked to the fairy-tale dwarfs of the Brothers Grimm. The following section begins with a hermeneutic reading of what are perhaps the best-known dwarf stories among the Grimms' tales: "Schneewittchen" ("Snow White," KHM 53), "Rumpelstilzchen" ("Rumpelstiltskin," KHM 55), and "Snow White and Rose Red." For the sake of coherence with the previous chapters, the focus lies primarily on films and television shows of the past two decades, such as the figures of Rumpelstiltskin and the dwarfs in *Once Upon a Time* (2011–18) and the films *Snow White: A Tale of Terror* (1997), *Snow White: The Fairest of Them All* (2001), *Sydney White* (2007), *Mirror Mirror* (2012), and *Snow White and the Huntsman* (2012).

Dwarfs in German Romantic Fairy Tales

Of all supernatural creatures, the dwarfs are the ones most common in the Grimms' fairy tales (Bühler and Bilz [1953] 1977, 38). Due to their ambivalent nature, they either appear as cranky and spiteful little men, as, for example, in the tales "Rumpelstiltskin" and "Snow White and Rose Red," or they are kindhearted and cooperative, as in "The Elves" or "Snow White." A closer examination of "Snow White" reveals, however, that the dwarfs were not always kind and helpful to everyone. In another variant of the tale, the dwarfs are known for killing any girl that approaches their dwelling in a cave in the woods. When Snow White enters the cave and encounters the dwarfs, she remains alive solely because the dwarfs are taken with her beauty. From the version of 1857, we learn that the dwarfs keep their little house neat and orderly. They live together in the companionship of seven but are otherwise isolated from the rest of society in the woods. They are diligent miners who work from dusk until dawn. Wilhelm Grimm added the detail that the dwarfs search for ore and gold in the mountains. In the manuscript of 1810 they are only described as miners, and in the first edition of 1812/1815 they are "in the mines and dig for gold." Gilmour surmises that Wilhelm interpolated this information to create a connection to the dwarfs in Germanic mythology and epic poetry where the dwarfs traditionally search for gold, silver, and ore (1993, 12).

Interestingly, the tale neither specifies the dwarfs' looks nor does it make mention of the creatures' stereotypical greed or lust for treasures. Quite the opposite seems to be true. The Grimms explicitly refer to the characters as "good dwarfs" who are not willing to sell Snow White's lifeless body to the prince "for all the gold in the world." Instead of having one dwarf watch over a vast fortune of gold and jewels, like Andavari in Norse mythology and Alberich in German mythology, one of the seven dwarfs watches Snow White's coffin every day for a "long, long time." This suggests that Snow White, the embodiment of beauty, is the dwarfs' true treasure. The high appreciation for beauty that the dwarfs have is also expressed in their artistry and workmanship. Already the *Edda* describes dwarfs as great craftsmen whose skill supersedes that of humans, thanks also to their magical powers. They forge fearsome weapons, such as Thor's hammer Mjölnir, Odin's spear Gungnir, and the magical swords Gram and Tyrfing; craft the mythical beverage called mead of poetry; and create such major treasures as the golden ring Draupnir, the golden hair of Sif (Thor's wife), and Freyja's precious necklace Brísingamen (Stephens 2008, 283). For Snow White, the seven dwarfs construct a transparent glass coffin on which they write the name and status of the princess with golden letters.

Compared to other dwarf figures in the Grimms' tales, the seven dwarfs are sensitive and display deep feelings. When they believe Snow White to be dead they mourn over her and cry for three days. They do not have the heart to bury the princess in the "black earth," and feel sympathy for the prince when he says that he cannot live without being able to see Snow White. The dwarfs' sense of empathy, compassion, condolence, and deep-felt devotion to Snow White, whose body they wash with water and wine before lying her on a bier, goes hand in hand with their caring character. Every time the seven little miners leave their house for work, they express their concern for Snow White's well-being and warn her not to open the door for anyone. Thus, the dwarfs function as parental protectors, providing guidance for the inexperienced child who is only seven years old when the evil queen decides to have her killed. Based on their concern for Snow White, the dwarfs repetitively deliver a warning that resembles a prophetic foreseeing of the danger to come: "Be careful about your stepmother. She will soon know that you are here. Do not let anyone in." The dwarfs' augural intuition conforms to their mythological reputation as repositories of wisdom and secret knowledge. In addition, they were credited with "having powers to foresee the future, assume other forms, and make themselves invisible."[7]

Although the seven dwarfs are good-natured, friendly, and kind in "Snow White," they do not shelter the fugitive princess without a service in return. The young princess enters into a verbal agreement with the dwarfs to take on the household chores, including cooking, making the beds, washing, sewing, knitting, and keeping everything clean and orderly. Only under this premise do the dwarfs agree to share their home with the beautiful maiden. This reciprocal relationship sharply contradicts Simon Gilmour's identification of "Snow White" as a tale of his first category of dwarfs in the Grimms' fairy tales, "the unexpected helper who demands no consideration" (Der unerwartete Helfer, der für seine Hilfe keine Gegenleistung verlangt; 1993,10–13). Due to the reciprocity between Snow White and the dwarfs, the tale belongs rather to Gilmour's third category, "the voluntary donor, who expects a consideration of similar value in return for a beneficence" (Der freiwillige Spender, der aber für seine Wohltätigkeit eine Gegengabe von gleichem Wert erwartet; 1993, 11). Into his third category Gilmour classifies the tales "Die drei Männlein im Walde" ("The Three Little Men in the Wood," KHM 13) and "The Golden Goose," "The Elves," "Das Wasser des Lebens" ("The Water of Life," KHM 97), "Der Jude im Dorn" ("The Jew in the Thornbush," KHM 110), and "Die Geschenke des kleinen Volkes" ("The Gifts of the Little People," KHM 182). The dwarfs in this category, according to Gilmour, are generous and return the favor of a benevolent deed or politeness by rewarding humans with magical gifts, beauty, wealth, or power (1993, 17). Exploiting the generosity of friendly dwarfs and self-indulgence, however, are punished harshly, for instance, with physical deformities, ugliness, or an unfortunate death. Within the communal living situation of the dwarfs in the tale "Snow White," every member is expected to contribute to the communal welfare. One might wonder how the seven dwarfs would have reacted if the princess had denied her services.

The dwarfs live in the forest, a marginalized living space far away from court and human society, which ties them to the status of outcasts and undesirable Others. Evocative of the fairy-tale witch, fairy-tale wolf, and other supernatural creatures dwelling in the woods, the seven dwarfs share a little cottage but are otherwise isolated in their habitat behind the seven mountains. Whether or not this isolation is by choice or by necessity can only be speculated upon. Did the dwarfs reject society or did society reject them, and if so, why? Santiago Solis hypothesizes that a societal rejection might be related to the dwarf's physical nonconformity: "The dwarfs are denied full citizenship because their bodies do not accommodate the architectural conventions of supposedly normal bodies. Consequently, since their stigmatization positions them as deviant, the dwarfs have no recourse but to segregate themselves from the rest of society" (2007, 124). Solis supports his conjecture by citing Rosemarie Garland-Thomson's reasoning on why society may shun disabled bodies. The disabled individuals, who are "at once familiarly human but definitively other," represent "a threatening presence, seemingly compromised by the particularities and limitations of their own bodies. . . . Cast as one of society's 'not me' figures, the disabled other" signifies vulnerability, somatic inadequacy, and loss of control and autonomy, which raises existential anxieties in the able-bodied (Garland-Thomson 1997, 41). Whether the dwarfs' seclusion is willing or unwilling, the mining dwarfs are a seemingly functioning group of workers and constitute, as such, an economically productive, autonomous, and self-sustaining small community.

According to Austrian psychoanalyst Bruno Bettelheim, the Grimms' *Märchen* are interspersed with hidden psychosexual conflicts, and "Snow White" is no exception. Bettelheim's emphasis on sexuality leads to a number of imaginative, if somewhat far-fetched, interpretations. He construes the dwarfs as "stunted penises" when he writes, "These 'little men' with their stunted bodies and their mining occupation—they skillfully penetrate into dark holes—all suggest phallic connotations. They are certainly not men in any sexual sense" (1976, 210). The dwarfs pose no sexual threat to the pubescent princess because their stunted growth alludes to their diminished sexual capacities. Sheldon Cashdan paraphrases Bettelheim, "Since they [the dwarfs] are unable to perform, they provide the child with a safe haven at a time in life when she is sexually vulnerable" (1999, 11). Instead of associating the dwarfs' bodies with male genitalia, they can also be interpreted to represent the desirable state of childhood and perhaps the wish to regress to a state of being physically little again. This consideration entails the notion of the dwarfs as innocent, childlike, asexual people who are bound to the domain of amity. Several authors and scholars of fairy tales have made similar observations. Bunny Crumpacker noted, "The poor little dwarfs, not men, not women, just like children, like good friends, cannot revive her" (2007, 90–91). Santiago Solis speaks of "the historical creation of the innocent, incognizant, childlike, and unsexed dwarf" (2007, 125). The release of Walt Disney's *Snow White and the Seven Dwarfs* (1937) certainly propagated the reputation of dwarfs as childlike and comical characters. With a primary audience of children in mind, Walt Disney and his team gave the dwarfs childlike names (e.g., Dopey, Sneezy, Sleepy, Happy) and temperaments and portrayed them in playful interactions as if they were little boys rather than adults. Philip Pullman refers to the animated comic sidekicks as "bearded babies" and calls Disney's Snow White the "all-American mom" (2012, 219).

Although the Grimms' dwarfs, and perhaps even more so Disney's animated creatures, may come across as childlike and asexual, it would be misleading to speak of a "historical creation," as Solis does in the quote cited above. Indeed, several dwarfs in Norse and Germanic mythology are sexual predators who lust after goddesses (e.g., four dwarfs demand sexual favors from the goddess Freyja in exchange for the necklace Brísingamen) and abduct human women. Prime examples for such a rape or abduction plot can be found, for instance, in the thirteenth-century Middle High German heroic epics dealing with Dietrich von Bern (Verona).[8] One epic poem tells of Laurin the dwarf king and his abduction of the princess Similde to his rose garden. In the fragmentary epic poem *Goldemar*, the dwarf king Goldemar abducts the maiden Hertlin, whom Dietrich rescues and then marries. Valdimar Tr. Hafstein noted that mythological sources such as the *Völuspá*, the first and best-known poem of the *Poetic Edda*, "depict dwarfs as an all-male race of supernatural beings, residing in cliffs and stones, created asexually from the bones and blood of the primordial giants" (2003, 33). Additionally, Ármann Jakobsson has suggested the dwarfs to be "a unisexual race" given the "total lack of women" in the *Edda* (2005, 68).[9] A similar observation holds true for the Grimms' fairy tales, where female dwarfs are almost never mentioned. In the only exception, "The Gifts of the Little People," the small women are not described any further. The idea that dwarfs abduct or imprison human women ("Strong Hans," KHM 166) because they are a unisexual race correlates with their stealing of human children (as in the stories of changelings, such as "The Elves") or their general desire for human children, as in the infamous tale of "Rumpelstiltskin."

The Grimms' tale "Rumpelstiltskin" is known for the reciprocal pact between a miller's daughter in need and the mysterious dwarf Rumpelstiltskin, who offers his services of spinning straw into gold. In exchange, the miller's daughter gives her unnamed helper a necklace the first night, a ring the second night, and finally promises her firstborn child to the manikin once she becomes queen. When the dwarf returns to claim the child one year later, the new queen offers the little man all the wealth of the kingdom if he will let her keep the child. Reminiscent of the seven dwarfs, who refuse to part with the still-living body of Snow White for "all the gold in the world," Rumpelstiltskin emphasizes that something living is dearer to him than all the treasures of the world. This complicates the assumption that fairy-tale dwarfs are first and foremost after materialistic wealth. Significantly, the Grimms mention in their notes to the *Children's and Household Tales* influential stories in which the helper figure asks for the woman instead of her child. Most notably, the Grimms reference the important French source tale "L'Histoire de Ricdin-Ricdon" by Mademoiselle Marie-Jeanne L'Héritier de Villandon in *La Tour ténébreuse et les jours luninineux, contes anglois* (The dark tower and luminous days: English tales, 1705). According to Zipes, the French tale is the very first literary form of "Rumpelstiltskin" (1994, 67). Johann Gottwerth Müller published a German version thereof in the second volume of his *Straußfedern* (Ostrich Feathers) in 1790. L'Héritier's tale also served as a source story for Karoline Stahl's "Das Stäbchen" ("The Small Rod") in *Fabeln, Mährchen und Erzählungen für Kinder* (Fables, fairy tales, and stories for children, 1818).

The stories of L'Héritier and Stahl both foreground the sexual interest of the helper figure in women. In the French tale, Rumpelstiltskin is not a dwarf but a tall, well-dressed man of brown or black and frightening appearance (Mayer and Mayer 1785, 40).[10] The uncanny man, also identified as "demon" (*démon*) and "evil spirit" (*esprit malin*), helps the beautiful girl Rosanie, who hates spinning but needs to spin flax for the queen. There is no mention of spinning straw into gold. The man gives Rosanie a small, magical rod or wand of fine, polished wood, studded with gemstones, which does the spinning for her. Rosanie may borrow the rod for three months but is told that she must remember the man's name, Ricdin-Ricdon, when she returns the magical object to him. Otherwise, the man may take her wherever he pleases (and presumably do with her whatever he wants—for example, rape her). Rosanie forgets the name but is saved by the prince, who overhears the man's singing at night, revealing his name. In the end, Rosanie defeats the dark man by saying his name and marries the prince. Stahl replaces the horrifying man with the figure of a *garstiger Zwerg* (nasty dwarf) called Gebhard (inspired by Müller's earlier version who uses the name Göbhard). He gives the maiden Röschen (Müller uses the same name) a small, magical rod that does the spinning for her to impress the king and queen. If Röschen forgets the dwarf's name after three months she must return the rod and go with the dwarf. The ending is similar to that of L'Héritier's tale but instead of marrying the prince, Röschen confesses her situation to the queen, hands over the rod for a financial reward, and returns home to her mother. The fact that Gebhard wants to take Röschen with her in Stahl's variant recalls the dwarfs of the Eddic tradition (e.g., Laurin and Godemar and their abduction of women).

Although Rumpelstiltskin represents a supernatural helper figure and the Grimms' tale is categorized as such in the Aarne-Thompson-Uther tale-type index (ATU 500), the magical manikin is coded negatively, as a demonic, sinister imp. The Grimms refer in their notes to five source stories from Hesse, all of which feature the trope of a dwarf demanding a child in exchange for his help. In a sixth Hessian story, Rumpelstiltskin is called Flederflitz and is a dark man who comes out of the ground but otherwise resides in a cave made of cooking ladles. In 1808, Jacob wrote down the earliest version of the Grimms' tale under the title "Rumpenstünzchen" and sent it to his friend, professor, and mentor, Friedrich Carl von Savigny. With few alterations and the notation "mündlich" (oral) as the tale's origin, Wilhelm recorded "Rumpenstünzchen" for the "*Urfassung*" (original version), the *Ölenberg manuscript* (*Ölenberger Handschrift*) of 1810 (Grimm and Grimm [1810] 2007, 128). In this variant, the girl's dilemma is that she can only spin gold instead of flax and Rumpenstünzchen is a little manikin offering to help in exchange for her firstborn child. The magical dwarf dwells in the woods and rides on a cooking ladle around the fire at night. Reminiscent of a witch on her broomstick, the imp flies on a cooking ladle out the window after the girl calls him by his true name at the end of the tale.[11] Furthermore, his remark, "The devil must have told you that," ties the figure to satanic forces, since the dwarf himself reveals his secret identity in the story. The Grimms expanded and intensified the ending in their following editions, where Rumpelstiltskin shouts repeatedly "The devil told you that!" before angrily stomping his right foot so hard into the ground that he ends up ripping himself in two. The manner of his gruesome self-destruction alludes to the fact that Rumpelstiltskin is a creature of the earth and is affiliated with demonic forces of the underworld. His brutal death in tearing himself apart is the Grimmian punishment for the malevolent dwarf whose physical anomaly, as Ann Schmiesing has noted, is an important marker of his villainy (2014, 140).

Whereas positive characters are usually free of physical "defects," or the bodily abnormalities are remedied at the end of the story (e.g., the blind prince in "Rapunzel," KHM 12; the girl whose hands are amputated by her father in "Das Mädchen ohne Hände" ["The Maiden Without Hands"], KHM 31), negative characters are often punished with corporal deformities (e.g., the evil sisters in "Aschenputtel" ["Cinderella"], KHM 21) or die a horrible death (e.g., Rumpelstiltskin, and the sight-impaired witch in "Hansel and Gretel" [KHM 15]). Schmiesing borrows the term "supercripple" from José Alaniz and Tobin Siebers to describe the helper-turned-tormentor Rumpelstiltskin as a disabled protagonist ("freak") with supernatural powers ("superfreak") who defies pity (2014, 111–12). In contrast to other, positively connoted supercripples—for example, the protagonists in the tales "Hans mein Igel" ("Hans My Hedgehog," KHM 108) and "Das Eselein" ("The Donkey," KHM 144), Rumpelstiltskin's deformation is not magically erased due to his dubious, malicious nature. Schmiesing elaborates why the Grimmian dwarf can be interpreted as an agent of disease, illness, and death, not least

because of the queen's alternate name suggestions for the dwarf in the tale
(2014, 140–43). When Rumpelstiltskin comes to claim the queen's child, the
miller's daughter, now queen, first guesses the names Kaspar, Melchior, and
Balzer, German variants of the names traditionally given to the Three Wise
Men or biblical Magi who brought gifts, including gold, to the Christ child.
Then the queen guesses the derisive nicknames Rippenbiest (rib beast),
Hammelswade (ram/wether calf), and Schnürbein (string leg). Schmiesing
associates each name with physical disfigurements and illness, such as chest
injury, deformity or atrophy of the legs, and genital mutilation (142).

The German suffix "*chen*" in the names Rumpelstilzchen and Rumpenstünzchen serves as diminutive not only to emphasize the characters'
smallness but also to infantilize the protagonist, as in the German names
Rotkäppchen (Little Red Riding Hood), Schneewittchen (Little Snow
White), or Dornröschen (Little Briar Rose). The origin of the denomina-
tions Rumpenstilz and Rumpenstunz is not entirely clear. In their notes, the
Grimms mention the children's game "Rumpele stilt oder der Poppart"[12]
in Johann Fischart's *Geschichtklitterung: Gargantua* (1575) and believe it to
be evidence of the fairy tale's age (Grimm and Grimm [1856] 2007, 3:107).
The Grimms' *Deutsches Wörterbuch* (*German Dictionary*) defines "Rum-
pelstilz" as a noisy, spooky goblin (*lärmender, spukender Kobold*) similar
to a poltergeist, associating the word "Rumpel" with noise (*Lärm*) but also
with wrinkle, pucker (*Runzel, Falte*), and in the compound "Rumpelzau-
bertasche" with the magical bag of a wrinkly witch (*runzliche Hexe*). The
word "Rumpen" is a derivative of "Rumpf," meaning body (*Leib*) and
the word "Stunz" refers to the adjectives stump, round, short (*stumpf, rund,
kurz*). Hence, the name Rumpenstünzchen might indeed indicate an old,
stunted figure and the name Rumpelstilzchen could allude to the creature's
supernatural, uncanny, and mischievous nature.

Schmiesing's interpretation of Rumpelstiltskin as a potential agent of
disease, deformity, illness, and death is especially of interest when seen in
conjunction with Rosemarie Garland-Thomson's reflections on society's

psychological reactions to disabled bodies. If the supercripple embodies the deviant, nonconforming, threatening Other and social outcast, his self-destruction in the end of the tale might symbolize the desire of the able-bodied to see the "abnormal" or supernatural individual removed from the "normal" or human society. Schmiesing points to the irrational fear able-bodied people may have that "contact with disabled people will somehow lead to their own disability" (2014, 144). Because the nondisabled may perceive disabled individuals as signifiers of physical deficiency, fragility, and somatic loss, they might shun them or meet them with disability bias and ableism. Whereas L'Héritier's demonic figure Ricdin-Ricdon is a tall, dark man, or a spirit disguised as such, the Grimms chose to tie their villainous outcast Rumpelstiltskin to deformation and stunted growth. The tale of the malevolent supercripple evokes other tales in the Grimms' collection, such as "The King of the Golden Mountain," with its dubious pact between a black manikin and a merchant, and tales featuring evil dwarfs, such as "Strong Hans" and "Snow White and Rose Red." In both tales, the Grimms depict the dwarf as greedy and unthankful creature who dwells in a secluded cave or in the woods. Since the dwarfs are coded negatively, they both find their "deserving" death at the end of the tales, similar to Rumpelstiltskin.[13]

The Grimms' "Snow White and Rose Red" is based on Karoline Stahl's literary fairy tale "Der undankbare Zwerg" ("The Ungrateful Dwarf," 1818) and stands out for its detailed descriptions of the antagonistic dwarf and his outrageous temper tantrums. Already Stahl uses the adjectives *böse* (evil), *hässlich* (ugly), and *garstig* (nasty) to describe a grumpy and impolite dwarf. Convinced that Stahl's tale is "Surely a real, old dwarf legend" ("Gewiß eine ächte, alte Zwergensage"), as Wilhelm remarked, the Grimms published their own adaptation of Stahl's tale in Hauff's *Mährchenalmanach auf das Jahr 1827* and eventually in the 1833 and 1837 editions of their fairy-tale collection (Grimm and Grimm, [1856] 2007, 3:504). The Grimms' retelling centers on the two sisters Snow White and Rose Red rather than on the figure of the dwarf, as indicated by the tale's different title. In their reimagined variant, the Grimms foreground the good-hearted, diligent, and pious sisters who live in harmony with their natural surroundings. Whereas Snow White prefers to help their poor, widowed mother with the household chores and read to her, Rose Red likes to go out into nature. Together, the sisters represent the harmonious and divine unison of the two antithetic spaces, the domestic cottage and the wild forest. This is supported by the fact that the sisters are at home in both places, are close to all forest creatures, and sleep in the woods under the supernatural protection of a guardian angel. Their pet lamb and white dove evoke innocence, purity, and the Christian symbolism of Jesus Christ and the Holy Spirit. The tale romanticizes the sisters' encounter with a he-bear who asks for shelter during the winter in their cottage and becomes their playmate. Whereas the bear appears as a noble creature whose true identity as enchanted prince augments his nobility even further, the dwarf represents his ignoble counterpart.

The ending of the tale reveals that the enchanted prince and his antagonist have a history, since the "godless" (*gottlos*) dwarf bewitched the prince into becoming a bear and stole his treasure. The bear identifies the dwarfs early on as an evil and thieving subterranean race that is greedy for treasures. When spring arrives he says to Snow White, "I must go into the forest and guard my treasures from the wicked dwarfs. In the winter, when the earth is frozen hard, they are obliged to stay below and cannot work their way through; but now, when the sun has thawed and warmed the earth, they break through it, and come out to pry and steal; and what once gets into their hands, and in their caves, does not easily see daylight again." Some time after the bear has left the sisters, they encounter an old, helpless dwarf with a withered face whose long, snow-white beard is caught in a crevice of a tree. The text compares the "little fellow" (*der Kleine*) with a little dog tied to a rope jumping backward and forward, thereby empathizing his inferiority. His red and fiery eyes endow the creature with demonic features. The dwarf's magical powers appear limited, since he cannot free himself from the predicament of his self-inflicted, awkward situation after chopping down a tree. Although the sisters try to help him, he only screams and insults them by calling Rose Red a "stupid, prying goose" and both of them "odious," "silly, sleek, milk-faces," and "crazy muttonheads."[14] After Snow White cuts off the end of his beard, the ungrateful dwarf seizes a bag of gold and grumbles, "Uncouth people, to cut off a piece of my fine beard. May the cuckoo [the devil is implied] reward you."[15]

Fairy-tale scholar Cristina Bacchilega ties the cutting of the dwarf's beard to a symbolic emasculation, as the beard traditionally represents strength and manhood (2015, 84). One can only speculate about other potential metaphors associated with the cutting of the beard, such as the loss of (magical) power, infamy, and, from a psychological perspective, symbolic castration. Perhaps more obvious is the assumption that the dwarf exhibits signs of vanity and shame for having a shorter beard. At their second encounter, the sisters help the dwarf, whose beard got entangled with his fishing line. This time, Snow White and Rose Red rescue the dwarf from the imminent danger of being drowned, since a big fish threatens to pull him under water. When Snow White cuts off a little piece of the dwarf's beard, he yells angrily, "Is that manners, you toads (*Lorche*[16]), to defile one's face? Not enough that you have clipped the end of my beard, now you have cut off the best part of it. I dare not be seen by my people. I wish you had been made to run and had lost the soles of your shoes!"[17] The Grimms also use the peculiar curse of the dwarf in their tale "The Jew in the Thornbush," where a Jew curses a servant, "I want to chase you that you may lose the soles of your shoes" ("Ich will dich jagen, daß du die Schuhsohlen verlieren sollst"; Grimm and Grimm [1856] 2007, 2:127). Although there is no evidence that the Grimms associated the ungrateful dwarf in "Snow White and Rose Red" with the negatively stigmatized figure of the Jew in their fairy tales, the two characters are connected linguistically through the curse they both speak. This, perhaps coincidental, commonality also recalls Tolkien's linkage between dwarfs and Jews.[18] The Grimms may have been inspired by the writings of Hans Jakob Christoffel von Grimmelshausen (1622–76), who employed the expression "began to run away that the soles of his shoes may have fallen off" in his novel *Trutz Simplex* (1670).[19]

Similar to Stahl's literary hypotext, the sisters rescue the dwarf from the dangers of three different elemental beings: a tree (earth), a fish (water), and a bird (air). When an eagle seizes the dwarf to carry him off, Snow White and Rose Red, full of pity, save his life once more by pulling against the eagle until he lets go of the booty. Angry that his coat is torn to shreds, the dwarf screeches "clumsy riffraff" at the sisters, grabs a bag of precious stones, and disappears. Whereas Stahl presented the dwarf only as an ungrateful and impolite creature, the Grimms intensified the character's negative persona by portraying him to be verbally abusive, insulting, and aggressive. The dwarf's malicious nature is most prominent when the he-bear appears at the end of the tale, threatening to kill him. After attempting to buy his life free with his treasures and jewels, the dwarf selfishly tries to save his own skin by suggesting the bear kill Snow White and Rose Red instead: "Take these two godless girls, they are tender morsels for you, fat as young quails; eat them in God's name." In Stahl's story, the wild bear is a nonmagical creature that devours the greedy dwarf simply because, as Stahl remarked, he deserved his fate and no one mourned him. The Grimms' tale foregrounds the enchantment of the magically cursed prince, thereby adding a dimension of wonder and another layer of meaning pertaining to the significance of animal-bridegrooms. The enchanted bear kills the evil creature in an apparent act of revenge with "a single blow of his paw" for transforming him into an animal and stealing his riches. The death of the wicked dwarf is an essential prerequisite to breaking the spell of the enchantment.

The crude behavior of the adverse dwarf in the Grimms' "Snow White and Rose Red" evokes the misbegotten, ugly character Klein Zaches of E. T. A. Hoffmann's anti-Enlightenment tale "Klein Zaches, genannt Zinnober:[20] Ein Mährchen" ("Little Zaches, Named Zinnober: A Fairy Tale," 1819). The malevolent dwarfish creature, first introduced as a misshapen, repulsive changeling, has a spell cast on him by the fairy Rosabelverde so that others find him beautiful and adorable. Thanks to the fairy's magic, everything good is attributed to Klein Zaches, whereas his tyrannical actions and ugly features are attributed to other people. In reality, the grotesque "dwarf," who curses and screeches when he talks, treats people in mean, barbaric, and nasty ways. The magic surrounding Klein Zaches (now named Zinnober) lies in three red hairs but disappears once the student Balthasar tears them off the manikin's head and throws them into the fire. At the beginning of the tale, the wicked creature is identified to be a changeling with features resembling those of the Grimms' changeling in "The Elves": "the boy was three-and-a-half and he can't walk, he can't run on his spidery little legs, and instead of talking, he growls and miaows, like a cat. Yet for all that the deformed wretch eats like the strongest eight-year-old lad, without putting on any weight at all" (Hoffmann [1819] 2005, 2). In his descriptions, Hoffmann especially highlights the physical deformities and abnormalities of the dwarfish being, who is only two spans high as an infant and crawls and growls like an animal. The literary fairy tale then merges the dwarfish figure of the changeling with the legendary mandrake (*Alraune, Alräunchen*) and ties it to somatic disability.

Hoffmann dehumanizes and objectifies the misshapen body of Klein Zaches by labeling him to be a mandrake and "a thing."

The thing's head was set deep between its shoulders, it had a pumpkin-like outgrowth in place of a back, and its hazel switch-thin little legs hung down directly beneath its breast, so that the boy resembled a split radish. A dull eye would discover little about the face, but looking more closely, you would become aware of a long, sharp nose jutting out beneath shaggy black hair and a pair of small, darkly flashing eyes that seemed—especially when one considered the otherwise quite old, furrowed facial features—to reveal a small alraun. (2)

Later on, the tale reveals that the "dwarf" is "neither a mandrake nor an Earth Spirit, but an ordinary human" (64). Once the magic spell is broken that made Klein Zaches, now Minister Zinnober, lovable to everyone, the people react with disgust and ridicule at his sight. The crowd throws stones, fruits, and vegetables at him, and screams derogative terms, such as smart little baboon, hideous little monster, little beast, fantastic freak, hop-o'-my-thumb, and little witch's imp. The angry mob calls for Minister Zinnober's downfall, suggesting that he should be locked in a cage, shown for money at the fair, or given to the children for a toy (105). Klein Zaches/Zinnober remains a figure of ridicule until the end of the tale. After he drowns in a silver-handled pot in the bathroom, his birth mother wants to stuff him like a little bird or squirrel and display his corpse on her cabinet (106–8).

Negative connotations of physical disability and deformity in connection with dwarfish figures also loom large in Wilhelm Hauff's literary fairy tales "Der kleine Muck" ("Little Muck," 1825) and "Zwerg Nase" ("Dwarf Long Nose," 1826). Only Hauff's "Das kalte Herz" ("The Cold Heart," 1827) features a good-natured, centuries-old forest spirit, the bearded, smoking, and wish-fulfilling glass manikin named "Schatzhauser" (treasure-keeper). The protagonists of "Little Muck" and "Dwarf Long Nose" are both social outcasts due to their bodily abnormalities and strange appearances. Muck's physical deformity (he is the size of a dwarf with an extraordinarily large head) and bizarre clothes (he wears an immense turban, a shabby little cloak, wide pants, and broad slippers that cause his feet to drag) provoke hostile reactions, teasing, and ridicule. Muley, a merchant of the tale's framing narrative, confesses, ashamed, how he used to make fun of Muck with his friends by singing: "Little Muck, little Muck, what an awful fright you look! In a big house you reside, only once a month outside. You are a plucky dwarf, but still your head is almost like a hill; do but just turn around and look, run and catch us, Little Muck" (Hauff [1825–27] 1890, 59). Thanks to his supernatural items, a pair of slippers that carries its wearer swiftly wherever he wishes to be and a magic walking stick that locates buried treasures, Muck manages to enter the services of a king. However, after the king confiscates the supernatural objects and chases Muck away, the little man takes revenge on the royal household by smuggling magic figs on the king's table that cause donkey's ears and long noses. Only after consumption of a different kind of magic figs the facial deformities disappear again.[21] Like the Brothers Grimm, Hauff uses the trope of corporal disfigurement as a form of punishment and ties it to societal stigma. Although Muck is a victim himself of disability discrimination in public, he leaves the disloyal king with his deformed face behind and returns to his home town. There, Muck lives in prosperity but remains lonely as he despises other people. Muck's misanthropy results from his disillusionment and disappointment about the greed and malice of his fellow men but also their stereotypical, negative attitudes towards disability. Hauff's moral lesson embedded in the tale's framing narrative denunci-ates the stigmatization of people with physical abnormalities since Muley repented of his unworthy conduct towards "the good little man" and he and his friends respected Muck as long as he lived (75).

Whereas Muck's dwarfish growth and oversized head are natural impair-ments, the protagonist Jakob in "Dwarf Long Nose" becomes a social outcast because of a magically induced long nose and grotesquely misshapen figure. An ugly old woman with red eyes abducts the handsome, twelve-year-old boy after he chafed at her behavior at the marketplace and openly scorned her looks. The boy's haughty remarks cause his downfall. The old woman is the wicked fairy Kräuterweis who bewitches Jakob into slavery as a squirrel in her household. When he awakes from a dreamlike state, he finds that seven years have passed and that his body has been transformed to that of a hunchbacked dwarf with a thick, long nose, brown hands, and spider-like fingers. Hoffmann gives a very detailed description to highlight Jakob's dras-tic physical deformation:

His eyes had become as small as pig's eyes, his nose was enormous, and hung down over his mouth and chin; his neck seemed to have disappeared altogether, for his head was deeply stuck on his shoulders, and it was with the utmost pain he could turn it to right or left; his body was the same size as seven years ago when he was twelve years of age, but while other grew in height from twelve to twenty, he had grown in breadth, his back and chest were broad and expanded, and looked like a little but well-stuffed sack, this enormous upper part of his body was supported by his little legs, which did not seem suitable for such a burden . . . He had changed into a deformed dwarf. (121–22)

Whereas his mother no longer recognizes Jakob and rejects her son by calling him "ugly dwarf" and "hideous monster," the people laugh at his unsightly appearance and make a public spectacle of him (118). Having learned the art of cooking during his servitude for the fairy Kräuterweis, Jakob is able to raise his social standing by obtaining the position of head chef at the duke's court. His excellent culinary skills ultimately save his life and render him useful in the eyes of higher society. However, due to his dwarfish size, Jakob has to prove his worthiness over and over. When he first arrives at court, the duke's chief cook looks at the dwarf from head to foot, bursts into a hearty laugh along with the other servants, and claims that Jakob could not even reach the fireplaces in the kitchen because of his stunted growth. The duke even threatens to chop off Jakob's head and put it on display if he fails to prepare the *souzeraine*, the queen of all pies. Finally, Jakob (now called *Zwerg Nase*) must find the secret herb *Niesmitlust* (Sneeze-with-pleasure) to bake the complicated pie and to break the fairy's spell, which he does with the help of Mimi, the daughter of a magician. Although Jakob defies the stigmatizing and prejudicial attitudes of the people around him, the protagonist's reward is his deliverance from his grotesque body and return to a "normal" physique. The ending of the tale thus perpetuates two significant aspects: firstly, the classic trope in German Romantic fairy tales of linking deformity and disability with punishments and bad, sinful, or improper behavior, and secondly, the portrayal of the dwarf as a negative figure characterized by ugliness and physical deficiencies. The following section will shed light on how contemporary North American media have reinterpreted the figure of the dwarf, based hypertextually on the Grimms' fairy tales, in an imaginative makeover tailored to popular culture.

Dwarfs in Postmodern American Media

The Grimms' tales portray dwarfs generally as ambivalent and reciprocal figures, oscillating between the ugly, nasty, devilish, and ungrateful imp and the benevolent, infantilized, domesticated, asexual manikin. Of all the Grimms' tales featuring dwarfs, the one most frequently adapted in postmodern American media appears to be the fairy tale "Snow White," which has seen a multitude of recastings for film and television. For the purpose of analysis, it is helpful to narrow the scope of research to media adaptations of the past two decades, as already done in Chapter Two. Further, it is crucial to focus on a diverse range of genres, including Michael Cohn's horror television film *Snow White: A Tale of Terror* (1997), Caroline Thompson's adventure television film and Hallmark production *Snow White: The Fairest of Them All* (2001), Joe Nussbaum's teen romantic comedy *Sydney White* (2007), Tarsem Singh's family comedy *Mirror Mirror* (2012), Rupert Sanders' action-loaded fantasy film *Snow White and The Huntsman* (2012) and ABC's popular drama television series *Once Upon a Time* (2011–18). Although fairy-tale scholarship has devoted attention to some of these recastings of "Snow White" already, for example, in *Channeling Wonder: Fairy Tales on Television* (2014) edited by Pauline Greenhill and Jill Terry Rudy and in *The Enchanted Screen* (2011) by Jack Zipes, the portrayal of the dwarf figure in these retellings remains largely unexplored. Of interest to me in particular is how these postmodern representations depart from, complicate, and subvert the conventional image of the fairy-tale dwarf as a small, old, long-bearded, wealth-obsessed, and deformed creature.

Most interestingly, there seems to be a trend in American media adaptations to subvert the idea that fairy-tale dwarfs and reimaginings thereof have to be represented in the media by little people or child actors. In other words, postmodern retellings of "Snow White" increasingly employ average-height actors and cast them in the roles occupied traditionally by "dwarfs." Whereas in some retellings, such as the productions by Cohn and Nussbaum, average-sized actors appear alongside a reincarnated Snow White without being labeled as "dwarfs," the television series *Once Upon a Time* draws heavily on that archetypal fairy-tale designation. Other productions also use average-height people to play fantastic dwarfs but digitally fit their full-sized bodies to dwarf size via computer-generated imagery (CGI) and special effects, such as Sanders' *Snow White and The Huntsman* and Jackson's *Lord of the Rings* and *Hobbit* films. The casting of big people to fill the iconic fairy-tale roles instead of able-bodied little people has stirred severe controversy and protests among advocates for little people, such as the representatives of Little People of America, Inc., "a national nonprofit organization that provides support and information to people of short stature and their families" (LPA 2017). Actor Danny Woodburn, who had a popular, recurring role on the television show *Seinfeld* as Mickey Abbott and played a dwarf in *Mirror Mirror*, went so far as to call the casting of average-sized actors for the role of dwarfs "akin to black face" (Li 2012). However, the producers using CGI-augmented versions of average-sized actors to create dwarfs in their films have counterargued that their casting preference was based on actors' talent and recognizability rather than body size. Sanders, for example, emphasized in an interview that the actors playing dwarfs in *Snow White and The Huntsman* "are some of the best character actors in the world. And that's why I cast them" (Ryan 2012). One might wonder, of course, how little people can gain recognizability if they are not cast in the first place and whether the phrase "talent and recognizability" serves merely as a convenient justification for some directors to exclude able-bodied little people. In a different interview, actor Warwick Davis, who is perhaps best known for his roles in *Star Wars* and the *Harry Potter* series, acknowledges that producers' casting decisions hinge greatly on the pool of actors from which to choose. He commented on

Jackson's casting choices, "I kind of understand why Peter Jackson did what he did—there wasn't the range of short actors to fill the roles" (Gilber 2011).

Michael Cohn's *Snow White: A Tale of Terror* abstains from the identifier "dwarf" altogether and portrays six average-sized actors and one little person (Bart, played by John Edward Allen) in the role of seven rough, combative gold miners who live as criminal outcasts in the forest. Instead of a homey cottage, they dwell in castle ruins in the woods, where Snow White, a.k.a. Lilli (Monica Keena), seeks shelter and spends the night. When the miners find her, they immediately threaten not only her life but also her sexuality:

WILL (Gil Bellows): If you want to live, don't make a sound.

BART: Are you here alone?

SCAR (Andrew Tiernan): She could be lying.

WILL: Who are you? Why are you here?

FATHER GILBERT (Bryan Pringle): What's your name, child?

LARS (Brian Glover): She is no child.

BART: Maybe she can't speak.

CONRAD (Christopher Bauer): Can't speak.

SCAR: Then she won't make a fuss when the wolves eat her. I say we throw her out.

CONRAD: She smells good.

ROLF (Anthony Brophy): I bet she tastes good, too.

Instead of offering Lilli hospitality, the miners deny her food, ridicule her, and make insinuating remarks. Whereas Bart and Scar only threaten sexual advances and obscenities, Rolf is depicted as a sexual predator who attempts to rape Lilli but only gets as far as tearing her blouse and forcing a kiss on her before Will puts a knife to his throat. The community of outcasts, led by Will, kick Rolf out and he grudgingly leaves.

Remarkably, Cohn highlights the heterogeneous nature of the miners' physicality by portraying seven bodies of different ages and height, with attractive and unattractive features, some slender, clean-shaven, with short

hair or bald head, others chubby, bearded, and with long hair. The striking fact that three of the miners, Will, Scar, and Lawrence, are marked by
facial disfigurement and scarring recalls the idea of dwarfs as misshapen and
deformed creatures. Conrad, the biggest miner, is portrayed as a childlike
simpleton and gentle giant, suggesting some form of mental impairment.
In contrast to the Grimms' tales, where magical and divine powers ensure
villains' punishment, Cohn ties disability and somatic disfigurement in his
adaptation to punishment executed by secular and religious powers. The film
implies that the miners are the victims of a cruel and unjust feudal system,
since the judges of Lilli's father, Lord Hoffman (Sam Neill), ordered their
corporal disfigurements as penalty for stealing food. Because Will refused
to join the cause of the Crusaders, they tied him to a stake, burned his
family while he watched, and then placed a red-hot cross of iron on his face.
Cohn also eroticizes some of the miners, since Lilli watches the shirtless,
muscular bodies of Will, Scar, and Conrad while they are slaving away in
the mines. Another sexually charged scene is the passionate kiss in the rain
between Lilli and Will, whose relationship continues to grow as the diegesis
evolves.

Overall, the film elevates the significance of the miners in the story by
turning Will into the hero figure and by adding two dramatic death scenes
of Lars and Father Gilbert, who fall victim to the attacks of the "evil queen,"
Lady Claudia (Sigourney Weaver). From the outset of his character introduction, Will is no Prince Charming, either by his looks or by his background
and conduct. Lilli rejects him at first, calling him an animal, a criminal, and
a savage. Will, in return, shows some aggressive tendencies by grabbing
her throat and only lets go of her once she tells him that he frightens her.
Will's "bad boy" behavior around Lilli is laced with flirtatious innuendo and
starkly undermines the traditional archetype of the fairy-tale prince:

LILLI: Why are you staring at me?
WILL: It hadn't occurred to me to look anywhere else.

LILLI: It's very rude.

WILL: It's one of my better habits.

LILLI: I take it you have no manners then.

WILL: No manners then . . . and no manners now.

LILLI: Are you trying to be funny?

WILL: I was just wondering what it would take . . . to make a princess smile.

Beneath the rough shell, however, Will conceals a kind heart. He cares about his fellow miners and goes out of his way to protect Lilli even when there is nothing in it for him. Finally, it is not the handsome, well-groomed "prince," Dr. Peter Gutenberg (David Conrad), who saves Lilli from being buried alive in a glass coffin but the defaced, fierce pariah Will. He revives Lilli by shaking her lifeless body, which dislodges the piece of poisoned apple stuck in her throat, and by repeatedly urging her to breathe.

Of the seven miners supplanting the Grimms' dwarfs in *Snow White: A Tale of Terror*, only four remain alive at the end of the story. Bart, Lars, and Conrad wish Lilli a friendly farewell when her "prince," Peter, comes to bring her home. Similar to the Grimms' tale, the "prince" offers the "dwarfs" monetary compensation for "the princess." Contrary to the Grimmian version, however, Will hesitantly accepts Peter's financial reward, which can be interpreted as an attempt to bribe the rival in love to not pursue Lilli. Despite taking the money, Will follows Lilli and Peter back to the castle to stop Lady Claudia and to rescue Lord Hoffman. After the "evil queen" kills Peter by pushing him out a window, Lilli defeats her stepmother, Claudia, and joins Will, who brought her father to safety. Because Cohn's horror adaptation adds psychological depths and sexually explicit aspects to a very diverse portrayal of the miners, thereby catering to an adult audience, it stands in stark opposition to its source tale as well as to the popular Disney narrative. The superficial, cheerful, childlike, asexual, cartoon dwarfs may have served as a blueprint for Thompson's portrayal of the "seven little men" in *Snow White: The Fairest of Them All*.

Thompson's live-action, made-for-TV film features a most original plot and depiction of Snow White's (Kristin Kreuk's) little helpers, who appear not only child-friendly but quintessentially infantilized. The dwarfish characters, each one displaying a different rainbow color and named for a different day of the week, are a motley and highly diverse crew. Thanks to their weather-controlling, magical powers, they can transform into a rainbow and transport themselves anywhere in the kingdom as long as they are all together. Monday (Michael Gilden), Tuesday (Mark J. Trombino), Friday (Martin Klebba), Saturday (Warwick Davis), and Sunday (Michael J. Anderson) are all portrayed by little men, whereas the insatiable Thursday (Penny Blake) is played by a little woman, and pessimistic Wednesday is played by the very tall actor Vincent Schiavelli. As Zipes points out, "They are obviously intended to make a mockery out of the Disney dwarfs and are comic appendages to the main plot" (2011, 126). In a subplot of the "Snow White" story, the seven weather dwarfs, who do not concern themselves with human affairs, are searching for the gnomes of the kingdom, which have mysteriously disappeared. The gnomes are responsible for such mundane things as delivering the daily mail and milk. The viewer learns that the wicked Elspeth (Miranda Richardson) has petrified the gnomes and turned them into decorative figurines for her garden. The white-bearded, grinning garden gnomes or *Gartenzwerge* with their colorful pointy hats, as Zipes remarks, "resemble those ghastly cute Disney dwarfs that some people love to place on their lawns in America as if they were objects of beauty or hominess" (126). When Sunday, the leader and oldest of the beardless weather dwarfs, comes across Elspeth's run-down shack, the wicked witch magically transmogrifies him into a petrified garden ornament as well and places the sculpture next to the other gnomes on her lawn.

The tradition of the German *Gartenzwerg* is rooted in the fashion for keeping little people, hunchbacks, cripples, or other orthopedically impaired individuals at court as so-called *Hofzwerge* (court dwarfs). The popular custom of owning dwarf servants as "human pets" lasted from medieval times to the end of the eighteenth century at European courts. Considered rare attractions and freaks, the court dwarfs were traded, sold, and gifted among rulers throughout Europe. "Due to their small stature and not uncommon deformity, their presence reinforced the idea of perfection and superiority of the ruling dynasty" (Ivanova 2013, 5). Their functions at court were diverse, ranging from entertainment and amusement purposes in the role of carnivalesque jesters to companionship for the monarch's children and lucky charms. In some cases, rulers surrounded themselves with court dwarfs like extravagant collectibles as an expression of wealth. Especially during the Renaissance, the employment of court dwarfs was considered "en vogue." As a substitute, dwarf statues made of white limestone or sandstone could be placed in the palace gardens. The oldest dwarf statues in Europe today are the twenty-eight baroque sculptures in the *Zwerglgarten* or "Dwarf Garden" at Castle Mirabell in Salzburg, Austria.

Elspeth's magically imprisoned gnomes evoke the court dwarfs, since she takes her gnome collection with her to the castle once she becomes queen and Snow White's stepmother. For amusement purposes, the court society uses them as expendable bowling pins at a royal banquet. Following the folk belief that rubbing the head of a dwarf brings good luck, Elspeth considers the gnomes to be lucky charms. After her brother, a genie-like creature known as the Green-Eyed One (Clancy Brown), transforms her from an ugly crone into a beautiful and young woman without demanding anything in return, she happily turns to her gnomes. Because she cannot believe her good fortune, she asks the mute companions to "look at her" and then touches four of the gnomes on their heads as if they were responsible for her unexpected change of luck. Later in the film, she repeatedly touches the head of Monday, the weather dwarf, before turning him into one of her statues bereft of any mobility. Further, the film intensifies the association with court dwarfs and disability through the portrayal of Sunday's partial deliverance from Elspeth's evil spell, leaving half of his face and body transfixed as garden gnome. Due to his magical impairment, he must walk with the aid of a wooden crutch. Reminiscent of the court dwarfs in their role as jesters and fools, the weather dwarfs also add a good portion of slapstick comedy to Thompson's adventure television film. Most prominently, Schiavelli, in his role as Wednesday, the yellow weather dwarf, comes across as a buffoon, emulating Disney's dwarf Grumpy and, perhaps coincidentally, conjuring up D'Aulnoy's gruff "yellow dwarf."

For Snow White's protection, the kind weather dwarfs go so far as to turn on one another. When the princess seeks refuge in their cottage in the woods, everyone except Wednesday wants to help the beautiful damsel in distress. Whereas the weather dwarfs applaud Snow White's plan to rescue her father, the prince, and the gnomes from the evil clutches of the queen, Wednesday protests strongly.

SUNDAY: It's brilliant.

SATURDAY: It's courageous.

WEDNESDAY: Phooey. It's stupid and we are stupid to let you stay here. The queen knows where we live. She was here and tried to kill her, remember? Think of what she'll do when she finds out that she's still alive. Think of what she'll do to us when she finds out that we're helping her.

TUESDAY: Stuff it, Wednesday.

WEDNESDAY: But does anyone consider this? No! It's just "How are you my dear?", "Can I do anything for you my dear?", "Can I polish your butt . . ."

SATURDAY: Why don't you shut your big mouth?

The disagreement escalates when the weather dwarfs tackle their tall companion, shackle his hands, and lock him up in a small closet. Only after Snow White secretly frees Wednesday in the middle of the night does the "gigantic dwarf" come around and change his mind about Snow White. Once the curse of the wicked queen is broken through the destruction of her mirror, the gnomes become freed from their enchantment and angrily attack Elspeth, a scene perhaps inspired by the ending of Disney's *Snow White and the Seven Dwarfs.* Ironically, Elspeth's "lucky charms" are her demise. The film closes on a romantic-comedic note of the weather dwarfs waving their farewell to Snow White and her prince, announcing that they are "On to Sleeping Beauty" next.

Unlike most American commercial "Snow White" adaptations, Joe Nussbaum's teen romantic comedy, *Sydney White,* is not set in a medieval period or narrative but takes place in the twenty-first century instead. The seven dwarfs in this adaptation are seven dorks, a group of average-sized, male college students and socially inept outcasts who live together in a dilapidated house on the campus of Southern Atlantic University (SAU). The dorks are misfits not because of their body sizes but primarily because they exhibit odd and quirky behaviors: Lenny (Jack Carpenter), a likeable, hyperallergenic student with manifold health issues requiring high maintenance; Terrence (Jeremy Howard), a genius and post-grad who still attends classes to satisfy his thirst for knowledge; Jeremy (Adam Hendershott), a very shy guy who saw several therapists as a child and still relies on his therapy puppet dog Skoozer to talk to people; Gurkin (Danny Strong), a hot-tempered blogger; Spanky (Samm Levine), who likes to hit on girls but lacks experience with the opposite sex; George (Arnie Pantoja), an immature boy scout who still believes in Santa Claus and does not know how to tie a knot; and Embelakbo Akapaktumbe or "Embele" (Donté Bonner), a Nigerian exchange student who still suffers from jet lag after three years and sleeps most of his screen time.

The film follows Sydney White (Amanda Bynes), a.k.a. Snow White, who is off to college to follow in her deceased mother's footsteps by becoming a member of the Kappa Sorority, headed by the vain, Barbie-like Rachel Witchburn (Sara Paxton). Rachel's "magic mirror" is the university's website "SAU Hot or Not," which reveals daily who has been voted "fairest of them all" by the students. When Sydney's popularity rises and she also attracts the attention of Rachel's ex-boyfriend Tyler Prince (Matt Long), Rachel publicly humiliates the tomboyish freshman and banishes her from the sorority.

Sydney finds refuge in the half-timbered, cottage-style home of the dorks, the run-down house Vortex, which is so named because it "sucks in losers." Sydney soon discovers that Rachel is controlling the student council budget appropriations and that her plan is to replace the Vortex with a luxury center that will benefit only the Greek sororities and fraternities. Sydney convinces the dorks to run against Rachel's sorority at the next student council election and spearheads their newly founded Freedom to the 7th Power Party.[22] Thanks to earning the respect of other outsider clubs on campus, Sydney wins the election whereas Rachel is kicked out of her sorority for exhibiting behavior unsuitable for a Kappa. With the help of Sydney's father and his construction workers from the company Royalty Plumbing, the seven dorks fix up the Vortex together with their newly made friends and live "dorkily ever after."

Nussbaum's romantic comedy highlights the story of the seven dorks to celebrate Otherness and to convey the moral message that diversity and equality trump sameness and elitism, especially the kind of exclusivism based solely on superficial appearances. Throughout the film, the dorks are ridiculed as freaks and systematically oppressed by the Greek student organizations. They are depicted as not only socially inept but also sexually inexperienced. In one scene, the dorks gather in awe around one of Sydney's bras to the music of Richard Strauss's *Also sprach Zarathustra*, behaving as if they were looking at a most mystical object:

SPANKY: Dudes . . . that thing has touched boobs.
TERRENCE: Of course. The sturdy, breathable fabric is designed to maintain mammary elasticity.
SPANKY: Shut up, Terrence! You're ruining the moment for me.

At the same time, the dorks are very protective when it comes to Sydney's love life and her blossoming relationship with her "prince" Tyler. At their first date, the dorks encourage Sydney and advise her on what outfit to wear.

When Tyler arrives at their house, the dorks go so far as to threaten him, should he try to take advantage of Sydney:

TERRENCE: Three quarters of first dates end in disappointment for one or both parties, studies show. I hope you beat the odds.

TYLER: Me, too.

GURKIN: If you try any funny stuff I will unleash the power of the internet on you. I will register you as a sex offender in all fifty states and Canada.

TYLER: Wow. Yeah!

GEORGE: And I'll kick your ass.

As in the Grimms' tale, the relationship between Sydney and the dorks is a symbiotic one. While the dorks allow Sydney to stay at the Vortex, she manages their political campaign, teaches George how to tie a knot, sets the alarm clock for Embele, introduces the couch potatoes to the campus fitness center, and helps them to socialize at a SAU football game. Sydney's strategy to connect the dorks with other outsiders on campus pays off in the end. At the debate, different minority clubs, such as the Southern Atlantic Pacific Islanders Association, the Reserve Officers' Training Corps, the Jewish Student Union, the Gay, Lesbian, Transgender, and Searching Alliance, the Marching Band, and the Gothic community, support the cause of the dorks. Sydney's debate speech defends diversity and incites a number of students, including members of the Greek fraternities and sororities, to proclaim their own "dorkyness."[23] Thanks to Sydney's positive influence, the seven dorks ultimately overcome some of their inhibitions. Gurkin and Lenny both have girlfriends at the end of the film, Terrence leaves college and becomes a millionaire, and Jeremy can speak publicly without his therapeutic puppet.

Although there is no magic at work in *Sydney White*, the film is intertextually and hypertextually linked to both the Grimms' tale and the Disney version of "Snow White." When the seven dorks return home and find a sign that the Vortex has been condemned, Gurkin says, "Things are looking grim, brothers" as a wordplay on the German folklorists. Further, the characters of the seven dorks relate directly to the identities of the popular Disney dwarfs: Lenny is Sneezy; Terrence is Doc; Jeremy is Bashful; Gurkin is Grumpy; Spanky is Happy; Embele is Sleepy; and George is Dopey. Another allusion to Disney's *Snow White and the Seven Dwarfs* is a scene depicting the seven dorks carrying wooden campaign signs (instead of pickaxes) over their shoulders. As they pass Rachel one by one, the first dork says "Hi Ho," and the last dork says "Bye Ho." Interestingly, what separates Nussbaum's recasting of "Snow White" from previous revisions is its multicultural portrayal of the "dwarfs." The director's choice to have African-American actor Donté Bonner play the Nigerian student Embele underscores the film's principal messages of promoting difference and celebrating heterogeneity, including ethnic, racial, and global cultural diversity.

Director Tarsem Singh also foregrounds a group of multicultural dwarfs as outcasts in *Mirror Mirror*, his modernized, edgy reimagining of

The seven dorks in *Sydney White* (2007) are intertextually linked to the dwarfs in Disney's *Snow White and the Seven Dwarfs* (1937).

the classic fairy tale featuring a self-determined, sword-wielding heroine. In this production, Snow White (Lily Collins) encounters seven courageous rebel dwarfs who are played by little people. The dwarfs live as brigands in the woods, which recalls the motif of the seven bandits in the Sicilian "Snow White" variant "Maria, die böse Stiefmutter und die sieben Räuber" ("Maria, the Wicked Stepmother, and the Seven Robbers"), included in Laura Gonzenbach's volume of Sicilian folk tales (1870). Singh's fairy-tale dwarfs once were honest workers with legitimate trades, such as teacher, butcher, and innkeeper, before the wicked queen Clementianna (Julia Roberts) banished all the "uglies" and expelled them as "undesirables" from the kingdom. Because none of the townspeople stood up to defend them, the dwarfs decided to turn to thievery and to steal the gold from anyone, whether poor or rich, who crossed their way. Believing that they had no other chance in life but to steal, the dwarfs learned how to fight on bouncy stilt-like contraptions, which make them appear to be much taller than average-sized humans. The band of little robbers consists of: Will Grimm (Danny Woodburn), the leader of the dwarfs who wears battle armor and a helmet; Butcher (Martin Klebba), a bald dwarf wearing a leather cowboy hat and whip; Wolf (Sebastian Saraceno), a dwarf dressed in a wolf-skin cape; Napoleon (Jordan Prentice), a fashionable dwarf wearing a bicorne; Half Pint (Mark Povinelli), a dwarf who has a crush on Snow White; Grub (Joe Gnoffo), a gluttonous dwarf who wears a French beret and a scarf; and the always cheerful Chuck, called "Chuckles," played by Korean-American actor Ronald Lee Clark.

As social outcasts, the dwarfs reside in a rustic cottage, made in a hollow, uprooted stump of a tree, somewhere in the middle of a birch forest caught up in an eternal winter. Singh's boisterous highwaymen provide comic relief in the way they squabble, joke, and fight acrobatically wearing their giant accordion pantaloons. A warning sign at their hideout's entrance reads, "NO entry over 4 feet," although several of the dwarfs are over four feet tall, including Butcher, who says the line "I never trust anyone over

Tarsem Singh's *Mirror Mirror* (2012) features seven multicultural dwarfs, played by little people, who live as social outcasts and bandits in the woods.

four feet." In an interview with the director, Singh stated his reasons for casting little people in the role of the seven little woodland bandits and the challenges associated with that decision:

> I said we should use real dwarves because I don't have the time and money needed to do something like *Lord of the Rings* where you shrink people. I want the dwarves to be real, and I don't want them to look at all artificial, no matter how good the technology is. . . . But they still said the dwarves had to fight. That was a problem, because it's really hard for people with the particular handicaps of dwarfism to do that type of thing. Everyone who I liked could barely walk fast, so I had to come up with a completely different technique. (Marshall 2015)

Hence, Singh contrived to solve the issue through wardrobe and have his fairy-tale dwarfs fight on stilts, which was done by stuntmen in masks. The pugnacious dwarfs join forces with Snow White to take back her kingdom from the wicked queen and transform the fair-skinned princess into a war-rioress. Although Snow White is an agent in her own self-empowerment, the dwarfs teach her fighting skills and train her in the ways of banditry. Whereas the dwarfs instruct the young woman in the art of swordplay, sling-shooting, hand-to-hand combat, throwing rocks, deception on the battle-field, and playing the shell game, Snow White, in return, brings a moral compass to the dwarfs. She returns the stolen gold to the poor and starving people of the kingdom and lets the dwarfs take credit for it. Snow White's public proclamation declaring that the dwarfs are brave men and the true heroes, earns them the people's loyalty and gratitude.

Because the dwarfs were ostracized by others for being different, short, and deformed, their messages in the film defy stigma connected with physi-cal disability and ableism. Grimm instructs his new "student," Snow White, about the misconceptions the dwarfs are faced with in society, "People think you can't be tall if you are short. That you can't be strong if you are not." He also instills in her a new way of thinking about personal disadvantages and how to overcome them: "A weakness is only a weakness if you think of it that way." Insecure about her own strengths, weaknesses, and leadership skills, Snow White plans on leaving the dwarfs to go someplace far away where the evil queen cannot find her. The dwarfs, however, convince the princess that she is not a little girl anymore but in fact a leader who can defeat her wicked stepmother. Together, Snow White and the dwarfs crash the wed-ding of Clementianna and kidnap the prince (Armie Hammer) to break the love spell the evil queen has put on him. Representing a racially diverse community with very different interests, opinions, and styles of dress, the dwarfs' role in the film is "firmly to support contemporary views of diversity and multiculturalism," as Gordon Slethaug states (2014, 244). At the end of Singh's adaptation, the dwarfs receive special honors from the king (Sean Bean) for being the "most valiant soldiers" of the prince, and they accom-pany Snow White's Bollywood-infused dance performance at her wedding. Captured in sepia-tinted pictures, the end credits of the film offer a glimpse into the future of each of the dwarfs: "Butcher became a flyweight champ; Napoleon brought hair to new heights; Wolf returned to his pack; Grub ate lunch; Chuckles joined the Royal Circus; Grimm wrote a book of fairy tales; and Half Pint found love."

Rupert Sanders' dark and gritty live-action retelling *Snow White and the Huntsman*, which could be described as the antithesis of Singh's gaudy, visually ornate reimagining, offers a striking parallel to the depiction of the dwarfs as petty robbers. The looks of the Celtic-named highwaymen bear some resemblance to Jackson's full-bearded, burly dwarfs in his cinematic adaptations of Tolkien's works. Because Sanders' dwarfs are former gold miners and drink from precious goblets, they also evoke the "classic" dwarfs of Norse and Germanic mythology associated with smithing, mining, and crafting. About halfway into the film, they are introduced as a band of eight angry bandits: Beith (Ian McShane), the leader of the dwarfs; Muir (Bob Hoskins), the blind elder dwarf who possesses the powers of premonition; Gort (Ray Winstone), an ill-tempered dwarf and drunkard; Nion (Nick Frost), who is Beith's right-hand man; Coll (Toby Jones), a tracker and Duir's brother; Duir (Eddie Marsan), a tracker and unscrupulous killer; Quert (Johnny Harris), Muir's son, who is very musical; and Gus (Brian Gleeson), the youngest of the dwarfs. They capture the fleeing Snow White (Kristen Stewart) and huntsman (Chris Hemsworth) in the dark woods by hanging them upside down in a tree. Since the dwarfs have an old grudge against the huntsman, they are about to kill the travelers when Muir uses his powers of premonition and identifies Snow White as the one destined to end the darkness caused by the evil queen, Ravenna (Charlize Theron).

Ravenna's reign of terror has not only turned the dwarfs into outcasts but has made them the sole survivors of an outright genocide committed against the dwarf race. The film indicates that the small band of robbers is the remainder of a species of potentially hundreds or thousands of dwarfs. Once noble gold miners, they returned one day to the surface and found that the land was blackened, with everything gone and everyone dead. Now, the dwarfs dwell in an enchanted but isolated part of the forest called "the sanctuary," the realm of the fairies. The eight little robbers, some of them related by blood, guide Snow White and the huntsman to their secret home, gather around a bonfire, and begin to drink, play music, and sing. Gus, who has taken a liking to Snow White, boldly asks the princess for a dance and she happily accepts. The scene appears to pay homage to Disney's animated adaptation in which the seven dwarfs also make music together, sing, and dance merrily with Snow White in their home. Further, Sanders embedded intertextual links to the Disney film. When the dwarfs partake in the final assault on the evil queen and climb up a sewer of the castle, Beith says, "Hi-ho lads, it's off to work," and Duir replies, "If he starts whistling, I'll smash his face in."

The dwarfs in Sanders's revision exhibit a wide spectrum of emotions and character traits. They are clever, quick-witted, angry, annoyed, grumpy, feisty, mistrusting, and nostalgic, but also team-oriented, bold, musical, loyal, devoted, respectful, and spiritually attuned. To protect the princess, Gus throws himself in front of her and thus sacrifices himself by taking an arrow meant for Snow White. In a ceremony of burning the dead body on a funeral pyre followed by an elegiac song, the companions mourn the death of the youngest dwarf, which reduces their number in the film to the conventional number seven. As Luke Hockley notes, "The dwarfs symbolize and embody for Snow White the ability to live life in a manner that is attuned to its realities and which also recognizes the importance of ritual and symbol. As such, they are figures of neither solely good nor evil" (2015, 44). Indeed, if the prophetic Muir would not have recognized Snow White in time as the chosen one, Duir sternly admits that he would have killed her. Hence, Sanders' live-action dwarfs are far removed from the Grimms' harmless helpers and diametrically opposed to Disney's comic, spoofed characters. What is more, the dwarfs are highly spiritual in that they believe in the prophecy of a savior figure that will come to heal the land. Here, the dwarfs' bodies suffering from physical infirmities become a metaphor for the "wounded" land in need of restoration. Because Snow White represents "life itself," her presence suffices to heal the dwarfs' physical ailments, such as Nion's gout and Coll's cough. Even Gort admits, "I've felt peculiar, queer almost. I'm not tingling all over, but I feel lovely. I feel lovely." The dwarfs' motivation for helping Snow White to fulfill her destiny is based on their spirituality rather than their desire for a materialistic reward. When Muir remarks "Can't you feel it? Are your ailments not gone? Gold or no gold, where she leads, I follow," the dwarfs unanimously pledge their allegiance to the princess.

Whereas the dwarfs in *Snow White and the Huntsman* are played by actors of average height who had their faces digitally superimposed onto small bodies, the dwarfs in *Once Upon a Time* (*OUaT*) are of average body size. Because of the strong Disney influence, it is no coincidence that the fairy-tale dwarfs in *OUaT* share the same names with their seven animated forerunners: Grumpy (Lee Arenberg), Happy (Michael Coleman), Doc (David Avalon), Sleepy (Faustino di Bauda), Bashful (Mig Macario), Sneezy (Gabe Khouth), and Dopey (Jeffrey Kaiser). However, the television show fleshes out the character of the dwarf Grumpy, significantly elaborates on the backstory of the seven dwarfs, and puts a new spin on the portrayal of the fairy-tale characters.

One of the most interesting and revealing episodes in the story arch of the dwarf characters in the show is episode fourteen of the first season, titled "Dreamy." In contrast to Disney's film adaptation, which portrays dwarfs predominantly as childlike, innocent, asexual beings, thereby reducing little men to the friend zone and platonic relationships, *OUaT* challenges the assumption of the dwarfs as diminutive men on one hand and undermines the notion that they are a homogeneous group of naive, harmless, and unmanly people on the other. The show's basic framework spans two separate worlds: the magical world of the Enchanted Forest and the realistic world set in present-day Storybrooke, a small (fictional) town in Maine.

The episode "Dreamy" interweaves two narrative strands, one featuring a flashback of Grumpy's (a.k.a. Dreamy's) past life in the fairy-tale land, the other following the relationship between the hospital janitor Leroy and Sister Astrid (Amy Acker), who have both forgotten about their true identities as Grumpy and Nova due to a magical curse. The flashback portrays how the fairy-tale dwarfs once hatched, full-bearded and clothed, from human-sized eggs in the mines of the Enchanted Forest. Shortly after their "birth," the dwarfs receive a personalized pickax that reveals each dwarf's name. The episode follows the story of the dwarf Dreamy, who hatched prematurely because the inexperienced fairy Nova accidentally dropped a large amount of fairy dust on his egg. His first interest as a newly hatched dwarf is to determine the identity of the woman whom he dreamed of:

DREAMY: Who is the woman I saw?

BOSSY (Richard Ian Cox): What woman?

DREAMY: The one I saw right before I hatched. She was beautiful. I want to see her again.

BOSSY: Ha! You must be dreaming—there are no female dwarfs. Dwarfs don't fall in love, dwarfs don't get married, and dwarfs don't have children. Why do you think you were hatched from an egg?

Bossy's remarks reflect the canonical portrayal and popular conception of fairy-tale dwarfs as asexual beings without interest in romantic love. Dreamy, however, feels that he is different from his fellow brethren because he has fallen in love with the fairy Nova. After Nova kisses him passionately on their first date, he decides to leave the mine behind and run away with the woman he loves. When Bossy reminds him that he has the responsibility of mining diamonds, Dreamy protests:

DREAMY: BUT, I LOVE HER.

BOSSY: You're a dwarf, Dreamy. We're not capable of love. It's not how we're made.

DREAMY: But, what if I'm different? What if you're wrong?

Nova's teacher, the Blue Fairy (Keegan Connor Tracy), convinces Dreamy that he stands in Nova's way of becoming a great fairy. For the sake of Nova's wish to be a fairy godmother one day, Dreamy abandons the crying Nova, claiming that he is a dwarf, incapable of love. Heartbroken, he returns to the mines and grabs a new pickax, which gives him the name "Grumpy."

The episode humanizes the figure of the dwarf by portraying Dreamy/Grumpy as a character with whom the audience can identify and relate. His tragic love story invites viewers to emphasize with the fairy-tale figure as an emotional being suffering from heartache. At the same time, "Dreamy" appears to critique the larger issue of how socially constructed norms about differences and diversity—for example, in race, ethnicity, ability, age, gender, sexual orientation, social class, religion, and culture—may interfere with personal relationships. The Blue Fairy and Bossy are authority figures who represent society's pressures and influences on the individual. Although dwarfs are stigmatized in *OUaT* as beings who cannot feel love or sexual attraction, evoking society's stereotypical beliefs about disabled men and women as "dependent, incompetent, and asexual," Dreamy/Grumpy clearly loves Nova and vice versa (Ostrove and Coffman 2012, 100). Instead of sailing away together and living their lives independently as a couple, Dreamy/Grumpy succumbs to the societal constraints and returns to his band of dwarf brothers in the mine, whereas Nova remains in the fairy collective under the supervision of the Blue Fairy. Although the parallel narrative of Leroy and Sister Astrid in Storybrooke ends on a more positive note, their romantic relationship is hindered by the fact that Sister Astrid is a devoted nun in a convent.

OUaT's postmodern portrayal of the dwarfs on television mirrors several of the reimaginings in the "Snow White" film adaptations. Similar to Sanders's revision, *OUaT* increases the number of Snow White's (Ginnifer Goodwin's) companions to eight by adding the dwarf Stealthy (Geoff Gustafson) to the group of miners. He dies, like Gus in *Snow White and the Huntsman*, from a hostile arrow in the episode "7:15 A.M." (season 1, ep. 10). Another episode, "An Apple Red as Blood" (season 1, ep. 21), depicts the dwarfs' sharpshooting skills, evoking the seven bandits from Singh's *Mirror Mirror*. The dwarfs in *OUaT* are also interracial because the actor playing Bashful, Mig Macario, is Filipino. They are willing to fight and die for the protection of Snow White, wielding their pickaxes in an attack on the castle of the malicious King George (Albert Spencer) and killing his soldiers in the Enchanted Forest. In Storybrooke, the dwarfs are humanized by their everyday occupations, clothes, behaviors, and life struggles. Sneezy, for instance, takes on the identity of Tom Clark the pharmacist, and Sleepy becomes Walter, a security guard at the Storybrooke Hospital who dozes off occasionally. Leroy/Grumpy is not only the hospital custodian but also the disreputable town drunk. As Hay and Baxter have noted, "the fairy-tale characters' contemporary counterparts grapple with problems typical of the white American middle class—not coincidentally, the show's key intended viewership" (2014, 320–21). After the dark curse of the town is broken, the dwarfs become miners again but not everyone remains in Storybrooke, breaking with the traditional occupation of dwarfs. In the episode "The Other Shoe" (season 6, ep. 3), Leroy complains to his therapist: "I'm stuck toiling in the mines and Dopey goes off and gets his master's degree? Now I got to pick up his slack? He's flirting with coeds." Ultimately, what makes *OUaT* so compelling is the creators' interweaving of humanized traditional fairy-tale characters, such as the dwarfs, with real-life problems in a modern-day environment.

Rumpelstiltskin Reloaded

More than any other American media production, *OUaT* fleshes out the Grimmian figure of the imp Rumpelstiltskin, played by the average-sized Scottish actor Robert Carlyle, and makes it a lead character. Although he is first introduced as one of the show's main antagonists, his character undergoes significant personality changes throughout the series and thus maintains an ambivalent role in the unfolding events. In the Enchanted Forest, he goes by the names of Rumplestiltskin (the different spelling is intended), Rumple, and The Dark One, representing a powerful magical wizard. Further, he takes the place of the Beast from the French fairy tale "Beauty and the Beast" and the identity of the Crocodile that cost Captain Hook (Colin O'Donoghue) his left hand in *Peter Pan*. In addition to his overlapping fairy-tale-inspired personas, Rumple's counterpart in present-day Storybrooke is Mr. Gold, the owner of a pawn shop and the town's wealthiest resident. Not only is he a ruthless businessman and landlord, but also a licensed attorney, which allows him to broker many of his Storybrooke deals. Whereas the character's associations with gold, materialistic wealth, and contracts strongly allude to the manikin in the Grimms' story, the looks of Mr. Gold and Rumple are far removed from the image of the traditional fairy-tale dwarf. Rumple is beardless, has green, glittery skin, gigantic pupils, ugly teeth, long fingernails, and shoulder-length, curly hair. His long-sleeve, reptilian leather jacket gives his character an exotic appearance befitting his alternate identity as Crocodile. In contrast, the clean-shaven Mr. Gold wears a dark business suit with a tie and his smile reveals a golden tooth.

The fact that Mr. Gold has a noticeable limp and must walk with a cane ties the character Rumplestiltskin in *OUaT* to physical disability and disease, which, in turn, evokes the notion of the deformed dwarf. In the episode "Manhattan" (season 2, ep. 14), the viewer learns in a flashback that his disability comes from a self-inflicted wound after being drafted into the Ogres War in the Enchanted Forest. Once an ordinary man without magical powers, Rumple was eager to free himself of his father's legacy of cowardice. However, after a seer tells him that his wife, Milah (Rachel Shelley), is pregnant with a son who will grow up without a father, Rumple assumes that he is going to die on the battlefield. He crushes his own leg with a hammer and is sent home to his wife as a disabled ex-service man. His wife leaves him for being a coward and Rumple raises his son, Baelfire (Dylan Schmid), as a single father. Thirteen years later, Rumple wants to protect his son from being drafted to war by killing the malevolent powerful creature known as The Dark One, thus making him the new Dark One in his place. He gains magical powers that allow him to temporarily heal his limp, but the power also corrupts Rumple and turns him into a villainous, power-craving "junkie." Once transported to Storybrooke, a place without magic, Mr. Gold can no longer use his supernatural powers to conceal his walking impediment and therefore uses a fancy cane with a golden derby handle as a walking aid.

On the one hand, the figure of Rumple/Mr. Gold conjures up the image of the disabled, demonic dwarf, but on the other hand, his character is far removed from the sinister manikin in the German fairy tale. In their reimagined version of the Grimms' ominous Rumpelstiltskin, Kitsis and Horowitz portray the fairy-tale character as a victim of his own power addiction who means well but fails time and again to find his personal happy ending. Most importantly, Rumple's/Mr. Gold's character in *OUaT* centers on familial relationships, romantic attachment, parental abandonment, pursuit of revenge, and individual redemption rather than on the figure's superficial binary oppositions between good and evil, or helper and adversary. To humanize the character, the creators depict Rumple/Mr. Gold as a troubled family man (e.g., a son, a father, a grandfather, a husband), and as a star-crossed lover. His backstory is a tragic one that invites viewers' sympathy and offers an explanation for why he turned to the dark side. Once destined to be a savior, his own mother, Fiona (Jamie Murray) chose power over love by magically severing Rumple from his heroic fate and by abandoning him so that she might become the Dark Fairy in the Dark Realm. Rumple's father, Malcolm (Stephen Lord), in turn, rejected his infant son because he believed him to be the reason for Fiona's presumed death. When Rumple was still a child, Malcolm abandoned his son as well for regaining his youth and becoming Peter Pan. Despite his traumatic past, Rumple was a decent person and a loving husband and father in his early years. Further disappointments in his life and the corruption through power and magic ultimately turned Rumple into a "beast."

Throughout the series, *OUaT* continues to defy stereotypical portrayals of the dwarfish, solitary creature Rumpelstiltskin—for instance, by foregrounding the character's humble beginnings as a human being and his amorous relationship with Belle (Emilie de Ravin) and other female characters. The companion guide to the hit show, *Once Upon a Time: Behind the Magic* (2016), features an interview with the actor Robert Carlyle, who states that the real saving grace for Rumple/Mr. Gold has been "the revelations about his past, which have steered him away from just being a bad guy" (Edwards and Clubb 2016, 76). *OUaT* reinvents Rumple as a multifaceted character with profoundness and depth to his personality, allowing audiences to connect with his human side. As Carlyle stated, "People at that point suddenly saw he has a heart. Belle began to peel away some of his mask. With the kiss, she peels away the mask and you see the person, a nice guy with his boy. I think from that point on people looked at Rumplestiltskin with a different eye" (76). Although Rumple is a flawed character, he feels a lot of love for Belle and his sons and wants to become a better person for it. Fan websites indicate that the "Rumbelle" couple has become a fan-favorite specifically because viewers of the show relate to Rumple as an imperfect man and can identify with his rocky love relationship. Fan "Joanne" noted,

> Personally, I think that people can relate to Belle and Rumple's relationship much more than they can to Snow and Charming's. Snowing is the perfect ideal romance. Rumbelle is anything but perfect. Belle is an optimist and sees the best in everyone. Rumpelstiltskin is an imperfect man who has been broken by life. Like most women, Belle loves Rumple for his potential. She knows that he can be a better man if he chooses to do so, but he is always making the wrong choices. Few of us have a perfect relationship like Snowing. Most of us have been in a relationship like Rumbelle. We can relate to them more. (Once Upon a Fan 2016)

Another fan, "Lori," commented on why the episode "Skin Deep" (season 1, ep. 12), a retelling of "Beauty and the Beast," struck a chord with audiences:

> I think it resonated so much with the audience because it caused a high point in the emotions that were evolving as we watched the progression of Rumplestiltskin's character. We saw him at his worst in the first few episodes of Season One ("You know what you love, now go kill it!"), and then we began to understand and empathize with him through "Desperate Souls." So when "Skin Deep" aired, I think it was the possibility that even the Dark One could be loved and love in return that completely captured our hearts. It was the possibility not only for love, but for redemption and a return to goodness. It was hope, and basically everything that the show stands for. (Once Upon a Fan 2016)

Like many postmodern villains in American pop culture and media productions, it is Rumple's/Mr. Gold's striving for redemption and struggle for rehabilitation that seems to resonate with viewers.

The creators of *OUaT* not only reinterpret the Grimms' figure of Rumpelstiltskin in fresh and innovative ways by demonstrating that even the darkest villain can potentially be redeemed and save the day, they also endow the character with an antiheroic bent. Characterized by moral ambiguity, Rumple/Mr. Gold exhibits a certain Machiavellianism with regard to achieving his goals. During his time as The Dark One in the episode "Crocodile" (season 2, ep. 14), he goes so far as to kill his first wife, Milah, by ripping out her heart and crushing it for betraying him and leaving their son. He also severs Captain Hook's left hand in the hope of getting hold of a magic bean. Indeed, Rumple/Mr. Gold displays several significant antiheroic tendencies: first, his personality is flawed, as it is marked by imperfections (e.g., selfishness and furtiveness); second, his character lacks certain positive qualities, such as courage and honesty; third, Rumple/Mr. Gold exhibits "dark traits" that usually belong to villains (e.g., violence, deception, and greed for power). However, despite being the scheming, conniving master manipulator of the series, Rumple/Mr. Gold also possesses some heroic qualities that shine when he repetitively protects the fairy-tale community of Storybrooke from destruction. In the episode "Going Home" (season 3, ep. 11), he sacrifices his life for the sake of Belle and his first son, Baelfire/ Neal Cassidy (Michael Raymond-James), by killing himself along with his father, Peter Pan/Malcolm, one of the main villains in season three. In the episode "The Final Battle" (season 6, ep. 22), Rumple/Mr. Gold kills his evil mother, Fiona/The Dark Fairy, the villainess of season six, in order to protect his second son, Gideon (Anton Starkman). In yet another episode, "The Bear and the Bow" (season 5, ep. 6), Rumple/Mr. Gold transforms into a genuine hero when he manages to pull out the sword Excalibur from the stone. Although his noble actions and underlying benevolence are driven by his own interest, the desire to keep his loved ones safe, they represent nevertheless the heroic side of his character.

Since most of the lead characters in *OUaT* have faced decisions between good and evil, it would be a superfluous task to try to separate them into pure heroes and villains, as can be done effortlessly in the Grimms' tales. Presenting fairy-tale characters such as Rumple/Mr. Gold with a profound complexity that defies easy division and classification into a binary system of opposites is a significant aspect of what makes the show so compelling to many viewers. As Rumple/Mr. Gold states in the episode "Her Handsome Hero" (season 5, ep. 17), "That's the thing about dark and light—it depends on your point of view." By resisting overly simplistic binaries and absolute dichotomous concepts, the show contributes to questioning the very common ethical, religious, psychological, and philosophical dichotomy of good and evil. Further, it offers its audience different viewpoints on perceived goodness and wickedness. Rumple's quote, "Evil isn't born dearie, it's made," in the episode "Heart of Darkness" (season 1, ep. 16), which invokes the discourse of nature versus nurture, is just one example of the pedagogical messages embedded in the show that invites viewers to reflect on moral beliefs and issues in contemporary societies.

Moreover, Kitsis and Horowitz foreground Rumple's/Mr. Gold's masculinity and virility, thereby challenging the image of the Grimms' imp as a solitary, emasculated creature. The scope of Rumple's/Mr. Gold's role as sexual partner vacillates between the romantic suitor for Belle's affections and the "bad-boy" type sensual seducer. In the episode "The Miller's Daughter" (season 2, ep. 16), the baby-bartering sorcerer offers to spin straw into gold for the young Cora (Rose McGowan), a poor miller's daughter. When Cora asks him to teach her the craft instead, the act of magically spinning becomes sexually charged. Rumple sits behind Cora at the spinning wheel, softly strokes her arms, and caresses her shoulder with his mouth. Cora, dressed in a provocative red dress, allows herself to be seduced sexually on the one hand and to use dark magic on the other. Rumple whispers in Cora's ear, kisses her cheek, and ultimately begins a love affair with her. On the day before her wedding to the prince, Rumple kisses Cora passionately on the mouth as she is trying on her wedding dress. He then amends their contract so that he will father the baby she promised to give him for spinning straw into gold. Rumple's amendment, which is sealed with a kiss, makes his sexual intentions explicit. In the episode "Bleeding Through" (season 3, ep. 18), Rumple/Mr. Gold uses his erotic charms as a "gentleman" to seduce the Wicked Witch/Zelena (Rebecca Mader), kissing her fervidly on a kitchen table, and in season six, Rumple/Mr. Gold has a secret love affair with Regina Mills's dark half, the Evil Queen (Lana Parrila).

Another contemporary, live-action, American media production that endows the lead character Rumpelstiltskin with sex appeal is Jeremy M. Inman's action adventure film *Avengers Grimm* (2015). The film is a mockbuster of *OUaT* and of the Marvel Studios superhero film *The Avengers* (2012). Produced by the Asylum, a low-budget film company, *Avengers Grimm* stars regular-height actor Casper Van Dien, known perhaps best for his role in *Starship Troopers* (1997), as the slick businessman/ supervillain Rumpelstiltskin. In this Brothers Grimm–inspired, comic-book-style fairy-tale mash-up, the princesses Snow White (Lauren Parkinson), Cinderella (Milynn Sarley), Sleeping Beauty (Marah Fairclough), and Rapunzel (Rileah Vanderbilt) join forces with Little Red Riding Hood (Elizabeth Peterson) to stop Rumpelstiltskin from taking over the modern world. The five physically attractive women match Rumpelstiltskin's male-model looks, emphasized by his dark eyeliner, clean-shaven face, and stylish short hairstyle. In the film, Rumpelstiltskin uses the magic mirror as a portal to transport himself from the realm of fairy tales to Earth, a world without magic, where he intends to "live like a god." Once on the other side of the portal, Rumpelstiltskin takes over Los Angeles as Mayor Heart and turns the city into a scummy, corrupt cesspool. Thanks to his hypnotic, brain-controlling powers, he can force his will onto other people, such as the city's police units, and enslave them. The fairy-tale women, all well trained and endowed with some magical powers, must fight Rumpelstiltskin and his brainwashed army of thralls to thwart his plan of world dominion.

In an interview with Inman, the director emphasized that Casper plays a perverted Prince Charming who is malicious, yet appealing. This explains Rumpelstiltskin's lavish, aristocratic gown in the fairy-tale world when he storms Snow White's throne room to inform her that he killed her husband, the real Prince Charming. Inman remarked, "I didn't want an impish Rumpelstiltskin cowering in sewers and speaking in riddles, I wanted someone who was maybe just one step away from royalty, so I made him a crooked politician with a great smile and a genuine, if twisted, charm" (Asylum Fan 2015). In stark contrast to the Disney-friendly version of Rumple/Mr. Gold in *OUaT*, *Avengers Grimm* couples Rumpelstiltskin's wickedness with sexual aggression. In one scene, he keeps Snow White tied up as his captive in his living room. To demonstrate his dominance, he takes off his glove and slowly starts stroking her cheek, hair, and knee. The conversation that follows is charged with strong sexual innuendo: "We'll just have to warm things up ourselves, won't we? . . . If you had just given me what I wanted. You realize, I always get what I want. Your husband gave me what I wanted. Why won't you?" Rumpelstiltskin then offers to make Snow White his queen, making his sexual desires explicit. After an unsuccessful surprise attack by Snow White with a magically created icicle, Rumpelstiltskin throws her onto a large ottoman and bends over her as if to rape her. Before this can happen, however, the other feisty fairy-tale women come to Snow White's rescue. *Avengers Grimm* and *OUaT* are two primary examples of the innovative ways in which American media productions of the twenty-first century subvert and physically augment the Grimms' fairy-tale creature Rumpelstiltskin.

Conclusion

In the German language, the common term *Giftzwerg* (poison dwarf) is used as a derogatory label for a nasty, spiteful, or short-tempered person and especially for someone who exhibits this type of negative behavior to compensate for physical shortness. The word *Giftzwerg* evokes not only Wagner's portrayal of the Nibelung dwarf Alberich of Germanic mythology but also the German fairy-tale figures Rumpelstiltskin, Little Zaches, and the unnamed dwarf from the Grimms' "Snow White and Rose Red." As this chapter has demonstrated, the archetypal figure of the dwarf as a small, aged, long-bearded, and wealth-obsessed creature derives primarily from the influences of Germanic and Norse mythology. For centuries, the image of the "classic" dwarf with a stunted body that appears physically misshapen in relation to humans found its way into countless narratives and pictures, first and foremost folkloric stories, legends, fairy tales, and more recently, the fantasy genre. The Brothers Grimm incorporated the figure of the mythological dwarf into their popular *Märchen* as an ambivalent character, a helper figure or trickster and adversary. In the twentieth century, modern fantasy writer J. R. R. Tolkien drew on the Grimms' fairy tales and Germanic and Norse mythology for his conception of the dwarf race in his fantastic literature. In American pop culture, most notably in the twenty-first century, the innovative portrayals of dwarfs in fairy-tale-inspired adaptations unsettle the notion of the archetypal dwarf. In fact, there is a developing trend of portraying fairy-tale dwarfs in contemporary media without their characteristic features, particularly without their defining physical traits concerning height, age, and looks. Instead, we see increasingly regular-seized actors in the roles of dwarfs who are humanized, of complex character, at times sexualized, or generally endowed with special skills that enable them to achieve heroic tasks. Hence, it is conceivable that the decline of stereotypical portrayals of dwarfs as deformed, ugly, asexual, or helpless beings in today's American media productions is an expression of society's changed attitude toward people with disabilities. The turnaround of depicting dwarfs as little, shriveled, full-bearded creatures can metaphorically be read as a social rethinking about people with disability and as a societal movement against disability bias.

From a historical point of view, people with disabilities were shunned by society as undesirable freaks and abnormal Others. For hundreds of years, they were considered socially unhealthy, defective, and deviant. People with disabled bodies, for instance, were marginalized and treated as objects of fear and pity, not least because they were considered incapable of participating in or contributing to society as valuable members. Since the laws of any nation reflect societal values, a closer look at the laws of the United States reveals how the social stance in America toward people with disabilities has changed over time. As disability rights activists Rhonda Neuhaus and Cindy Smith have highlighted,

Historically, the laws of the United States devalued persons with disabilities as society as a whole viewed such persons as a group of people to be pitied, ridiculed, rejected, and feared, or as objects of fascination. Persons with disabilities were seen as objects of charity or welfare or as needing to be subjected to medical treatment or cure. . . . Early laws and actions through the late 20th century reflected these beliefs. Since that time, the country's laws and policies have evolved and have been enacted with the growing assumption that persons with disabilities should be full and equal participants in all aspects of society. (Neuhaus, Smith, and Burgdorf 2014, 46)

Since the 1960s and 1970s, there have been numerous changes in American society with respect to the management and treatment of people with disabilities. Of all the legislative and societal changes that occurred over the past decades, perhaps the Americans with Disabilities Act (ADA) of 1990 had the most significant impact on the treatment of and attitudes toward people with disabilities since the Civil Rights Act of 1964. The ADA is a civil rights law that prohibits discrimination based on disability and attempts to guarantee the rights of full inclusion into the mainstream of American life for all persons with disabilities. Molly Burgdorf, senior advisor for the Administration on Intellectual and Developmental Disabilities in the U.S. Department of Health and Human Services, has pointed out,

Over the past 60 years, the legal landscape in the United States has undergone a fundamental transformation with respect to the rights of people with disabilities, a shift toward independence and full participation and away from pervasive institutionalization and exclusion. This transition, including the emergence of the disability rights movement, is reflected in many ways, including the built environment (for example, curb cuts and ramps), the availability of accessible public transportation, changes in the public school classroom and the working world, and the increased visibility of people with disabilities in popular culture and in the community. (Neuhaus, Smith, and Burgdorf 2014, 49)

Due to the growing humanization and heterogeneity in contemporary depictions of the dwarf, this supernatural creature appears less and less as a marginalized, oppressed identity that is socially constructed as a "disabled," abnormal Other. A final case in point for this trend of reimagining the dwarf's physicality and foregrounding its potency is Peter Jackson's presentation of the fantastic beings in his *Hobbit* film series.

For his *Hobbit* trilogy, Jackson took extreme liberties with the source material and Tolkien's vision of the dwarfs by portraying thirteen dwarfs with different personalities, looks, and styles. Whereas some dwarfs have bulbous noses, bushy beards, and unkempt, wiry nests of hair, others are well groomed and of neat appearance with finer facial features similar to humans. Among the most attractive dwarfs are the brothers Fíli (Dean O'Gorman) and Kíli (Aidan Turner), the youngest of a band of dwarfs led by their uncle, Thorin Oakenshield (Richard Armitage), who set out on a quest to reclaim the Lonely Mountain for the dwarfs of Middle-earth. Whereas Fíli has long, golden hair and a braided moustache, Kíli has long dark hair and only a stubble instead of a full beard. Being the youngest of the band of travelers, they are also the most active dwarfs, have the keenest eyesight, and are therefore often sent to scout ahead. Thorin, a majestic dwarf warrior with long dark hair and a short beard, could easily pass for a human with his height of five-foot-two. *Hobbit* fans and the media have repeatedly referred to the three dwarfs, Fíli, Kíli, and Thorin, as the "hot" and "sexy" dwarfs of the posse. According to a Tolkien wiki website, Warner Brothers describes Kíli in the following way: "Handsome and physically able, Kíli possesses the invincible courage of youth. He is a skilled fighter and expert archer, having been trained with weapons from an early age. As one of the youngest in The Company of Dwarves, Kíli is determined to make his mark and prove his worth" (lotr wikia 2017). Kíli's figure is especially interesting because throughout the films, a subplot develops involving romance between Kíli and the beautiful wood-elf maiden Tauriel (Evangeline Lilly).

On the one hand, one could argue that the handsome dwarfs are little more than a shrewd marketing choice to make these three characters more appealing to the audience, especially the female followers. On the other hand, however, one can argue that Jackson's *Hobbit* trilogy is a celebration of extraordinary bodies. The films focus on a world from the perspective of little people and tell a tale in which non-normative bodies need not be ridiculous, cute, or domestic. Geographically and physically, dwarfs and hobbits are not out of place here and are made neither childish nor naïve. Jeffrey J. Cohen, professor of English and director of the Medieval and Early Modern Studies Institute at George Washington University, calls Jackson's *Hobbit* films a "disability epic," emphasizing that the director presents the epic story from a point of view that is not the traditional gaze of the camera and viewer. In an online blog, he asks the questions,

> What happens when scale and point of view are forced to adjust, so that bodies supposed to be ridiculous and not overly martial and not at all sexual reveal themselves to be all those things? What of a world in which a dwarf can be battle-machine not in a way that offers whimsical contrast with an adept elf (Gimli and Legolas), but straightforwardly and without contrast (dwarves versus orcs . . .)? What of a world in which being a dwarf does not necessarily entail inhabiting a disfigured body . . . ? (Cohen 2014).

Cohen hypothesizes in his blog that the cinematic gaze of Jackson's *Hobbit* trilogy re-orients epic, "away from the tall and conventionally beautiful people who are its usual eye candy, thereby making it a suitable genre for extraordinary bodies" (Cohen 2014). Cohen's line of argument further substantiates my claims that I have elucidated in this chapter. One thing is certain, contrary to my LEGO set mentioned in the introduction of this chapter, there is not "one design to fit them all," as dwarfs these days come in all shapes and sizes: small and tall, blockheaded and nerdy, hideous and handsome, cowardly and heroic, harmless and dangerous, blended and colorful, hairy and bald, magical and nonmagical, and with ordinary and extraordinary physicality.

CONCLUSION

Supernatural creatures surround us everywhere. In fact, we have always shared the world with them, as they dwell in our belief systems and mythologies, sometimes taking human shape. Today, however, we live in a world inhabited by magical beings, or rather the visual representations thereof, that populate a wide variety of new cultural terrains and spaces. Fantastic creatures, whether that includes witches, monsters, unicorns, dwarfs, or other magical beings, penetrate the public and private spheres of our society in novel and multifaceted ways. They appear in our houses on cereal boxes and television screens, in our schools on backpacks, binders, and pencil sharpeners, and in our stores on towels, pajamas, and home décor. They entertain masses in movie theaters and are celebrated as the new heroes in the visual culture of the twenty-first century. Indeed, our media is overflowing with supernatural creatures and fairy-tale figures, many of which are traditionally associated with uncanny, villainous, monstrous, and freakish attributes. In this study, I have demonstrated how fantastic Otherness featured in German Romantic fairy tales is linked intertextually and hypertextually to contemporary North American fairy-tale adaptations and have emphasized how North American society is moving toward the appreciation and celebration of the supernatural Other as expressed in today's media culture. The monster has become beautiful, the villain appears attractive, the freak is now cool, and the uncanny Other seems very familiar all of a sudden. Is it a coincidence that girls are into dolls who are representing the daughters and sons of classic monsters and fairy-tale creatures? That fashion fans buy their clothes from a model called Zombie Boy who is covered in tattoos that make him look like the living dead? That iconic singer Lady Gaga is stylized as Mother Monster who refers to her devotees lovingly as "little monsters"? That people are chasing fictional creatures called Pokémon (Pocket Monsters) with their smartphones in the real world? Wherever we turn our heads, we see people craving, chasing after, adoring, collecting, buying, and even impersonating supernatural creatures.

Our society makes room for fantastic beings, or supernatural Others, and firmly integrates them into our pop culture. But far more interesting is the consideration of the type of space they occupy. Magical Others appear in many guises in our culture but are not relegated to the areas of the grotesque, the villainous, the horrific, and negatively connoted characters. Instead, they oftentimes appear in humanized forms, with human flaws, emotions, and identities mirroring the human self, or in augmented, idealized, and admirable shapes, reflecting a form of apotheosis. In today's fairy-tale reimaginings, we see witches and evil queens who are seeking redemption, forgiveness, and friendship rather than casting wicked spells. We see wolves and werewolves that are romantic instead of big and bad. There are reincarnations of automatons, golems, and doubles who are funny and comedic rather than uncanny or scary, and there are fairy-tale dwarfs who defy their clichéd reputation of being small, old, and physically inferior. The list of rehabilitated fairy-tale villains and reimagined fantastic creatures in postmodern pop culture is long. Not only is there room for humanity in these embodiments of difference but contemporary society presents them as extensions of ourselves rather than as agents of Otherness, deviation, abnormality, and aberration. North American visual culture, including films, television shows, video games, comic books, and the internet, portrays many of the fairy-tale creatures and supernatural Others with a pronounced "human" side, which suggests a new approach to difference. Magical and monstrous beings are accepted and celebrated for their diversity, which I read as a cultural push to overcome stereotypical, adverse attitudes toward societal differences, including race, ethnicity, religion or belief, age, disability, class, gender, and sexual orientation.

Therefore, it is not surprising that the toy and entertainment industries in North America are launching products that center on promoting diversity and fuel the growing trend in pop culture of celebrating difference in an unprecedented fashion. Mattel's glamorized, beautified, and trivialized Monster High and Ever After High dolls are representative examples. Among these "freaky-fab" dolls, we find grotesquely deformed bodies, such as the conjoined twin Peri and Pearl Serpentine Doll with two female heads resting on a reptilian, snake-like body. The Monster High homepage advertises the doll, "With two heads and one body, the daughters of the Hydra have their own minds but not their own bodies! They have cool glow-in-the-dark bioluminescent effects in the fins, and a scaly tail that curls so the two-headed body can stand on its own. A colorful top has an iconic print, and the accessories are twice as nice for the bling-loving duo" (Peri-Pearl 2017). The chimera doll is in the companionship of other hybrid species with physical abnormalities, such as the Kala Mer'ri Doll, featuring four arms, purple skin, and tentacle feet. The promotion on Mattel's website reads, "The misunderstood character uhh-mazes with two sea-sational sets of arms decorated with bangles! A colorful print top looks boo-tiful, while accessories are scary cool" (Kala Mer'ri 2017). In the collection "Garden Ghouls," the Tree Monster Doll Treesa Thornwillow displays corporal deformations in her tree-textured skin and extremities, which sprout sparkling branches. Twisting the knob in her back makes her torso grow twice the size and more branches lift up from her backside. Mattel not only advertises the dolls' unique, creepy, and freakish bodily deviances as cool, fabulous, sensational, and amazing, but also markets Monster High as a place where students embrace and celebrate Otherness.

Interestingly, this movement toward embracing diversity, as expressed through channels of the fantastic, the monstrous, the supernatural, and the fairy tale, has brought about remarkable synergies between the toy and entertainment industries. Monster High, for instance, has teamed up with Lady Gaga to create an adult collector doll "in celebration of bravery, kindness and acceptance" (Zomby Gaga 2017). Influenced by the singer's famous "Born This Way" video, Mattel's Zomby Gaga doll is meant to inspire her audience to find their own inner strength. On its official website, Monster High has pledged to make a donation to the Born This Way Foundation (BTWF) to further the mission of empowering young people to create a kinder and braver world. In 2011, Lady Gaga founded the BTWF as a nonprofit organization with the mission to foster a more accepting society, where differences are embraced and individuality is celebrated. Gaga created the foundation in response to a series of LGBT teenagers committing suicide after being bullied about their sexual orientation and in response to the tragic death of a fan, Jamey Rodemeyer, on September 18, 2011. The Gaga fan tweeted a message to the pop icon on Twitter shortly before taking his life at the age of fourteen: "Bye mother monster, thank you for all you have done, paws up forever" (IBT 2011). Rodemeyer's tragic death is a reminder of the ongoing oppression and marginalization LGBTQ people still face in the United States and globally. Only one year earlier, Lady Gaga had made an appearance at the MTV Video Music Awards in her infamous red, raw-meat dress and hat, evoking a twisted version of Little Red Riding Hood as wolf bait. As the self-proclaimed "Mother of Monsters," Lady Gaga could dress in such an outrageous, fleshy attire, yet at the same time speak emotionally about the release of her new album "Born This Way."

Within North America's capitalist socioeconomic structures, the Disney Corporation, which has managed to gain a cultural stronghold and corporate monopoly on the fairy tale, is at the forefront of the new trend of embracing Otherness in pop culture. On July 31, 2015, the company released the musical fantasy television film *Descendants*, watched by

6.6 million viewers on the day of debut on the Disney Channel and by 12.2 million viewers in the following week. On July 21, 2017, the sequel *Descendants 2* was viewed by 8.92 million viewers across six networks on the night of its premiere and by 21 million viewers in delayed viewing (Otterson 2017). The films, both directed and choreographed by Kenny Ortega, revolve around the offspring of Disney's most infamous villains and most beloved royalty. *Descendants* introduces viewers to the United States of Auradon, a present-day alternate universe that is the homeland to all Disney characters and came into existence twenty years before the film. Prince Ben (Mitchell Hope), the teenage son of Queen Beauty (Keegan Connor Tracey) and King Beast (Dan Payne), is poised to take the throne. He offers a chance for rehabilitation to the troublemaking teen descendants of defeated Disney villains exiled to the remote, slum-like Isle of the Lost. Among them are the sons and daughters of Maleficent (daughter Mal played by Dove Cameron), the Evil Queen (daughter Evie played by Sofia Carson), Jafar (son Jay played by Booboo Stewart), and Cruella De Vil (son Carlos played by Cameron Boyce). The villains' descendants have been granted permission to attend prep school in the kingdom together with the Disney heroes' children. The film, which can be interpreted as a postmodern gaze of Disney at its own iconography and stories, follows these "rotten" teenagers adjusting to life outside their island prison.

The redemption story of *Descendants* is embedded with moral messages critiquing prejudice against Otherness, highlighting that evilness is not hereditary, and illustrating that one's identity and destiny are not defined by past mistakes, origin, or personal background. The opening of the film features the song "Rotten to the Core," in which the teenage mischief-makers revel in their reputation of being wicked, yet sing about their painful life experiences as misunderstood misfits and outsiders who grew up without love. Whereas Carlos suffers from a lack of self-worth, singing "They think I'm callous, A low-life hood, I feel so useless," Mal emphasizes her individuality, singing "Call me a schemer, Call me a freak, How can you say that? I'm just . . . unique!" Although the teenagers start out as "rotten," they choose not to follow in their villainous parents' footsteps by the end of the film. Happiness, as Mal realizes in one of her final monologues, comes with friendship and goodness rather than with destruction, thievery, and evilness. In a magical staring contest between Mal and her mother Maleficent, who transforms herself into a dragon, Mal casts a spell of love and goodness ("The strength of evil is good as none, when stands before four hearts as one!") and transforms her mother into a little lizard. The finale of the film culminates in the song "Set It Off," which contains the line "We were born this way" and thus strongly evokes Lady Gaga's album, foundation, campaign, and motto of embracing different identities.

Descendants 2 centers on Mal's suffering under the societal pressures to be the royally perfect girlfriend of Prince Ben. She returns to the Isle of the Lost, where her archenemy Uma (China Anne McClain), the daughter of Ursula from "The Little Mermaid," has taken her spot as self-proclaimed queen of the run-down town. Uma is angry at Prince Ben for not inviting her to Auradon Prep and creates a pirate gang including Harry (son of Captain Hook and played by Thomas Doherty) and Gil (son of Gaston from "Beauty and the Beast" and played by Dylan Playfair) to break down the magic barrier of the island prison and unleash evil into Auradon. The sequel follows the thread of redemption and rehabilitation of its predecessor, zooming in on Mal's identity crisis to find her true self. Whereas the remaining three villain kids, Evie, Jay, and Carlos, are happily settled in Auradon with little attention to their past ways, Mal struggles with her inner demons and sense of belonging. Initially, Mal attempts to hide her problems instead of working through them in healthy ways before turning to her friends for help. In the end, though, Mal embraces her uniqueness and the offspring of the notorious Disney villains continue to be positive examples of living life by their own moral compass instead of by what others tell them to believe.

Remarkably, Uma and Mal stand out not only for their villainous heritage but also for their magical abilities and somatic heterogeneousness. Uma metamorphoses at will into a cephalopod hybrid creature, a giant octopus with tentacles and a human upper body, and Mal can transmogrify into a fierce dragon. Their monstrous side aligns the two characters of Disney's *Descendants* with Mattel's Monster High and Ever After High franchise but also evokes the imaginary beings in J. K. Rowling's *Harry Potter* universe, including the prequel to the *Harry Potter* film series, *Fantastic Beasts and Where to Find Them* (2016). In Rowling's magical universe, familiar creatures from antiquity and the Middle Ages, such as werewolves, dragons, hippogriffs, centaurs, unicorns, sphinxes, and phoenixes, are crowded in with supernatural creatures from different traditions of fairy tale and legend, such as house-elves, merpeople, boggarts, basilisks, giants, goblins, trolls, gnomes, and pixies. In addition, *Fantastic Beasts and Where to Find Them* introduced an array of novel types of marvelous monsters to its audiences, including the adorable platypus-like animal niffler, the magnificent, eagle-faced thunderbird, and the sapphire-blue insect billywig. In a catalogue accompanying the exhibit *Fairy Tales, Monsters, and the Genetic Imagination*, organized in 2012 by the Frist Center for the Visual Arts in Nashville, Tennessee, British scholar Marina Warner observantly asked, "Has there ever been, since the triumph of the gargoyle in the Middle Ages, such fascination with the monstrous? Why have monsters returned with such force and taken such hold again of the popular imagination? What can they tell us? Why are young readers, adult filmgoers, and artists and writers today drawing on fairy-tale fantasy and mythological symbolism from the past to fashion new sports and wonders?" (2012, 24).

The exhibition, curated by Frist Center Chief Curator Mark W. Scala, featured works by contemporary artists such as Patricia Piccinini, Kiki Smith, Saya Woolfalk, Charlie White, and Cindy Sherman, who invented human-like, animal, or hybrid creatures to symbolize life's mysteries, desires, and fears. Inspired by sources ranging from Aesop's Fables, fairy tales, and folklore, to the products of genetic experimentation, the artists in the exhibition blurred the boundaries between human and animal as a way of emphasizing the fluid nature of identity. Their artworks dissolved distinctions between reality and artifice and expressed interactions between nature and humanity in the context of oral and written lore, psychology, ethics, and visions of the future in both science and science fiction. For their "monstrous creations," artists employed anthropomorphism (the projection of human characteristics onto animals) and zoomorphism (the attribution of animal traits to people). One of the first artists chosen for the exhibit was Australian artist Patricia Piccinini, whose sculpture *The Long Awaited* (2008) shows a young boy snuggling up with a manatee-like grandmother figure. The sculpture foregrounds the love relationship between the child and his "monstrous" grandma, who resembles a Dugong, a threatened species of marine mammals. The relationship between the fantastic being and the boy is intimate and beautiful, and their embrace of sleep reflects trust and a sense of nurturing. Although the grandmotherly creature is from the realm of fantasy, the closeness of this relationship is human in nature.

The topic and artworks of the exhibition by the Frist Center for the Visual Arts fit in well with the growing movement in North America of adopting fresh viewpoints on difference and diversity in society. In many ways, fairy-tale beasts, supernatural creatures, fantastic villains, and marvelous monsters can operate as mirror reflections of mankind, open the human self to reexamination, and allow us to recognize ourselves in the Other. In classic fairy tales and myths, animalistic monsters are ugly creatures with insatiable appetites and frightening physical features and are frequently associated with death and sexual threats. Beastly metamorphoses are linked with fear and aversion, recalling medieval representations of monstrous bodies as sinful, demonic, devilish, and grotesque. Today, however, as Marina Warner noted, "The eventuality of falling outside the human species altogether no longer holds such a threat, and contemporary artists are actively engaged in this work of reconfiguring monstrosity. To achieve these realignments of meaning and feeling, artists are making works that communicate empathy and identification with the monsters; they perform inversions, parodies, and ironical takes on conventionally assigned values; they give reign to carnivalesque riot and comedy" (2012, 25–26). A similar observation holds true about fantastic Others and supernatural creatures in postmodern pop culture, as I have elucidated in this book.

Whereas traditionally the princess was horrified to find the Frog Prince sitting on her pillow, Little Red Riding Hood was gobbled up by the Big Bad Wolf, and Hansel and Gretel were imprisoned by the cannibalistic witch, today's monsters and ogres have become loveable and funny and are heaped on children's beds in the form of soft toys. Young and adult filmgoers worship animal-human hybrid bodies equipped with magical powers when they make their pilgrimages to the movie theaters to see the X-Men, Spiderman, or J. K. Rowling's fantasy world. At home, audiences enjoy quirky fairy-tale retellings on television or in the forms of video games and comic books, which subvert the illusion of a coherent, homogeneous world and promote tolerance of Otherness in all shapes, colors, and sizes. In rehabilitating monsters and villains by embracing diversity, we are seeing an ideological shift, although not fully realized yet in our society, that values alterity and Otherness. The trend may suggest that the twenty-first-century American consumers of fairy tales are longing to see the transition from celebrating fictional representations of diversity in pop culture to cherishing actual, nonfictional diversity in areas of their everyday life. Unfortunately, many people are still faced nowadays with marginalization, harassment, bullying, and other challenging struggles in their day-to-day lives due to their race, ethnicity, religion, disability, sexual orientation, age, and so forth. However, the craving of supernatural creatures and the growing embrace of fantastic Otherness in North American popular culture may indeed represent a promising sign of a dawning era of increased mutual tolerance, acceptance of differences, and appreciation of heterogeneity.

NOTES

Notes to Introduction

1. My definition of "supernatural" or "fantastic" creatures is a very broad one, including any imaginative being that does not exist in real life. Such creatures may range from magical beings and those with superhuman powers to talking animals, hybrid species, monsters, artificially created creatures, and so forth.
2. See also Cristina Bacchilega's "Sketch 2: Field of Fairy Tale Cultural Production (early 2000s)" (2014, 17).

Notes to Chapter 1

1. Letter by Friedrich Schiller to Wilhelm Reinwald, dated April 14, 1783.
2. For the sake of easier readability I will refrain henceforth from using the obligatory quotation marks.
3. See also Richard Kearney's *Strangers, Gods, and Monsters: Interpreting Otherness* (2003) and Julia Kristeva's *Strangers to Ourselves* (1991).
4. As Todorov states, "The fantastic occupies the duration of this uncertainty. Once we choose one answer or the other, we leave the fantastic for a neighboring genre, the uncanny or the marvelous. The fantastic is that hesitation experienced by a person who knows only the laws of nature, confronting an apparently supernatural event" (1973, 25).
5. The term "android" appears in US patents as early as 1863 in reference to miniature human-like toy automatons (U.S. Patent and Trademark Office).

6. For the German Romantic fascination with the automaton, see Heinrich von Kleist's 1810 essay "Ueber das Marionettentheater" (On the marionette theater). He notes that grace appears purest in that human form that has either no consciousness or an infinite one, that is, in a *Gliedermann* (puppet) or in a god (261). Hence, Kleist creates the paradoxical link between the automaton or puppet and god, between inanimate matter, madness, and death on one side and the sublime power of transcending consciousness on the other. "Only a god could equal inanimate matter in being beyond the limitations of consciousness" (Wai-yee Li 1993, 125).

7. Mechanical toys also play a role in Clemen's Brentano's "Gockel, Hinkel, Gackeleia" ("Rooster, Hen, and Little Cluck," 1838). Adapted from a fairy tale collected by Neapolitan poet Giambattista Basile, Brentano's tale deals with a mechanical figure that is a *Kunstfigur* (artificial figure) rather than an inanimate *Puppe* (puppet). However, as it turns out, this dancing mechanical toy is not simply an automaton, a purely mechanical construction, but it houses a real living creature and is therefore a combination of organic and inorganic matter. The mechanical construct that only appears to be a beautiful doll on the outside is in reality a prison for the mouse princess Sissi, who was captured by an old and sinister Jew. Ultimately, the playful child Gackeleia frees the little white mouse from its involuntary masquerade and imprisonment inside the artificial construction. Thus, the fairy tale codes the automaton negatively because it is symbolic of seduction, deception, confinement, and enslavement.

8. E. F. Bleiler and Riou, among other scholars, argue that the tale reveals Hoffmann's own critique of mechanistic science and his own strong feelings when he describes the horror felt at the possibility of mistaking an automaton for a human being (Bleiler 1967, xxi; Riou 2004, 222). Other scholars, such as Katherine Maree Hirt, have refuted the common interpretation of Ludwig's opinions as Hoffmann's own views (2010, 35).

9. After seeing Olimpia's "bloody eyes" on the floor, her glass eyes covered in Spalazani's blood, Nathanael jumps at Spalazani's throat, intending to kill him. Nathanael's state of madness, his confusion between mechanic fabrication and natural life, between robot and human being, reaches a climax when he climbs up a high steeple with Clara and her brother Lothar. Nathanael gazes through Coppola's spyglass sideways, sees Clara through

the lens, and tries to hurl her from the steeple. She is saved by Lothar, but in the crowd that gathers below, Coppelius appears. Upon seeing him, Nathanael cries "pretty eyes, pretty eyes!" and jumps off the parapet to his death while Coppelius watches. While Nathanael lies on the paving stones with a shattered skull, Coppelius vanishes in the throng.

10. Although neither the novel nor the film adaptations of *The Stepford Wives* are directly based on the Charles Perrault's fairy tale "Bluebeard," *The Stepford Wives* can be interpreted as an intertextual transformation of the tale. Similar to the men behind the killings of women, monstrous crimes hidden behind the pretty facade of the "white picket fence" town Stepford, the villain Bluebeard in the fairy tale is a serial killer of his wives who tries to cover up his murders by concealing the dead bodies in a secret room of his beautiful castle. In both stories, husbands demand complete obedience from their wives and discourage female curiosity, a sign of independence of mind. Following the monster bridegroom tale type found also in the myth of Cupid and Psyche, marriage condemns these unfortunate women to imprisonment and loneliness, but also puts them in immediate danger from their own spouses, who are supposed to protect them.

11. After Monica performs the imprinting process, David feels never-ending love for the woman he calls "mommy."

12. On his journey, David is captured for a grotesque "Flesh Fair," a carnivalesque spectacle of massacring mechas for the amusement of anti-mecha fanatics. David sways the audience into believing he is a real boy and manages to escape together with Gigolo Joe (Jude Law), a male prostitute mecha on the run after being framed for murder. David tells Joe about the Blue Fairy, convinced that she will transform him into a human boy whom Monica will love and welcome back home. Their journey leads them eventually to the office of David's creator at Cybertronics, where David discovers that he is not unique but merely a replicated automaton with special programming. Although the authorities of a futuristic, flooded New York City capture Joe, David and Teddy escape in an amphibicopter. They land the craft within a *Pinocchio*-themed attraction at the submerged Coney Island amusement park. At the sight of a statue of the Blue Fairy, David repeatedly wishes to become a real boy, until his internal power source drains away.

13. There are several elements in this postmodern film that reinforce certain fairy-tale conventions, such as the omniscient narrator or the popular fairy-tale motifs of child abandonment and of the birth, death or long sleep, and rebirth cycle. First, Monica abandons David in the middle of a dark forest, similar to the events that take place in the Grimms' fairy tales "Hansel and Gretel" and "Snow White." Psychologist Sheldon Cashdan describes the act of abandonment as "perhaps the most dreaded fear of childhood," which might explain its occurrence as famous fairy-tale trope (1999, 14). Evoking the tales "Sleeping Beauty" or "Snow White," in which the main character undergoes a long period of dormancy that can be interpreted as a figurative death, David spends two thousand years submerged in a frozen sleep state. Confined to an amphibicopter with a large windshield, recalling Snow White's glass coffin, the automated boy remains in a dark, underwater world and "survives" a second ice age. But when David is freed from his rimy, casket-like entrapment, humankind has long died out and the resurrection of his mother, David's personal "spring," lasts for only one day. Another fairy-tale parallel is, of course, Carlo Collodi's story of *Pinocchio* and that of Pinocchio's little helper figure, the talking cricket, who advises and warns the puppet about the perils of disobedience. In *A.I.,* it is Teddy, David's toy automaton, who takes it upon himself to care for the well-being of the android boy and offers helpful advice whenever possible.

14. *Edward Scissorhands* shares striking parallels with the fairy tale "Beauty and the Beast," including the Beast's mansion or castle, Beauty's (Kim's) initial fear of the Beast (Edward), the growing love relationship between Beauty and the Beast, and the kindhearted Beast of monstrous appearance. Whereas Disney's adaptation features a character called Gaston as Beast's adversary, Burton's film features Kim's overbearing boyfriend, Jim (Anthony Michael Hall), as Edward's foe.

15. In *Edward Scissorhands*, Burton's own feelings of isolation as a "very tortured" teenager growing up in the Los Angeles suburb Burbank come to the fore. "I felt like an outcast," Burton admitted in an interview with Dave Itzkoff, published by the *New York Times* on September 23, 2012. "I think a lot of kids feel alone and slightly isolated and in their own world. . . . That's where 'Edward Scissorhands' came from" (Itzkoff 2012).

16. Encyclopædia Britannica Online, n.d., s.v. "golem," accessed January 24, 2016, http://www.britannica.com/topic/golem-Jewish-folklore.

17. "Unglücklicher König Sekakis, der du das Verständnis der Natur verschmähtest, der du, verblendet von dem bösen Zauber des arglistigen Dämons, den falschen Teraphim erschautest, statt des wahrhaften Geistes."

18. The Biedermeier period refers to an era in Central Europe during which the middle class grew and arts appealed to common sensibilities in the historical period between 1815 and 1848. Elfriede Neubuhr adds: "Man verstand unter Biedermaier einen Menschentyp, der die Idylle, die Behaglichkeit, den kleinen Bereich des Häuslichen liebte und in stiller Bescheidenheit und Selbstzufriedenheit lebte" (1974, 8) (Biedermaier defined a type of person, who loved the idyll, the comfortableness, the small domain of domesticity, and who lived in quiet humility and self-sufficiency) (my translation).

19. The Gypsy Duke Michael was wrongly accused and hanged as a casualty of the persecuted gypsies in Europe.

20. In their efforts to unearth hidden treasures, Cornelius, Bella, and Braka are assisted by the Bearskinner, the ghost of a slave who sold his soul to the devil.

21. In the end it is Bella, not her son, who leads the Gypsies back to Egypt. During the journey, she gives birth to her son Lrak. After Bella's departure, Charles becomes emperor but ultimately retires to a monastery. Charles and Bella both die on the same day and by their own will. Bella dies in her homeland after a long and successful reign, surrounded by the praise and love of her people. Charles deceases after a vision of his beloved Isabella.

22. Cathy S. Gelbin discusses the relationship between German Romanticism, anti-Semitism, and the golem in *The Golem Returns* (2011), pointing out that "the golem becomes the sign of the uncanny Jews' disfigured body and soul" in the works of German Romantic literature (19).

23. A golem-like creature can also be seen in the 1999 episode "Arcadia" (season 6, ep. 15).

24. Goethe also mentions the doppelganger as harbinger of death and bad luck in his novel *Wilhelm Meisters Lehrjahre* (*Wilhelm Meister's Apprenticeship*), published in 1795–96: "To a certainty, the old fool believes that

he has seen his ghost! He dreads that the vision may betoken some misfortune, perhaps death, to him" (1824, 316).

25. This also recalls fairy tales of the false bride, where a slave or servant takes the place of the true bride.

26. The show's spelling of the name "Rumplestiltskin" is slightly different from the more common spelling of the Grimms' character "Rumpelstiltskin."

Notes to Chapter 2

1. This quote by famed comic book author Peter J. Tomasi is taken from the comic book *Batman and Robin*, Volume 1: Born to Kill. His words imply that our world is not made of the overly simplistic black-and-white patterns that we find, for instance, in many fairy tales. Rather, the perception of the concepts of "good" and "bad," or what makes a hero and a villain, lies in the eye of the beholder, as it is a matter of perspective.

2. Taken from the second book of her Horrorscape Series, Nenia Campbell's quote suggests that our tendency to villainize is closely connected to our lack of understanding and thus to our fear of the unknown, the mysterious, and the unfathomable. Hence, fairy-tale villains are perhaps only misunderstood characters whose background stories and motivations are unknown and incomprehensible to us.

3. ATU refers to the Aarne-Thompson-Uther Index used in folkloristics to classify folktales.

4. According to Propp, the princess and her father "cannot be exactly delineated from each other according to functions" (79).

5. In the first two editions (1812/15 and 1819) the queen is described as "proud" (*stolz*) and in editions three to seven (1837, 1840, 1843, 1850, 1857) the queen is described as "proud and arrogant" (*stolz und übermütig*).

6. Her looks evoke Arthur Rackham's 1909 illustration of the witch in the fairy tale "Hansel and Gretel" because Joe Grant, Disney artist and creator of the evil queen, was influenced by European illustrative sources, including Wilhelm Busch and Arthur Rackham (Girveau 2006, 144).

7. Also Cohn's and Singh's "Snow White" adaptations associate the evil queen with ravens, which have long been considered in Western culture a bird of ill omen, of death, of mysticism, and of magic due to their black plumage,

croaking call, and diet of carrion. In the Grimms' tales "The Seven
Ravens" and "The Twelve Brothers," young men turn into ravens because
of a curse or evil enchantment.

Notes to Chapter 3

1. Atwood's quote may suggest that although the archetype of the wolf is
traditionally seen as villainous and associated with male sexuality, there
is the possibility of a wolf lurking in all of us, in each "civilized" individual. If anyone can potentially turn into a wolf or rather, if we all carry
"the wolf" within us, then perhaps a rethinking is necessary of what that
means, especially in a diverse society.

2. "Il faut mourir pour réparer cette faute; je ne vous donne qu'un quart d'heure
pour demander pardon à Dieu" (Leprince de Beaumont [1756] 1860, 44).
Unless otherwise stated, the translations in this chapter are my own.

3. See also Marianne Rumpf's doctoral dissertation, "Rotkäppchen: Eine
vergleichende Märchenuntersuchung" (1951) and Mariano Soriano's *Les
Contes de Perrault: Culture savante et traditions populaires* (1968).

4. Telltale Games plans the release of Season Two of *The Wolf Among Us* for
2018.

5. In the twentieth century, "Dirne" (originally a euphemism) has also developed toward meaning "prostitute."

6. En passant dans un bois, elle rencontra compère le Loup, qui eut bien
envie de la manger; mais il n'osa, à cause de quelques bûcherons qui
étaient dans la forêt.

7. Willem de Blécourt notes that the English term "werewolf" might also be
etymologically related to the "warg"-wolf, "warg" meaning "strangler" or
more generally "killer" or "murderer" (2016, 71).

8. Zipes pointed out that the *Jäger* was associated with the police, since
he protected the property of a feudal lord from intruders and poachers
(Zipes 1983, 17). *Jäger* is also a German military term adopted in 1631
and associated with soldiers and infantry up until today. Out of the
Grimms' 211 tales, the hunter, hunt, and hunting are mentioned 31 times,
that is, in approximately every seventh fairy tale. In contrast to German
legends of the same time period as the *Children's and Household Tales*,
where the figure of the hunter is mostly "evil" (*böse*), "cruel" (*grausam*),
and coded negatively, the *Jäger* in the Grimms' fairy tales is a positive,

good-natured character, a lifesaver and loyal servant (Röhrich in *Enzyk-lopädie des Märchens*).

9. The Grimms mention the forest eighty-one times in their tales, more frequently than every third tale. Twenty-eight times the forest is described as "big" (*groß*), and five times as "dark" (*dunkel*) or "louring" (*finster*).

10. The German term "*Maul*" implies the mouth of an animal rather than a human being.

11. Although the spelling *wieder* (again, return to) is the commonly endorsed spelling for its use on *Grimm*, it could have been an incorrect translation of the German word *wider* (against). Logically, the latter spelling makes more sense for a reformed Blutbad who is "against blood bath."

12. The killer's house contains a collection of Hummel figurines, suggesting that he is the collector and also destroyer of innocent, fragile children.

13. http://grimmforum.com/forum/Thread-Who-is-your-Favorite-Character-on-Grimm-Poll?page=1 (accessed December 7, 2016).

14. https://www.reddit.com/r/grimm/comments/37dej3/who_is_your_favorite_character/? (accessed December 7, 2016).

15. For further examples of overlapping characters and doubling in recent retellings of "Little Red Riding Hood," see also the work of Pauline Green-hill and Steven Kohm, particularly their articles "Criminal Beasts and Swan Girls: The *Red Riding Trilogy* and Little Red Riding Hood on Television" (2014) and "*Hoodwinked!* and *Jin-Roh: The Wolf Brigade*: Animated 'Little Red Riding Hood' Films and the Rashômon Effect" (2013).

16. *Merriam-Webster's Collegiate Dictionary* (2012), s.v. "teensploitation."

Notes to Chapter 4

1. Reprinted in *Collected Letters: Books, Broadcasts and War 1931–1949* (2004, 242).

2. In the 2005 film adaptation *The Chronicles of Narnia: The Lion, the Witch and the Wardrobe*, this conversation takes place between the faun Mr. Tumnus, played by James McAvoy, and Lucy Pevensie, played by Georgie Henley. Based on Lucy's small size, Mr. Tumnus misconceives Lucy to be a type of dwarf since he has never seen a human child before.

3. *Merriam-Webster's Encyclopedia of Literature* (1995), s.v. "Alberich."

4. The book was first published in English between 1880 and 1888 under the title *Teutonic Mythology*.

5. Other sources speak of additional physical deformities. According to Leander Petzold, dwarfs often have an oversized head and only four toes on each foot ([1990] 2003, 196). Wilhelm Schaub describes the dwarf in the German folktales also with a big head, with a withered face, at times with red hair and beard, and with goat feet (1904, 6). The goat feet could allude to a connection with demonic forces.

6. Because *Wichtel* and *Wichtelmänner* usually refer to helpful little house gnomes, they are associated with the *Heinzelmännchen*, a race of creatures connected with a legend of Cologne, Germany, written down by Ernst Weyden (1805–69).

7. *Merriam-Webster's Encyclopedia of Literature* (1995), s.v. "dwarf."

8. The city of Bern was named after the Italian city of Verona, which at the time was known as Berrn in Middle High German.

9. The absence of dwarf women is also discussed in Anatoly Liberman's article "What Happened to Female Dwarfs?" in *Mythological Women. Studies in Memory of Lotte Motz (1922–1997)*, published by Rudolf Simek and Wilhelm Heizmann in 2002.

10. Descriptions of Ricdin-Ricdon: "un grand homme brun fort bien vêtu, d'une phisionomie assez sombre" (Mayer and Mayer 1785, 40); "un home vêtu de noir, & d'une phisionomie fort sombre" (Mayer and Mayer 1785, 124).

11. After the first edition of the Grimms' tales, the cooking ladle disappears but references to baking and brewing remain in Rumpelstiltskin's song:

    "Today I'll bake; tomorrow I'll brew; the day after tomorrow I'll fetch the queen's child. Oh how good it is that no one knows, that I'm called Rumpelstiltskin."

    "Heute back ich, morgen brau ich, übermorgen hol ich der Königin ihr Kind; ach, wie gut ist, daß niemand weiß, daß ich Rumpelstilzchen heiß!" (Grimm and Grimm [1856] 2007, 1:287). The household crafts of cooking, spinning, baking, and brewing, traditionally associated with females, emasculate the manikin.

12. Jacob Grimm writes in *Teutonic Mythology*: "A pophart, identical with rumpelstilt in Fischart, is to be derived from popeln, popern, to keep bobbing or thumping softly and rapidly" ([1887] 2004, 505).

13. In contrast to the Grimms' fairy tales, where justice prevails in the form of the death of malicious dwarfs, the adverse and ugly dwarf in Madame

Marie-Catherine d'Aulnoy's French literary fairy tale "Le nain jaune" ("The Yellow Dwarf," 1698) triumphs in the end.

14. "Dumme, neugierige Gans . . . Da lachen die albernen glatten Milchge-sichter! Pfui, was seid ihr garstig . . . Wahnsinnige Schafsköpfe" (Grimm and Grimm [1856] 2007, 2:281–82).

15. "Ungehobeltes Volk, schneidet mir ein Stück von meinem stolzen Barte ab! Lohn's euch der Guckuck!" (Grimm and Grimm [1856] 2007, 2:282). The word "cuckoo" (*Kuckuck*) is used in German to avoid naming the devil directly because, according to superstition, like the expression "to speak of the devil," the naming of evil may conjure it up. The *Kuckuck* and the *Geier* (vulture) are slandered in association with the devil, also because the cuckoo is considered a treacherous bird for laying its eggs in the nests of other birds.

16. "Lorche" is the German plural form of "der Lorch," defined in the Grimms' *Deutsches Wörterbuch* as "Kröte" ("toad"). In modern German, the word is written as "der Lurch" in singular and as "die Lurche" in plural and refers more generally to amphibians.

17. "Ist das Manier, ihr Lorche, einem das Gesicht zu schänden? Nicht genug, daß ihr mir den Bart unten abgestutzt habt, jetzt schneidet ihr mir den besten Teil davon ab: ich darf mich vor den Meinigen gar nicht sehen las-sen. Daß ihr laufen müsstet und die Schuhsohlen verloren hättet" (Grimm and Grimm [1856] 2007, 2:283).

18. In his work *Versuch über Wagner* (1952) German philosopher Theo-dor W. Adorno interprets the dwarfs Alberich and his brother Mime in Wagner's opera cycle as caricatures of Jews, "Der Gold raffende, unsichtbar-anonyme, ausbeutende Alberich, der achselzuckende, geschwätzige, von Selbstlob und Tücke überfließende Mime—all die Zurückgewiesenen in Wagners Werk sind Judenkarikaturen" (24). "Alberich, obsessed with gold, invisibly anonymous, and quick to exploit others, and his brother Mime, shoulder-shrugging, garrulous, and bub-bling over with deceit—all of the rejected characters in Wagner's work are caricatures of Jews."

19. "Er paßte auf und schlug auf den Reuter an und brachte ihn mit Bedro-hung dahin, daß er mir nicht allein den Rucken wendet, sondern auch anfing darvon zu laufen, daß ihm die Schuchsohlen hätten herunter fallen mögen . . ." (Grimmelshausen 1670, 134).

20. "Zinnober" is the German word for "cinnabar" but also means "nonsense, rubbish."

21. The motif is also found in the Grimms' tale "Die lange Nase" ("The Long Nose"), which was only published in the second part of the first edition of 1815 and replaced with the tale "Der Krautesel" ("The Donkey Cabbage," KHM 122) thereafter.

22. When Rachel finds out that Sydney has replaced her number one position on the "SAU Hot or Not" ranking, she decides that her competition must die a social death. First, the Kappa "queen" arranges a humiliating spectacle at a college party where the seven dorks are exposed naked to the campus students. Then, she hires a hacker who unleashes a computer virus called "poisoned apple" to erase Sydney's computer hard drive. Sydney must work all night through to rewrite her lost paper, which is due the next day, and, in exhaustion, falls asleep. Tyler kisses her awake just in time for her to get to the student debate to compete against Rachel.

23. The film's plot and ending share strong parallels with Jeff Kanew's *Revenge of the Nerds* (1984).

WORKS CITED

adevilishdiva. 2012. "Will You Feel Sorry For Regina?" *ONCE Podcast*, April 19.
    http://oncepodcast.com/forums/topic/will-you-feel-sorry-for-regina/page/3/.

Adorno, Theodor W. 1952. *Versuch über Wagner*. Berlin: Suhrkamp.

Aldred, B. Grantham. 2016. "The Queen." In *Folktales and Fairy Tales: Traditions
    and Texts from around the World*, edited by Donald Haase and Anne Duggan.
    2nd ed. 3:841–43. Santa Barbara: ABC-CLIO.

Amidi, Amid. 2009. "The Director of *Hoodwinked* Speaks," *Cartoon Brew*, March 3.
    http://www.cartoonbrew.com/cgi/the-director-of-hoodwinked-speaks-11828.html.

Andermatt, Michael. 2008. "Artificial Life and Romantic Brides." In Romantic
    Prose Fiction, edited by Gerald Ernest Paul Gillespie, Manfred Engel, and Ber-
    nard Dieterle, 204-25. Amsterdam: John Benjamin's Publishing Company.

Apel, Friedmar. 1993. "Italien mit Hoffmanns Augen—Carl Blechen." In *E.T.A.
    Hoffmann-Jahrbuch 1992–93: Deutsche Romantik im europäischen Kontext*,
    edited by Hartmut Steinecke, 145–58. Berlin: Erich Schmidt Verlag.

Aquino, Tara. 2012. "Interview: 'Snow White And The Huntsman' Director Rupert
    Sanders Talks Dark Fairy Tales & Kristen Stewart's Toughness." *Complex*,
    June 2. https://www.complex.com/pop-culture/2012/06/interview-director
    -rupert-sanders-talks-snow-white-and-the-huntsman.

Arnim, Achim von. 1997. *Ludwig Achim von Arnim's novellas of 1812*. Translated
    by Bruce Duncan. Lewiston: Edwin Mellen Press.

Asylum Fan. 2015. "Jeremy M. Inman Interview and review of his Aveng-
    ers Grimm." March 19. https://asylumfan.wordpress.com/2015/03/19/jeremy
    -m-inman-interview-and-review-of-his-avengers-grimm/.

Avengers Grimm. 2015. Directed by Jeremy M. Inman. United States: The Asylum.
    Film.

Bacchilega, Cristina. 2014. *Fairy Tales Transformed? Twenty-First-Century Adapta-
    tions and the Politics of Wonder*. Detroit: Wayne State University Press.

———. 2015. "Fairy Tale Adaptations and Economies of Desire." In *The Cambridge Companion to Fairy Tales*, edited by Maria Tatar, 79–96. Cambridge: Cambridge University Press.

Badley, Linda. 1995. *Film, Horror, and the Body Fantastic*. Westport: Greenwood Press.

Bailey, Michael D. 2007. *Magic and Superstition in Europe: A Concise History from Antiquity to the Present*. New York: Rowman & Littlefield.

Bär, Gerald. 2007. "Perceptions of the Self as the Other: Double-Visions in Literature and Film." In *Processes of Transposition: German Literature and Film*, edited by Christiane Schönfeld and Hermann Rasche, 89–118. New York: Rodopi.

Barrie, James Matthew. 1911. *Peter and Wendy (Peter Pan)*. London: Hodder & Stoughton.

Barzilai, Shuli. 1990. "Reading Snow White: The Mother's Story." *Signs* 15(3): 515–34.

Baumeister, Roy F. 2001. *Evil: Inside Human Violence and Cruelty*. New York: Holt Paperbacks.

Beastly. 2011. Directed by Daniel Barnz. United States: CBS Films. Film.

Beauty and the Beast. 1991. Directed by Gary Trousdale and Kirk Wise. United States: Walt Disney Productions. Film.

Beckett, Sandra L. 2002. *Recycling Red Riding Hood*. New York: Routledge.

———. 2004. *The Child in French and Francophone Literature*. French Literature Series, edited by Buford Norman, 31:1–24. New York: Rodopi.

———. 2016. "Little Red Riding Hood." In *Folktales and Fairy Tales: Traditions and Texts from around the World*, edited by Donald Haase and Anne Duggan. 2nd ed. 2:585–90. Santa Barbara: ABC-CLIO.

beekee404. 2012. "Once Upon A Time Question." *fanpop*. http://www.fanpop.com/clubs/once-upon-a-time/answers/show/387885/can-anyone-join-on-feeling-bad-regina-todays-epic-finale.

Beit, Hedwig von. 1956. *Symbolik des Märchens: Gegensatz und Erneuerung im Märchen*. 2:34–42. Bern: A. Francke AG Verlag.

Benvenuto, Maria Raffaella. 2007. "German Folktale: Deutsche Mythologie." In *J. R. R. Tolkien Encyclopedia: Scholarship and Critical Assessment*, edited by Michael D. C. Drout, 236–37. New York: Routledge.

Berkowitz, Lana. 2012. "Are You Team Snow White or Team Evil Queen"? *Houston Chronicle*. March 28. https://www.chron.com/life/article/Are-you-Team-Snow-White-or-Team-Evil-Queen-3438997.php.

Bettelheim, Bruno. 1976. *The Uses of Enchantment: The Meaning and Importance of Fairy Tales*. New York: Vintage Books.

Bibbiani, William. 2011. "Exclusive: Tarsem Singh Reveals 'Snow White' Plot Details!" *Crave*. October 30. http://www.craveonline.com/site/177133-exclusive-tarsem-singh-reveals-snow-white-plot-details.

BillyGoat3. 2005. "Reviews & Ratings for Hoodwinked!" IMDb. November 23. http://www.imdb.com/title/tt0443536/reviews?start=0.

Bilski, Emily D. 1988. *Golem! Danger, Deliverance and Art*. New York: The Jewish Museum.

Black, Joel. 2000. "Scientific Models." In *The Cambridge History of Literary Criticism: Volume 5, Romanticism*, edited by Marshall Brown, 115–37. Cambridge, UK: Cambridge University Press.

Blackford, Holly. 2012. *The Myth of Persephone in Girls' Fantasy Literature*. New York: Routledge.

Blade Runner. 1982. Directed by Ridley Scott. United States/Hong Kong: The Ladd Company/Shaw Brothers/Blade Runner Partnership. Film.

Bleiler, E. F. (1967) 2012. Introduction to *The Best Tales of Hoffmann*, by E. T. A. Hoffmann. New York: Dover Publications.

Bosch-Roig, Gloria. 2013. "From Folk to Children's Literature: An Ideological Analysis of the Grimms' Contribution to the Fairy Tale Genre." In *De-Centring Cultural Studies: Past, Present and Future of Popular Culture*, edited by José Igor Prietto-Arranz et al., 305–20. Newcastle Upon Tyne, UK: Cambridge Scholars Publishing.

Braidotti, Rosi. 2002. *Metamorphoses: Towards a Materialist Theory of Becoming*. Cambridge: Polity Press.

Brave. 2012. Directed by Mark Andrews, Steve Purcell, and Brenda Chapman. United States: Pixar Animation Studios. Film.

Breuer, Heidi. 2009. *Crafting the Witch: Gendering Magic in Medieval and Early Modern England*. New York: Routledge.

Bridgwater, Patrick. 2013. *The German Gothic Novel in Anglo-German Perspective*. New York: Rodopi.

The Brothers Grimm. 2005. Directed by Terry Gilliam. United States/United Kingdom/Czech Republic: Mosaic Media Group/Daniel Bobker Productions. Film.

Bruce, Susan. 2005. "Sympathy for the Dead: (G)hosts, Hostilities and Mediums in Alejandro Amenábar's *The Others* and Postmortem Photography." *Discourse* 27, no. 2/3 (Spring and Fall): 21–40.

Buckley, Michael. 2004. "Stage to Screens: A Chat with Wicked Nominee and TV Veteran Winnie Holzman." *Playbill*. June 6. http://www.playbill.com/article/stage-to-screens-a-chat-with-wicked-nominee-and-tv-veteran-winnie-holzman-com-120118.

Bühler, Charlotte, and Josefine Bilz. (1953) 1977. *Das Märchen und die Phantasie des Kindes*. 4th ed. Berlin: Springer.

Business Wire. 2011. "Monster High™ and the Kind Campaign Partner to Bring the Power of Kindness to Girls." May 18, 2011. http://www.businesswire.com/news/home/20110518005606/en/Monster-High™-Kind-Campaign-Partner-Bring-Power.

Caligor, Eve, Kenneth N. Levy, and Frank E. Yeomans. 2015. "Narcissistic Personality Disorder: Diagnostic and Clinical Challenges." *American Journal of Psychiatry* 172 (5): 415–22.

Callahan, Maureen. 1999. "Forever Young," *SPIN* 15(2): 62–65.

Carter, Angela. (1979) 1993. "The Company of Wolves." In *The Bloody Chamber and Other Stories*, 110–18. London: Penguin Books.

Cashdan, Sheldon. 1999. *The Witch Must Die: How Fairy Tales Shape Our Lives.* New York: Basic Books.

Cavallaro, Dani. 2011. *The Fairy Tale and Anime: Traditional Themes, Images and Symbols at Play on Screen.* Jefferson, NC: McFarland.

Chouinard, Vera. 1997. "Making Space for Disabling Difference: Challenges Ableist Geographies." *Environment and Planning D: Society and Space* 15: 379–87.

The Chronicles of Narnia: The Lion, the Witch and the Wardrobe. 2005. Directed by Andrew Adamson. United Kingdom/United States: Walt Disney Pictures/Walden Media. Film.

A Cinderella Story. 2004. Directed by Mark Rosman. United States: Warner Bros. Pictures. Film.

Cohen, Jeffrey J. 2014. "Peter Jackson, Epic Dwarves and Extraordinary Bodies." *In the Middle.* January 2. http://www.inthemedievalmiddle.com/2014/01/peter -jackson-epic-dwarves-and.html.

The Company of Wolves. 1984. Directed by Neil Jordan. United Kingdom: Palace Productions. Film.

Cornfeld, Li. 2014. "'The Sanitation Man': Erasing Evil in Walt Disney." In *A History of Evil in Popular Culture: What Hannibal Lecter, Stephen King, and Vampires Reveal about America*, edited by Sharon Packer MD and Jody Pennington, 2:125–36. Santa Barbara, CA: ABC-CLIO.

Coryedwards. 2007. "Living In A Satirical World." May 19. http://coryedwards .com/?p=62.

Crumpacker, Bunny. 2007. *The Sex Life of Food: When Body and Soul Meet to Eat.* London: Macmillan.

Dahl, Roald. 1982. "Little Red Riding Hood and the Wolf." In *Revolting Rhymes*, illustrated by Quentin Blake, 30–33. New York: Knopf.

Davis, Amy M. 2014. *Handsome Heroes and Vile Villains: Masculinity in Disney's Feature Films.* Bloomington: Indiana University Press.

De Blécourt, Willem. 2016. "The Werewolf Pack: A Cinematic Metamorphosis." *Contemporary Legend* 2014(4): 59–75.

Deadpool. 2016. Directed by Tim Miller. United States: Marvel Entertainment/Kinberg Genre/The Donners' Company/TSG Entertainment. Film.

Delanty, Gerard, and Peter Millward. 2007. "Post-Liberal Anxieties and Discourses of Peoplehood in Europe: Nationalism, Xenophobia, and Racism." In *Discursive Constructions of Identity in European Politics*, edited by Richard C. M. Mole, 137–48. New York: Palgrave Macmillan.

Derjanecz, Agnes. 2003. *Das Motiv des Doppelgängers in der deutschen Romantik und im russischen Realismus: E.T.A. Hoffmann, Chamisso, Dostojewski.* In *Diplomica*, edited by Björn Bedey. Vol. 7. Marburg: Tectum Verlag.

Descendants. 2015. Directed by Kenny Ortega. United States: Bad Angels Productions/5678 Productions/Disney Channel. Television film.

Descendants 2. 2017. Directed by Kenny Ortega. United States: Disney Channel. Television film.

Dinello, Daniel. 2013. *Technophobia!: Science Fiction Visions of Posthuman Technology.* Austin: University of Texas Press.

Douglas, Susan, and Meredith Michaels. 2004. *The Mommy Myth: The Idealization of Motherhood and How It Has Undermined All Women.* New York: Free Press.

DPIC. 2016. "Women and Death Penalty." *Death Penalty Information Center.* http://www.deathpenaltyinfo.org/women-and-death-penalty.

Drux, Rudolf. 2009. Afterword to *Der Sandmann*, by E. T. A. Hoffmann. Stuttgart: Reclam.

Dumas, Philippe, and Boris Moissard. 1977. "Le Petit Chaperon Bleu Marine." In *Contes à l'envers*, illustrated by Philippe Dumes, 15–26. Paris: L'École des Loisirs.

Dundes, Alan, ed. 1989. *Little Red Riding Hood: A Casebook.* Madison: University of Wisconsin Press.

Edwards, Neil, and Natalie Clubb. 2016. *Once Upon a Time: Behind the Magic—Companion to the Hit TV Show.* London: Titan Comics.

Ella Enchanted. 2004. Directed by Tommy O'Haver. United States/Ireland/United Kingdom: Blessington Film Productions/Jane Startz Productions/Miramax. Film.

Entertainment. 2010. "Tasty Bites: The Vampire Diaries Cast Dishes." *Popsugar.* January 19. http://www.popsugar.com/entertainment/Exclusive-Interview -Vampire-Diaries-Nina-Dobrev-Ian-Somerhalder-Paul-Wesley-7103021.

Ewen, Frederic. 2004. *Heroic Imagination: The Creative Genius of Europe from Waterloo (1815) to the Revolution of 1848.* New York: NYU Press.

Ex Machina. 2015. Directed by Alex Garland. United Kingdom/United States: Film4/DNA Films. Film.

ExpendableMan. 2007. "Reviews & Ratings for Hoodwinked!" IMDb. February 13. http://www.imdb.com/title/tt0443536/reviews?start=40.

Extreme Ghostbusters. 1997. Developed by Jeff Kline and Richard Raynis. United States: Adelaide Productions/Columbia TriStar Television, Kids WB Nickelodeon/Qubo. Television series.

The Fall. 2006. Directed by Tarsem Singh. India/United States: Googly Films. Film.

Fantastic Beasts and Where to Find Them. 2016. Directed by David Yates. United Kindgom/United States: Warner Brothers. Pictures/Heyday Films. Film.

Farr, Louise. 2015. "Partners in Crime." *WrittenBy: The Magazine of the Writers Guild of America, West* 19(4): 26–33.

Forbes, Daniel. 2011. "The Aesthetic of Evil," in *Vader, Voldemort and Other Villains: Essays on Evil in Popular Media*, edited by Jamey Heit, 13–27. Jefferson, NC: McFarland.

Forrest Gump. 1994. Directed by Robert Zemeckis. United States: Wendy Finerman Productions. Film.

Freud, Sigmund. 1917–19. "The Uncanny" in *The Standard Edition of the Complete Psychological Works of Sigmund Freud, Volume XVII*, translated by James Strachey, 219–52. London: Hogarth Press.

———. (1919) 2003. "The Uncanny." In *The Uncanny*, translated by David McLintock, 123–62. New York: Penguin Books.

Frozen. 2013. Directed by Jennifer Lee and Chris Buck. United States: Walt Disney Productions. Film.

Gans, Andrew. 2016. "Broadway's Wicked Celebrates Major Milestone Today!" *Playbill*. February 14. http://www.playbill.com/article/broadways-wicked-celebrates-major-milestone-today-com-386153.

Gargoyles. 1994–97. Directed by Dennis Woodyard, Frank Paur, Kazuo Terada, Saburo Hashimoto, and Bob Kline. United States: Walt Disney Television/Disney Television Animation, Syndicated/ABC. Television series.

Garland-Thomson, Rosemarie. 1997. *Extraordinary Bodies: Figuring Physical Disability in American Culture and Literature*. New York: Columbia University Press.

Gelbin, Cathy S. 2011. *The Golem Returns: From German Romantic Literature to Global Jewish Culture, 1808–2008*. Ann Arbor: University of Michigan Press.

Genette, Gérard. (1979) 1992. *The Architext: An Introduction*. Translated by Jane E. Lewin. Berkeley: University of California Press.

Giesen, Rolf, and J. P. Storm. 2012. *Animation Under the Swastika: A History of Trickfilm in Nazi Germany, 1933–1945*. Jefferson, NC: McFarland & Company, Inc.

Gilber, Gerard. 2011. "Size Matters: Warwick Davis is no Small Talent." *Independent*, October 21. http://www.independent.co.uk/news/people/profiles/size-matters-warwick-davis-is-no-small-talent-2372841.html.

Gilbert, Ruth. 2015. "Jewish Gothic." In *The Encyclopedia of the Gothic*, edited by William Hughes, David Punter, and Andrew Smith, 375–78. West Sussex, UK: John Wiley & Sons Ltd.

Gilbert, Sandra M., and Susan Gubar. 1979. *The Madwoman in the Attic: The Woman Writer and the Nineteenth-Century Literary Imagination*. New Haven: Yale University Press.

Gilmour, Simon J. 1993. "Die Figur des Zwerges in den Kinder- und Hausmärchen der Brüder Grimm." *Fabula* 34, no. 1–2: 9–23.

Girveau, Bruno, ed. 2006. *Once Upon a Time—Walt Disney: The Sources of Inspiration for the Disney Studios*. Munich: Prestel.

Goethe, Johann Wolfgang von. 1808. *Faust: Eine Tragödie (Der Tragödie erster Teil)*. Tübingen: Cotta.

———. 1824. *Wilhelm Meister's Apprenticeship: A Novel*. Vol. 1. Translated by Thomas Carlyle. Edinburgh: Oliver & Boyd.

———.1832. *Faust: Der Tragödie zweiter Teil*. Stuttgart: Cotta.

Gonzalez, Sandra. 2013. "Sleepy Hollow recap: Just Me and My Golem." *Entertainment Weekly*. December 10. http://www.ew.com/recap/sleepy-hollow-season-1 -episode-10/3.

Gonzenbach, Laura. 1870. *Sicilianische Märchen. Aus dem Volksmund gesammelt*. 2 vols. Leipzig: Wilhelm Engelmann.

Goodman, Martin. 2006. "Dr. Toon: A Peek Under the Hood." *Animation World Network*. February 3. http://www.awn.com/animationworld/dr-toon-peek -under-hood. Accessed on April 12, 2017.

Gordon, Neta. 2016. *A Tour of Fabletown: Patterns and Plots in Bill Willingham's Fables*. Jefferson, NC: McFarland.

Greenhill, Pauline, and Jill Terry Rudy, eds. 2014. *Channeling Wonder: Fairy Tales on Television*. Detroit: Wayne State University Press.

Greenhill, Pauline, and Sidney Eve Matrix, eds. 2010. *Fairy Tale Films: Visions of Ambiguity*. Logan: Utah State University Press.

Greenhill, Pauline, and Steven Kohm. 2013. "*Hoodwinked!* and *Jin-Roh: The Wolf Brigade*: Animated 'Little Red Riding Hood' Films and the Rashômon Effect." *Marvels & Tales: Journal of Fairy-Tale Studies* 27(1): 89–108.

———. 2014. "Criminal Beasts and Swan Girls: The *Red Riding Trilogy* and Little Red Riding Hood on Television." In *Channeling Wonder: Fairy Tales on Television*, edited by Pauline Greenhill and Jill Terry Rudy, 189–209. Detroit: Wayne State University Press.

Greenwalt, David, and Jim Kouf. 2012. "Grimm and Bear It: Q & A with *Grimm's* David Greenwalt and Jim Kouf." *The Morton Report*. February 1. http://www .themortonreport.com/entertainment/television/grimm-and-bear-it-q-a-with -grimms-david-greenwalt-and-jim-kouf/.

Grimm, Jacob. (1887) 2004. *Teutonic Mythology*. Translated by James Steven Stallybrass. Vol. 2. Mineola, NY: Dover Publications.

Grimm, Jacob, and Wilhelm Grimm. (1810) 2007. *Kinder- und Hausmärchen: Die handschriftliche Urfassung von 1810*. Edited by Heinz Rölleke. Stuttgart: Reclam.

———. (1812) 1974. *Kinder- und Hausmärchen gesammelt durch die Brüder Grimm*. 3 vols. Frankfurt am Main: Insel.

———. 1815. *Kinder- und Hausmärchen. Gesammelt durch die Brüder Grimm*. Vol. 2. Berlin: Realschulbuchhandlung.

———. 1854–1971. *Deutsches Wörterbuch*. 16 vols. Leipzig: S. Hirzel. http:// woerterbuchnetz.de/DWB/.

———. (1856) 2007. *Brüder Grimm: Kinder- und Hausmärchen. Ausgabe letzter Hand mit den Originalanmerkungen der Brüder Grimm*. Edited by Heinz Rölleke. 3 vols. Stuttgart: Reclam.

———. 1860. "Doppelgänger." In *Deutsches Wörterbuch. Zweiter Band*. Leipzig: S. Hirzel.

———. 1988. *Complete Fairy Tales of the Brothers Grimm*. Translated by Jack Zipes. 2 vols. New York: Bantam Books.

Grimm. 2011–17. Created by Stephen Carpenter, David Greenwalt, and Jim Kouf. United States: GK Productions, NBC. Television series.

Grimmelshausen, Hans Jakob Christoffel. 1670. *Trutz Simplex: Oder Ausführliche und wunderseltzame Lebensbeschreibung Der Ertzbetrügerin und Landstörtzerin Courasche/ Wie sie anfangs eine Rittmeisterin/ hernach eine Hauptmännin/ ferner eine Leutenantin/ bald eine Marcketenterin/ Mußquetirerin/ und letzlich eine Ziegeunerin abgegeben*. Nürnberg: Felsecker.

Gritten, David. 2013. "Hansel and Gretel: Witch Hunters 3D, review." *Telegraph*, February 28. http://www.telegraph.co.uk/culture/film/filmreviews/9900136/Hansel-and-Gretel-Witch-Hunters-3D-review.html.

Gschwandtner, Christina M. 2012. *Postmodern Apologetics?: Arguments for God in Contemporary Philosophy: Arguments for God in Contemporary Philosophy*. New York: Fordham University Press.

Gymnich, Marion, and Klaus Scheunemann. 2010. "'A World Without Gender'?— Robots, Androids and the Gender Matrix in Films and TV Series." In *Gendered (Re)Visions: Constructions of Gender in Audiovisual Media*, edited by Marion Gymnich, Kathrin Ruhl, and Klaus Scheunemann, 181–202. Göttingen: Vandenhoeck & Ruprecht Unipress.

Hafstein, Valdimar Tr. 2003. "Groaning Dwarfs at Granite Doors: Fieldwork in Völuspá." *Arkiv för nordisk filologi* 118: 29–45.

Hansel and Gretel: Witch Hunters. 2013. Directed by Tommy Wirkola. United States/ Germany: Gary Sanchez Productions/ MTV Films/ Studio Babelsberg. Film.

Harris, Jason Marc. 2016. "We All Live in Fabletown: Bill Willingham's *Fables*—A Fairy-Tale Epic for the 21st Century." In *Humanities*, edited by Claudia Schwabe, 180–211. Basel, Switzerland: MDPI AG.

Harry Potter and the Sorcerer's Stone/Harry Potter and the Philosopher's Stone. 2001. Directed by Chris Columbus. United Kingdom: Warner Bros/Heyday Films/1492 Pictures. Film.

Harry Potter and the Chamber of Secrets. 2002. Directed by Chris Columbus. United Kingdom/United States: Warner Bros/Heyday Films/1492 Pictures. Film.

Harry Potter and the Prisoner of Azkaban. 2004. Directed by Alfonso Cuarón. United Kingdom/United States: Warner Bros/Heyday Films/1492 Pictures. Film.

Harry Potter and the Goblet of Fire. 2005. Directed by Mike Newell. United Kingdom/United States: Warner Bros/Heyday Films. Film.

Harry Potter and the Order of the Phoenix. 2007. Directed by David Yates. United Kingdom/United States: Warner Bros/Heyday Films. Film.

Harry Potter and the Half-Blood Prince. 2009. Directed by David Yates. United Kingdom/United States: Warner Bros/Heyday Films. Film.

Harry Potter and the Deathly Hallows: Part 1. 2010. Directed by David Yates. United Kingdom/United States: Warner Bros/Heyday Films. Film.

Harry Potter and the Deathly Hallows: Part 2. 2011. Directed by David Yates. United Kingdom/United States: Moving Picture Company. Film.

Hauff, Wilhelm. (1825–1827) 1890. *Tales: The Caravan. The Sheik of Alexandria. The Inn in the Spessart.* Translated by S. Mendel. London: George Bell and Sons.

Hay, Rebecca, and Christa Baxter. 2014. "Happily Never After: The Commodification and Critique of Fairy Tale in ABC's *Once Upon a Time.*" In *Channeling Wonder*, edited by Pauline Greenhill and Jill Terry Rudy, 316–35. Detroit: Wayne State University Press.

Hill, Mark C. 2009. "Negotiating Wartime Masculinity in Bill Willingham's *Fables.*" In *Fairy-Tales Reimagined: Essays on New Retellings*, edited by Susan Redington Bobby, 181–95. Jefferson, NC: McFarland.

Hirt, Katherine Maree. 2010. *When Machines Play Chopin: Musical Spirit and Automation in Nineteenth-century German Literature.* New York: Walter de Gruyter.

The Hobbit: An Unexpected Journey. 2012. Directed by Peter Jackson. New Zealand/United States: WingNut Films. Film.

The Hobbit: The Desolation of Smaug. 2013. Directed by Peter Jackson. New Zealand/United States: Metro-Goldwyn-Mayer (MGM)/New Line Cinema/WingNut Films. Film.

The Hobbit: The Battle of the Five Armies. 2014. Directed by Peter Jackson. New Zealand/United States: Metro-Goldwyn-Mayer (MGM)/New Line Cinema/WingNut Films. Film.

Hockley, Luke. 2015. "Snow White and the Huntsman: The Fairytale of Gender and the Female Warrior." In *The Happiness Illusion: How the Media Sold Us a Fairytale*, edited by Luke Hockley and Nadi Fadina, 33–49. New York: Routledge.

Hoffmann, E. T. A., C. W. Contessa, and Baron Friedrich de la Motte Fouqué. 1817. *Kinder-Mährchen.* Vol. 2. Berlin: Realschulbuchhandlung.

———. (1816) 1967. "The Sand-Man." In *The Best Tales of Hoffmann*, edited by E. F. Bleiler. Translated by J. T. Bealby. New York: Dover Publications.

———. (1819) 2005. *Little Zaches, Great Zinnober: A Fairy Tale.* Translated by Michael Haldane. http://www.michaelhaldane.com/kleinzaches.pdf.

———. 2008. *The Sandman. The Elementary Spirit. Two Mysterious Tales.* Translated by John Oxenford. New York: Mondial.

———. 2010. *The Nutcracker and the Strange Child.* Translated by Anthea Bell. London: Pushkin Press.

Hoffmann, E. T. A., and Alexandre Dumas. 2007. *The Nutcracker and the Mouse King.* Translated by Joachim Neugroschel. New York: Penguin Books.

Hoffmann, E. T. A., and E. F. Bleiler. (1967) 2012. "Automata." In *The Best Tales of Hoffmann*, translated by Alexander Ewing. New York: Dover Publications.

Holmes, Sally. 2014. "Angelina Jolie Says Violent *Maleficent* Scene Was a Metaphor for Rape." *Elle*. June 12. http://www.elle.com/culture/celebrities/news/a15426/angelina-jolie-maleficent-scene-metaphor-for-rape/.

Hoodwinked! 2005. Directed by Corey Edwards, Todd Edwards, and Tony Leech. United States: Weinstein Company. Film.

Hoodwinked Too! Hood vs. Evil. 2011. Directed by Mike Disa. United States: Weinstein Company. Film.

Hugo. 2011. Directed by Martin Scorsese. United States: GK Films/Infinitum Nihil. Film.

The Huntsman: Winter's War. 2016. Directed by Cedric Nicolas-Troyan. United States: Roth Films/Universal Pictures/Perfect World Pictures. Film.

IBT. 2011. "Jamey Rodemeyer's Suicide Gets Lady Gaga Angry, 'Bullying is Hate Crime.'" *International Business Times.* September 22, 2011. http://www.ibtimes.com/jamey-rodemeyers-suicide-gets-lady-gaga-angry-bullying-hate-crime-648033.

Into the Woods. 2014. Directed by Rob Marshall. United States: Walt Disney Pictures/Marc Platt Productions. Film.

Itzkoff, Dave. 2012. "At His Home in His Own Head." *New York Times*, September 23, AR1.

Ivanova, Elena. 2013. "Human Pets at the Royal Court." *Issue: The Arts Magazine of the Art Studio, Inc.* 9, no. 5: 4–5.

I, Robot. 2004. Directed by Alex Proyas. United States: Davis Entertainment/Laurence Mark Productions/Overbrook Films/Mediastream IV. Film.

I Was a Teenage Werewolf. 1957. Directed by Gene Fowler Jr. United States: American International Pictures. Film.

Jack the Giant-Slayer. 2013. Directed by Brian Singer. United States: New Line Cinema. Film.

Jackson, Michael C. 2002. *Systems Approaches to Management.* New York: Kluwer Academic Publishers.

Jackson, Rosemary. 1981. *Fantasy: The Literature of Subversion.* New York: Methuen.

Jäger, Hans-Wolf. 1989. "Is Little Red Riding Hood Wearing a Liberty Cap? On Presumable Connotations in Tieck and in Grimm." In *Little Red Riding Hood: A Casebook*, edited by Alan Dundes, 89–120. Madison: University of Wisconsin Press.

Jakobsson, Ármann. 2005. "The Hole: Problems in Medieval Dwarfology." *Arv* 61 (2005): 53–76.

Jameson, Fredric. 1975. "Magical Narratives: Romance as Genre," *New Literary History* 7(1): 135–63.

Jones, Alan. 1997a. "In the Black Forest: The Fairy Tale Returns to Its Roots in Showtime's Gothic Chiller." *Cinefantastique* 29(3): 24–26.

———. 1997b. "Weaver on Her Wicked Star Turn as the Evil Queen." *Cinefantastique* 29(3): 27–30.

Joosen, Vanessa. 2014. "Snow White and Her Dedicated Dutch Mothers Translating in the Footsteps of the Brothers Grimm." *Marvels & Tales* 28 (1): 88–103.

Jorgensen, Jeana. 2007. "A Wave of the Magic Wand: Fairy Godmothers in Contemporary American Media." *Marvels & Tales* 21(2): 216–27.

Joshi, S. T., ed. 2007. *Icons of Horror and the Supernatural: An Encyclopedia of Our Worst Nightmares*. Vol. 1. Westport: Greenwood Publishing Group.

Kala Mer'ri. 2017. http://shop.mattel.com/shop/en-us/ms/monster-high/monster -high-great-scarrier-reef-down-under-ghouls-kala-merri-doll-dhb49.

Kearney, Richard. 2003. *Strangers, Gods, and Monsters: Interpreting Otherness*. New York: Routledge.

Keegan, Rebecca. 2010. "'Red Riding Hood' director Catherine Hardwicke explains the big, bad sexy secret." *Hero Complex*. November 16. http:// herocomplex.latimes.com/movies/red-riding-hood-director-catherine -hardwicke-explains-the-big-bad-sexy-secret/.

Kleist, Heinrich von. 1810. "Ueber das Marionettentheater." In *Berliner Abendblätter*, 247–61. Berlin: Julius Eduard Hitzig.

Kristeva, Julia. 1991. *Strangers to Ourselves*. Translated by Leon S. Roudiez. New York: Columbia University Press.

L'Héritier de Villandon, Marie-Jeanne. 1705. *La Tour ténébreuse et les jours luninineux, contes anglois*. Paris: Veuve de Claude Barbin.

Lawson, Corrina. 2014. "Maleficent: Feminist Fairy Tale." *GeekDad*. June 2. https://geekdad.com/2014/06/maleficent-feminist-fairy-tale/.

Lee, Tanith. 1983. "Wolfland." In *Red as Blood: Or Tales from the Sisters Grimmer*, 106–36. New York: DAW Books.

Leprince de Beaumont, Jeanne-Marie. (1756) 1860. Le magasin des enfants. Paris: Morizot.

———. (1756) 1818. *Magasin des enfans, ou dialogues d'une sage gouvernante avec ses élèves: dans lesquels on fait penser, parler, agir les jeunes gens, suivant le génie, le tempérament et les inclinations de chacun*. Gent, Belgium: G. De Busscher et Fils.

Leviant, Curt. 2007. "Introduction." In *The Golem and the Wondrous Deeds of the Maharal of Prague* by Yehudah Yudl Rosenberg, xiii–xxxiv. New Haven: Yale University Press.

Lewis, C. S. 2004. *Collected Letters: Books, Broadcasts and War 1931–1949*. Edited by Clive Staples Lewis. New York: HarperCollins.

Li, David K. 2012. "Shortchanged: 'Snow White' Disses Dwarfs." *New York Post*, June 6. http://nypost.com/2012/06/06/shortchanged-snow-white-disses -dwarfs/.

Li, Wai-yee. 1993. *Enchantment and Disenchantment: Love and Illusion in Chinese*. Princeton, NJ: Princeton University Press.

Liberman, Anatoly. 2002. "What Happened to Female Dwarfs?" In *Mythological Women. Studies in Memory of Lotte Motz (1922–1997)*, edited by Rudolf Simek and Wilhelm Heizmann. 257–63. Wien: Fassbaender.

Lis. 2012. "Evil Disney Queens Are Doing It For Themselves." *Autostraddle.*
  July 18. http://www.autostraddle.com/evil-disney-queens-are-doing-it-for
  -themselves-141596/.
Lotr wikia. 2017. "The One Wiki to Rule Them All." Accessed July 23. http://lotr
  .wikia.com/wiki/F%C3%ADli_and_K%C3%ADli.
loYol. 2012. "Once Upon A Time Question." *fanpop.* http://www.fanpop.com/
  clubs/once-upon-a-time/answers/show/387885/can-anyone-join-on-feeling
  -bad-regina-todays-epic-finale.
LPA. 2017. "Little People of America." Accessed June 24. http://www.lpaonline.org.
Macey, Samuel L. 1987. *Patriarchs of Time: Dualism in Saturn-Cronus, Father Time, the
  Watchmaker God, and Father Christmasa.* Athens: University of Georgia Press.
Maguire, Gregory. 1995. *Wicked: The Life and Times of the Wicked Witch of the
  West.* New York: Harper.
Malarte-Feldman, Claire L. 2016. "Adaptation." In *Folktales and Fairy Tales:
  Traditions and Texts from around the World*, edited by Donald Haase and Anne
  Duggan. 2nd ed. 1:4–5. Santa Barbara: ABC-CLIO.
Maleficent. 2014. Directed by Robert Stromberg. United States: Walt Disney
  Pictures/Roth Films. Film.
Marshall, Rick. 2015. "*Mirror Mirror* Director Tarsem Singh Talks Visual Effects,
  Fighting Dwarves, Music Videos, and Superheroes." *Digital Trends.* April 20.
  https://www.digitaltrends.com/movies/mirror-mirror-director-tarsem-singh
  -talks-visual-effects-fighting-dwarves-music-videos-and-superheroes/.
The Martian. 2015. Directed by Ridley Scott. United States/United Kingdom: Scott
  Free Productions/Kinberg Genre/TSG Entertainment. Film.
Mathière, Catherine. (1992) 2015. "The Golem." In *Companion to Literary
  Myths, Heroes and Archetype*, edited by Pierre Brunel, 468–87. New York:
  Routledge.
Mayer, Charles-Joseph, and Charles Leopold Mayer. 1785. *Le cabinet des fées,
  ou, Collection choisie des contes des fées, et autres contes merveilleux, ornés de
  figures.* Amsterdam/Paris: Hôtel Serpente.
Metropolis. 1927. Directed by Fritz Lang. Germany: Ufa. Film.
Miller, Jeffrey. 2013. *The Structures of Law and Literature: Duty, Justice, and Evil in
  the Cultural Imagination.* London: McGill-Queen's University Press.
Mirror Mirror. 2012. Directed by Tarsem Singh. Canada/United States: Relativity
  Media. Film.
Mitchell, Silas Weir. 2015. "'Grimm's' Silas Weir Mitchell talks Monroe's fate
  and Hexenbiestiality." *Entertainment Weekly Community.* January 21. http://
  community.ew.com/2015/01/21/grimm-silas-weir-mitchell-interview/.
Mücke, Dorothea von. 2003. *The Seduction of the Occult and the Rise of the
  Fantastic Tale.* Stanford: Stanford University Press.
Müller, Johann Gottwerth. 1790. *Straußfedern.* Edited by Siegfried von Linden-
  berg. Vol. 2. Berlin/Stettin: Friedrich Nikolai.

Neubuhr, Elfriede. 1974. *Begriffsbestimmung des literarischen Biedermeier*. Darmstadt: Wissenschaftliche Buchgesellschaft.

Neuhaus, Rhonda, Cindy Smith, and Molly Burgdorf. 2014. "Equality for People with Disabilities, Then and Now." *GPSolo* 31(6): 46–51.

Neumyer, Scott. 2013. "Marilyn Manson Joining 'Once Upon a Time' Cast." *RollingStone*. October 18. http://www.rollingstone.com/music/news/marilyn -manson-joining-once-upon-a-time-cast-20131018.

Nikolajeva, Maria. 2005. *Aesthetic Approaches to Children's Literature: An Introduction*. Lanham, MD: Scarecrow Press.

Once Upon a Fan. 2016. "Favorite Episodes." December 2. http://www .onceuponafans.com/roundtables/favorite-episodes.

Once Upon a Time. 2011–18. Created by Edward Kitsis and Adam Horrowitz. United States: Disney, ABC Television Group. Television series.

"Once Upon a Time: Why Does the Queen Hate Snow White?" 2012. *The Fairy Tale Site*. YouTube. April 9. https://www.youtube.com/watch?v=4bKBSZWBU5g.

Orenstein, Catherine. 2002. *Little Red Riding Hood Uncloaked: Sex, Morality, and the Evolution of a Fairy Tale*. New York: Basic Books.

Ostrove, Joan M., and Stacey L. Coffman. 2012. "The Psychology of Love in the Context of Physical Disability: Reframing Culture, Exposing Oppression, Narrating Resistance." In *The Psychology of Love*, edited by Michele E. Paludi, 4:95–110. Santa Barbara: ABC-CLIO.

Otterson, Joe. 2017. "'Descendants 2' Rises to 21 Million Viewers in Delayed Viewing." *Variety*. July 26, 2017. http://variety.com/2017/tv/news/descendants -2-delayed-viewing-ratings-1202507508/.

Pape, Walter. 1981. "Doppelgänger." In *Enzyklopädie des Märchens: Handwörterbuch zur historischen und vergleichenden Erzählforschung*, edited by Kurt Ranke, 3:766–73. Berlin: Walter de Gruyter.

Paul, Jean. 1796. *Jean Pauls Werke, Zweiter Teil: T. Quintus Fixlein. Siebenkäs*. Edited by Paul Nerrlich. Berlin and Stuttgart: W. Spemann.

Peri-Perl. 2017. http://shop.mattel.com/shop/en-us/ms/monster-high/monster -high-great-scarrier-reef-peri-pearl-serpentine-doll-dhb47.

Petzold, Leander. (1990) 2003. *Kleines Lexikon der Dämonen und Elementargeister*. München: C.H. Beck.

Pickard, Roy. 1978. *The Hollywood Studios*. London: Frederick Muller.

Pinkowitz, Jackie. 2014. "No More Evil Step-Mothers: Motherhood as Redemption for Female Fairy Tale Villains." *FLOW*. http://www.flowjournal.org/2014/07/no -more-evil-step-mothers/.

Poniewozik, James. 2007. "The End of Fairy Tales?" *Time* 169(21): 83–85.

Propp, Vladimir. (1928) 1968. *Morphology of the Folktale*. 2nd ed. Translated by L. A. Wagner. Austin: University of Texas Press.

Pullman, Philip. 2012. *Fairy Tales from the Brothers Grimm: A New English Version*. New York: Viking.

Rank, Otto. 1971. *The Double: A Psychoanalytic Study*. Translated and edited by Harry Tucker Jr. Chapel Hill: University of North Carolina Press.

Red Riding Hood. 2011. Directed by Catherine Hardwicke. United States/Canada: Appian Way Productions. Film.

Renaud, Jeffrey. 2015. "Interview: Bill Willingham & Mark Buckingham Bid Farewell To 'Fables.'" *Comic News*. July 22. http://www.cbr.com/interview-bill -willingham-mark-buckingham-bid-farewell-to-fables/.

Revenge of the Nerds. 1984. Directed by Jeff Kanew. United States: Interscope Communications. Film.

Riou, Jeanne. 2004. *Imagination in German Romanticism: Re-thinking the Self and Its Environment*. Bern: Peter Lang.

Robbins, Trina. 2010. "Feminism." In *Encyclopedia of Comics and Graphic Novels*. Edited by M. Keith Booker. 1:212–18. Westport, CT: Greenwood.

Röhrich, Lutz. 1993. "Jagd, Jagen, Jäger." In *Enzyklopädie des Märchens. Handwörterbuch zur historischen und vergleichenden Erzählforschung*. Edited by Rudolf Wilhelm Brednich, Hermann Bausinger, Wolfgang Brückner, Lutz Röhrich, Klaus Roth, and Rudolf Schenda. 7:394-411. Berlin/New York: De Gruyter.

Rumpf, Marianne. 1951. "Rotkäppchen: Eine vergleichende Märchenuntersu-chung," PhD diss., Universität Göttingen.

Rushkoff, Douglas. 1996. *Playing the Future: How Kids' Culture Can Teach Us to Thrive in an Age of Chaos*. New York. HarperCollins.

Ryan, Mike. 2012. "'Snow White and the Huntsman' Director Rupert Sanders on Kristen Stewart and his 'Mirror Mirror' Fears." *Huffpost*. May 31. http://www .huffingtonpost.com/2012/05/31/snow-white-movie-the-huntsman-rupert -sanders_n_1559890.html.

Sale, Roger. 1979. *Fairy Tales and After: From Snow White to E. B. White*. Cam-bridge: Harvard University Press.

Sauer, Lieselotte. 1990. "Romantic Automata." In *European Romanticism: Literary Cross-currents, Modes, and Models*, edited by Gerhart Hoffmeister, 287–308. Detroit: Wayne State University Press.

Schanoes, Veronica. 2015. "Doubling and Multiplying the Self/Story in Cath-erynne M. Valente's *The Ice Puzzle*: Readers, Writers, and the Best of All Girls." *Marvels & Tales: Journal of Fairy-Tale Studies* 29 (2): 195–208.

Schaub, Wilhelm. 1904. "Über den Ursprung der deutschen Zwergsage." In *Königliches Wilhelms-Gymnasium in Berlin (1866): Schuljahr 1903/1904*. Berlin: Trowitzsch & Sohn.

Scheck, Ulrich. 2004. "Tales of Wonder and Terror: Short Prose of the German Romantics." In *The Literature of German Romanticism*, edited by Dennis F. Mahoney, 8:101–23. Rochester, NY: Camden House.

Schlegel, Friedrich. 1958-. *Kritische Friedrich-Schlegel-Ausgabe*, 28 vols. to date. Edited by Ernst Behler et al. Paderborn: Schöningh.

Schmiesing, Ann. 2014. *Disability, Deformity, and Disease in the Grimms' Fairy Tales*. Detroit: Wayne State University Press.

Schneidewind, Friedhelm. 2007. "Biology of Middle-Earth." In *J. R. R. Tolkien Encyclopedia: Scholarship and Critical Assessment*. Edited by Michael D. C. Drout, 66–67. New York: Routledge.

Schmitz-Emans, Monika. 2008. "Night-Sides of Existence: Madness, Dream, etc." In *Romantic Prose Fiction*. Edited by Gerald Ernest Paul, Manfred Engel, and Bernard Dieterle. 139–67. Amsterdam: John Benjamin's Publishing Company.

Scholem, Gershom. 1969. "The Idea of the Golem." In *On the Kabbalah and Its Symbolism*, 159–204. New York: Schocken Books.

Schuck, Peter H. 1998. *Citizens, Strangers, and In-betweens: Essays On Immigration and Citizenship*. Boulder, CO: Westview Press.

Schwabe, Claudia. 2014. "Getting Real With Fairy Tales: Magic Realism in Grimm and Once Upon a Time." In *Channeling Wonder: Fairy Tales on Television*, edited by Pauline Greenhill and Jill Terry Rudy, 294–315. Detroit: Wayne State University Press.

———, ed. 2016. *The Fairy Tale and Its Uses in Contemporary New Media and Popular Culture*. Basel, Switzerland: MDPI.

Senn, Bryan. 2017. *The Werewolf Filmography: 300+ Movies*. Jefferson, NC: McFarland.

The Shape of Water. 2017. Directed by Guillermo del Toro. United States: Fox Searchlight Pictures/Double Dare You/Bull Productions. Film.

Shaver, Phillip R., ed. 1984. *Review of Personality and Social Psychology: Emotions, Relationships, and Health*. Beverly Hills: Sage Publications.

Shelley, Mary. 1818. *Frankenstein; or, The Modern Prometheus*. London: Lackington, Hughes, Harding, Mavor & Jones.

Shippey, Tom. 2004. "Light-elves, Dark-elves, and Others: Tolkien's Elvish Problem." *Tolkien Studies* 1:1–15.

Short, Sue. 2015. *Fairy Tale and Film: Old Tales with a New Spin*. New York: Palgrave Macmillan.

Shrek. 2001. Directed by Andrew Adamson and Vicky Jenson. United States: DreamWorks Animation. Film.

Shrek 2. 2004. Directed by Andrew Adamson, Kelly Asbury, and Conrad Vernon. United States: DreamWorks SKG. Film.

Shrek Forever After. 2010. Directed by Mike Mitchell. United States: Pacific Data Images. Film.

Shrek the Third. 2007. Directed by Chris Miller and Raman Hui. United States: DreamWorks Animation. Film.

The Simpsons. 1989–present. Created by Matt Groening. United States: Gracie Films/ 20th Century Fox Television/Klasky Csupo/Film Roman/Fox Television Animation/The Curiosity Company/AKOM/Rough Draft Studios, Fox. Television series.

Simrock, Karl. 1864. *Handbuch der deutschen Mythologie mit Einschluss der nor-dischen*. Bonn: Adolf Marcus.

Sinyard, Neil. 1988. *The Best of Disney*. Greenwich, CT: Twin Books; Portland House: Distributed by Crown Publishers.

Sleeping Beauty. 1959. Directed by Walt Disney, Clyde Geronimi, Les Clark, Eric Larson, and Wolfgang Reighterman. United States: Walt Disney. Film.

Sleepy Hollow. 2013–17. Created by Alex Kurtzman, Roberto Orci, Phillip Iscove, and Len Wiseman. United States: Mark Goffman Productions/Sketch Films/ K/O Paper Products/20th Century Fox Television, Fox. Television series.

Slethaug, Gordon E. 2014. *Adaptation Theory and Criticism: Postmodern Literature and Cinema in the USA*. New York: Bloomsbury.

Snow White and the Huntsman. 2012. Directed by Rupert Sanders. United States: Universal Pictures. Film.

Snow White and the Seven Dwarfs. 1937. Directed by David Hand. United States: Walt Disney Productions. Film.

Snow White: A Tale of Terror. 1997. Directed by Michael Cohn. United States: PolyGram Filmed Entertainment/Interscope Communications. Film.

Snow White: The Fairest of Them All. 2001. Directed by Caroline Thompson. Canada/Germany/United States: Hallmark Entertainment. Film.

Solis, Santiago. 2007. "Snow White and the Seven 'Dwarfs'—Queercripped." *Hypatia: A Journal of Feminist Philosophy* 22(1):114–31.

Soriano, Mariano. 1968. *Les Contes de Perrault: Culture savante et traditions populaires*. Paris: Gallimard.

Star Trek: The Next Generation. 1987–94. Created by Gene Roddenberry. United States: Paramount Domestic Television, First-run syndication. Television series.

Stephens, John. 2008. "Dwarf, Dwarves." In *The Greenwood Encyclopedia of Folktales and Fairy Tales. Volume One: A-F*, edited by Donald Haase, 286–87. Westport, CT: Greenwood Press.

Suicide Squad. 2016. Directed by David Ayer. United States: DC Entertainment, RatPac Entertainment, Atlas Entertainment. Film.

Supernatural. 2005–present. Created by Eric Kripke. United States: Kripke Enterprises/Wonderland Sound and Vision/Warner Bros. Television, The WB/The CW. Television series.

Surmelian, Leon Z. 1968. *Techniques of Fiction Writing: Measure and Madness*. New York: Anchor Books.

Suvannasankha, Emily. 2016. "Regina Mills: B*tch Mayor of Storybrooke & Official 'Once Upon a Time' Punishing Bag." *Study Breaks*. June 3. https:// studybreaks.com/culture/once-upon-a-time/.

Swain, Virginia E. 2016. "Beauty and the Beast." In *Folktales and Fairy Tales: Traditions and Texts from around the World*, edited by Donald Haase and Anne Duggan. 2nd ed. 1:106–10. Santa Barbara: ABC-CLIO.

Sydney White (Sydney White and the Seven Dorks). 2007. Directed by Joe Nussbaum. United States: Clifford Werber Productions/SW7D Productions. Film.

Tatar, Maria. 1985. "From Nags to Witches: Stepmother's in the Grimms' Fairy Tales." In *Opening Texts: Psychoanalysis and the Culture of the Child,* edited by Joseph H. Smith and William Kerrigan, 28–41. Baltimore: Johns Hopkins University Press.

———. 1987. *The Hard Facts of the Grimms' Fairy Tales.* Princeton, NJ: Princeton University Press.

———. 1992. *Off with Their Heads: Fairy Tales and the Culture of Childhood.* Princeton, NJ: Princeton University Press.

———, ed. (2004) 2012. *The Annotated Brothers Grimm.* New York: W.W. Norton & Company.

———, ed. 2015. *The Cambridge Companion to Fairy Tales.* Cambridge: Cambridge University Press.

The Terminator. 1984. Directed by James Cameron. United States: Hemdale/Pacific Western Productions/Cinema '84. Film.

Terminator 2: Judgement Day. 1991. Directed by James Cameron. United States: Carolco Pictures/Pacific Western Productions/Lightstorm Entertainment/Le Studio Canal+ S.A. Film.

Terminator 3: Rise of the Machines. 2003. Directed by Jonathan Mostow. United States: Intermedia/C2 Pictures. Film.

Terminator: The Sarah Connor Chronicles. 2008–9. Created by Josh Friedman. United States: Sarah Connor Pictures/Bartleby Company/C2 Pictures/The Halcyon Company/Warner Bros Television, Fox. Television series.

Terminator Salvation. 2009. Directed by McG. United States: The Halcyon Company/Wonderland Sound and Vision. Film.

Terminator Genisys. 2015. Directed by Alan Taylor. United States: Skydance Productions. Film.

Tieck, Ludwig. (1800) 1985. *Leben und Tod des kleinen Rotkäppchens.* In *Schriften in zwölf Bänden,* edited by Manfred Frank, 6:1337–40. Frankfurt a.M.: Deutscher Klassiker Verlag.

Tiffin, Jessica. 2016. "Snow White Films." In Folktales and Fairy Tales: Traditions and Texts from around the World, edited by Anne E. Duggan, Donald Haase, and Helen J. Callow, 2nd ed. 945–49. Detroit: Wayne State University Press.

Todorov, Tzvetan. 1973. *The Fantastic: A Structural Approach to a Literary Genre.* Translated by Richard Howard. Cleveland, OH: Press of Case Western Reserve University.

Tolkien, J. R. R. 1937. *The Hobbit, or There and Back Again.* London: George Allen & Unwin.

———. 1954–55. *The Lord of the Rings.* London: George Allen & Unwin.

———. 1977. *The Silmarillion.* Edited by Christopher Tolkien. London: George Allen & Unwin.

———. (1981) 2014. *The Letters of J. R. R. Tolkien*. Edited by Humphrey Carpenter. Boston/New York: Houghton Mifflin Harcourt.

The Twilight Saga. 2008–12. Directed by Catherine Hardwicke, Chris Weitz, David Slade, and Bill Condon. United States: Temple Hill Entertainment/ Maverick Films/ Imprint Entertainment/ Sunswept Entertainment. Film series.

U.S. Patent and Trademark Office. 1863. "Toy Automation." Patent #40891. https://www.google.com/patents/US40891?hl=de&dq=patent:40891%7C.

Ungerer, Tomi. 1974. *A Storybook*. New York: Watts.

Uther, Hans-Jörg. 2013. *Handbuch zu den "Kinder- und Hausmärchen" der Brüder Grimm: Entstehung—Wirkung—Interpretation*. 2nd ed. Berlin: Walter de Gruyter.

Vitaris, Paula. 1997. "Howard Gordon's 'Kaddish'–X-Files Remakes the Golem Legend As a Love Story." *Cinefantastique* 29 (3/5): 38–39, 124.

Warman, Brittany. 2016. "I Am the Wolf: Queering 'Little Red Riding Hood' and 'Snow White and Rose Red' in the Television Show *Once Upon a Time*." In *Humanities*, edited by Claudia Schwabe, 98–113. Basel, Switzerland: MDPI AG.

Warner, Marina. 2012. "Metamorphoses of the Monstrous." In *Fairy Tales, Monsters, and the Genetic Imagination*, edited by Mark W. Scala, 24–36. Nashville, TN: Vanderbuilt University Press.

Willingham, Bill. 2002. *Fables: Legends in Exile*. Vol. 1. New York: Vertigo DC Comics.

———. 2005. *Fables: The Mean Seasons*. Vol. 5. New York: Vertigo DC Comics.

———. 2006a. *Fables: 1001 Nights of Snowfall*. New York: Vertigo DC Comics.

———. 2006b. *Fables: Wolves*. Vol. 8. New York: Vertigo DC Comics.

———. 2008. *Fables: War and Pieces*. Vol. 11. New York: Vertigo DC Comics.

———. 2014. *Fables: Camelot*. Vol. 20. New York: Vertigo DC Comics.

Wilson, Eric G. 2012. *The Melancholy Android: On the Psychology of Sacred Machines*. Albany: State University of New York Press.

The Wizard of Oz. 1939. Directed by Victor Fleming. United States: Warner Bros. Film.

Wright, Andrea. 2014. "A Dark Story Retold: Adaptation, Representation, and Design in *Snow White: A Tale of Terror*." In *Channeling Wonder: Fairy Tales on Television*, edited by Pauline Greenhill and Jill Terry Rudy, 229–47. Detroit: Wayne State University Press.

Wührl, Paul-Wolfgang. 2003. *Das deutsche Kunstmärchen: Geschichte, Botschaft und Erzählstrukturen*. Hohengehren: Schneider.

The X-Files. 1993–2002; 2016–18. Created by Chris Carter. United States: Ten Thirteen Productions, 20th Television/20th Century Fox Television, Fox. Television series.

Yair, Gad, and Michaela Soyer. 2008. *The Golem in German Social Theory*. Lanham, MD: Lexington Books.

Zanhar1. 2012. "Once Upon a Time Question: Can Anyone Join Me on Feeling Bad for Regina in Today's Epic Finale?" *Fanpop*. http://www.fanpop.com/clubs/once-upon-a-time/answers/show/387885/can-anyone-join-on-feeling-bad-regina-todays-epic-finale.

Zipes, Jack. (1979) 2002. *Breaking the Magic Spell: Radical Theories of Folk and Fairy Tales*. Lexington: University Press of Kentucky.

———. 1983. *The Trials & Tribulations of Little Red Riding Hood: Versions of the Tale in Sociocultural Context*. South Hadley: Bergin & Garvey Publishers.

———, ed. (1983) 1993. *The Trials & Tribulations of Little Red Riding Hood*. 2nd ed. New York: Routledge.

———. 1987. *Don't Bet on the Prince: Contemporary Feminist Fairy Tales in North America and England*. New York: Routledge.

———, ed. and trans. (1987) 2003. *The Complete Fairy Tales of the Brothers Grimm All-New Third Edition*. New York: Bantam.

———. 1994. *Fairy Tale as Myth: Myth as Fairy Tale*. Lexington: University Press of Kentucky.

———. (1999) 2013. *When Dreams Came True: Classical Fairy Tales and Their Tradition*. New York: Routledge.

———, ed. (2000) 2015. *The Oxford Companion to Fairy Tales*. Oxford: Oxford University Press.

———. 2006. *Why Fairy Tales Stick: The Evolution and Relevance of a Genre*. New York: Routledge.

———. 2011. *The Enchanted Screen: The Unknown History of Fairy-Tale Films*. New York: Routledge.

———, ed. and trans. 2014a. *The Original Folk & Fairy Tales of the Brothers Grimm*. Princeton, NJ: Princeton University Press.

———. 2014b. "Today's Fairy Tales Started Out (Even More) Dark and Harrowing." Interview, NPR, November 16. https://www.npr.org/2014/11/16/364089661/todays-fairy-tales-started-out-even-more-dark-and-harrowing.

———. 2015a. *Grimm Legacies: The Magic Spell of the Grimms' Folk and Fairy Tales*. Princeton, NJ: Princeton University Press.

———. 2015b. "Media-Hyping of Fairy Tales." In *The Cambridge Companion to Fairy Tales*, edited by Maria Tatar, 202–19. Cambridge: Cambridge University Press.

Zipes, Jack, Pauline Greenhill, and Kendra-Magnus Johnston, eds. 2015. *Fairy Tale Films Beyond Disney: International Perspectives*. New York: Routledge.

Zolkover, Adam. 2008. "Corporealizing Fairy Tales: The Body, the Bawdy, and the Carnivalesque in the Comic Book *Fables*." *Marvels & Tales: Journal of Fairy-Tale Studies* 22(1): 38–51.

Zomby Gaga. 2017. https://shop.mattel.com/shop/en-us/ms/monster-high/monster-high-zomby-gaga-doll-fcd09.

INDEX

www.ingramcontent.com/pod-product-compliance
Lightning Source LLC
Chambersburg PA
CBHW051100030726
47504CB00006B/1711

* 9 7 8 0 8 1 4 3 4 1 9 6 4 *